Surviving Zeptulgar

The Personal Journal of Johlnz Dezlond Zavix *I*

J J Eckhardt

This is a work of fiction. All characters, organizations, and events portrayed in this novel are either products of the author's imagination or are used fictitiously.

Copyright © 2022 by J J Eckhardt

For information regarding permission, please write to author@jjeckhardt.com.

ISBN: 979-8-9863632-3-3

The Personal Journal of Johlnz Dezlond Zavix *I*

Forward by Johlnz Dezlond Zavix *II*

100 Cycles – Jantnelnu 1, 0100 AC

One hundred cycles ago, our planet ended.

If my statement above were true, you wouldn't be holding in your hand or reading on your vid, a firsthand account of what our ancestors endured to survive and build a new civilization from almost literally the ashes of the old.

I hadn't yet joined this planet when my Gryn-JarPypzie passed away fifty-five cycles ago. My Pypzie, Robarz and JarPypzie, Jacol told me many stories about Johlnz Dezlond Zavix *I*, and his life. He lived when comet *X/3012 ZI IXON*, later called comet Zeptulgar, hit Tanacun, and he had a significant role in rebuilding our civilization. He is todaz, not well known in the history taught to our liltanz, but my hope is for Tanans to know his name in the future, thanks to this, his personal journal.

You will read here the manuscript of his journal, which he started soon after he arrived at Reswoll Camo. My JarPypzie Jacol mentioned it many times and always insisted it existed somewhere hidden. He did not know where it could be and eventually stopped trying to find it; still, I never gave up hope that one daz I would find the journal.

I knew my Gryn-JarPypzie worked primarily in the underground cizay of Nel Experza, the first of the three underground sprawling cizaes we now have in this area. Since it was not in any of his old possessions, I figured he had to have placed it somewhere, maybe as part of a time capsule. According to my JarPypzie, Johlnz had mumbled something about a secret place before he died from a severe form of Moniasar Disorder in 0046 AC.

To remind those who do not remember, Moniasar Disorder had been an almost always fatal respiration condition, which killed many when Johlnz I was an infant. He had a minor form of the disorder when five cycles old. The affliction mutated from a remnant of the Monuasatin Plague, which wiped out more than half the planet's population over twenty cycles before Johlnz *I*, joined the planet. The scientist did not know where the disorder originated; even so, many rumors were suggesting it had extratana origins. No one ever took the stories seriously, according to all the research I could gather.

Over the cycles, I looked through old records and found Johlnz *I* was involved with the new cybez center they were building almost fifty cycles ago. It is in this center, much expanded now, where I work. I looked carefully over the old project plans and noticed some discrepancies. After some exploring, I found a hidden compartment behind an old, no longer used cybez monitor station on the schematics of the project.

It took much effort and endless forms for permission before I could pull the old system out of the wall, but my perseverance rewarded me with success. The journal was dusty from being hidden away for over fifty cycles in the little compartment, carefully wrapped and well preserved. The simple note found enclosed with the journal, had the handwritten message, 'This journal is a present from one generation to another'.

I read the journal as soon as I got off shift. I felt enthralled to have a firsthand account of what happened almost one hundred cycles ago when the comet struck Tanacun. I held in my hands a personal account of one of the beginnings of our new civilization.

As we know now, there are at least seven main areas of Tanacun where Tanans gathered, trying to rebuild. To my Gryn-JarPypzie and the others in the community, for all they knew, they were the lone survivors remaining on the planet, trying to rebuild from the ashes the comet left behind. A task they certainly thought almost impossible.

The scientists and other leaders of the time, who became the first Council, were too busy building the new society to keep any journals or supplementary written records. It was not until many cycles later, at Johlnz *I* urging, that they realized they should be maintaining a formal written record of events. They needed it not merely for history but also to establish a permanent framework for the new civilization.

I became amazed to learn that in later cycles, when Johlnz *I* served on the Council, he became instrumental with the push north and south to found the two newest cizaes. Nel Monrot, located in northern Donhurex, and later after he died, New Medellax in Old Bolumtia.

He also led the push to start work on reopening the Matabas Canal, to give us access to the Narral Ocean. The reopening that happened recently will be beneficial to our new civilization as it will help us move goods and have better contact with the additional surviving communities.

My Gryn-JarPypzie was vocal about not ever considering ourselves a country. He believed the concept would lead to trouble many cycles in the future like it had many cycles in the past. Although we have been in contact with others who consider themselves a country, we still debate the concept to this daz, as you know.

Something I knew, yet many may not, is he helped create the new calendar of ten mooncazts of the cycle; the system now adopted by over half of the communities on the planet. This mooncazt of Jantnelnu, he insisted on, since many of the original inhabitants of this cizay were from the old United Provinces of Jantnel.

He was the first to suggest ten mooncazts instead of the old nine mooncazts, with thirty dazs each mooncazt and a twenty-zaka daz. I can't imagine the old system or even the old planet. I wish this journal had more information about life preceding the comet, but history pre-comet was not his priority.

So, it is on the first daz of our new centspan and new cycle, Jantnelnu 1, (Nemvaz 19 BC), 0100 AC, that I dedicate this book to our future generations and my Gryn-JarPypzie, Johlnz Dezlond Zavix I, Joined Lant 4, 3961, Died Kult 24, 0046 AC.

Johlnz Dezlond Zavix *II*   Nel Experza
Jantnelnu 1, 0100 AC

The Personal Journal of – Johlnz D. Zavix *I*

Published Jantnelnu 0100 AC, Nel Experza

by Johlnz D Zavix *II*

PART 1 – Reswoll Camo

Five Mooncazts Ago – Nemvaz 18, 3988

Five mooncazts ago, this cycle, the planet Tanacun changed forever.

I find it odd I still track the dazs and mooncazts as if nothing has changed. The cycles mean nothing now, just as the zakas of the dreary dark dazs mean nothing.

A short time ago, it meant so much to so many, but we found now time is fleeting, and it is merely a way to measure the distance to what could be the end of all life on Tanacun. We should have learned from the time of the Monuasatin Plague; life is precious and can be taken away in the blink of an eye.

In reality, the planet changed many more than five mooncazts ago. For many, it was closer to eighteen mooncazts. Some knew of the possibility the end could happen, and more choose to ignore the threat, maybe out of arrogance or perhaps out of fear.

I remember a little of the first time I heard of comet *X/3012 ZI IXON*. It was a quick little promo of sorts on one of the nationalized inform broadcasts. "When the comet approaches Tanacun, it will be brighter than the moons and be visible during the daz," is what she said. "We will be here to keep you updated and provide you with views of the great event." I wonder where she is now.

As the time drew closer, the scientist named the comet, Zeptulgar. The name means 'Bringer of Light' in ancient Zeltian; however, it also means 'Bringer of Foreboding' in the old Pelton language, long forgotten by most.

As the comet came closer still and the small dot of light grew, the stories began to come out. One doomsayer after another saying, "the One was going to smite the planet." Others said, "The Authority knows the truth but are afraid to tell the individuals." Amateur astronomers were saying, "A near miss if not a direct hit was nonetheless certain."

However, the professionals always debunked those claims with facts only they understood. "Trust us," they said. "We have nothing to worry about; sit back and watch the show." Where are they now, and how much did they know or suspect?

The greedy were ready to play on the fears, real or not. To many individuals, they sold backspace shelters, and others went deep into the darklands to construct their own as if the overabundant canopy would offer some form of protection.

I am sure many prepared quite well with their shelters buried deep in the ground. How long can they last? How many have they killed in defense of their little piece of paradise lost? Luckily, I had never run into any or trespassed on what they still considered their land.

How many survive at places like NELAD and other deep Authority bunkers? How many are alive still outside the bunkers, trying to survive on their own? Are there enough survivors to rebuild enough to start over, assuming the possibility of starting over exists? The plague wiped out so many; our population was already less than half its one-time peak.

Many questions may never be answered, at least not by me. Does it even really matter? We may know soon, although nothing is ever certain.

The sky I can occasionally see is strikingly different. The moons look out of sync, and the sun and the stars appear out of place.

It's almost the full sun season here in the north, but it feels more like early warming. What must it be like in what's remaining of the southern hemisphere where the comet glanced and scooped out part of Tanacun?

I have not met anyone who knows for sure, not even those I am with now. The reports that came in before all went nuts did not say for sure. Most satellites were down, blinded by the pulse the comet caused as it entered our atmosphere. Orbital Station I, OS-I, had been out of contact since the daz before the comet, and Station II, OS-II, was believed to be in the comet's path.

I have felt many tanaquakes here in what was once the backlands of Ahito. Sometimes three or four tremors a daz can be felt, although they seem to be getting less as the time passes.

I do not know if this area had many quakes in the past since I was an east coast Rilody and Lertay tan for many cycles. I headed inland away from the coast when we started to grasp the truth.

Many left the coasts as they were afraid of large tidal waves sweeping across the land from the oceans of the planet. After the plague, most of the planet's populations moved closer to the coast and then, thanks to Zeptulgar, had to flee for their lives back inland, where in many towzs and vilogges, only ruins remained.

I heard stories from individuals I encountered in my travels, and most sounded just like that, stories. I doubted anyone witnessed anything they lived to tell. Only some of us who now survive have seen second-hand some of the truth.

Yes, five mooncazts todaz, I wonder if any of us will make it to a full cycle. Will I be caring enough even to bother to track time if I am still alive?

Hello, My Name Is Johlnz

I must stop here and beg your forgiveness. I am rambling along, and I have not yet introduced myself.

My name is Johlnz Dezlond Zavix, formally of what was once known as Jurlton, Nel Lertay, in the great country once known as the United Provinces of Jantnel. As I have eluded too earlier, I joined this planet and was raised for the first twenty-four cycles of my life in Rilodfia, Renvania, all meaningless to me now in this cycle 0 AC (After Comet).

My Muzie named me after my JarPypzie, Jacol, though she opted for Johlnz instead. My parents were both big Jopagengo fans and liked the name Dezlond, hence my middle name. Their music will now most likely be forgotten.

My parents raised me in a fine Athix family, and I went through fourteen cycles of Athix education. I have to wonder why the One, if itz exists, would bring this down upon us. Were we evil and deserving of such a punishment? Truth be told, when I think back on life before the comet, I think maybe we were. It's possible the universe would be better off without us. Past events certainly indicate it to be the universe's desire.

Prior to Zeptulgar, I lived in a camo with my soon-to-be partner, Monharat, dreaming of the life we were going to start together. We had a modern new camo, and we both had excellent jobs. I am; was an Electrical/cybez Engineer, and my espoused worked for a credit exchange in Renvania.

I should have known it all was too good to last.

Six mooncazts before the comet's coming, the news started to spread; this might be far more than a good show. The comet's trajectory was not as the scientists predicted; it became erratic and did not follow the standard codes of physics. Being new to Tanacun, the scientists had no idea what material made up the comet or even if it was a traditional, mostly snowball-like object. They could not explain its behavior, and some whispered the notion of extratana influences.

It became clear as the sun's light and heat ripped the ice away; this comet held a destructive secret inside. It measured at around the size of Lake Ponchit in Bousiana, and the basderz was coming right at us, maybe. Eventually, scientists realized the most recent approach angle would cause it to miss us or give merely a glancing blow to our planet and not a full-on impact.

A direct hit would have been sudden death for much of Tanacun, with the planet barren long before the five mooncazts, which have since passed. With this new information, some thought we might be okay after all.

Unfortunately, the news came too late to save my espoused. Monharat left me a note explaining she felt so sorry, yet she was not brave and could not sit around waiting daz by daz for her death to come. I found her sitting in a chair on our porch. The authorities did not know where she could have gotten the poison she took, but we had our suspicions. Like I mentioned earlier, maybe the universe is better without us.

With Monharat gone, I found myself alone on the planet, and with the impending doom, society went downhill quickly.

Many stopped working to stay camo and pray, while others went around raping and destroying all they could lay their hands upon with a vengeance. The Tana race at its lowest. What was the point? If the planet were to end, the credits and jewels would mean nothing. Does it become okay to rape and torture just because you can get away with it while the Authority is busy with the looters and everyone is concerned only for themselves?

As I mentioned, I had been alone on the planet. My parents had died a few cycles earlier, and I was an only liltanz. Monharat had been the best thing I had in my life, and with her now gone from my life forever, I almost wished some thug would kill me so I could be at peace.

As the comet drew closer, many scientists were again concerned. The comet could fly by a few zilos above our outer stratosphere, or it could be dragged down into our atmosphere, brush across the land, and become a tiny moon burning around our globe.

The only thing they knew for certain; the most significant effects would happen in the southern hemisphere and possibly along all the coastlands of the planet. Not knowing what to expect and with nothing keeping me in Nel Lertay, I headed west, two mooncazts before the coming.

The Daz of the Comet

What happened on the daz of the comet, I did not know at the time. Based on the abundance of debris in the air, the tanaquakes, and the strange realignment of the moons and stars, I believed it to be more than a glancing blow to the planet. I think it may have been better if we were hit dead on. I would most likely be dead now and with my love. I do not have it in me to take her way out.

The daz the comet was to strike or pass by felt warm for the mooncazt of Nemvaz; a cloudy, rainy daz, as if Tanacun waited in mourning for the impending death and destruction. I was not sure of the exact time Zeptulgar was due and decided I would sit in a gazebo in a nice little park I found in Besamer, a small towz just east of the Ahito border. The towz was one of the small communities, which did not move to the coast after the plague, and it had been a vibrant place to live. The park stood empty except for a few querzlas eating and playing in the trees.

The camoz, which remained undamaged from the earlier riots and looting, were mostly quiet. I could see lights in some, and I could imagine the scene of families huddled together. I wondered how many had taken Monharat's way out todaz or the dazs and weezs prior.

No decorations or lights hung to celebrate the coming Spark of Light holidays in towz or anywhere else along my travels. Individuals were scared and in no mood for festivities. The present the universe was sending we did not want or appreciate.

Late in the pastmid, I believe it happened. The azians flew out of the trees, and I heard a rumbling, which seemed to be coming from nowhere and everywhere. I felt slightly dizzy, as if the ground had moved under my pads.

I wondered if I was far enough from the coast to avoid any tidal waves, part caring and part not. I did not know what to expect and realized I held my breath waiting for what, I did not know.

I felt more tremors in the ground and a lot of noise from flocks of azians flying in all directions at once. The querzlas, which had been playing, had run into the trees and hadn't been seen since. I could hear many clars yowling around the area and in the distance. After some time had passed, I realized nothing else was going to happen; the ground was not going to swallow me whole, and the ocean probably was not speeding toward me.

I heard stories later; large waves did destroy the major cizaes. Any cizay close to the coast or near a river close to the coast, I thought, was probably gone. I have recently seen images showing evidence of how bad it became after the impact. Had I not gone west, I would now be dead and buried under debris.

The next daz, the sun shined, but sunrise and sunset did not seem quite right to me. And when the moons came up, they were not near where they had come up two dazs earlier. The sky remained mostly clear; however, I did notice a slight haze in the air, and the sunrise and sunsets were much more colorful than usual.

A few dazs later, things began to change. The sky became dark, and it was not from normal-looking clouds. It appeared as if a blanket overhung everything, blocking out the sunlight. The moons and the stars were downright gone. Five mooncazts later, the skies are clearer on some dazs, and even the brighter stars are occasionally visible through the haze, even so, most dazs are dark and dreary.

Another thing I noticed in the first few dazs after the comet was the air seemed to be thinner, as if some of our atmosphere had been ripped away or thrown into space. Too much exertion caused me to feel light-headed, and I had more headaches than ever before. Across the land moved a constant wind, which at times became intense, blowing towards the south.

My Travels Westward

I stayed around Besamer for about six weezs after the events of the daz. Those who remained in their camoz offered me shelter from the cold, as well as food and water. I made some friends, which tempted me to stay longer; nevertheless, I became restless and had to go. I did not feel I could merely sit around to see what would happen next.

Since the planet did not immediately end, individuals in towz began to try and find a new ordinary life. I considered the idea of normalcy a bit too optimistic, considering the sky remained dark and the temperatures were dropping. The tanaquakes were, I thought, a bad sign even though they were mild. Having so many quakes was not typical for this area, the long-time residents told me, with concern in their voices.

I decided to continue west for no other reason than that is where I had been going. I ventured more to the south to stay away from the large cizay of Loungston. Even small cizaes were a dangerous place to be since the comet. I felt better in the countryside, where individuals were scarce. I met a few individuals on my way. Some were going east to find family, and others, going south to get away from the cold. I should have gone more toward the south considering the temperatures, but then I would not be here to know the horrors of that daz. Maybe it would have been better.

Nobody had any specific information, just theories on what had happened. A few individuals had battery-powered radios; however, we heard nothing beyond static. I passed through a few towzs where those in charge told me in no uncertain terms, I was not wanted there, and I should keep moving. In many other formerly abandoned towzs, it had become a police state.

At one point, I came to a refugee camp controlled by an Authority Defense troop, and I decided to stay for rest and get some better food. They were doing their best to keep order and keep out troublemakers. They were hoping to hear something from the Authority, but even their radios were full of static. One of the deftanmen was sure the static was because of the comet's effects and not the fact that the Authority ceased to exist. I stayed in the camp for almost a mooncazt before deciding to move on, as the camp no longer felt safe.

It had been over three mooncazts since the comet, and I learned it best to stick to the main byways. Animals, once pets, were roaming around, and some were near starvation. A couple of times during my journey, I had to fight off or scare away hungry clars.

Zolves and other predators must have understood something had changed. They were much more brazen and willing to be out in the open. I hadn't yet had a problem with any zolves; nonetheless, I was always sure to have some shelter every nitz.

I had not seen anyone for well over a weez, and I was glad. Meeting individuals in my travels was not something I looked forward to anymore. You would think I would long for the company, yet nowadaz, you never knew what to expect; even someone traveling with liltanz, was not above pulling a gun and demanding food, water, or clothes. Usually, if I heard someone ahead or heard a transport, I would scurry into the woods until they passed.

The Camo in Reswoll

I traveled for a weez without seeing anyone or coming upon any occupied or previously occupied towzs. Reswoll was a small towz with a central small country style downtowz with single-family camoz scattered around. The towz would have been a pleasant place to live and raise a family before the plague; nevertheless, now, only a few homes looked occupied from a distance, and I could see many signs of conflict and looting. I passed a couple of bodies along the byway. One was in what appeared to be a confine uniform.

On the far side of towz, it seemed more preserved and less damaged. I saw no direct signs of individuals, though the area seemed a bit cleaned up. I thought the scene odd, but who knows what it was like here after the impact. I did hear what I thought were conversations when the wind blew from a particular direction, and I felt like someone watched my every move.

I needed a safe place for the nitz, and after walking about a half-zaka out of towz, I saw a rather large camo down a dead-end byway that looked abandoned, yet something about it was not right. As I approached the camo, I noticed it looked cleaned up and taken care of, as if someone lived inside. It looked abandoned from further away, simply because of all the brush and bushes allowed to grow large in front of it, partially blocking the view from the main byway.

I again sensed that someone watched my every move. I am not usually one to have such feelings, and maybe it was the oddness of the area causing me to be nervous. I started to turn and walk away when I noticed an unusual amount of satellite dishes on the roof further down the byway, which looked like someone deliberately hid from view. I also observed what looked like antennas hidden in the trees.

I wanted to start walking in another direction, thinking I needed to find somewhere else for the nitz, yet at the same time, my curiosity got the better of me. As I approached the camo, I still did not see any Tana activity; nevertheless, a querzla dug through some trash from a fallen can. A full can with fresh trash by what appeared to be an abandoned camo; that made no sense? As the thought entered my mind, someone grabbed me from behind; everything went black, and I next woke up in a bed feeling pain in the back of my head. I was tied down to the bed and could not get up. It appeared dark outside, and on a small table, a lamp provided light. I knew no power flowed through the grid, so the light indicated the camo had a generator. Later I found they had a very sophisticated power system set up for the camo, powering many cybez units.

I listened intently but could not hear the hum of a generator or any other noise from the camo. I could have been alone, and I suddenly panicked; what if whoever left me tied to the bed also left me alone to die? I realized it did not make sense. If I was left to die, why did a lamp remain turned on in the room?

I noticed a mirror flush against the wall and figured it was probably a two-way mirror. Someone watched me from another room. "Hello," I said and realized my mouth was dry, and my voice sounded extremely weak and timid, so I spoke more loudly. "Hello, is anyone there? Why am I tied to this bed? I mean you no harm; I was only passing by."

I received no immediate response, and I did not want to waste my strength, screaming and struggling with my bonds.

The bed—the warmest and most comfortable sleeping accommodation I had in a long time, eventually put me back to sleep.

An older tanmen with a thick groz beard, shook me awake. Two large tanmen with guns were standing behind him. "Why did you come to this camo?" He asked. I gave a brief account of my journey. He did not care how I got there; why was more important to him. After hearing the details, he instructed the tanmen to make the camo look less inviting and hide it more from the byway. What have I gotten myself into, I thought?

"I'll deal with you later." He said as he abruptly left, followed by the guards. I remained tied to the bed and was getting even more worried, yet again, I managed to fall asleep.

When I awoke the next premid, I found they had removed my bonds, and I could leave the bed. Some fresh food and juice sat there for me on a table in the corner, so at least I was not left there to die.

I noticed an open door on the far side of the room leading to a bathroom. I took advantage of the facilities and washed up a bit. The bathroom had a working shower, though I was not comfortable with the idea of being so vulnerable, especially if they still watched.

When I came out of the bathroom, which had no windows, I went to one of the windows in the room and found it barred with a fancy grate, and the glass frosted so no one could see in or out.

Since I had nothing better to do and needed nourishment, I decided to sit down and eat. The tray included what I believed to be freshly crushed zale juice, a planx berry, some bread, and cheese. As I ate, I began to wonder what had happened to my backpack. I did not have many possessions; all the same, it would have been nice to have my other clothes.

It was at this time I first thought about keeping a diary or journal of some kind, if only so I could remember the events of my life—forever changed. Or, I thought, if the planet somehow survives and rebuilds, it could be a lasting piece of history for future generations. I decided if it were possible in the future, I would begin what you are now reading.

I was lost in thought and startled when I heard the door suddenly and quickly open behind me. As I turned, the two tanmen who were there before, with guns strapped now to their sides, entered the room. One of them, a large built tanmen with blonden hair, tossed my backpack on the bed. "Here are your things; Dr. Moxron will be here in a while to talk to you." That is all he said, quick and to the point.

The second tanmen, not as tall, but also adequately built for the job, sporting a full verm beard with hair to match, said nothing. They left me alone in the room, and I wondered if talk to would be more like interrogated again, but I had nothing to hide, and if they wanted me dead, they could already have killed me. Of course, I thought, they may want to hear what more I know from out there before they kill me. Why then feed me? Many thoughts ran through my head before Robarz, the same tanmen from the nitz before, finally came into my room.

The Horror

Dr. Robarz Moxron was an older tanmen with well-groomed light groz hair and a tired face. I later found out he had a Doctorate in Astronomy and Tanacun sciences from Trinton University.

Robarz began by asking me the usual questions, who are you, where are you from, and again, he inquired why I approached the camo. After I filled him in on the important details of my recent life, and I assured him I was just a weary traveler, we moved to a more comfortable room. The tanmen with the guns disappeared; however, I was sure they were close. I did not blame them for not completely trusting a stranger.

When I told him I had worked as a cybez Engineer, he became very interested. "We can't afford to have guests here, so your choice is to be escorted away from here or stay, join us, and work on our cybezs units."

I felt sure, for some reason, if I choose to be escorted away, it would be the last choice I would ever make in this life. I had nowhere really to go, so I decided to stay. After I made my decision, he explained to me what was happening in the camo. As he began to explain, I realized I made the correct choice.

I found out a group of over thirty individuals lived in the camo. Most, like Robarz, were scientists; the rest were the muscle. They had power and access to some fresh food but mostly relied on frozen and canned supplies, plus Authority rations.

When the truth started to be known, they gathered here from universities up and down the coast. Some were in Authority programs, and a few amalgam types were working in the satellite collective. Many groups like them existed across the country and a few in other countries around the planet. One group had been in Austran and another in southern Braza, though they are no longer there, the camoz or the countries. Robarz informed me they believed the comet glanced Tanacun right over South Orisa, basically ripping land and water right off the planet and throwing a lot of it into the atmosphere, and some even out into space.

He showed me images taken from some northern satellites, which showed what looked like a massive cloud ripping out of Tanacun and into space. It was a horrible sight to see. Zeptulgar ripped apart the southern hemisphere, and huge waves of water swamped most of the South Jantnel continent as pieces of the wounded planet smashed to the ground.

The oceans rushing in to fill the void had made the title waves less in the north; nonetheless, they still did much damage. Cizaes close to the coast, all basically gone, all now lifeless. The empty wreckage of severely damaged buildings is all that remains. As the oceans slowly stopped oscillating, the sea levels of the planet ended well below normal. As heavy rains fell, mostly on what remained of the southern hemisphere, the water level started to come back up; however, the planet had lost water to space, never to come back again.

One of the other scientists told me there were much larger chunks of the planet and comet still orbiting in space, mostly invisible because of the debris in the atmosphere. Eventually, they will all fall back to Tanacun, some causing even more damage to the north than the first impact.

Almost all the satellites they could access before the comet were either destroyed or damaged and will also soon fall. They had tried repeatedly to contact the orbital stations, but neither one was responding. They are sure OS-II is gone.

The group had been monitoring conditions as best they could with the technology remaining. What they learned hadn't been good. They believed the planet had been slightly jogged out of its standard orbit, causing it to become a bit oval rather than round. A slight distortion doesn't have a significant weather impact since our temperatures are more controlled by the angle of the sun than our distance from the sun. What concerned the scientists was the fact the long-term effects on the moons and planets were unknown. The solar system has been in this balance for many millennia, and no one knows how much a slight shift in one planet will affect the others. Based on the limited availability of observations, they thought the moons had almost entirely adjusted and were back on a close to normal pattern, be that as it may, they were not one hundred percent sure of anything.

The bad news they saved for last. Everyone knows Tanacun revolves on an axis tilted at 17.65 degrees with respect to the orbital plane. One scientist used a bunch of big words about gravity and force I did not understand, in any event, what it came down to was they thought the planet might have been knocked off its axis by the comet. The tilt that had been at 17.65 degrees had changed as best they could tell to around 31 degrees.

They are not sure, but they think this is ongoing, and the planet is still tilting and moving out of its normal position. What does it mean? Imagine if Tanacun kept tilting more and more, never stopping. Temperatures at what were the polls could reach over 100 degrees, and the areas that were the equator being at sometimes well below zero. If the axis of Tanacun did not stop moving, it would continue to turn in two directions at once, alternately baking and freezing the planet forever. Normal daz and nitz cycles, as well as the seasons, would be gone as the planet's axis continued to shift. We would not survive for long as almost every spot on Tanacun would go from endless daz to endless nitz—baking and freezing, over and over.

How do we go on? How do I go on? I don't have an answer I only know we must.

Reswoll, Ahito Province   **Lant 18**

(((*)))

Working and Waiting

Johlnz sat on one of the rockers, which still lined the porch of the camo, enjoying the breeze. He found it a great place to take a moment to breathe and finish the first entry of his new journal. Much work continued at the camo, not least of which was his work on the cybez units. The group had boxes of cybez, some old and some new, which needed to be configured or repaired, and it kept him busy.

"Yo, lazy tan, what are you doing out here?"

"Lazy, I remained up until five this premid fixing the cybez for Dr. Moxron. When the Doc speaks, I listen."

The tanmen standing in front of Johlnz was Tolz Bezler, one of the security guards who patrolled the area and protected the camo. He was a large tanmen, with verm hair and a bushy grown-out beard to match, which led him to have the nickname of Big Verm.

Tolz was one of the two security guards who captured him and brought him to the room where he awoke a mooncazt prior. When not out on patrol, Tolz could be found in the basement working out or cleaning his guns. He became Johlnz's first real friend at the camo, and he constantly tried to get Johlnz to start exercising his body as much as he had exercised his mind.

"Speaking of the Doc, he is looking for you. Something about the junk being too slow to get any work finished."

"Not much I can do about that issue, Tolz. I can't manufacture new processors. Probably nobody can."

"So, what are you doing out here, and what do you have there? You can't possibly have time to read."

"Well, I promised myself back when you and your friend had me tied to a bed, if I got out of the room alive, I would start a journal of my travels. I do not expect anyone will ever care to read it, but if we do survive, it could be a good historical reference."

"Yes, if we survive. It's exceedingly grim down below. I do not think the big guys like what they are seeing."

Johlnz put down his pen and sighed before responding. "Thanks for depressing me even more on this overly dark greyz daz."

"What are friends for?" He said as he walked back into the camo, chuckling along the way.

Johlnz sat for a moment missing his old life, and most of all, Monharat. He sat there a moment longer to get his emotions in check and then went inside to talk some sense into the Doc.

Lant 28

It has been a mooncazt since the daz I first saw the images of the devastation caused by the comet.

I have been allowed to stay here in exchange for help maintaining the cybezs and other systems. It seems they did not think to include any engineers in their group.

We have experienced more tanaquakes since I have been here. Most were small, yet we had a strong one last weez, and it caused us to lose power from our zolatron generators for a few zakas. Since then, Tanacun has been quiet.

The scientists are continuing to monitor as best they can. They are limited in the ways they can measure and are relying on some of the old-fashioned methods of measuring the position of the sun, which is very difficult when, on most dazs, the sky is still not clear, and has hazy sunshine at best. All we can do is continue to wait and maybe pray.

Even if Tanacun doesn't move back to its traditional position, all may not be lost. The planet may tilt slightly more before stopping or reversing, no one knows with any certainty. We hope it does stop or reverse its movement, or most of this planet is doomed. If we cease tilting farther, and seasons still exist on this planet, they will be different but not necessarily deadly.

I think I am starting to ramble on and repeat myself. It's been a long daz, a long few weezs.

While monitoring the planet, our scientists have also been monitoring radio frequencies, trying to find out what's happening on the rest of the planet. They have monitored Authority communications, talking about trying to restore some order and form of temporary Authority management. Gangs and militias control many smaller towzs. A few provinces have partial Authority management; however, society has mostly broken down. We have had some gangs wander by here, but none have come close to the camo. We try to hide our presence here as much as possible.

They have picked up some communications from others, not part of our larger group, discussing the orbit and axis of the planet. Apparently, our scientists here are not the only ones concerned.

Enough for todaz, time for bed.

Lant 30

We had some excitement last nitz. A couple of tanwez stumbled upon the camo and decided to come in for a look around. They were grabbed by security and locked in a couple of bedrooms—sounds familiar. I do not know what their status is at the moment. We can only support so many here and still stay hidden.

When Johlnz went down in the premid for breakfast, he ran into Arten, one of the security guards; the one who had thrown Johlnz's backpack on the bed the first daz he stumbled upon the camo. Johlnz did not know his last name; he never volunteered it, and Johlnz never asked. He did not consider him a friend, like Tolz; nevertheless, he was fine to talk to and prod for information. It was Arten who told him about the young tanmen.

"We caught them snooping around the same way you were when we grabbed you, except they made it into the camo. They put up a little bit of a fight, but eventually, they saw reason and did not have to be knocked out."

Arten paused for a bit, held out his hand to Johlnz, and then continued. "By the way, sorry about what happened. I did not mean to strike you so hard that daz. You were the first person to stumble upon us here, and I got a little carried away."

Johlnz took his hand and shook it while saying, "So it was you who knocked me out. Well, no harm done, apparently. What are you going to do with the tanwez?"

"I do not know, not my decision to make. The young tanmen are currently locked in a couple of extra bedrooms. We can only support so many individuals in this camo even so, if we let them go, then what? They could come back with others and overrun the place just to get some food."

I had a busy premid but was free by early pastmid. I went for a little walk around the area to clear my head and keep all the thoughts of despair and hopelessness from bringing me down. I dream about Monharat all the time and wonder for how long it will hurt.

We can't walk very far from the camo for fear of running into someone bent on trouble. I found out many other individuals still live in the area, mostly in towz, though we try not to have contact with them. The local Sharoz of the Authority believes an old tanmen, Dr. Moxron, and his relations live alone in the mansion.

We have resources and supplies most others in the area do not have access to, and they could be worth a person's life in todaz's reality. Even the Sharoz cannot be trusted.

Nully 04

After breakfast, the Doc invited me to join the status meeting concerning what the scientists have learned to date. Dr. Moxron is hard to read, but there was no mistaking the look on his face when he entered the room.

"Hi Arten, good premid."

"Good premid Johlnz, hopefully, it will be. You were invited to this meeting as well?"

"Yes," he continued as they walked together, "I do not know if that is a good thing or not. Do you usually attend these meetings?"

"No, this is my first. Usually, the head of security, Malcolz, attends the meetings and fills us in, but he's busy this premid with a . . . another matter."

"The tanwez?" Johlnz said. "I have not heard anything about their status, and I was wondering."

"I really can't say."

Johlnz was about to press Arten more for answers, but the leaders entered the dining room, now serving as the meeting room. He was not happy about the secrecy surrounding the tanwez, and he hoped those in charge were not going to do something rash.

A few minzakas later, Dr. Moxron entered the room and stood at the head of the large table. He looked tired as he slumped a bit before using the table to rest his hands. Johlnz moved to stand in the back since not enough seats were set up for all in attendance, and he sat long enough already working on the cybezs.

"Our worst fears appear to be coming true. Tanacun has not started moving back on its axis. In fact, it has not even slowed down. We believe it is still moving at about the rate of 2-3 degrees per mooncazt. We are monitoring the situation constantly, as best we can, and this could be just a temporary deviation. We can't be one hundred percent sure of anything since our tools are crude compared to what we would have had before the comet. If the planet does correct itself, it could still be devastating for the environment. The disruption to the wildlife still in existence could cause extinction for many species, and it could be a cascading event.

"We will give another update in a couple of dazs, or sooner if we learn anything new. Please continue at your assigned task, and if you are religious — pray."

The pastmid was filled with violent thunderstorms as if Tanacun knew things were not well for its inhabitants, and the planet was throwing a temper tantrum of anger and despair. If the Tana race were to die off and disappear, Tanacun would still be here, moving through space. We did not always treat the planet well in the past, and maybe it would be happy to be rid of us for good.

Nully 06

The only update todaz is a bit disconcerting. I had not seen Tolz or Arten todaz, and I was curious about the tanwez who had stumbled onto the grounds and into the camo. I ran into one of the other guards whose name I did not know, and I asked him about the two young tanmen caught last weez. He ignored my question for a while, then, after more prodding from me, he said, "They have been taken care of; that is all I am at liberty to say." He could mean a lot of things, and I decided not to push the issue. I know we have a delicate balance here, but I hope we have not sunk so low as to do what his comment implied. Even if they are locked up somewhere, it still causes me a lot of concern.

Nully 10

I managed to have a brief conversation with Dr. Moxron todaz while I worked on one of the cybez power systems giving us some issues.

"Hello Johlnz, good to see you. Are you going to be able to get this old tan back up and running for us?"

Johlnz paused and shook the Doc's hand. "Well, a few extra parts would not hurt, be that as it may, I think I have come up with a solution to get the job done."

After a brief pause, Dr. Moxron continued.

"I wanted to apologize to you if I came off a bit harsh when we first met. I am always afraid of disruptions to our work, and I worry about everyone we have assembled here to help us. We do not know what is to come, but we need to remain as civil to each other as possible in these difficult dazs. I hope, all things considered, you are happy with your role here as part of our group."

"Yes, I enjoy my work, and of course, my life could be a lot worse. I hope I am not too presumptuous; even so, I would like to ask you about the two tanwez caught last weez. Are they okay? What is going to happen to them?"

Dr. Moxron did not immediately answer as he was reading a report from one of the monitors. "I did talk to them; still, I do not know where they are now. I trust my security, and I need to leave those decisions up to them, but I do understand your concern."

He quickly changed the subject before Johlnz could ask another question.

"I do have some good news for you. We have been able to pick up some signals from a few countries in Iurox. A couple of small Iuroxan countries have restored limited power and are trying to rebuild. Hopefully, it will not be in vain.

I have no news todaz on the movement of the planet. I did not ask, figuring someone would have told me if anything changed.

Nully 12

We had more violent storms come through last nitz. The fierce gales knocked down some trees, and we spent all daz restoring the storm-damaged communication equipment.

If the planet does survive, I have new skills in climbing and working in trees, as well as fixing missing roof shingles. From cybez engineer to handytan, whoever would have thought? Whoever would have expected our civilization could be coming to its end?

Nully 16

The last few dazs have been hectic and strenuous. I have been back in the trees fixing some of our antennas and working on the cybezs.

Dr. Moxron is in contact with the Malod and Authority Sharoz from the towz. They are trying, with some success, to restore order and the rule of code to the area. He did not inform them of what was happening. He acted as if it were just himself and a few of his relations living in the camo. He felt they were more like warlords than a legitimate Authority.

Then the update we were all waiting to hear happened todaz.

"Nothing has changed," he began. "The planet is still tilting away from its normal position, and the movement has not slowed. All we can do is continue to monitor the situation as best we can.

"Plans are underway in some communities to move as many supplies as possible into underground facilities. One such facility mentioned was the superfuse in Turoz, Iurox. We can be sure other preparations are happening in our provinces plus in many of the Authority's facilities. None of that will help us here, and most of it will be for nothing if the planet continues to tilt further.

"There are some places on Tanacun where we could endure the extreme temperature changes, and maybe in those areas, is where our civilization will survive, if at all.

The problem is the area would be along the equator. A huge amount of damage occurred in and below those regions of the planet, and in land area, it is also not large, compared to the provinces."

I had the feeling while listening to the last part of what he said; they do have some plans to evacuate us from the camo if necessary. It would be an extended trip; nevertheless, if it is the only way to survive, we will have no choice.

Nully 18

We were hit by another strong tanaquake todaz, lasting almost one minzaka. The scientists are saying tanaquakes could be another outcome of the planet's shift and could also signify Tanacun's core exerting its influence over the planet's tilt. The tilt should also be affecting Tanacun's magnetic field, which is, in part, connected to the spinning of the core. They know the magnetic poles have shifted; still, they have no way to measure the magnetic field itself.

Last nitz I had to help with guard duty since some guards have been ill for a few dazs.

"Johlnz, can I talk to you for a minzaka?"

"Sure, Tolz, what's up? I have not seen you in a few dazs."

"I have been out on patrol duty a lot lately since we have a few guys out sick and confined to bed. I have had to do double shifts," he said as he slowly sank into the chair next to Johlnz.

"I heard there were a lot of us getting sick this weez," Johlnz said. "We do not get out much, so it spreads fast. I know some of the Doc's team has been stuck in bed as well. Part of my job has become disinfecting the cybez systems as well as repairing them."

Tolz laughed as he continued, "Well, Johlnz, I have another job for you, that is why I wanted to talk to you. Malcolz asked me to ask you if you would be willing to help out on guard duty tonitz."

"Guard duty, me? I am a six-pad three-inz skinny weakling who has never held a gun before."

"I know, I know, I keep trying to get you to work out with me, yet you always have an excuse."

"It's called work."

Johlnz paused for a moment and started walking back and forth across the room before continuing.

"I can't say I am comfortable with the idea."

"I can tell, but Malcolz said he would have Arten go over things with you, including gun safety and usage. I am sure it will just be a handgun, nothing serious like our Z94's. They require some special training."

"Okay," Johlnz said reluctantly, perspiring a bit in the process. "I do not get off shift until five. Where and when would I meet with Arten?"

"Six o'clock, in the basement. He will be waiting."

"Sounds like you already anticipated my answer."

"Well, sort of. I do not think you really had a choice," Tolz said as he stood up.

He scurried away before Johlnz could respond to his last comment. He felt glad Johlnz agreed. He did not want to have to tell his friend he had no choice. Tolz was sure this would not be the last time Johlnz would have to expand his duties.

(((*)))

A few zakas later, Johlnz found himself down in the basement waiting for Arten, with his heartbeat accelerated. He was surprised to find a full arsenal of weapons in the basement, most of which he did not recognize, as well as a four-station shooting range. Also, in the basement, he saw a significant weight and training room—Tolz's favorite place to unwind.

A few minzakas later, Arten arrived.

"Hi, Johlnz, good to see you again, and glad you can help out."

"I am not sure how much help I will be. I am not strong enough to fight off anyone, and I have never held a gun before."

"Even so, you do have eyes, and you will have a talkie to communicate anything you see. You will have a gun; all the same, I doubt you will have to use it. We have never had to fire our guns here. We just beat individuals over the head," he said while laughing.

Arten's humor helped make Johlnz feel better about the situation, and he came to realize he worried about nothing. He still did not know Arten's last name, but at least he earned some respect with the tanmen.

Arten gave Johlnz a pistol and spent the next zaka and a half showing him how to use the weapon. How to properly holster the gun, engage and quickly disengage the lock, and how best to load the projectiles. His training included twenty minzakas of shooting on the gun range, and he found out firing a gun; at least that one was not too bad, and he was a decent shot for never having done it before.

In addition to the gun and holster, Arten gave him a talkie, nitz vision assists, and a projectile-proof vest. Arten explained that the vest was more for protection against friendly fire. Arten told him to keep all the equipment and consider it his, which only emphasized to Johlnz the fact this was not a one-time event. His heartbeat quickened again.

Johlnz's patrol shift started at seven-thirty, which at that time of cycle would still have been dazlight, though tonitz, on top of the usual dark skies because of the comet, there were also clouds and a chance of rain.

He, of course, never wore nitz vision assists before and was having some fun with them until he inadvertently looked at one of the porch lights, nearly blinding himself. He realized it might take some time to remember not to look at any light sources while wearing the assists.

His patrol area started behind the camo and out to about one hundred yarzs away from the back door. He stood fifty yarzs away from what was at one time considered the main byway. He now found it littered with debris and rarely saw any transports. If anyone were going to approach the camo, this would be one possible direction they would take.

After three zakas on patrol, he started to get hungry since he only had time between shift one, training, and now, shift two, for a small sandwich. Luckily Arten had also given him a small utility pouch, stocked with a couple of snack bars and some water. The nitz was cool; however, the added layer of a projectile-proof vest helped to keep him warm. Never in his wildest dreams did he ever think he would be wearing such a vest.

He was making another pass along the back of his assigned area when he almost jumped out of his skin when his talkie came to life with one of the other guards checking in. Even though it wirelessly connected to a speaker in his ear, he had forgotten he had the device.

"This is Robarz, area one checking in, all areas report."

Johlnz was area four, so he waited. After two and three finished, he reported in.

"This is Johlnz, area four, all quiet."

The report meant he was halfway through. Four zakas to go. He enjoyed the sounds of the insects and nitz flyers he could hear. The noise kept him from feeling alone in the darkness. He started getting tired, and his pads were getting sore when he was startled by a zearen jumping through the woods a short distance in front of him. His heart pounded while he hoped someone in the woods hadn't disturbed the zearen. He waited behind a tree, listening, but heard no sound, except noises expected from animals on the hunt and now the beginning of the rain.

When he got back to his room, he was too cold, wet, and fatigued to update his journal and decided to do it sometime the next daz after the update from the Doc.

Before going to sleep, he said a prayer to the One. Something he had not done in many years.

Nully 19

Todaz is Nully 19, and the start of full sun in the northern hemisphere. Even though Tanacun's axis is off tilt, most individuals would probably not notice, even if the clouds and debris did not obscure the sun. It should be the start of the warm time; even so, temperatures have been below normal thanks to the continuing cloud cover and fine debris floating in the atmosphere. As we approach the hot time based on dazs, it feels more like late cooling time. The sky is still not clear, and on most dazs, we experience a ray of abysmal hazy sunshine at best. If the planet's axis shift doesn't stop or somehow reverse, the concept of seasons and even dazlight and nitz zakas will be meaningless, as meaningless as the terms northern and southern. I wonder at nitz when I look up if I will ever see stars again, and if not, will I even care.

Nully 21

Dr. Moxron informed the group of positive developments todaz. Since this all started, they have been monitoring radio and televid signals, and todaz received a message from the Federated Authority's emergency system.

Dr. Moxron walked into the room, looking a little better than usual. He did not have the heavy look in his eyes and face, now so familiar. Before taking the podium, he had a small side conversation with one of the other scientists already in the dining room waiting.

"Good premid, everyone, I do have a bit of good news todaz. Early this premid, we picked up a signal from the U.P. emergency broadcast system—no direct communication, just the emergency background image, and a voice signal.

"According to the broadcast, the Federated Authority remains intact and is urging calm and asking everyone to work together and not take advantage of the situation.

"They talked about working with power controllers to start bringing back limited electricity and gas service. There was no mention of what happened or the current state of affairs, which I am sure they must understand. Our group here in Reswoll and our colleagues around the planet will still try to remain hidden. We can't be certain if everything we heard was truthful, and we do not want to acknowledge our presence until we are sure a legitimate Authority system is in control.

"As to the matter concerning the axis of the planet, nothing had changed. All we can do is to continue monitoring the situation as best we can. I know I keep saying the same thing, but we are helpless.

"My associates have suggested I open up the floor to questions, so if anyone has a question they would like to ask, please raise your hand.

"Yes, Ralitan, go ahead."

Ralitan Oberan was one of the mechanics who worked on the generator systems and kept the transports on-site in working order in case needed.

"Thank you, Dr. Moxron. I am wondering if there is a point of no return, a point where it would be too late for the planet to correct itself?

"Unfortunately, we do not know. If the planet does keep tilting, it will be a couple of mooncazts before we would be drastically affected. We do not know what will happen, and admittedly, it worries us a great deal.

The room remained quiet, with no other questions. I think we were all afraid of the answers.

After the update, I went outside to look at the barely visible sun and sky, hoping for some blucyn, and experienced nothing beyond disappointment. I wondered if the animals could notice the odd position of the sun, and wondered how long before the populace left alive began to notice.

There were a few small tanaquakes again todaz and even one while I was daydreaming about the life I could have had if the universe did not hate us so much.

Nully 24 - AT

I awakened a few zakas ago to the sound of gunfire and loud voices. A group of tanmen and tanwoz, five in all, managed to get past the guards outside and into the camo. I am glad I was not on duty. I am sure the guards will be in hot water with Malcolz.

To date, no one has formally introduced me to Malcolz; however, I have seen him on occasion. He's a large tanmen in his mid-forties, larger than Tolz and Arten. He joined and was raised in Orisa and learned how to fight and how to kill early in life. I have heard he was a fighter for the jungle nation resistance until the killing became too much for him to accept. He fled his camo country and came to the United Provinces a little over six cycles ago.

We are not sure if the intruders know what we are doing in the camo, or if they noticed the activity and thought we had something worth stealing. When the group entered the camo, they set off an alarm quickly answered by the guards inside. They refused to put down their weapons and began to fire at our guards. We have superior firepower, and all five ended up dead, even the two who tried to escape outside.

I fear this is another sign of how bad things have gotten. Even though small groups and some Authority's are trying to restore normalcy, society has all but fallen apart. It has become everyone for themselves or their little group, and they will steal and kill to get what they need or want.

The guards did an extensive search around the grounds, yet they did not see any sign of others watching from the woods. It's almost 3:00. I think it is time to go back to sleep.

Nully 24 - PT

Our little firefight last nitz did not go unnoticed. The Malod, Waltez Johlant, the local Authority Chief, Walkir, and his Duzen, Chriz, drove out—yes, drove, some individuals do still have access to fuel—to pay us a visit. Since they were known, they were allowed to approach the camo, and the guards remained unseen. They got out of the transport, heavily armed

—which was not surprising considering how the Provinces had changed—and knocked at the door. I happened to be in the front area of the camo when they came to the door, so Arten asked me to answer while someone else went off to fetch Dr. Moxron.

Johlnz stood at the door a few seconds and waited till they knocked a second time before opening it and greeting the guests.

"Hello, I am Johlnz. How can I help you?"

The first tanmen to speak was the Malod, a short, well-fed individual who had dark circles under his eyes. Having to deal with the aftermath of the comet was probably more than he could handle.

"Hello, I am the Malod of Reswoll, Waltez Johlant, and this is the Authority Chief, Walkir and his Duzen, Chriz.

After shaking hands and a few pleasantries, Johlnz introduced himself as one of Robarz Moxron's relations and invited them to come in. As they entered, they looked around, on guard, and even a bit nervous, having realized Johlnz was sure that things at the camo were not as previously represented.

The Malod began to ask a question when to Johlnz's surprise, Dr. Moxron approached with his relation Thereza, who served as his assistant, and one of the other scientists whose name he did not know.

"Hello Malod, I am Dr. Moxron, the owner of this property, how may I help you?"

"Hello, Doctor," the Malod began. "We received reports of gunfire from out this way last nitz, and the formants were sure it came from this property."

Johlnz wondered why they did not come to investigate last nitz before he understood they probably did not hear about the confrontation until the premid. The intruders probably had an accomplice who was hiding in the woods as a lookout.

The two scientists glanced at each other and then asked the guests to join them in the parlor, located on the opposite side of the camo from our group's usual meeting area. It appeared the group was ready for this situation and had a plan. Johlnz followed them even though not specifically asked, and it appeared the Doc did not mind. He remained standing by the doors as the others all sat down.

To Johlnz's surprise, they started by telling the Malod and his two companions the truth about how many individuals were in the camo and what they were doing, without mentioning too many specifics.

Dr. Moxron proceeded to give them the details about the events of the previous nitz and informed the guest they had already buried the bodies in the backlands.

As Johlnz stood nervously leaning against the doorframe, he waited for an outburst from the Authority Chief, but it seemed he was allowing the Malod to take the lead.

The Malod uncomfortably shifted in his seat before speaking.

"I must say, I am not comfortable about how you handled the situation or about the presence of so many individuals here with guns. I admit the planet being the way it is, you need to protect yourself, and we are not in a position to do anything about the attacks. We certainly cannot deny individuals the right to defend themselves, be that as it may, we must insist, however, of being informed of such activity."

The Malod paused and then continued as if talking to himself, "It is now a different place."

As Johlnz stood watching, he could tell the Duzen was not happy about how the Malod was handling the situation, and although he felt the Malod to be sincere, Johlnz expected possible trouble from the group in the future.

Or maybe not; as to Johlnz's surprise, Dr. Moxron looked over at the other scientists who had accompanied him and nodded his head. Johlnz knew then they had decided to tell their visitors everything.

Dr. Moxron had already explained they were a group of scientists monitoring the situation, so he started by filling them in on the scientific network the scientists established, followed by explaining what had happened when the comet hit.

Time for the hard part. The Doctor stood up and walked over to the window to look out before proceeding. He was so tired, and so often, giving bad news to individuals was becoming more than he could handle. He turned back to the guest and provided them with the complete story.

As the Doctor progressed with the details, Johlnz could see the color draining from the faces of the tanmen sitting before them. They were reluctant to believe what they were hearing and did not fully understand until Dr. Moxron used a handy globe to show them how some parts of Tanacun would be in sunshine or darkness for many mooncazts at a time if the movement did not stop or go back. The Authority Chief Walkir became the first to speak.

"Well, that is some story, but in the meantime, while we wait to see if any of what you told us is fact, we need to continue trying to restore order."

The Chief was about to continue when the Malod interrupted.

"We do not have access to any generators, so we have made arrangements to tap into the old windgen farm a few zilos away. It will bring a small amount of electricity to the towz if it works after all these cycles.

"You should know we sent a group of tanmen to Xumbus Cizay, to see if the Provincial Authority existed. They departed over three weezs ago, and we are beginning to get worried they may have come to harm. We are thinking of sending another group with an armed transport and a good supply of fuel.

"It would be helpful if maybe one of your guards could go along or at least give us some guns and projectiles. Our supplies are low, and we have had to use more than half of what existed."

As Johlnz stood listening, he noticed how the Duzen's demeanor had changed. He went from looking angry to looking like he wanted to cry. He appeared lost in his thoughts, his eyes when opened, looking down on the floor, and Johlnz wondered if he had a family waiting for him back in towz.

Dr. Moxron interrupted Johlnz's thoughts when he began to respond to the Malod's request. "I will certainly discuss it with the others to see what help we may be able to offer."

There was more discussion of what to do if individuals started to notice the lengthening of the dazlight zakas. They decided it was a conversation for later after more information about the planet's movement could be ascertained.

Johlnz escorted the group to the door and saw them out. As he started back to work, he heard the other scientist remark to Dr. Moxron; their guests were suffering from a severe case of denial.

Johlnz suspected they were not alone. He remained sure others have noticed the changes but refused to acknowledge the danger.

Nully 26

I have not seen Dr. Moxron since the meeting with the Malod, and I am beginning to get worried he has only bad news to share.

The Malod had come by again yesterday, by himself, asking for an update. Thereza answered the door and told him the Doctor was not available, and we had no updates to report. The Malod did not seem pleased, and I feared he might try to force his way into the camo, thankfully, he merely left and indicated he would be back.

Autnar 01

We experienced another strong tanaquake last nitz. More trees fell, and the camo had some damage to the food prep.

Another group of scientists and support personnel—deftanmen—joined us yesterday. They came with a few bulk- transports and Authority lisks. I found out we have a variety of other transports hidden in garages and barns in the area. I knew we had some, though we have far more than I had imagined. Apparently, I am not trusted enough for all the secrets.

Except for the quakes, it has been quiet, too quiet. I fear the tanmen from the towz are planning some trouble, and I am worried by the fact there have been no updates. I see the scientists when I work on the cybezs, but even that work has been slow, and I have been doing more guard duty.

Everyone looks tired and depressed. I wish maybe the end would come. Mercy from the universe.

Autnar 04

7:00 AT

Does the United Provinces of Jantnel still exist? Do we have a Provincial Federated Authority with Larsitol gone? What will become of what's left of the UPJ? The country will have no celebrations todaz, and no fireflames in the nitz sky. The nation created almost 245 cycles ago todaz is probably never coming back.

I have allowed my pessimism to get the best of me, as I am not expecting good news. The notice went out last nitz there would be a meeting at 8:00 in the premid. That is it, no other news, and no further updates. I did not know what to expect, and I had a hard time sleeping. I woke early and could not manage breakfast. They would have informed us by now if the news were good. I am sure nothing except terrible news is about to be divulged.

Johlnz walked into the large space where the meeting was to be held and saw the Malod and Authority Chief also in attendance.

This is it, one way or another; we are getting the final answer to what will happen to the planet.

In a sense, he was relieved, no more guessing or false hope. As soon as Dr. Moxron walked into the room, Johlnz had confirmation the news would not be good.

"Tanacun has not stopped moving on its axis," he began, "and we do not feel; well, actually, we are certain, it is not going to stop. Our instruments have measured the tilt at around 37 degrees, and we are positive at this juncture; there is no turning back. We will be monitoring the situation going forward, but nothing is going to change."

Johlnz watched the Malod and Authority Chief as the Doctor spoke, and he could see a mixture of disbelief, confusion, and a bit of fear on their faces.

"Is there anything we can do to get through this," the Malod asked?

"No," Dr. Moxron replied. "When this part of the planet is in constant sunlight, with the sun directly overhead, temperatures could approach 200 degrees. How do you prepare for such an extreme? We do not have any suggestions for what to do other than heading as far south as possible. The safest, best possible chance for survival will be at the planet's equator."

Johlnz watched as reality suddenly set in, and they both quickly said goodbye and hurried out the door. After the Malod had left, Dr. Moxron proceeded to tell everyone; they were heading south early in the premid.

"We have planned our departure for some time now. We have bulk-transports hidden we will load with the equipment and supplies for the move. The advice I gave to Malod Johlant was the truth. To survive, we must go south, or we will surely die.

"Please see my assistant Thereza for your instructions and assignments. We do not have much time, but we do have a lot to do.

"Thank you, all."

Everyone attending lined up to receive their instructions from Thereza and then began preparing all the food and water supplies to be packed and loaded. All the electronics, except for communications equipment, were to be left behind. It would be up to the other sites to monitor the situation and keep in contact with our group.

Tolz approached Johlnz and informed him that everyone would be armed and ready to fight if necessary. He had never even fired the gun Malcolz gave him for patrol except during the first practice session, and now he would be expected to help defend the group if they ran into trouble. Tolz instructed this friend to report for a quick lesson with a new gun in the evening, and then they would provide more training as the group proceeded south into the unknown.

8:00 PT

After a meager dinner, I received instructions to go down to the basement, where I met another guard who gave me a machine gun and a small supply of projectiles. He did not volunteer his name before he instructed me on how to load the weapon and the basics of operation. We went into a shooting gallery I never knew existed—more extensive than the one I used before. I took my first shots, and the power of the gun nearly knocked me over. The instructor gave me further lessons on how to aim, and I took additional practice shots with little success. The weapon was more challenging to aim, shoot, and control than I would have imagined, and it gave me a new appreciation of those who fought in the Provincial Guard.

"Not the most graceful shooting I have ever seen; nevertheless, I am sure you'll get the hang of it with practice."

Johlnz turned around to see Tolz standing behind him with a big smile on his face, which Johlnz found odd considering the situation.

"Oh, hi, Tolz. Hopefully, I will not ever have the opportunity to get better at shooting this damn thing. If I never have to fire it again, I'll be happy."

After a brief pause, Johlnz continued, "Wipe that grin off your face; what are you smiling about anyway. There's nothing to be smiling about."

"Do not be so glum," Tolz said. "I look at it this way, we live, or we die; little we can do other than continue on our way. We may be the last hope this planet has."

"I do not think our little group is going to save the planet," Johlnz said with some sadness in his voice.

"It's not merely us, I hope, and we are not just running for our lives. We will meet others along the way, and a place is already set up down at the equator. We only need so many to preserve the Tana race, and we are not alone on the planet."

Tolz walked over to Johlnz and put his hand on his friend's shoulder. The gesture of friendship did make Johlnz more at ease.

"Stay positive and stay strong. I have been through worse, and I will be around to help you.

"Now go take your new sleeping companion to bed and get some rest! We are leaving at 2:00 in the premid. See you then?"

PART 2 – Travel South

Autnar 05

It has been a long daz; even so, I do not expect to get much sleep.

Our convoy of bulk-transports left the camo at two in the premid as promised. I felt a twinge of remorse at having to depart the camo, as it represented the promise of a better future. I believe leaving is a sign of failure, a sign of giving up, even though Tolz had told me otherwise. But also, as he said to me last nitz, "we live, or we die," there was not anything more we could do at this facility or in the Provinces.

Tolz told me we would be following back byways along Rz 800 as much as possible until, at some point, we would be on the main. We did not plan to use any major byways since we did not want to be too much out in the open, and many jar-tranways were sure to be blocked with abandoned transports. Most of all, we wanted to stay away from any big cizay or towzs along the way.

Around middaz, the convoy split, and the second group took a different routway. The strategy would give us a better chance since if one convoy was attacked or had problems, the second group could hopefully provide a rescue. We were in constant, coded communication with each other, and each bulk-transport also included a transponder.

The daz remained uneventful; we were able to keep moving with little problems. We were about 600 zilos away from Roswell when we decided to stop for the nitz at around eight. One of the guards instructed me to sleep in the back of the transport tonitz, but tomorrow nitz, it would be my turn to help patrol while at Riczland, a small towz outside of Jackzon.

The transport and bedding are uncomfortable, so I do not expect to get much sleep as I wrote in the beginning.

Autnar 06

I must have fallen asleep eventually because, at around six in the premid, another guard brusquely awakened me for breakfast, which was simple and not satisfying. We were on the move again a zaka later, heading to the camo in Riczland, where we would reunite with the second group and gain some more members and various transports.

As we neared Riczland, more individuals were around, and many saw our convoy, yet no one caused any trouble. One thing I have failed to mention so far is all of our transports have a fake logo and name, which makes us look like an official Authority Emergency Management team. Those with weapons are in a Provincial Guard uniform to frighten off anyone who might have ideas about trying to stop or rob the convoy.

We arrived without incident in the early evening. The other convoy arrived ahead of us, and most of the bulk-transports were in large garages to keep them out of sight. Our transports were a few hundred yarzs away on the opposite side of the camo. Better to still stay apart in case we had to make a quick getaway.

We arrived to find a good, plentiful dinner in the camo, and after dinner, we had a large group meeting to discuss our routway and plans. We would be in three groups as we advanced south. A small, well-armed group would go out two zakas in advance and check out as much of both routways as possible. Although there were places where we would use the same byways, the two main convoys would travel about a zaka apart.

I discovered later, the first convoy did have some trouble on the byway, but they quickly dispatched of the problem. That is all the details we received, and it did not make me comfortable, as I imagined how they handled the incident. I would continue to be in the second convoy, which was being well protected, and I would be traveling with Tolz, which made me feel better. At least I will have a good friend to talk to about our possible futures.

Our next major stop would be about 775 zilos away in Morzey-Sanzez, Zexan Province, a tiny towz on the Tezacian border. Our routway would take us west about 75 zilos around Touzton. As suspected, the tidal waves hadn't completely washed away the surroundings, and we wanted to avoid any places that could still have a sizable population.

My patrol shift started a few zakas after dinner. We would be doubling up, and I was happy to find out my partner would be Tolz.

"Hello Tolz, I am glad to see you, although you may not feel the same; after all, this little puppy I am carrying is not exactly familiar to me."

"I can always count on you for a laugh Johlnz. Do not worry; I am sure you will have my back if necessary. Just make sure you are not pointing at my back."

"Very funny, friend."

They walked out to their designated assignment, tightening their jackets as they went in the last of the early twilight. They both had nitz goggles they put on and activated when the last of the light slipped away.

The camp remained quiet, with a couple of fires burning to give the mechanics some warmth. Johlnz made sure not to look at the fires while he wore the goggles.

The mechanics were performing some last-minzaka maintenance and double-checks before heading out again, and Johlnz realized their job was one of the most important.

"It's a little cold tonitz," Johlnz said, only to make some small talk before broaching the intended subject. "So, what do you think of our chances of getting down to our final destination?"

"I think as long as there isn't too much damage along the byways, we should be okay. The plan is to drive as close to the coast as possible since most survivors have moved inland. I do not expect much trouble from anyone, at least not here or in Tezaci. When we leave Tezaci, things could change. They were never safe areas in the past, especially since the uprising and revolution."

"So, relax now and worry later. Is that what you are telling me, Tolz?"

"You've got it, buddy."

"Oh, I have some news you might not be aware of," Tolz continued. "Those two tanwez we caught sneaking around the camo are with us. We gave them the option of joining our group or being locked up in the camo, with no promise anyone would ever find them. They, of course, opted to join the group."

"That is a relief. Based on what I heard, I thought maybe the tanwez were; well—you know."

"Killed," Tolz said. He continued without waiting for confirmation. "You will need to prepare yourself for the fact we may have to do things, like kill fellow Tanans; individuals who are only like ourselves, trying to survive. The group we work with is not evil, but they will protect this mission, and the security force is prepared to do whatever we must."

"I know, Tolz. I know what the planet has become. So where are the tanwez, I have not seen them?"

"They are still locked up in one of the bulk-transports and will stay there until we leave the Provinces. They will be less likely to try anything when outside of the country."

"Makes sense," Johlnz replied as they silently continued their patrol.

A few minzakas later, a piece of debris sailed well overhead on its way west, blazing a trail of fire in the sky. Johlnz wondered if it was an omen.

Autnar 08

We continued our journey south in the early premid before the sun came above the horizon. With the northern hemisphere continuing to tilt toward the sun, the nitz zakas are getting shorter. The sun was up by four-thirty this premid, not that you could see it as anything other than a bright fuzziness.

We were close enough to the coast to see large areas of tidal wave damage in the distance. We passed over a small river, and when I looked down, I could see Tana remains lying along the banks. The tidal waves probably carried the bodies up the river before receding to the ocean.

Around three in the pastmid, we were startled by a loud boom, followed by a bright light trailing across the sky, lighting up the clouds below. What the scientists feared had started to happen. A chunk of the planet or comet, which had been thrown up into orbit, was coming down. Larger than the one the nitz before, this one had to be huge based on the brightness. I have never been more afraid in my life. Not even the daz of the comet frightened me in this way. The chunk moved over our heads, heading west. After a few minzakas, we saw a bright flash, as the piece of debris hit Tanacun. Minzakas later, a huge gust of hot wind blew over us, followed by a tremendous crashing sound. We were lucky. Had the piece of debris been fifty or so zilos closer, we might very well have not survived.

A few zakas later, we met up with the second group and stopped to camp for the nitz. The advance team would remain about ten zilos in front of us, and a small team moved back about five zilos behind.

I did not have guard duty, so I am looking forward to some rest. It's disconcertingly quiet tonitz. After what happened earlier, no one feels in the mood to talk or play any card games.

Autnar 09

It remained quiet when we broke camp to move on early in the premid. Again, we would travel as two groups with an advanced team out ahead. Everyone remained a little on edge after the debris fall yesterdaz. By lunch, things lightened up a bit, with some joking around.

Our lives were likely to come to an end sooner rather than later, yet we joked around merely to stay sane; our attempt at normalcy did not last long.

We stopped for a lunch break around 11:00, and some of the team went off on patrol to check the area as usual.

Johlnz sat on the end of the transport he had been riding in since premid, with Tolz and Arten, finishing the lunch of Authority P-paks. They were not as bad as he expected, but he would be happy when dinnertime came.

He spent the premid working on cybezs in the transport, set up as a work area, so Johlnz could perform minor repairs as they traveled. Tolz and Arten had joined him after they finished their patrol.

While they were cleaning up, the Doctor's assistant, Thereza, passed by and said a quick hello, to the guys sitting around the vehicle. After acknowledging her with his own hello, Johlnz watched her walk away, admiring the view.

"Put your eyes back in your head, buddy tan, a guy like you has not a chance with her."

Oh, really, Tolz, and I guess you think you do?"

"Your both nuts," Arten said as he got up, unbuttoned his shirt, and posed like a bodybuilder. "Look at this body; abundant muscle, blonden hair, cobalt eyes, and plenty of chest hair. What's not to love about me?"

"I would say," said Johlnz, "your lack of common sense caused by your pea-sized brain."

"And lack of style, sophistication, humility, and manners," added Tolz."

"I am sure Thereza is the kind of tanwoz who wants a full package starting with intelligence and overall good looks. Any dimwit can push weights around."

While Arten and Tolz laughed at his comment, Johlnz thought how good it felt to laugh, if just for a little while. Arten was about to respond to Johlnz's last comment when all doxx broke loose.

A series of explosions followed by gunfire erupted from the back of the convoy. Tolz and Arten quickly grabbed their guns and went running toward the commotion as a moment later, a couple of non-security tanmen came running past Johlnz yelling, "someone set off a trap; it is an ambush!"

The essential team members; the scientists, who were not trained to fight, were sent into the more heavily protected bulk-transports as the rest of the non-security personnel ran for cover. Since Johlnz was not currently on security duty, he had stowed his gear a couple of vehicles back where he had bunked the nitz before.

Johlnz could not hide in the work transport while his friends were risking their lives, so he started working his way back to the bulk-transport where he could get his vest and weapon. The gunfire had stopped, and it had become eerily quiet when a rocket shell passed overhead, which luckily landed about thirty yarzs behind his position.

His transport lay only a few more yarzs away and in sight. Crouching behind the supplies transport, he encountered Bartlex Joaxton, a cook and general maintenance crewman Johlnz had spoken to a few times. He was hiding there, shaking with fear.

"Bart, have you seen who is attacking?"

"No, Johlnz, I was working under this transport when I heard the explosions."

Johlnz was about to tell him he should have stayed under the transport when more gunfire erupted as one of the unknown assailants attacked again, and Bart—hit in the head, fell to the ground. With his heart pounding, Johlnz quickly ran the rest of the way back to the transport, jumped in and grabbed his gun without putting on the vest, and headed back in the direction of where he thought the assailant hid. He saw movement in the woods, which he knew was not one of his group, so he fired into the trees, hoping at the very least, to scare the person away.

He heard more gunfire from the front of the convoy; heart pounding, he quickly ran in that direction and saw two tanmen with machine guns being swiftly brought down by one of the convoy's guards. Another assailant had made it around the front of the convoy before being shot, and three others running away were taken down quickly as well.

Johlnz stopped and leaned against one of the bulk-transports as he scanned the heavy brush while thanking the One; unlike him, most of the security trained often for combat. He knew, if they did not have these tanmen, they would probably all be dead by now. As he finished the thought, he saw movement in the shadows of the trees.

A few moments later, a hand explosive flew towards him from the brush. The small but dangerous bomb landed next to him and rolled under the transport. Without thinking, he reached under the transport, picked up the explosive, and threw it back toward the trees. The device exploded before it hit the ground; even so, he believed pieces of debris ended up hitting one of the attackers as he heard a scream come from the direction of the explosion. Johlnz was shocked and surprised he did such a stupid thing; still, in all, it probably saved his life as well as one of the bulk-transports.

He heard someone in the woods yell retreat, and the small amount of gunfire he was hearing, quickly stopped. However, the convoy's security teams did not stop as they ran into the trees after the attackers, with Johlnz following behind. He heard more gunfire from ahead of him as he ducked behind a tree, and then there was silence.

Along with one of the other deftanmen, Arten came walking through the trees in his direction.

"Johlnz, are you unhurt?"

"I am, yes."

"Where the doxx is your vest? You could have gotten yourself killed."

"I guess back where I bunked last nitz. I did not even think to stop to grab it; I just grabbed my gun and headed out."

"You get yourself killed; the Doc will not be happy. It's not like we can find another cybez geek wandering around," he said with a smile. Let's head back and check around the far end of the convoy for more assailants. Five of our guys are out checking the perimeter and going over the bodies for spoils."

"Spoils?" Johlnz asked.

"Yes, you know, weapons, ammunition, clothes, food, anything we can use."

Johlnz tried to push the thought out of his head. The individuals who attacked them were their countrymen, citizens of the Provinces, and now their enemies. *Why did it have to come to this?*

He told Arten he wanted to check on Bartlex. After Johlnz explained what happened, Arten told him to keep his eyes open and sent him on his way.

Johlnz saw no additional assailants as he returned to where he had left Bartlex lying on the ground, wounded. He found the young cook lying dead, with his blood trailing down the hill into the trees. The young tanmen lived barely twenty-one cycles, and now he was gone, just like that, for no damn good reason. He was unsure if Bart had died immediately or bled to death while he ran off trying to be something he was not.

He died utterly alone, lying in the dirt. The realization caused Johlnz to lose control of his emotions as he fell to his knees and wept.

(((*)))

A half a zaka later, Johlnz went looking for Tolz, hoping he was okay. He found Tolz, and the other tanmen returning from their scavenging, carrying guns and ammunition.

"Spoils from the dead," he said, a bit more sarcastically than intended.

"No, and glad to see you are alive too, Johlnz."

"I am sorry Tolz, I am not cut out for this. I spent the last half zaka crying over the body of Bartlex Joaxton. I can't imagine someone picking over his young body for a few trinkets."

Tolz's expression changed to one of despair. "He was a great kid. I am sorry, and no, these are from the attacker's camp. I know you do not want to hear this right now, but I need your help bringing back more of their equipment we can use; and where the doxx is your vest?"

"Yes, I know, stupid thing to do. Arten already read me the riot act."

A few minzakas later, Johlnz and a few other tanmen followed Tolz back to the camp, where they took everything useful and headed back to the convoy. When they arrived, Malcolz informed them they needed to move right away in case any others heard the noise.

A couple of tires, flattened by projectiles, had been changed while they gathered the supplies from the camp. None of the bulk-transports had significant damage, so they were back on their way, moving faster than usual to get out of the area.

We continued moving southwest between Touzton and what was Corzus Batt, an old swanky seaside resort, until a couple of zakas after dark. We proceeded to make camp and re-inspected the bulk-transports to look for additional damage. Some further problems were found and quickly fixed before dinner. The Doc had called a short meeting to regroup and evaluate our situation, which I considered grim at best.

We lost three good tanmen in the fighting. One, Franlix Anders; killed by the explosive he tripped, another, Josex Delpox; shot in the woods during the fighting, and the final casualty, Bartlex Joaxton.

I include their names here, so if anyone someday reads my journal, at least their names will not be lost. They died in service to what little remains of civilization.

There was a moment of silence, and afterward, Doc informed the group we should be in Morcey-Sanchez by tomorrow nitz. We darkened the camp and went to our assigned areas to sleep. I am barely holding my emotions in check. We could not properly bury the bodies of our friends, and the thought of them lying on the open ground waiting for the animals to take their spoils is making me sick.

Autnar 10

Autnar 10, what does it mean now? Why do I keep using dates? The daz, the zaka means nothing as the planet continues to turn in two directions at once while moving around the sun. I guess we, or at least, I need something, some marker to define the events of our lives, even as our lives might be nearing the end.

I wonder if what is remaining of the Tanacun population has noticed yet. Do the survivors know they will soon die a possibly slow and painful death?
Such thoughts are not helpful, I know, but how can I not think them?

The daz stayed uneventful. We traveled with the other convoy, thinking our combined strength might be more critical, and we somehow picked up additional transport along the way. They added three large-size all-terrain transports, which will help us cross the border and traverse the backlands.

We arrived at Morcey-Sanchez in the early evening, although the warmer, extremely hazy sun hung far above the horizon. The cooler evenings were getting notably shorter every daz.

Morcey-Sanchez was a tiny towz on the Tezacian border. There appeared to be no individuals around the area any longer, all fleeing to some supposed safe place. We made camp and settled down for the nitz, while the group leaders held a meeting, with no additional information shared.

In the premid, we will head south on Rz 83 to Zalcon Heights. We hope to go around the south end of the reservoir to cross the border.

Zalcon Heights

I have decided to track my life by location going forward. I do not expect it to last much longer anyway, and I feel places, as meaningless as they are now, describe in a better way, this journey.

We reached Zalcon Heights and were greeted by gunfire, although it was not directed at us this time. We ended up driving almost directly into a small civil war to control what remained of the towz. We headed around the northeastern side of towz and then down below toward the river when we realized the situation.

We did not go unnoticed. One of the groups fighting for control of the towz, blocked the byway with a few old Authority lisks, forcing us to stop.

"Johlnz, you need to gear up, with your vest on this time, and come with me to the front of the convoy."

"What's going on Tolz, why have we stopped?"

"A couple of lisks from one of the groups fighting in Zalcon have blocked the byway, not letting us pass. I am not sure what they want, but we need to be showing some firepower up there. Most of the security is flanking them on the side or guarding our back. Let's get going."

"Okay, I am ready, I guess."

"Not holding your gun that way, Johlnz. You need to look at least like you know what you are doing."

Tolz showed Johlnz the proper way to hold the weapon, so he looked ready to use it in a split second. When they arrived at the front of the convoy, they found Malcolz and Dr. Moxron talking to three tanmen, two of whom with weapons of their own held in the same manner Tolz had just shown to Johlnz.

Here I go again; I am a damn engineer, not a deftanmen. What if I have to shoot this gun at someone; what if I actually kill someone? I do not know if I can handle killing another Tanan. I do not know if I can continue —

"Be ready, Johlnz!"

The instruction from Tolz woke him from his thoughts, and he saw two large-sized open-back delivery bulk-transports had now joined the lisks blocking the byway with a driver behind the wheel in each one — Johlnz assumed, in case they have to make a quick getaway. They do not appear to have guns, he thought, though they might be hiding them on their laps. He felt surprised his mind was starting to work like a deftanmen.

Tolz directed Johlnz to stand at the front left side of their lead transport while he took up position to the right. Johlnz tried not to appear nervous, but he knew he was sweating and his heart pounding. Sweat ran down his face and into his eyes as he watched. They appeared to be having a friendly conversation until Malcolz spoke up loudly.

"We told you, we are merely passing through on important Authority business. We are not going to help you or whomever it is you are fighting against."

One of the tanmen spoke up just as loudly.

"The tanmen we are fighting are drug dealers from across the border. They are trying to take over the towz and use it as a base to import more drugs. Do not you care enough to help protect your own country?"

"So, you say," Malcolz responded, "nevertheless, as far as we know, you are the drug smugglers trying to take over the towz. Either way, we cannot help in any way; now move your equipment so we can continue."

"No," responded the tanmen, obviously in charge, as he raised his gun and pointed it at Dr. Moxron. It was the last word he ever said, the final move he would ever make, as the two with weapons were shot dead on the spot by the security tanmen hiding behind a dumpster on the side of the byway. The remaining tanmen ran, jumped into one of the bulk-transports, and the drivers quickly headed back to towz, leaving the bodies where they fell.

"Thank the One," Johlnz said, "I did not need another gunfight. One a weez is enough. In fact, one a lifetime is enough."

Tolz walked over and put his hand on Johlnz's shoulder. "Maybe you need to lay down and die, cause the other daz will surely not be the last."

Johlnz did not know what to make of Tolz's comment. He was about to respond when Malcolz ordered the convoy to start moving and told Tolz and Johlnz to watch the sides as they moved by and then join the guards in the rear transport. When they got into the vehicle, four guards were already inside, so Johlnz could not talk to Tolz, and he decided to let it go.

They proceeded a little farther south and then along the Zia Tranda River, looking for a good spot to cross, when they came upon a makeshift bridge of dirt and debris. Large pipes were placed under the rubble to allow the river to flow through; however, the makeshift bridge had started eroding in many places.

The leaders put everyone to work, including themselves, to make repairs and spent the next three zakas, making it more robust, so they could cross. They also pulled all the fake UPJ Authority logos and nameplates off the bulk-transports and toned down the UPJ Authority look of their clothes. They had some Tezacian license plates, which they quickly placed on the transports, with plans to acquire others after they crossed the border.

When it came time to cross, Doc gave instructions to move as fast as possible. A few bulk-transports got stuck a couple of times; eventually, though, they got through and were welcomed to Tezaci by the sight of another piece of debris falling from the sky, thankfully heading far west of their location. The convoy proceeded a few zilos further south away from the river and made camp for the nitz.

Tezaci

I have little to write about this evening since I had an uneventful daz. I wish all dazs could be slow, but I know it is not likely. In the early premid, before we moved on, a meeting was called to discuss the plans for proceeding. To everyone not already equipped, they gave a bulletproof vest, and told everyone to always wear them and keep them close at nitz.

Malcolz expected we would encounter more problems in Tezaci, and we should be ready always to defend ourselves, be alert, and be prepared to fight. His exact words were 'to shoot first and keep moving.'

I am sickened by what we have become and again thought it would be better to die now. Maybe a piece of debris should fall on us and finish us off. The One if Itz exists, surely has sent the message we are not worthy. Or maybe as individuals have suggested, someone in the universe or the universe itself finds us worthless.

I sat on the back of my transport, feeling depressed during my break. While I sat there despondent, Tolz came over to apologize for his comment the daz before. He said he was sorry and out of line. He told me he values our friendship and needs to remember I was never trained for any of this excitement, as he jokingly called our travels. Our conversation made me feel a lot better.

So far, there are no signs of any other inhabitants. The towz of Montezzey to the west may be still standing and not destroyed, and farther south, Sal Luiz Potozi. We headed south and a little east to the ocean since it is not likely to be populated after the waves. We tried to avoid any towzs, which was easy as we went closer to the coast since nothing remained.

We saw much evidence of the destruction as we approached within fifty zilos of the east coast of Tezaci. The convoy used existing byways as much as possible, but the waves have wiped out many, and those remaining were full of debris.

By nitzfall, we had progressed over three hundred zilos, and we stopped outside what was once the vilogge of Panuzco.

Tezaci – Panuzco

Well, that was fun. Not really; anyway, I am feeling the need to add some humor to my journal. I hear tell, hilarity is the best remedy, and I need some damn good remedies.

I awoke this premid to an ashen sky filled with intermittent heavy rain. The rain slowed the convoy, and the transport I rode in heated up and became unbearable, so when we stopped to clear the byway, I stepped outside for some air. As we prepared to move on, I felt a terrible pain in my chest, as I was knocked backward, hitting my head hard on the thankfully soggy ground. All I could feel as I hit the ground was relief because, for me, it would all be over.

I remember hearing a lot of shouting and gunfire before I passed out, and when I awoke for the second time todaz, I lay on a cot in one of the bulk-transports. I could see my vest, which I had forgotten I wore, and my shirts tossed on a chair. Wrapped tightly around my chest, I felt cloth, and it hurt to take a deep breath; still, I did not think I broke any bones. They had bandaged my head as well, and it hurt like doxx. The medic noticed I awoke, so she came over to check my condition.

"Hello, Johlnz, I see you are awake. How are you feeling?"

"My head hurts like doxx, and my chest isn't much better. What happened?"

"Do not worry about what happened; you need to get some rest to feel better. Your vest stopped the projectile, with no apparent broken bones; however, you may have a mild concussion. Lucky for you, your head fell into a muddy puddle, which helped cushion the blow. I will be back to check your vitals, but Tolz is waiting outside."

As he lay waiting for Tolz to come in, Johlnz realized he was happier to be alive than he expected. Even in the worst of times and life, something in us makes us want to live, even if for only one more miserable, rainy daz.

"Why you lazy piece of shizz, what are you doing in here just laying around?"

"Love you too!"

"Oh, dear maker, do not get all mushy on me, Johlnz. How are you doing?"

"No broken bones and I can always use some extra sense knocked into my head. What happened?"

"A group of eight fighters ambushed us. We lost three good individuals, and we eliminated all the assailants. The Doc sends his regards, and oddly enough, Thereza asked me to pass on her regards as well."

"Malcolz is worried we might run into more trouble since this was a more populated area before the comet than what we have gone through before, so we are heading a little closer to the coast, if possible, to encounter fewer individuals.

"Move on, kiss, and get out, the party is over," the medic said as she came back and approached the bed, pushing Tolz aside.

"I need to check his vitals, and Arten is looking for you.

"Arten also asked me to say hello to you, Johlnz, and wants to know if you would like to do a guard shift tonitz?"

"Always the comedian," Johlnz thought as Tolz sheepishly waved goodbye.

We could not stay close to the coast for long before we had to go back west and take the pass through the Vexacruz Mountains. We stopped for the evening without any more problems, other than the rain, after having gone only about one hundred more zilos south of where we were before the attack. I heard through the grauavine; Doc was not happy about our progress.

Tezaci - The Premid After

They permitted me to stay in my usual bunk last nitz, but I remained sore this premid. I found myself able to be mobile for a while until all doxx broke loose again.

This time the universe was trying again to take us out. We advanced almost twenty-five zilos cross country, east of Martex Torre, heading for the byway through the mountains when we heard a loud boom from far overhead and to the east.

A short time later, we saw a flash of light in the eastern sky and heard another loud noise like an explosion, as all doxx broke loose.

The radios scattered throughout the convoy all came to life at once. "Move as fast as possible to the southwest towards the pass. Do not stop for any reason; we have to get the bulk-transports through."

It became apparent to everyone a large piece of debris had fallen in the Gulf of Tezaci, and a tsunami probably headed our way. We had no way to know how large; nevertheless, this was relatively flat land below the mountains to the south, and even a foot or two of fast-moving water could wipe us out for good.

The convoy moved at well over fifty zilos a zaka, across rough terrain, giving Johlnz a lot of pain in his chest and head as he lay on the cot in the back of the transport. He could do nothing beyond worry about what could be heading their way, more death and destruction from above.

Eventually, the ride smoothed out, and Tolz said they were now on a dirt byway, and Johlnz silently thanked the One. Tolz had managed to jump in the transport before they had started booking it for the mountain pass. It was good to have him there, Johlnz thought, especially if the transport became washed off the byway.

A moment later, the radio came to life with bad news. One of the bulk-transports flipped over before they made it to the dirt byway. The vehicle had been empty except for the driver and two passengers since they had just picked it up at the border. Ralton Xsine, the driver, was dead; however, the two passengers were safe but injured. One of the support lisks stopped and quickly picked them up.

A half-zaka later, the first bulk-transports made it to the byway going through the mountains; even so, they were not all safe yet. The last of the convoy remained in harm's way.

"Damn it to doxx," Arten said, "I see the wave coming. It doesn't look too big, all the same, we are only fifteen zilos from the coast, and this land is flatter than a sail cake. It's likely to overtake us before we all get to higher ground."

"Always the bringer of bad news. Do you have any good news, Tolz?"

"Umm, not really, oh yes, the byway we are on is raised a few pads, so that is something."

"So, if we run off the byway, we are not likely to get back on. Who's driving this bucket?"

"No idea, buddy, but the wave is getting closer and is just about to hit the end bulk-transports. It reminds me of the images I saw from Xazan a couple of cycles ago when a tanaquake struck them and caused multiple tsunamis to hit the island. The scene here looks similar to those videos. It's not a wave like you would see in the ocean. It's just water; it starts at a couple of inches and quickly gets deeper and deeper."

The water swamped the byway behind them, which meant it was well over four pads and climbing. They were now moving close to seventy zilos a zaka since they were back on the byway, which continued slowly rising, though not fast enough. The water began to overtake the last vehicle of the convoy, only three bulk-transports behind.

The wave rose a pad around the last transport's wheels, and the vehicle started to slow down when the water's advance slowed and began to recede down the slope.

They barely made it. If the convoy had been on the plain, the water would have swept them away. Anyone still on the flats or down below ahead of the travelers would no longer be a problem, for they would no longer be alive.

"We just made it in time, Johlnz. We were damn lucky."

"Yea, this time. Will we be so lucky next time? If the power or powers that be, keep picking us off one by one, who will be left to make it to possible safety?"

"You keep talking doom and gloom, and I am going to recommend we drop you off at the first shrivel we can find, and you can be their problem."

"Good luck finding one."

They continued for another ten zilos before stopping to regroup and discuss their next obstacle. Johlnz felt restless, useless, and claustrophobic.

"Help me get up, Tolz; I want to get out of this damn thing and hear what's going on."

Tolz helped Johlnz get out of the transport, which was not as bad as expected. Thankfully, his head no longer hurt, but his chest still throbbed, and every step he took shot a spasm of pain through his body. He moved a bit slow along the convoy, and they got to the gathering spot as the Doc started to speak.

"We are five zilos away from the towz of Mixantla. This byway passes right through the middle of towz, so there is no way to avoid it and keep a low profile. Our advance scouts came back with what's happening at the towz."

"Because the towz was in the mountains, it probably survived the first tsunamis and is now a haven for individuals too afraid to go back down the mountains. We do not know how many live in the towz, how well armed they are, or if they will cause trouble. The scouts saw many liltanz and tanwez, with no obvious guards, Authority, or enforcers.

"I hope, Johlnz, we can get through without incident; I do not want to have to shoot a liltanz's parent."

Security issued a weapon to everyone not already equipped, and Tolz told Johlnz to get his vest on and grab his gun. He would be back in the same transport he rode in before and hopefully would not be needed. Tolz was going to be upfront in the lead vehicle with Arten.

The convoy moved along the byway as fast as possible and had no intention of stopping for anything. Since Johlnz was in the back of the transport, he could not see where they were, but the driver yelled back as they entered Mixantla.

They continued on a bit slower as the convoy went through the damaged towz. Gunfire erupted, and one projectile ripped through the canopy over Johlnz as he then heard return gunfire from the convoy.

They made it most of the way through the towz when forced to stop. Johlnz did not know why they stopped, and he received orders to stay in the transport unless he heard other instructions over the radio. He was happy to oblige since he remained tired from the pain medication, and after being stopped for a while, he drifted off to sleep.

Yes, I fell asleep, something Tolz will never let me forget. After he finished laughing, Tolz told me we had to stop because the byway had been blocked by barricades and guarded by tanmen with guns.

Dr. Moxron used the loudspeaker to say we intended no harm; we were only passing through on our way south. The tanmen responded they were not going to let us through without payment. They wanted food supplies, medicine, and of course, guns.

After a couple of zakas negotiating and the death of one of the tanmen blocking the byway, they decided to let us through if we gave them some food. Their individuals were running out of supplies and were dying. We ended up giving them food and medicine we thought we could spare before they let us pass.

Tolz believed it was a little too easy. He figured they probably did not have many projectiles, and when they realized we were well-armed and willing to use the weapons, they backed down.

We traveled another four zakas, passing through other smaller towzs without any trouble before stopping for the nitz near the end of the pass in the vilogge of Zilotepex.

Tezaci – Zilotepex

Premid came, as did the pain from my previous injuries. I think all the shaking around yesterday was not good for my body.

The advance team dispatched before dawn, which is around 4:00 AT, presently. The mission, check out the towz and, if possible, inspect the byway below. They reported the vilogge looked deserted. It had received some flood damage from the first tsunami and also appeared to have had a tanaquake. The byway through the vilogge remained passable; however, the byway below is at some places still covered with water or deep mud.

The leaders decided we should move to the other side of the vilogge and wait for a daz or two for the valley to dry out. Teams were sent into towz to look for useful supplies; however, there was not much to be found. I had volunteered to go, but the medics instructed me to rest. Later I had to look at some of the cybezs, which were acting up. The fast, bumpy ride yesterday was not kind to them either. Wish I had someone to make me all better.

Tezaci – Leaving Zilotepex

We stayed above the valley for two dazs waiting for the mud to dry, and I spent most of the time resting or working on the cybezs. The medics again did not want me helping on patrols until I was one hundred percent unless we had an emergency. Thankfully, no difficulties reared their ugly heads, and I started to feel better.

The plan was to use the jar-tranways in some areas, though most of our travels would be off-byway going forward, which is why we had to delay our movement.

I am writing this journal entry on the evening of the first daz we resumed heading south. The sun was barely visible this premid when I awoke and prepared for guard duty. I am not sure if the sky was filled with clouds or debris this premid, but I have noticed the farther south we go, the sky is getting darker.

Malcolz assigned me a position in the back transport vehicle along with a couple of other guards I did not know well. We traveled along the former central jar-tranway south until later in the day when the way became blocked, and we had to divert to back byways in not much better condition. The two tsunamis we know of caused a lot of damage to the infrastructure. As expected, we did not see anyone in the area since the floods would have swept away anyone here, most likely to their death.

The advance team moved ahead and cleared some of the debris blocking our intended routway. Progress continued to be slow due to the massive amounts of damage. Below the now ruined towz of Rinzonaxa, we had to divert and go along even smaller side byways. The central way headed too far toward the gulf, and one of the advance teams confirmed the substantial damage, which would have slowed down the convoy.

We moved across the flat and scrubbed clean plain until we approached the next central byway in great shape and thankfully deserted. The convoy made significant progress and continued forward until nitzfall.

Dr. Moxron wanted to proceed in the dark; however, security advised our lights would be visible for a long distance, which could draw out anyone still in the area. The Doc realized the risk to be considerable, so the advance team stayed ahead of us a couple of zilos while we stopped along the byway until premid.

Tolz had stopped by to give me all the details of the daz I might not have heard since he knows I am keeping this journal. We spent a few minzakas talking about the last few dazs' events and joking around with my recent travel companions.

Tezaci – Out in the Open to Tuxtla

We had to leave the central byway again todaz and go cross-country to where the central intersected with our next planned way forward. The plan was to go across the plains to our next way south, about eighty zilos away. We would then move across more open land until we came to the next small byway needed to shorten our journey.

Our plans quickly changed when we found most of our intended way blocked by heavy debris. Malcolz ordered two advance teams out to find the best pathway through, and we were on the move a bit before middaz.

This area of Tezaci is less than one hundred zilos wide and was most likely inundated with water after the comet struck, except for in the mountains. If another piece of debris fell and hit in the gulf or Narral Ocean, the area would be quickly covered with water again, so we had to move at a quick pace.

It was another bumpy ride, though not as bad as before, and we made it to a small un-named byway, so covered with dirt, you could barely see the byway at all. A few zakas later, we made our way to higher ground without any incidents. We proceeded west to the towz of Tuxtla, and we are staying here for the nitz.

Tolz, Arten, and I had dinner together, and we talked about, of all things, the One.

As they finished with dinner, another piece of debris was first heard like prolonged thunder, then seen falling toward the Narral Ocean. They knew they were safe where camped, but the land they had been crossing a few zakas ago, would soon be underwater.

"Did you ever stop to wonder why?" Tolz said, surprising both Johlnz and Arten.

"Wonder what?" asked Johlnz.

"Why this happened? Why now? Are we being punished for our sins, or is the universe just tired of us? I grew up in a religious Roztant camo, and my parents always told me the One had a plan. Either Itz doesn't exist, or the One is a malicious Muzie Flutar!"

Johlnz was the first to answer.

"I grew up in an appropriate religious camo as well. Jozna Athix; basilic every weez, twelve cycles of Athix education, and for what? Will I go to the light if this kills me or when I die of old age? When my fiancé took her life, I was ready for the planet to be over."

"Shizz, I did not know; I am sorry," Arten and Tolz both replied. Johlnz could detect the sincerity in their voices, so he decided to tell them the entire story. When Johlnz finished, Arten spoke first.

"I understand Johlnz, why you would think the individuals of this planet deserve to die, still not everyone is, or maybe I should say, was out for their individual interest above all. I do not talk much about my past, and I plan on keeping it that way, yet I must say, in my travels, I have seen many decent individuals doing good for others while sacrificing for themselves."

Before Johlnz could respond, Arten continued.

"I hope neither the final light nor doxx exists and hope the universe doesn't hold a grudge because I have done many things, which could send me to damnation."

The three of them sat in silence for a few minzakas before Arten spoke up again.

"We should probably get some rest. I believe we are together tomorrow on team one scouting."

"Me, scouting," Johlnz said? "That is new; what happened to the usual team?"

"Rantal sprained his pad yesterday, and Brazner got knocked out of the lisk earlier when they hit some debris, so he is out a few dazs. Get some rest, be sharp tomorrow, and do not forget your vest, Johlnz."

"You will never let me live that down."

"Absolutely not, goodnitz!"

As I watched them both head back to their bunks, I thought about becoming a deftanmen unwittingly, and I was unsure how I felt about my new responsibility. At least my pains are gone, so I am hoping to have a good nitz's sleep. I think I will need to be well-rested.

Tezaci – Horror on the Byway

I awoke to the sounds of more debris falling nearby, but thankfully these were much smaller pieces. If anything hit Tanacun, they were minimal by the time they hit.
We were near what had been moderately large population areas before the comet, so they decided to send a couple of scout bulk-transports out ahead while the convoy waited. Although we could see signs of flood and tanaquake damage around us, there could still be a lot of individuals in the towzs, which were at higher elevations.

As I had written in yesterday's entry, I was to be part of one of the scouting groups. What we found was beyond anything I had seen before or could ever in the past have imagined.

They had been driving in the lisk for about twenty minzakas when they found access to a central way and continued without seeing any signs of life other than the carrion eaters circling above. After ten minzakas, they diverted to check out a couple of small towzs less than a zilo from the exit. Most of the first towz was in ruin from the tanaquakes; even so, a basilic remained standing with only damage to a wall now scattered on the ground.

"Tolz, drive on over to the basilic. If anyone is alive, that might be where they would go," Arten said.

Johlnz and Arten went in to check out the structure but found it empty, and it looked like it had been that way for a while. Johlnz found gilt ceremonials lying on the floor by the dais rail and carefully picked them up and put them back on the dais, silently saying a prayer.

"You know we might have use for that gilt Johlnz."

"No, Arten, it just would not be a correct thing."

Arten did not argue, so they went back to the list and checked some more areas of the towz; nevertheless, it appeared entirely deserted.

A few minzakas later, they were higher up the mountain in the next small towz and were horrified by what they found. Most of the towz had been devastated like the first one, and not even the basilic remained standing. As they were slowly driving, Johlnz yelled for Tolz to stop, and he jumped out of the list.

As he walked closer to what had caught his eye, he could not believe the sight. He stood in disbelief while a tear fell from his eye, followed by another. The sight shocked him like nothing before, as he took in row upon row of half-eaten, decomposed remains of approximately one hundred tanmen, tanwoz, and liltanz. The bodies lying in the dirt now had carrion-eaters walking among them, not at all bothered by Johlnz, as he stood close, watching as they were picking the remaining decayed meat off the bones.

He could do nothing except stand and cry, his legs weak and trembling. Thankfully, Tolz and Arten came by his side to give support.

"How could they do this to their liltanz? How could they lose all hope?" Tolz said as he put his hand on Johlnz's shoulder.

"I have seen this before," Arten said. "In war zones, individuals would decide there was no hope, and they would commit mass suicide. It looks like it happened a couple of mooncazts ago, maybe after additional floods or tanaquakes, or they just decided to give up."

His voice quivering with emotion, Johlnz spoke.

"I know, I . . . I have felt like giving up many times, especially after my own experiences, even so, I could never do this. I am too much of a coward to do it myself; that is why I have prayed for the One to end it and drop a rock on my head."

"Come on, Johlnz, it is time to head back to the convoy. Nothing remains here for the living."

Tolz walked beside his friend, ready to give whatever support he needed. He had also seen many things in his life as a deftanmen, but this was a horror he would not soon forget.

They traveled back to the convoy in silence, and when they returned, Johlnz and Tolz, let Arten make the formal report. Johlnz walked a short distance from the convoy, bent down, and threw up. He found it hard to believe it did not happen sooner, and he had no idea how he would get the image out of his head.

I have had to stop several times while writing tonitz, merely to cry, and calm my stomach before continuing. I know the scene disturbed Tolz more than he wants to admit, and I hope we all can get over it and work to save the lives we all still have. It's easy to give up, not easy to go on.

When the second group came back, they did confirm there was a sizeable group of individuals still living in the larger towzs farther along the central, so we would go mostly off the byway for the remainder of the daz.

Tomorrow, we head farther south to the next border crossing, as we hope no one is around to cause us any trouble. We've had more than enough already, or at least I have.

Time for bed, I have nothing more to say. I hope to the One, I do not dream.

Guazemax - At the Border

Thank the One, I did not dream the last nitz.

We made good progress todaz, and the daz ended amid a conversation with Tolz.

The convoy only had to go a hundred zilos to get to the border, but they were moving at an extreme slow pace since the byway was in bad condition and blocked with burned-out or broken-down transports littering the intended way south.

After a zaka of traveling, they heard a tremendous boom from above as another piece of debris flew overhead and struck the ground well over one hundred zilos away to the northwest. It was a reminder death could come from the sky at any time and end their trip permanently.

On the way, the convoy had to abandon one of the bulk-transports when the engine gave out, and they did not have the supplies necessary or the time to get it running again. They lost a zaka just moving the supplies it carried to another transport and pushing the broken-down transport out of the way.

At one point, the byway crossed a small river, which flowed backward due to waves coming up from the Narral Ocean. It was evident a sizeable piece had fallen somewhere out in the ocean, and the waves continued to move against and over the coastland. The water flowing back up the river contained debris from washed away camoz and other buildings, plus numerous bodies of animals and tanans.

As the convoy neared the border, a small lisk started approaching them from behind, and they could see four well-armed individuals in the vehicle. One of the convoy's larger; also well-armed Authority lisks moved behind the group and slowed down to head off the threat. When the security tanmen started firing warning shots, the approaching lisk backed off.

The convoy continued to within three zilos of the border as nitz started to descend, so they would wait until premid to cross. As usual, two teams went out behind, in case the lisk tried to come again at nitz, and another team went ahead to patrol closer to the border and look for any signs of life.

The daz ended as it began; another piece of debris fell to the planet north of the convoy's position, striking land about one hundred zilos away.

Johlnz sat on a chair he pulled out of a transport, enjoying the fire roaring in front of him when Tolz came up from behind.

"Did you order the fireflames?"

"Hey Tolz, good to see you; how was your daz?"

Tolz sat on the ground next to Johlnz and stuck his hands out to warm them on the blazing fire.

"Fine, dear, how was yours?"

"Do not be a smart ass Tolz, at any rate, since you didn't ask. I spent the daz riding up front with Theoxdore Yancez in the spare cybez parts transport. He's a genuinely nice guy."

"I do not think I know him."

"He joined the group before we crossed the border out of the Provinces. He has his partner and eight-cycle-old somz with him. I believe they are the only family with us on this wonderful excursion south."

"Now I know whom you are talking about, Johlnz. He used to be an equit-agent and learned to drive big transports because he always liked them."

"That is the guy. He told me he came to the Provinces when he turned twenty-two cycles old. He grew up an orphan in Iurox and was one of the last groups allowed in under the old lottery system. I would say he is lucky, but look where he is todaz."

"It could be worse, Johlnz; he could be dead; they could all be dead. At least they have some chance at survival."

"What kind of survival, Tolz? What awaits us down south, an actual life, or a life of waiting to die?"

"Enough depressing thoughts, time to change the subject. I spent my daz in the Authority lisk going after our friends who were following. From what we could see when we got closer, they were well-armed. I was surprised when they backed off, and I hope they are not planning something for tonitz."

"Isn't Arten out behind us tonitz," Johlnz asked.

"Yes, and he would never let anything happen to his best buds, so we probably have nothing to worry about.

"Hey, Johlnz, shouldn't you be updating your journal?"

"Maybe not tonitz, aside from meeting Theoxdore, it had been a boring daz. The best kind."

"I'll second that," Tolz said as he got up. "Good nitz Johlnz."

"Good nitz, Tolz. Do not let the bed duzgens bite."

Well, as apparent, I changed my mind about the journal. I realized after Tolz left, that even the most annoying and mundane of events have a place in our lives if only to balance out the hectic dazs.

Guazemax - Beyond the Border

The premid started with a meeting to discuss how we would proceed, and word, Dr. Moxron had spoken again to the group in Nizarax. They had managed to grow their facility and make it more secure than it had been the last time the group made contact. They encountered some hostility and had clashes with the locals, but things had died down, and they were starting to work together. The team in Nizarax hadn't yet revealed to the locals the complete truth.

"We have been in contact with the Nizarax compound and gave them our position. They have urged us to proceed with extreme caution since they are aware of warlords who have patrols in the area and are taking everything they can for themselves."

The person giving the update was Dr. Moxron's assistant, and Johlnz found himself paying more attention to her than the information.

"Why are they fortifying that compound? I thought we were going all the way to the equator," Arten asked.

"The team has informed Dr. Moxron the way farther south is no longer safe to travel, and the facility itself is smaller than what may be needed. They moved no equipment or supplies down to the south base, so all equipment is still in Nizarax. It may be possible at some point to have another settlement down in Matabas. Still, the way will not be safe for some time since the single way to the facility is currently below water because a lot of debris has fallen to the west, causing more waves, making it far inland. The settlement we are going to is only seventy zilos farther north, so it will make very little difference weather-wise, and it was always the intention to keep a presence in Nizarax."

When Thereza finished, Malcolz got up to speak.

"We need to be prepared to move out again in half a zaka. Everyone will be required to wear a bulletproof vest, and everyone trained will be armed. I will be in the forward scout group, along with our best-trained guards. Please see me up here for your assignments if you are not already assigned."

"Thank you, and good luck!"

A half-zaka later, they were on the move, and Johlnz was in the middle of the convoy with Tolz, in one of the supply bulk-transports. Usually, this time of cycle, riding in a covered transport like they were in would be like riding in an oven, however with temperatures well below average and the sun barely visible, it felt reasonably comfortable.

It became an active premid overhead in the sky, and Johlnz worried they were about to be hit. One piece of debris flew close overhead and landed somewhere to the west, probably in the ocean. The following waves would have killed anyone still along the coastland about fifty zilos to the west of the group's current position. The convoy was about a quarter-zilo above the present sea level, so even if fifty zilos were not safe enough, their height would keep them safe. A zaka later, more noise came from overhead as some smaller pieces of debris landed close enough to be heard and felt.

"That is getting way too close for me, Tolz. We may need stronger helmets."

Tolz laughed, "Well, Johlnz, if it is our time, then it is our time. I have decided I am no longer going to worry about it."

The convoy stopped for lunch, and Arten came back to their transport to join them.

"Talk about a close call. Did either of you tans shizz your pants?"

"No," replied Tolz, "I almost lost my dentures, and Johlnz stayed down on the floor, awaiting the end."

"Very funny Tolz, I almost died laughing."

"Oh, come on, Johlnz, at least it would be a happy death," Arten replied, and they all had a good laugh.

They finished lunch and were about to get in the bulk-transports to move forward when another large piece of debris fell less than a zilo behind the convoy. Arten felt sure it hit the byway on which they had recently traveled. The debris was not large enough to create any excessive heat or shock wave; even so, a couple of minzakas later, some small hail-sized pebbles and dirt did fall on top of them. Luckily, they were not significant or dense enough to cause any damage.

The convoy proceeded on its way again a few minzakas later and, Johlnz was going to try and rest a little, though Tolz wanted to talk. More accurately, he wanted to tease.

"So, Johlnz, I caught you staring at Thereza this premid, and you looked like you were fantasizing about getting a piece. It's a pity a guy like you will never get to do her."

"Tolz, you are a porlz, and if you do not stop, I am going to have to slug you one."

"Sticking up for her honor, so cute. I think I should tell her, see what she thinks, see what she says, and remind her she's too good for you."

"Do not you dare talk to her about me ever, really, I mean it."

Johlnz's throat tightened, his hands moved on their own, and he began to sweat, merely thinking about what Tolz could say to her. His friend was correct; Johlnz did have an attraction to her.

"Relax, Johlnz, do not get your bowels in an uproar; I am only teasing you. That is what friends are for.

"In all seriousness, I think she does like you. I can't figure out why, nevertheless I did catch her back before we left the Provinces, watching you work, and I have it from an excellent source; she has been overheard talking about you."

Johlnz sat, not sure what to say or believe, with his heart wanting to leap out of his chest. Tolz and Arten both liked to tease their friend, but Tolz did appear to be sincere.

"You need to say something to her before it is too late. I think you two would make a great couple, and if we are going to rebuild, we need to do it with good families and good family values."

I do think Tolz was serious todaz. I never heard him talk that way before about values and families, and I think he is a bit jealous. He is probably right; I should say something to her so I may know if she does have an interest in me, as Tolz indicated.

Well, tomorrow is another daz, and hopefully, it will be as quiet as todaz, except for our attackers from above. Like a relentless fly bug they keep coming. One daz we will not be so lucky, and a piece of debris will end our civilization. The universe, or someone in it, unknown and unseen, is not done playing with us, I am sure.

Time to sleep and maybe dream about something nice like Thereza and me alone somewhere sunny and peaceful. Only in my dreams could it ever be possible.

PART 3 – Nel Experza

Guazemax - Almost to Nizarax

I am writing this entry almost two weezs after being attacked the following premid, about ten zilos from the Nizarax border. How many dazs exactly have passed, I do not even know. I am lucky, I guess, to be alive. Hopefully, I can remember everything clearly. Some of the details, which follow, are from my fellow captives.

Johlnz was assigned to a lisk about a third of the way back in the convoy and given a fully freematic weapon much more powerful than any he had used to date. He felt unsure he could handle such a large, powerful gun and hoped not to find out. He got what he wanted.

The convoy proceeded partially along the central byways, but mostly again off the central ways, which at times became difficult to navigate. They were going as close to the western coast as they could without putting the convoy in danger from waves that could come at any time, started by debris falls anywhere on the planet. The routway would take them out of their way a few dazs; even so, the reports they received from the Nizarax settlement warned them away from the direct approach.

The convoy traveled for two zakas and had received word from the scout lisk a few zilos in front of them; everything looked clear. They were wrong. A massive explosion erupted in front of the convoy, which destroyed the lead lisk and killed everyone riding.

Gunfire discharged from all around, along with a few more substantial explosions. Johlnz prepared to shoot at whatever moved when another smaller explosion came from behind, and he went flying through the air. Hitting the ground hard was the last thing he remembered until he awoke later in a confined cell with five other group members.

"Johlnz, try not to move too much; you look pretty banged up and may have some internal injuries. You've been out since the attack zakas ago. We were not sure you were going to wake up."

"Where are we?" Johlnz managed to ask. His head pounding and his throat dry.

"They brought us to some small towz, roughly northeast from where we were attacked, and stuck us in this confine cell. I am Raxdel, by the way. I know you, even though we have not worked together."

"Hopefully, we won't die together."

"I'll second that, Johlnz. There are six of us here, all from the security forces, no scientists or support personnel, unless they have them somewhere else. They took Danz out about a zaka ago."

Johlnz tried to move; which immediately caused pain so severe he again passed out. While Johlnz was unconscious, the captures brought Danz back, tossed him into the cell, and grabbed Raxdel. He tried to fight back as they seized him, and in response, one of the captures slammed him hard on the knees with a club. Raxdel fell to the floor, and they dragged him away.

Johlnz woke about two zakas later, feeling slightly better. When he looked around, he saw Danz lying unconscious in the corner. He was one of the younger guards, barely twenty, and Johlnz felt sure Danz never expected his daz to include the beating it looked like he received from their captors. When Johlnz realized the abductors brought Danz back while he remained unconscious, he looked around for Raxdel.

"What happened to Raxdel?" One of the other guards he did not know responded with the details.

"They took him when they brought Danz back. He put up a good fight until they were able to overpower him and drag him away, over two zakas ago."

A little later, when Danz was conscious, he told them their captures beat and tortured him, asking who they were and where they were going. He did not say what, if anything, he told them before he passed out again.

Johlnz knew his turn would come eventually.

When the captors returned, they did not bring anyone back; they merely walked in and grabbed the guard from the floor who had responded to Johlnz about Raxdel. When Johlnz asked where the tanmen was they had taken earlier; he responded with one word, and a smile on his face, "Dead!"

Johlnz tried to sleep though he could not; his mind raced, wondering how many others might be captive. *Where are Tolz and Arten, are they alive, did the convoy get to safety? Did we come all this way to be killed by individuals who will probably soon be dead themselves?*

Johlnz no longer cared what happened to him; he just wanted it to be over. He worried about what tomorrow would bring. He did not care if he died, but he did not wish torture to be the method of his death.

Eventually, because the many needs of his body overpowered the worry in his mind, he fell asleep.

The following daz he painfully managed to sit up and look around to see who remained in the cell. The guard taken the nitz before was not in the cell, and no one else appeared to be missing. He wondered if the guard was now dead or still being tortured.

Does it matter? We will probably all be dead soon anyway, either from torture or being left here to starve to death.

They hadn't received any food or water. Johlnz hadn't a thing to drink since the premid prior, and he felt sure dehydration was a big part of the throbbing in his head.

The cement floor of the cell, dirty and smelling of urine from past guests, felt cool and comforting to his head. He lay unmoving on his side, staring at the empty, bloodstained wall, listening to the conversation Danz was having with himself.

A zaka later, maybe two or maybe three, the guard the captures took the nitz before, was brought back and tossed to the floor, naked and bleeding from many wounds. The tanmen did not move, but he moaned between breaths, shallow and raspy. Johlnz believed the guard to be close to death.

Immediately after the thought of the young guard's death entered his mind, the captures grabbed Johlnz off the floor and pushed him out the door, which caused him to stumble and hit his head on the opposite wall. Blackness was back.

When Johlnz awoke, he sat naked in a cold metal chair, bleeding from many places on his body from what looked like knife wounds, which probably happened when they cut off his clothes. As he slowly regained his senses, all he could feel was pain and cold; pain in his head, pain from the cuts, pain in his shoulders from having them pulled so far behind him, and pain where his hands were tied together.

"Wake up, purg," someone said as a bucket of ice-cold water splashed on his head, followed by the pain of an electric prod being pushed into his chest and fired.

"We wanted make sure you wake," a thickly accented voice said to him. "Now answer question, maybe I let you die quick," he laughed as he fired the prod again into Johlnz's chest, and Johlnz screamed, now fully awake.

"Who you, and what you do here?"

"Water" was all Johlnz could manage to say. The interrogator snapped his fingers, and another bucket of ice water hit his body.

"Let us try again," the interrogator said, as the probe was again put against Johlnz's body, this time between his legs, and fired.

Johlnz screamed and cried out; my name is Johlnz, Johlnz Zavix. When he did not continue, the interrogator smacked Johlnz across the face with the butt of the probe. "You start answer question or end up dead like friends."

Friends, plural, he thought, as he wondered whom else they killed.

"Who are you, and where you go?"

Johlnz figured he had better say something, so he told the interrogator what he thought the tanmen would believe.

"I am not an original part of their group. I ran into them back in the Provinces while looking for some food. They did not appear happy to see me, and I thought for sure they were going to shoot me when an old tanmen came out and asked my name.

"They did not torture me, by the way."

His remark was met with another smack to the face, as he wondered to himself why he continued to be such an idiot. Before being smacked again, or worse, he continued.

"I told them my name and said I meant no harm, but I needed food. I told them I could work for them at whatever they needed. Apparently, they needed extra help with security. They gave me a weapon, only a small pistol at first, and some training on how to shoot. They made it clear I was not to ask questions, and I was expendable. All I know is we are heading south. I do not know why, and I did not care. I had a life."

Johlnz did not think he convinced the interrogator. He hated, in this instance, being correct.

"I do not believe you be innocent. We looked in transport we capture. What all the equipment for—what in Nizarax?"

"I do not know. I did not even know we were going to Nizarax."

"Liar," he yelled, along with other words Johlnz could not comprehend, as the frustrated tanmen hit him again with two more blasts from the probe, this time to Johlnz's head.

He became too weak even to scream, and the room commenced to spin. He started to explain about the planet and the sun, desperate to end his pain as the room exploded. Johlnz and the chair flew across the cold floor. As he began to lose consciousness and slip into sweet oblivion, he thought he heard gunfire.

Nizarax - The Dazs After

When I awoke, I found myself in bed, in a tent with others who looked like they had been injured or beaten by our captors, including Danz and the other guard I remembered from the cell. I quickly fell asleep again, until later when gently awakened by a nurse. She gave me some water and medicine and told me to rest.

I started to ask where I was and what happened, but she told me again to rest. "Plenty of time later for questions," she said as I drifted back to sleep. Regrettably, I dreamed of being beaten, followed by a fireball coming out of the sky and hitting my captures and me, which caused me to jump back awake. No one appeared to be around, no one saw me jump awake with sweat running down my face, so I closed my eyes and drifted back to a dreamless sleep.

When I woke again later, a different nurse came over and asked how I felt and if I was hungry. I said, "Yes," and she brought me some food consisting of a bowl of hot cereal and some fruit. I assumed it to be premid, though I did not know how many dazs had passed since the premid at the border. I asked the nurse if she had seen any of my personal belongings, and she told me they had found my backpack and placed it inside the table alongside the bed. I asked if she could get the journal out for me, assuming the book was still there with my stuff and not lost.

"No, Johlnz, you have had a very severe concussion, and you are to do nothing except rest. Reading or writing will cause you to overexert your eyes and brain, which need more time to recover.

"I also am not allowing visitors, even though they come by every daz, sometimes more than once asking about you. I tell them the same thing I am telling you; rest is what you need."

She gave me another pill, and I quickly fell back to sleep.

That was two dazs ago. It is now premid, two weezs after crossing into Nizarax as I finish writing this update.

I need a few more dazs to rest and recover, according to the Doctor who examined me todaz; I think he is correct. Adding these updates to my journal has given me a slight headache.

The good news todaz, is the nurses are allowing me to have visitors. They confirmed both Tolz and Arten are okay, and Malcolz and Arten led the raid to free us from our captivity.

Time to rest.

Nizarax - Visitors

Johlnz had finished his lunch when Tolz and Arten came in, grinning ear to ear.

"So, the rumors are true; you are alive. We thought maybe you never woke up or woke up and said, 'to doxx with all this shizz'."

"Do not make me laugh, Arten; it still hurts too much."

Johlnz sat up in bed, grimacing in pain and taking a moment before continuing.

"If I knew you two would be my first visitors, I would have stayed asleep longer. This is the first good rest since the damn comet hit," Johlnz said while coughing and flinching in pain.

"I guess I owe you a huge thanks, Arten? I heard you, and Malcolz led the team to rescue us. And where was Big Verm when they were having all the fun saving our hides and hinds?"

"I was almost exactly where you are now. I took a hit in the leg, nothing major; nevertheless, they sidelined me, and said I would slow them down. I think they wanted all the glory from themselves."

"So, how bad was the attack?"

"We managed to fight them off rather quickly, Johlnz, but by the time Malcolz got back in the recon list, the attackers were already retreating; unfortunately, with six of our tanmen. We wanted to follow right away; however, we needed to get the convoy to safety."

Arten continued, "Malcolz did not exactly follow orders. He stayed with the convoy a few zakas and then went to follow the trail before it got cold. As soon as things settled down here, I put together our team and headed out to rendezvous with Malcolz. He knew where they took you, and once we arrived, taking out your captors was a piece of cake."

"How many were lost?"

"We lost four tanmen in the lead list and one during the fight, plus four serious injuries. Everyone injured, including the confine six, as we are calling you, are well on their way to recovery."

"Raxdel is alive; they told us he was dead?"

"They lied," Arten said, "probably to scare you; regardless, they did leave him for dead in a pool of blood. Had we not arrived when we did, they probably would have left you all for dead."

Johlnz was about to ask Tolz a question when Thereza came in with a bright smile.

"Hello Johlnz, good to see you are doing better. We were all worried about you. My Onczle sends his regards. How are you feeling?"

Johlnz sat up a little straighter, hiding the pain.

"I am doing much better now, thank you. I am glad to see you are okay."

"Oh, you are so sweet, but you worry about yourself."

She came around to the head of the bed, gave Johlnz another big smile, and then kissed him before quickly heading out.

"If I knew that is what it took to get her attention, I would have volunteered to be captured and tortured. I guess she has the hots for you, buddy," Arten said while laughing.

"Johlnz, take it from Big Verm; I told you before, I think she is tired of waiting for you to make your move. I suggest you get out of here quick before somebody else grabs her from you.

"We have to get going; we are already late for patrol. Take care, bud."

After they left, Johlnz realized he never got a chance to ask them where they were.

Nizarax - The Compound

I had an interesting and informative daz.
I finally was released from the medical tent and told I should still rest, though I did not need to be there anymore. I gathered my things, as meager as they are, and Thereza greeted me to take me to my new camo.

"Good premid Johlnz, it is good to see you standing again."

Thereza went to hug Johlnz until she realized it might not be a good idea and kissed him on his cheek instead.

"Good premid to you as well, Thereza."

His heart raced while he wondered if she was only sympathetic or generally interested in him.

"It is good to be out and about. I am glad we are no longer on the byway traveling. Am I correct in thinking this is our final destination?"

"Yes, this is our new camo."

Thereza started walking Johlnz through the compound, pointing out areas he would need to know. As they walked, Johlnz was surprised to see liltanz running around playing. He was expecting a small group of individuals in a single camo, much like in Reswoll.

As they continued walking and Thereza pointed out a few buildings, she confirmed that families lived in the compound. They were mostly families from the local area and some from other research camoz that managed to make their way down.

"Well, here we are, camo sweet camo."

They were standing in front of a building, probably at one time an Authority barracks. It was a drab greyz color, made from corrugated metal sheets with windows all around the building.

Inside, the building was divided into small individual rooms, and Thereza led him down a short hallway to his room. The room had a bed, a desk with a lamp, and a closet. The building's flooring was cement, but the room had a couple of rugs on the floor.

"I know it is not much to look at; however, most of the scientists and support personnel are in the same type of quarters, and we have larger rooms for families. The security forces are in barracks-type quarters, much like this used to be, unless they have family here.

"I have to attend a meeting; however, my Onczle would like to see you in a zaka at the monitoring facility."

"Thereza, can I ask you a personal question?"

"Sure."

"Dr. Moxron looks a bit old to be your Onczle."

"That is because he is not actually my Onczle. It's a story for another time, but he took me in when my Muzie died. My Pypzie died a few cycles earlier from latent Moniasar."

"I am so sorry; I did not mean to pry . . . I . . ."

"It is okay, Johlnz; you did not upset me. It happened many cycles ago, and we have so much more to worry about todaz and beyond."

She gave him directions to the monitoring facility, gave him another kiss, and went on her way.

Johlnz watched Thereza walk down the hallway before going back into his room to unpack his little bag of belongings. When he left the medical tent, they gave him some clothes; medical scrubs basically, and a pair of sandals, his to keep.

He looked in the closet and found a few items of clothing, which appeared to be his size. The few pieces of clothing he brought with him from Reswoll were there, plus a pair of overalls with his name stitched on a pocket.

Have I been demoted to maintenance, he wondered as he tried on the overalls? They fit well; still, he did not want to be wearing them to meet with the Doc, so he changed into clothes he had from Roswell. He could find no clock in the room and noticed his old watch was missing, so he figured he would look around some more, and maybe he could find out the time.

The sky remained dark and greyz, and the temperature, which was a bit warm, remained nowhere near what it would have been normally. The fine dust and debris still in the atmosphere continued to cause temperatures to be much lower than the normal average.

As he wandered around, he did see more liltanz of varying ages. The younger ones were in what he thought to be a school, and he saw some tanwez in work clothes performing cleanup around the area and some young tanmen and tanwoz constructing additional buildings.

As he looked around, he felt something hit his foot. When he looked down, he saw a small starsow ball. He bent down to pick it up as a young liltanz came over to him and asked to have it back.

"Well, of course, I was not going to keep it. I do not have time to play games, plus I am too injured right now. What's your name?"

"I am Randalx, and I am four cycles old. Can I have my ball back now?"

"Sorry, I forgot I was still holding it."

He gave the ball to the little tan and watched him leave while wondering what kind of life the tan would have in the future. What kind of life will any of us have?

He continued walking around, taking everything in when he passed one building, they used as a vegcamo. He did not know what good it would do with so little direct sunlight getting through, but he saw some lights used to grow food indoors.

He still did not know the exact time; even so, he figured it had to be time to meet with Doc Moxron. If the Doc were not ready for him, he would wait. What else was he going to do?

The monitoring facility was inside an old plantation camo twice the size of the camo in Reswoll. More than half a dozen satellite dishes of varying sizes and what looked like radio and televid antennas were on its roof. He had to stop twice for directions before he found the monitoring facility, which was merely a large room with some equipment from Reswoll plus much additional monitoring equipment he did not recognize.

The Doctor looked exhausted and showed signs of having sustained some injuries, probably during the attack. He sat at a desk looking at some reports as Johlnz entered.

"Hello, Dr. Moxron, how are you?"

"Johlnz, it is so good to see you up and about. Forget about me; how are you feeling?"

"Still a little sore, yet much improved."

"I am so sorry about what happened to you and the fact it took so long to rescue you and the others. I wanted to come by the medical tent to see you, but things have been hectic around here. We have much to do to survive; getting here was merely half the battle."

"You have nothing to be sorry for, I completely understand."

He let Johlnz know nothing had changed, and the planet continued to move off its standard tilt.

"At this rate, the equator will be perpendicular to the plane of the solar system in roughly two cycles, with what was the North Polar Region facing the sun. Since the tilt doesn't move at a speed, which corresponds to our orbit around the sun, the damage to Tanacun's ecosystem will vary, be that as it may, long term, it will be disastrous. Here close to the equator, we will have the best chance at a more normal climate change that will be more predictable and adaptable. The twilight times will be our biggest problem going forward."

He admitted to Johlnz, the scientist had no idea what would happen to the magnetic fields of the planet. They might survive the temperatures to die of radiation poisoning if the magnetic fields changed or broke down. "All we can do," he conceded, "is to try to make a community and survive as best we can.

"The population here is made up of scientists and what's left of the local populace. They have come together to try and rebuild something from the ashes."

"You know, Dr. Moxron, at times, I think it is hopeless, and then when I see the liltanz here playing, I think it would be a sin not to try as hard as possible to find a way to survive."

Dr. Moxron sat as if lost in thought and then agreed with Johlnz's statement.

"I need to cut our conversation short Johlnz, I am fatigued and think I need more sleep. I will continue with the details of our new community with you tomorrow. Make sure you get some rest yourself as well."

I left the facility and wandered around some more, thinking about what the Doc had said. Hopefully, we can survive and build something here. I know we are not the only place on the planet trying, but it doesn't lessen our need for success.

Before heading back to this room, I found a large easy to climb rock formation, which afforded a magnificent view of the valley below. As I sat and watched, a few smaller pieces of debris shot overhead and exploded harmlessly in the sky like a small fireflames display. Hopefully, it is a good sign.

Nizarax - Nel Experza

I learned todaz; our community has a name. 'Nel Experza,' which means 'New Hope,' in Provincial. It is in the country known as Nizarax, fifty zilos from the border with Matabas. Over three hundred individuals now make up this community or towz, as I prefer to say. It's a very fitting name. I do hope, becomes a reality.

We are in a partial mountain valley, with high mountains off in the distance. The towz is about sixty zilos from the Battal Ocean and about thirty zilos east of the vilogge once known as Siuna, and we are about ten zilos from the small community of Rozita.

Most of our native population lived in Siuna or Rozita, but the tanaquakes and falling debris heavily damaged both communities.

I went back to see Dr. Moxron todaz, and he filled me in on everything concerning the towz and my role in its future.

After breakfast at the mezcaf tent, Johlnz went back to the monitoring facility at the plantation camo to see if Dr. Moxron remained in his office. Unfortunately, the Doc was in a meeting with Professor Kizermel and would be available after eleven.

Johlnz had no idea who Professor Kizermel was but figured he would find out later. Since the Doc was not around, he looked for Thereza with no luck and thought she was probably in the same meeting.

After walking around exploring to become more familiar with the towz, he met the little tan from the daz before. The tan did not recognize Johlnz at first, but after a moment, he again introduced himself as Randalx.

"Would you like to play ball with me?" he asked Johlnz.

"Of course, I would like to play. You stand over by the tree, and I'll stand over here. Toss me the ball whenever you are ready."

Randalx tossed the ball well to Johlnz, and he thought if ever there were a starsow game in the future, the tan would be a great launcher. After a few more tosses back and forth, the tan asked his name.

"My name is Johlnz, Johlnz Zavix. I am from the Provinces up north. Do you know about the Provinces?"

"I think my Pypzie did; I heard him talk about the nasty individuals from the Provinces."

"Oh, he did; well, I am not nasty."

"You are okay, I guess, still, you have a boring name."

Johlnz laughed at the comment and realized this was the most fun he had in a very long time, and he started to think about his future. He wondered if he would have any liltanz of his own someday. First, they had to survive, and that might not be easy. When the little tan spoke again, it brought Johlnz out of his thoughts.

"I lived in Guazemax before my Muzie brought me here with my Pypzie. I miss my friends; most of the other kids here are too old to play with me. They are all busy in school or helping to do things."

"Well, I am staying in the big greyz building, so if you need a friend, you can come looking for me, and if I am not busy, I will play with you."

"Okay, I would like that."

After a few more tosses, Johlnz told the tan he had to go to a meeting, and they said their goodbyes. As Johlnz walked away, he said a little prayer to protect the tan. He was not very religious anymore; nevertheless, he felt good doing it for the tan and himself.

A few minzakas later, he was back at the plantation camo waiting in the Doc's office.

"Hello Johlnz, good premid. How are you, todaz?"

"I am doing well, Dr. Moxron, less pain every daz. If you do not mind me saying you look better todaz. You appeared tired yesterday, and I see you also had some injuries from the attack."

"I did, nothing serious, and I slept quite well last nitz. I am glad you are here so we can continue our conversation from yesterday and bring you up to speed. Walk with me to the mezcaf tent for some lunch. I know it is a bit early; all the same, I missed breakfast this premid.

The Doc led Johlnz out the side door and started talking about the community. Johlnz didn't have the heart to tell the Doc; he knew some of the information already.

"While you were recovering, we all got together and decided on a name for this community. The name picked is Nel Experza, which means, New Hope, in Provincial. Professor Kizermel, whom I will have to introduce you to at some point, suggested the name. He was the head of the science department at Tezaci Cizay University before the comet. When he realized the extent of the comet's damage, he gathered a bunch of other scientists together to move down here and start this community.

"We have a stream near the community which brings us fresh water from the mountains, but food is one of the biggest problems. Groups have been sent out to find as much food as possible, though there isn't much to be found. Luckily many of the locals here now, were farmers, and although crops are a problem because of the sun, they do have animals, and we have the vegcamo."

The Doc continued without pause.

"We are working to move the animals to a more appropriate area away from the towz and expand grazing areas for the livestock so they can maintain a stable supply. We also have plans for more Vegcamoz;

however, we still need more sun. We only have so many sun lamps, and the bulbs will not last forever."

After a brief pause, while the Doc stopped to talk to one of the other residents he introduced as one of the teachers, he continued the conversation.

"The original farmers from the area also have a muzrool cave not too far away, which we are now working, as well as an experimental mazla field which, lucky for us, was modified to grow in dense forests, so the lack of sunlight has not slowed its growth.

"There is not going to be much left of our planet, but maybe small pockets can survive and someday have a real civilization again. It will be a much smaller civilization until maybe someday we move underground to get away from the extreme temperatures much of the planet will endure."

Johlnz wanted to interrupt and ask about the idea of living underground; however, the Doc quickly continued. Johlnz thought the idea of living underground would be horrible and difficult to achieve.

"The towz itself is growing as more individuals and families come from the surrounding area. Most of the families here came from the local area. They are allowed to join the community as long as they are willing to help build and defend if need be. We have not had any problems yet; nevertheless, you never know when another group like the ones in Guazemax could stumble upon us and want to cause trouble."

They arrived at the mezcaf tent and sat in a corner so they could continue the one-sided conversation. The Doc had a sandwich and a drink, but Johlnz was not yet hungry, so he only had cazzaa as he told the Doc about his game of catch with Randalx.

"I know him; he is a cute little kid. His Pypzie died last cycle, and his Muzie works in one of the vegcamoz.

His JarPypzie, or Pypz as he calls him, is a bit frail. He was a mechanical engineer before retiring, and he helps out where he can.

"Hopefully, you can keep your promise to play with him; that said, I guarantee you, Johlnz, you will be busy. In addition to working on the cybezs, there will be many other projects, which will need your expertise, and Malcolz asked he be able to borrow you on occasion to help where needed."

"I respectably hate the idea of having to use a gun again; even so, I, of course, will help where needed."

"He knows you are not comfortable with large guns, but he mentioned many low-security situations in which he could use your help.

When done, I will show you where the maintenance office is and introduce you to Stacel Zavaros; she oversees assigning maintenance projects and all the cybez system maintenance and repair. The office is back in the Kiz Camo."

"Kiz Camo," Johlnz said questioningly?

"Yes, it is the name we gave to the old plantation camo, where we located all the main offices and planning rooms. The leaders decided to name it after the Professor; however, he insisted on Kiz for short. He is a tanmen of few and short words."

After he finished lunch, the Doc showed me around a little more and talked about plans for the future. He then walked me over to the maintenance office to meet Stacel. In her early fifties, she was an older tanwoz with a touch of groz mixed into her jet-char hair. For some reason, I found her a little intimidating.

I spent the rest of the daz doing repair and maintenance around the towz to get electricity to be more reliable. We are about ten zilos east of an old small power plant; they had managed to get working again with help from former workers who have joined the towz. It used to belong to a muzrool and collon plantation abandoned a few cycles ago.

In addition to the power plant, we also have zolatron generators scattered around the towz. Between the two systems, power should not be an issue for our small community.

It's been a long daz, and I am still a little sore and in need of some rest.

More tomorrow.

Nel Experza - Death in the Sky

I was awoken early this premid by a considerable booming sound. Along with many others, I ran outside to see a large piece of debris fly across the sky heading southwest. A minzaka or so later, we saw a bright flash in the distance, followed many minzakas later by a substantial, warm gust of wind.

The wind was not strong enough to do any damage; just the same, we knew what it meant. The piece had most likely fallen onto land. A water landing would usually not cause as much warmth. Our location, about one hundred zilos from the Battal Ocean to the west, makes the impact what the scientist would consider a very close call.

"Way too close for me, Johlnz,"

Thereza came up behind him while he still faced the direction from which the windblast had come. The azians were now chirping louder than he had heard since being let out of the hospital tent. Their singing was a pleasant sound; however, he preferred the friendly voice that spoke behind him.

"Hello Thereza, good premid. I agree, way too close. Thankfully it was not a large piece, or being over a hundred zilos away would not have spared us at least some major damage."

"My Onczle says we can expect more debris falls over the next few cycles, which will make the skies take even longer to clear. It's bad enough now; we rarely get to see any blucyn or even a glimpse of unobstructed sunlight."

"Let's hope that is all the excitement for the daz."

Thereza agreed and then paused before continuing.

"Johlnz, would you like to join me for a cup of cazzaa at the mezcaf in about a zaka, if you are not working?"

"I do not have to report to the control center to hook up some new systems for another two zakas, so I would love to join you for cazzaa."

"Great, see you there."

Johlnz watched her walk away and recollected how his fiancée, Monharat, used to walk when she tried to be a little extra conty. He looked forward to having cazzaa, but it was not because of the drink.

A zaka later, Johlnz was washed and dressed in his best work coverall. At least that is what he told himself. He was proud of the fact, even with all that had happened, he could keep at least a bit of humor in his life.

Halfway to the mezcaf tent he heard his name called out by a familiar voice.

"Hello, Johlnz, and where would we be off to this fine greyz premid?"

"Tolz, it is great to see you. It's been a few dazs; I was wondering if you had forgotten about me."

"Forget you, never? I have been out on patrol every nitz, thinking of you, of course, and—"

"Thinking probably, you wished it were me instead of you."

"Yes, you know me too well."

As they were standing around laughing, Arten came over and told Tolz he needed him on a search mission. He informed them about two teams they had sent out on an exploratory mission, and the teams hadn't made contact since having left the towz.

"I know you were on patrol last nitz, Tolz, but I need you on this."

"Arten, you know you can always count on me."

They said their goodbyes, Johlnz wished them luck, and a few minzakas later, he stood in the mezcaf tent looking for Thereza.

He had to laugh to himself when he saw where she sat. She was in the same spot where her Onczle had taken him to sit yesterday. It must be their favorite spot. He grabbed cazzaa, a piece of toast, and sat across from her, thinking how nice she looked.

"Is this spot reserved for the Moxron-Zeleton family?" He asked Thereza, which caused her to have a questioning expression on her face.

"This is the same spot your Onczle sat yesterday when we came here to have lunch and talk about everything."

"I believe it is his favorite spot, as he always sits here when we come together. I think I sat here out of habit."

She paused for a moment while taking a sip of her cazzaa and then continued.

"So, Johlnz, have you settled into your stylish new accommodations?"

"Yes, I have, not that it took much to settle in. Remember the dazs when our possessions, transport, phone, and clothes were all so important? Things have certainly changed. I was never much into clothes, which annoyed my fiancée all the time. She always tried to get me to dress in the latest styles, while I preferred a basic shirt and pair of leglongs."

"I did not know you had a fiancée; what happened?"

He did not answer right away; not sure he could talk about it without getting emotional. Thereza regretted asking the question as she could see the memory caused him pain.

"I am sorry I shouldn't have asked. I did not mean to make you sad; I should have known it was a bad —; oh, I really put my foot in it this time, did not I?"

Seeing her all flustered and embarrassed brought a smile to his face as he grabbed her hand and told her she hadn't reason to be sorry.

"I brought her up, not sure why. We all have our past from before the comet. We all have to learn how to deal with it, or we will never survive."

He awkwardly pulled his hand back, recognizing it might have been a little inappropriate, even though he did notice she did not appear to mind. They spent the next few minzakas talking about the two groups who were out on patrol in the area the latest piece of debris had fallen, both hoping the news would be good.

It was not until later in the pastmid we found out where the piece of debris had hit. It crashed about eighty zilos south-southwest of towz, and we had two teams out in the area. Search parties found only one survivor.

He had been exploring a cave when the shock wave hit and was unsure what happened to the rest of the team, but based on the destruction of the forests, he doubted they could have survived. The search teams were not able to find their bodies.

Anything salvageable along the far southwestern coast was probably now gone. One day we may not be so lucky. There are still many large chunks of comet and planet fragments in low orbit; eventually, many will be coming down.

Nel Experza - Divulging the truth

Another premid. It has been a few dazs since my last entry. I have been busy working on cybez installations and repairs and doing security and other general maintenance tasks around the towz, leaving little time to sleep or write. My life is oddly starting to become routine, as one daz follows another with much work to be done to try and increase our odds of survival.

The locals remain unaware of the situation happening to the planet, and the leaders of the towz, including the Doc, have decided it is time. They have scheduled a large meeting for this evening and have asked those who have liltanz to drop them off at the school so their parents can tell them later if they think it is appropriate.

One of Johlnz's tasks for the daz was to help make sure all the locals were aware of the meeting about to start. He helped spread the word and put up a few signs around their little community. He discovered to his surprise, some individuals already knew the truth or part of the truth, which he thought was good. The news might not be as big of a shock to the individuals here as the leaders had feared.

Professor Kizermel was the one chosen to give the news.

"Hello, everyone. For those of you who may not know me, my name is Prof—forget the title, we are all equals here, and we all need to work together. My name is Mazjuen Kizermel, I am the temporary leader of the group of scientists who came here to form this community, and I know many of you have questions.

"I know one question is, why would a group of scientists from Tezaci, and the Provinces, want to come down here and build a community? Why here? It is a very reasonable yet difficult question to answer because the truth may scare many of you, all the same, we ask you to listen and save questions for after.

"When the comet struck Tanacun, it did far more than destroy Orisa, Austran, and most of the coastal cizaes around the planet, and it did more than cause the skies to be greyz and dark.

"The comet struck the planet at an unusual angle, which caused the planet to start moving off its normal axis. For those of you not familiar with the term, it is the tilt of the planet, which causes the seasons. The planet's tilt was constant and the seasons predictable; now, the situation has changed. We first thought the change to be temporary, and the planet would bounce back, but we know for sure now, it is not. In fact, what we found is the planet is continuing to move farther from the uniform standard.

"The planet now rotates slowly in a new direction, and this will cause devastation to much of Tanacun. The tilt is changing by almost three degrees per mooncazt, and we see no signs of it stopping."

The Professor then picked up a specially designed model of Tanacun and showed how the planet used to rotate and revolve around the sun. He then visually explained what was happening with the axis and showed how the planet would continue to tilt as it moved around the sun.

"What this means is what were the poles, the frozen ice caps, will at some point entirely melt as they face directly towards the sun for long periods, and the temperate zones, north and south, will do the same for long periods, and they will burn. At other times those regions will face directly away from the sun and freeze far worse than the poles ever have in the past."

He could see the look of shock, fear, and confusion on the faces of the crowd as he continued.

"Come what may, there is hope, which is why we are here. The areas along the equator will have a more livable climate, though not like what this area experienced in the past. The equatorial region will now experience seasons, but they may be drastically different from the familiar seasons of the past.

"The way our planet is currently tilted is causing temperatures more like what was the standard full sun in this region and in the northern hemisphere. The two areas should be approaching haz sun, but as the tilt continues, our planet will eventually rotate in such a way as to put us in perpetual twilight for mooncazts at a time. If the skies remain filled with debris, it could get extremely cold, and the difference between the hot side of the planet and the cold side could cause catastrophic storms in our area.

"This area here, where we live, will be at twilight point in about two cycles. We do not know one hundred percent what to expect; still, we do have a plan. We have many mooncazts before we experience the worst conditions, and we are working on plans to survive those twilight times in various ways. As we know more, we will keep you informed. I understand this is a lot of information and a lot to take in. Any questions?"

There were no questions. I think everyone felt too confused or even in shock to think of any questions to ask. I remember how shaken I was to learn the truth, and I realized it gradually as the scientists' understanding unfolded.

The Professor explained they were available to answer questions any time and to come to the camo and ask to see any one of them. He also informed everyone, counselors were available if needed, something I was not even aware of until that moment. It may be a service I need, as I sometimes have terrible dreams about my time in captivity.

Another nitz arrives; hopefully, the nitzmares do not.

Nel Experza - The Weezs Go By

I have not written much recently since I have been so busy around the towz. When I am not working security or fixing equipment, I give Provincial language lessons and take Guazel lessons.

The leaders have decided to have a bilingual towz. Provincial and this region's dialect of Guazel will be taught to everyone. At some point, one language must dominate, but that will be a discussion for another daz if we are lucky and survive long enough for it to matter.

There has not been much happening with security. A few groups of individuals have found us and became part of the towz, and we have had no trouble with unwanted persons or wildlife, which is a good thing.

We have teams farther out, patrolling around the area and working on a rudimentary perimeter byway to enable better transportation and patrols. A crude dirt way runs to the abandoned towz of Zan Buepco, where still useful buildings and supplies remain to be scavenged. All the surviving residents have moved to Nel Experza. Work crews have made clearing the main byway to the towz their first priority.

The cybez and monitoring equipment we have is in good shape, so I have been trying to repair those damaged in transit and starting an inventory of spare parts. We no longer require some of the old equipment, as knowing what's happening above is not of much use. If something is ready to fall on us, there's nothing we can do, nowhere to go.

The communications teams have been continuously trying to contact the Orbital Stations I and II; they still receive no answer. We do not have the right equipment, so maybe they are functional, but we can't reach them, and they would not know of our existence.

Johlnz sat in the mezcaf tent, having a light lunch while updating his journal and thinking about why he continued. It had been a couple of weezs, and he honestly became lazy about the updates; however, he believed in a way, it did help him cope with his new everyday life. He realized one reason why he hadn't updated it for a while was because it had been quiet—a very good thing.

One thing not the usual was the time he spent with Thereza. He would stop by her office only to say hello, and if she knew he was working in the camo, she would make an excuse to visit.

They would take walks around the community and stop to sit on the rocks looking over the lower valley, or walk up to the stream and sit by the little waterfall. Johlnz was not exactly sure of his feelings, as he still hurt from the loss of his fiancée, even though it had been over a cycle ago when she took her life.

He was sitting, lost in his thoughts when Thereza came over and gave him a small hug.

"Hello there, you looked like you were a million zilos away and could use a good hug. Oh, I see you are working on your journal. Am I in your little book somewhere?"

"Maybe, here and there. You know I do not kiss and tell."

"You do not kiss much at all. I sometimes feel you are holding back, and I do understand. You had someone in your life whom you asked to be your partner, and maybe you are feeling a little guilty."

"Since when are you a Psychologist, and is that a question or an observation?"

Johlnz felt a little put on the spot by Thereza, and he felt sure he was blushing. He never liked to talk about himself with anyone, especially not someone he still did not know well.

"I am sorry I did not mean to pry or to upset you. I do care for you, and I want to help you if I can."

Thereza was about to fill him in on some good news when Tolz came over with his lunch and asked if they would mind some company.

"Not at all," Thereza said, "Please join us. I have not seen you in a while; how have you been?"

"In a word, bored, yet I guess that is a good thing. I am bored because things have been nice and quiet; however, I did receive orders. I am heading south as the leader of a recon mission."

"When do you leave?"

"I leave first thing tomorrow premid, Johlnz, for two to three weezs, depending on what we find and how difficult it is to travel."

They both wished him good luck, and then they were all silent for a bit, but Johlnz could tell Tolz had something else he wanted to discuss.

"I can tell you have something else you want to say, so spill it."

"You know me too well; if you were not smitten with Thereza, I might want to espouse you."

"Very funny," Johlnz replied before Thereza could chime in. He knew his face was now verm.

"Smitten? Where did you pull that word from?"

"An old phrase my JarMuzie used to say, Thereza. When I went to my first school dance, she asked if I was smitten with my date. I miss her; I miss everyone who had been in my life before.

"Anyway, yes, I do have a question for Thereza. I have been wondering what you knew about Olania?"

"Why, are you smitten with her?"

"Very funny, Johlnz, nevertheless, maybe."

"Isn't she one of the nurses who took care of me when I was recovering," Johlnz asked?

"Yes, she was your head nurse," Thereza responded. "I did notice, every time I know of, when Tolz came to visit you, he spent time talking to Olania. I began to wonder who he was really visiting."

"Figures."

"I swear to the creator; I came to see you, Johlnz, she became—a bonus."

"Well, she might have mentioned your name a few times when I talked to her; maybe when you get back, we could have a double date walk up to the waterfall. After all, it is not like we have is a good oceanfood restaurant around here."

They all laughed for a moment, and Tolz said he had to get going to prepare for his trip. As the mission leader, he had to be well prepared and make sure they had everything they might need. On his way out, Tolz happened to see Olania in line for lunch, and he wished he had time to talk to her before he left, but he was already behind schedule.

Since I was interrupted earlier, not that I am complaining, I wanted to finish my update, which includes some good news. After Tolz left the mezcaf tent, Thereza told me a new group of almost fifty individuals, including four families with liltanz, were arriving tomorrow. They lived in the mid-western Province of Celoraza and were bringing some much-needed equipment and supplies.

The best news—they were also bringing a bulk-transport loaded with tri-dimensional printers and material for the printers, as well as more Zolatron generators. It's an odd assortment of supplies, and I wondered how they managed to get through the dangerous areas unharmed. Thereza told me I shouldn't ask.

It's now Nemvaz based on our position around the sun, and there were discussions of starting a new version of Hzalo-Multum for our towz, but it would probably not involve any special foods, at least not for a few cycles. Even though much of our population is not from the Provinces, most acknowledged it is a tradition they would like to adopt.

If we survive, a growing season of some kind will occur from time to time. The important thing is to be prepared to take advantage of the time when it comes. To that end, teams, continue to work on areas to be used as farmland, and other are figuring out the best crops to grow. The idea of a typical weather pattern is gone for good. In the future, if there is one for us, the complicated weather patterns may be determined, but it will not ever be as before. The new pattern would be more like a two to three cycle span as the planet continues to turn in two directions at once while orbiting our star.

Water-Water Everywhere. One Cycle
Nemvaz 19, 0001 AC

Well, not really, unless, of course, a wave wipes us off the face of the planet. The universe keeps trying, yet luckily, the debris falls have become smaller and farther from towz.

A tremendous amount of rain fell on us the last weez, and that is good since we now have a reservoir to fill. We have direct access to fresh water from the nearby spring and stream it supplies, plus the team finished a partial dam to hold the water in the reservoir. We do not need to worry about who is downstream since no one remains. We won't have any water wars in the near future.

The hope is to be able to have an irrigation system in place if needed for the growing season. We do not know if we will experience rainy and dry seasons like in the past, so best to be prepared. This part of the planet was once an equatorial jungle, but now many native plants are starting to die, and we are planting some new species, which will do better in the varying climate.

You may have noticed I am no longer tracking my life and entries by location. We are here for better or worse. I have decided to mark my existence by dates again since I do not expect to move.

I have one additional item before getting some sleep. Yesterdaz was Nemvaz 18 on the old calendar. One cycle since Zeptulgar struck. Who would have expected I would be alive and part of a towz trying to help rebuild the Tanan civilization; certainly not me.

The towz leaders held a memorial observance yesterdaz, and I attended with Thereza.

Thereza took hold of Johlnz's hand as they finished the memorial with a short prayer and a moment of silence. She began to cry as she remembered all the individuals she lost because of the comet. A lot of her relatives lived along the eastern coast, and although the waves did not hit the area as hard as the west coast of the Provinces, many individuals still perished.

She had cousins and friends from supreme school who had lived in Nel Lart, in high-rises they thought would be safe. She knew many fell when their supports washed away. She did not know if her friends and relatives were dead or alive. If they were alive and did not head south, they would not live for long.

Hzalo-Multum

Nemvaz 25

Todaz was our first celebration of Hzalo-Multum. The towz leaders decided a few dazs ago to start a new daz of gratmul based on the Hzalo-Multum celebration practiced in the Provinces for over two hundred cycles.

Our daz of gratmul will be one weez after the anniversary of the comet, so we always remember. The local population treated us to cuisine native to Nizarax, which is part of their old Ancestor-Gratitude daz—a celebration to recognize those who came before and the harvest of the cycle. The dish, prepared with mazla and wild muzrools was tasty, and I highly recommend you give it a try.

Look at me, being optimistic about our future.

Thereza and her Onczle invited me to sit at the main celebration table. The meal, also included locally, produced wier, a type of sweet alcoholic beverage we all enjoyed.

Afterward, we held a prayer service where many individuals expressed their gratmul to each other and the towz leaders. As the ceremony neared the end, I added my silent gratmul not only for Thereza but also for my friend Tolz, who made it back from his exploratory mission just in time for the celebration.

Update from Tolz
Nemvaz 28

I finally caught up to Tolz this premid. It's the first time since he made it back on Hzalo-Multum Daz I have been able to talk to him. He's been occupied reporting first to Malcolz, and then to the towz leaders. He complained about having to repeat it all for the third time, but I knew he was full of shizz and bursting at the seams to fill me in on the mission.

They had little trouble traveling, for most of the byways were passable for their smaller lisks. They found a vilogge higher up in the mountains called Calsandrax, about forty zilos farther south, still populated and in good condition. It's a small towz with less than one hundred residents. Tolz told me they had access to clean water and minimal electricity.

They were not very friendly at first; however, they appeared to have no weapons and were happy to be left alone. Tolz did not tell them about our towz, as that will be a decision for our leaders to make, but it is clear they will not make it through the twilight time on their own.

Calsandrax contained the only signs of life they had seen the entire time, though they did manage to find some excellent supply resources. They ventured as far into the eastern coastal valley as they could and found warehouses above the port towz of Bilwi, filled with non-perishable foods, building materials, and a few bulk-transports. The waves mostly destroyed the towz, yet the docks themselves, which were modern newer facilities, did not look severely damaged.

The team brought back two bulk-transports filled with building materials and food, as well as radio equipment. It was a successful mission.

Welcome to Towz
Tralmard 15

I am embarrassed by how little I have written in this journal. I wanted to update it at least weekly if not daily; even so, time is short, and I have much to do.

I met our newest citizens todaz. When the towz leaders heard of the individuals living in Calsandrax, they sent Arten back down with a team to offer them the opportunity to live here. The team did not tell them the truth about the planet's future, but four families did accept the invitation.

They were told of our predicament when they arrived and met Dr. Moxron. They are sure the rest of the towz will come when they know the truth, and the Doc indicated they would send another team down to tell those remaining when we have more space and before twilight makes travel more difficult.

Our population now is over four hundred.

Tanaquake & Spark of Light
Tralmard 24

I have been busy helping to catalog and store the supplies Tolz brought back from his mission as well as repairing our electronic equipment, which has been giving us more problems than usual lately.

If life had continued uninterrupted by the gift from above, todaz would have been The Spark of Light. Most of the original residents of this region are Athix, as are some of us new residents. The towz leaders planned a religious ceremony for this evening; unfortunately, they canceled it when another tanaquake struck.

We have no equipment to monitor the scale, but it was a moderate quake and lasted almost forty-five seconds. There were some minor injuries and damage to some structures; however, the most significant damage was to our dam. Part of the dam collapsed, and we lost more than half of our stored water. The collapse won't be an immediate problem for drinking water; regardless, we may need water for our crops when the warm weather returns.

Speaking of the weather, our nitz have been a few degrees above freezing and the dazs in the mid-fifties. It will get colder for a few more mooncazts, then will warm briefly before gradually getting colder as we approach our first twilight. The skies do continue to clear and allow more sunlight, so we hope to have a small growing season before twilight. We have recently experienced some partially clear dazs; all the same, we are a long way from normal.

Snow
Banlar 15

The planet has most certainly gone head over heels. It snowed last nitz for the first time in the region, once an equatorial rain forest. Many of the individuals here had never seen snow before and were amazed.

The snow only amounted to one-half an inz; still, a few unprepared individuals got hurt because they did not understand how slippery it would be. Hopefully, we will not see too much of this in the future, but I know this is just the beginning with twilight less than two cycles away.

Much of the vegetation which once thrived in this area is now gone. It's a good thing the scientist came prepared with seeds and seedlings for a large variety of vegetation. I hope many of the plants and trees can grow and adjust to the new strange seasons we will be experiencing.

As usual, one group of citizens enjoyed the snow more than most.

Johlnz walked to Kiz Camo the long way to enjoy the snow. He had several repairs to finish in the offices and communications room. The snow reminded him of better times when he was a liltanz living in Rilodfia, across from a playground with some decent hills for sledding. He and his friends would spend zakas out in the cold walking up and sledding down, or sometimes sliding down the hill without the sled when the hill got the better of them.

The snow stuck to the trees, and with so many trees dead, it reminded him of how the northern forest would look in the haz sun when a heavy snowfall would stick to the trees and create a beautiful haz sun wonderland.

You could tell by looking around who in the towz hadn't grown up with an occasional snowstorm. They were the ones walking extremely slow and having trouble keeping from falling. The scene was almost funny; still, Johlnz knew it could be dangerous as well.

He approached close to the camo when he saw the little tan he met before. It took a bit before he remembered the liltanz's name was Randalx.

"Hello Randalx, are you enjoying the snow?"

"Hi, mister. What am I supposed to do with this stuff?"

"Well, have fun, of course. When we get some more snow, you need to find a little hill and go sledding."

"What is sledding?"

"A sled is usually made out of wood with metal rails. You sit or lie on it and slide down the snow-covered hills. Sledding is fun, but you do not have to have a sled. You can use a trash can lid, a tray from the mezcaf tent, or even a piece of board."

Johlnz started to show Randalx how to make a snowman when he was hit in the back of the head by a snowball. Randalx thought it funny and laughed as Johlnz turned around just in time to see Arten launching another salvo, hitting Johlnz smack in the middle of the chest.

"Do I need to have my vest on when it snows to protect me from you, Arten?"

"All is fair when it comes to a good snowball fight Johlnz."

"You know, you are not setting a good example for this little tan here by hitting me with a snowball."

As if to prove the point, Johlnz got hit in the back, this time by Randalx, who again laughed like crazy as a little three-way snowball fight was now underway.

An Invitation

Marwe 01

Todaz, is the first daz of Marwe, and I had a pleasant surprise when I went to Dr. Moxron's office to fix a problem with one of his monitoring systems. We had a little conversation, and he asked me if I would be interested in joining the Towz Council as a non-voting community representative. I, of course, said yes, and I am looking forward to attending my first meeting next weez. I did not even know they were officially the Towz Council, as I previously referred to them as the towz leaders.

We had a little more snow and blessedly also a little more sunshine—a hazy sun, but at least it could be seen. Thereza and I took advantage of some free time to head up to the partially frozen waterfall. The view was beautiful, with snow on the ground and the sun shining off the water as it made its way over the falls.

I am not much of a romantic; nevertheless, the moment itself was romantic, and I think I may be starting to again fall in love.

The Matchmaking Doc
Marwe 07

Thereza and I have been spending a lot of time together. When we are not busy, we go for walks around the area and up to the waterfall. Unless there are schedule conflicts, we even have most of our meals together. It has not gone unnoticed, and some would say we are dating, a strange concept under the circumstances.

"Hello Johlnz, if you are not busy, would you like to join me for some cazzaa?"

Johlnz was on his way to help with building some new barracks for their increasing population and was taken by surprise when Dr. Moxron stopped him.

"I guess it will be okay; I am on my way to work on the new barracks, so I do not have too much time."

"Do not worry about it. Tell the supervisor you were with me," the Doc said as they walked to the mezcaf.

They sat with their cazzaa in the Doc's usual spot, making small talk, and Johlnz developed the impression Dr, Moxron wanted to say something, but he was not sure. The Doc appeared nervous to Johlnz, something he had never seen before. After a couple of minzakas, the Doc got to the point.

"Johlnz, I noticed you have been spending a lot of time with Thereza, and well, I . . . ah wanted to let you know, if you have any intentions toward her, it would not be a problem. She talks about you all the time when we are working, and you know if we are to rebuild our civilization, we need to have normal lives with partners and liltanz, and I ah, just want to say, I, um, I, have no problem, I merely wanted to let you know you have my blessing.

"I am late for a meeting. I have to go."

Dr. Moxron quickly got up and left the tent leaving Johlnz absolutely astounded. He felt glad the Doc had gone because he had no idea what to say. He knew he was falling in love with Thereza, but beyond those feelings, the thought of espousal had never occurred to him. There was too much happening, and life, was still one big crapshoot. He sat for a while, not sure what to think.

The Weezs Go By, Again
Marwe 27

I have not written for a while since the planet, at least in this area, has been wonderfully quiet. Aside from the daz to daz of trying to survive as the temperatures get colder, life is the new routine. We thankfully see a little bit more sunlight every weez.

The stars are becoming visible as debris continues to clear from the atmosphere. The many fireflames—debris from our near destruction—have added to our romantic evening walks as I continue to think about my conversation a couple of weezs ago with Thereza's Onczle.

I attended my first towz supervisors' meeting since my last entry. Being my first time, I simply sat in my chair, listening as the full members talked about supply shortages and plans for the future. They are working on a grand plan, as one member called it, to ensure our survival by using the local caves for shelter.

Thank the One for the Vegcamoz, mushroom caves, and limited livestock. They are providing just enough food to get by and survive without us using all our stores.

The Grand Plan
Eral 01

I returned moments ago from a meeting about the future of our community, or maybe the future of our species. Even though I am sure we are not the only survivors trying to rebuild, if we want this community to survive, we need to act now and hope others left on Tanacun do the same. Our location is one of the few places remaining on the planet to give us the best chance.

The scientists suspect the existence of numerous underground Authority facilities across the planet harboring survivors; even so, how long can they survive locked in bunkers? If they are up north, can they survive the many mooncazts of extreme hot and cold? How long will their supplies last?

Another question haunting me lately is how many individuals does it take to re-create a civilization? I did not pay much attention to my life science classes in school. Still, I know with not enough variation in the species, dramatic and dangerous deformities and disabilities can occur. Is our traits pool large enough to build a healthy and robust civilization? One thing is for sure, no matter what, I will not live long enough to know the answers.

The last few weezs have been difficult. The temperatures have been colder, and we have had some nearby debris falls. Some of the fragments hit the water and propelled sprays near us, which came down as snow. The cold spells are not unusual, considering the position and condition of the planet at this time, and the scientists are sure it will get warm again before the temperatures fall back for a more extended duration as we get closer to twilight.

As usual, with this journal, I digress from what I intended to be the main point of this entry; the grand plan.

Professor Kizermel stepped up to the podium in front of the room and called the meeting to order. He looked a little nervous, preparing to present the proposal to all the senior staff from the towz. It was a radical proposal, only hinted at during the last meeting, but he knew they could not survive just living in shacks on the surface.

"I will get right to the point of this meeting. The proposal you received when you came in has full details of all I will discuss. When I finish, we will have a one-zaka recess for you to look over the plan thoroughly; when we reconvene, we will need to have a formal vote.

"The hard reality is, we will not be able to survive living on the surface of this planet, one hundred percent of the time. As we approach and move away from twilight, our weather will most likely become unpredictable, often violent, and extremely cold.

"We recently discovered the caves in this area, which have been in the past and still used now for muzrool farming, are much more extensive than first thought. There are many large chambers in the caves with easy access and proximity to the surface.

"In addition, our teams have discovered two large underground pools with more than enough fresh drinkable water for our needs, especially coupled with our reservoir higher in the mountains. The caves have all the space and water we need to build an underground cizay.

"We will start small, of course. Even so, many cycles from now, I envision our ancestors living in a sprawling, brightly lit cizay filled with all the comforts we all knew before the comet took away the lives and communities, we all enjoyed.

"The plan is to begin by enlarging the smaller, closer caves and make them available for living space for the first upcoming twilight. We have thirteen mooncazts before total twilight, though I fear we will need to be in the new shelters in ten mooncazts, eleven at most. It will not be perfect, and it may be cramped and rough, but it will be warm and safe. By the time the second twilight comes, I envision clean, comfortable private spaces for all citizens, as well as space for recreation and community events; however, to make this a reality, we have much to accomplish."

The room remained silent as the members had begun leafing through the proposal. One member raised their hand to ask a question, but the Professor instructed them to wait until the end for questions.

"All the details are in the packet you received. This is the first blueprint, nothing is yet locked in stone, and we will modify the plan as needed. In addition to underground work, other tasks will need to be accomplished above ground first.

"The long-term plan is to begin manufacturing from the ground up, a new industrial base from the small factories, which still exist not too far away. One of our recon teams recently found a still secure and standing, clean-room facility, which we will greatly need to make replacement components for our electronics.

"We intend to start with making tools and support structures for the caves. Eventually, we will move to working on electrical generation, lighting supplies, and ventilation systems.

"You will also find in the report, our intention, after the first twilight, to clear an area for a small landing strip and work facility, to start building an old-style bi-plane to use for scouting and or emergency rescues."

The Professor paused for a moment to take a drink of water before continuing.

"We have the knowledge, in books and on cybezs, and we have some here with the skills. What we lack to rebuild a society quickly are the raw materials and industrial infrastructure. "It is a bold plan, and if our descendants and we can survive long enough, it will work, of that, I am sure."

There were a few basic questions asked before the break; nothing important. Everyone appeared to be in a hurry to read the full proposal. One zaka later, the meeting reconvened, and the plan was approved unanimously; however, the members did have a proposition of their own.

They strongly recommended a more formal Authority type body in charge of the community, and they nominated five individuals to be members of the First Council. Since I may be the only one documenting any of this and may someday be considered significant, I am listing the nominated and approved Council members here.

 Professor Mazjuen Kizermel

 Doctor Robarz Moxron

 Doctor Andrez Johlant

 Jox Bartle

 Commander Malcolz Predsen

After a few minzakas of debate, the new Council decided Professor Kizermel, would be the Chairtan for a term of two cycles. After two cycles, Council membership and the position of Chairtan will be put to a vote by the entire community, of anyone over the age of sixteen.

I remain a community representative of the Council, so I guess for that reason, they decided to give me a task. I have been assigned to the long-range planning committee to work with the other engineers and technical experts—the few we have—to map out the multi-decade long-range plan. It's the intention of the scientists who put together the plan to rebuild civilization based on communities predominantly underground. Only farming, industry, some recreation, and partial transportation would remain above ground. Implementing the plan will be a daunting task, and it will continue long after I am dead, even if I manage to die of old age.

A Plan for My Descendants
Eral 20

I have returned from the first meeting of what we are calling 'The Grand Plan Envisionment Committee' or GPEC for short. I am not sure envisionment is a word, but hey, if we are rebuilding a civilization, why not invent new words as well.

We elected Salerand Loxon as our committee leader. He was, or I should say, still is a Mechanical Engineer, who lived in Nel Lertay, Province, before the comet. If you have been paying attention to what I have written, you know it is where I lived as well before Zeptulgar, although he lived up north outside of Nel Lart Cizay.

He gave a very impassioned speech to set the mood for our committee.

"The first thing I would like to say is, thank you for the trust you have bestowed on me. I will do my best to lead and work us through the task at hand.

"We have ahead of us, an undertaking, which is lengthy and most likely complicated; nevertheless, the task is also the opportunity to shape the future of this community, or maybe the future of the planet.

"This plan we are to devise and institute, is not for us, and maybe not even for our liltanz. This plan will be for our descendants and those who will come long after we have left this planet, and our spirits have moved on to eternal rest. Our names will be quickly forgotten, and some may even curse us in the future, but we know a sustainable long-term plan for a viable underground community is essential for our survival and the survival of all we know.

"The vision we are to create is not meant to be temporary; others have the job of solving our immediate needs, and we will be expected to help them as well. We are going to devise a plan for a community, a towz, and a cizay, which will endure for decdecazs.

"We are now entrusted with creating a grand vision for the future.

"We can do it!

"We will do it!

"We must do it!

"Even the grandest of plans must start small. Cazzaa, anyone?"

Everyone laughed as Salerand walked over to the table and poured himself a cup of cazzaa as applause erupted. I considered his remarks a great beginning to something for which none of us will live to see the end.

Espoused with Liltanz
Lant 09

Speaking of descendants, as I did about two weezs ago, yes, shame on me again for not writing in this journal for two weezs. I am announcing here my commitment to Thereza. We have not set a date yet; still, the towz is excited since we will be the first couple to be espoused in Nel Experza. I am joking about the liltanz—for now. I have detailed my proposal below.

For our society to survive, we do need to have liltanz, but we cannot grow the population faster than we can sustain them. Life is more a balance now than it has been for many decdecazs. Every daz more individuals show up looking for help, and we certainly will never turn them away. Out towz now has a population of over 500.

As I prepare to detail my proposal, another small piece of debris has fallen westward into the ocean north of here. We can only hope our luck will hold out, and we will not become additional victims.

The daz started bright—meaning you could see a round brightness in the sky behind the clouds—as they walked hand in hand up to their favorite spot by the waterfall. There were azians in the slowly dying trees singing as if they had no care in the planet. Unfortunately for Tanas, they could not fly away to a better place with abundant food and shelter.

As Johlnz walked along the stream, he wished he could be an azian and fly away from all the problems. Fly away from responsibility, fly away from fear, and fly away from the question he wanted to ask Thereza. It was not that he loathed asking the question; only he was afraid of the answer he might receive. He believed she liked him; in fact, he also felt sure she loved him as he loved her; still, espousal is a big step, especially on the planet on which they now lived.

They arrived at the waterfall; Johlnz put down a little blanket and laid out the sandwiches he had asked Briontell to make for their lunch. Briontell knew something was up when Johlnz asked for the special order, but he did not want to pry, and Johlnz did not want to divulge his secrets.

"These sandwiches look great, Johlnz. Did you have them made special? I have never seen them offered for lunch before."

"Yes, I did; I thought it would be nice to have something different for todaz."

As they ate, they talked about life in the towz. They were both so busy, they barely had time to talk about the projects they were doing, and most times, work was the last thing on their minds. After lunch, they sat with

Thereza held in Johlnz's arms as they watched the water flow over the falls as the azians continued to sing. After a few minzakas, Johlnz got up and walked over to a bush, which still had some large bright verm flowers in bloom, and he pulled one off the bush and went back to the blanket and sat down.

"This is for you. A beautiful flower for a beautiful tanwoz."

Thereza experienced a bit of surprise, as Johlnz usually did not say those kinds of things when they were together. She felt certain she knew his intentions toward her, but he did not typically vocalize his thoughts or feelings. She was about to tell him thank you when he quickly continued.

"I have been thinking a lot lately about the future for this towz and the planet if we survive, though mostly I have been thinking about our future. I never thought I could ever have a happy moment in my life again after Monharat took her own life; I was wrong. I have managed to find happiness again when I am with you and when I think about you. I want to be with you as much as possible, even if our future ends up being short.

"Thereza Zeleton, I love you and would be honored if you would be my partner."

Thereza sat with a big smile on her face as she grabbed Johlnz and hugged him hard.

"Yes, yes, and yes again. No matter what happens, I love you and want to be with you and have you as my partner."

Tr. & Tiz. Popular

Nully 01

Thereza and I have become the hit of Nel Experza; the towz's first 'big thing' and the beginning of what some call the advance to normalcy. I am not sure who started calling it that but it will be a slow advance to be sure, and who am I to argue with popularity. It's only been a couple of weezs since we announced our espousement to our friends; still, individuals I do not know and have never met before are stopping to give me good graces.

We still have not decided when the big daz will be, though it will be soon. It's not like we have a lot of planning to do. We are sure the ceremony will be at Kiz Camo with just our friends in attendance. There will be no big party, no bonnaze throwing, no gartan pass, and no speeches. Our biggest concern right now is where we will live. Space has become a premium as more families have arrived from Calsandrax. The Council talked about creating a partner's barracks; however, right now, we do not have many official partners.

I am, of course, swamped with work. I still do security once a weez to keep sharp, and between maintenance and cybez repair, my dazs are full and exhausting. Even being espoused, Thereza and I may not see much of each other.

Spelunking Anyone
Nully 21

Wow, finally a chance to update my journal. I have been exceptionally busy, I know, I say it one way or another, almost every entry lately. Thankfully, I have been taken off the maintenance detail, which would free up some time if I were not constantly being dragged down to the caves to give my opinion on one thing or another. Yes, my edu-minor had been mechanical engineering. Still, my edu-major and my job before the near end of the planet was electrical engineering, specifically cybezs and electronics, which may be one of the last things to be moved below.

I ran into Tolz, and Arten yesterday. I do not see them much since I only work security once a weez, so it felt great to have some time to catch up.

Tolz officially has a dinfriend he has spent much time with lately; her name is Olania. Yes, for those who remember, she was my head nurse, and she also works as a teacher. He says he has no plans to follow down my path; we shall see what the future holds.

Arten is still determined to be a bachelor for life, and when he's not working security, he offers physical and survival training classes to the residents of the towz. He mentioned an old-fashioned bachelor party in my honor; date to be determined as soon as Thereza and I pick a date for our espousal.

In other news concerning the caves, I have been asked to join the next exploration team to map out the new section of cave recently discovered. The initial description of the new area is promising.

Johlnz had never explored a cave before and looked forward to the new experience. Each member of the seven-person team carried a portable zolatron lantern as well as a container of floratine bulbs, floor stands, and wire to extend the lighting system at least five hundred yarzs into the new cave.

The team, which found the new section, only went one hundred yarzs into the cave initially, but their radial-spatial readings showed the main chamber to be larger than could be measured.

"Johlnz, move up ahead with Ruzicka, and head out due north as far as you can go, placing a bulb every fifty yarzs. Keep moving out, however, no farther than seven hundred yarzs before making your way back."

The tanmen giving Johlnz directions was Nuzen Hultztrand. Nuzen was the leader of the expedition, as well as one of the primary section leaders working on the layout of the initial dormitory construction in the front portion of the cave system. As Johlnz and Ruzicka started on their way, Nuzen began giving the other team members instructions to move out in different directions.

"I do not know about you, Johlnz, but walking in darkness like this, not being able to see anything except total charness gives me the shivers. It reminds me of the old horror flickers I used to watch as a kid. I feel like something is going to jump out and grab me at any moment."

"Well, thanks a lot; I felt fine with this until now. It is odd; I have never done anything or experienced anything like this in the past. I would feel better if I could at least see a ceiling."

"They told me the cave ceiling in here is at least fifty pads above us. Some daz we could have five floors of living, working or recreation space in this section, at any rate, that is your job right, as part of the Grand Plan Envisionment Committee?"

"We probably won't immediately get into those kinds of details; however, I think you are correct about what will be here someday, but probably not till we are both very old or dead."

"Okay, Johlnz, this is the spot for the first bulb. Let's start with one from your pack, and I will start splicing the cable."

Johlnz took a bulb and stand out of his pack and positioned them on the wet soil. The damp ground, which made Johlnz think about the many challenges ahead to make these caves into a permanent camo. The stands they were placing were only a pad high; later, another team would replace the polls with higher, more permanent ones.

When they were done splicing in the power line, they lit the lamp and could still see nothing in the charness in all directions, except for the other lights shimmering behind them. There were mounds of dirt and piles of rocks now illuminated, but mostly around them remained just darkness.

Johlnz and Ruzicka continued for another two zakas, moving northward deeper into the giant cave as the ground swelled up and down below them like enormous frozen waves. Finally, they reached the end of the lighting supplies and connected the last lamp to the power line.

"Well, Johlnz, that takes care of our main task; even so, we still have another one hundred yarzs we can walk if we want."

"I say let's journey on into the darkness and discover a new land."

"A bit overly dramatic, I would say, Johlnz. The best we can hope to find is more dirt and rocks, which is far better than bumping into some big-eyed monster looking to devour us for dinner."

They journeyed on a short way when they noticed a shimmering up ahead. After a few more yarzs, they reached a wall. Without any light other than their respective lanterns, they still could not see the top of the cave or how far the wall ran, but they did at least know the cave had an ending.

The light from their lanterns bounced off the wall, which appeared to have shiny pieces of qurtzon rocks embedded. It created a beautiful display of color continually changing as they moved around their lanterns.

"Okay, Ruz, I guess we should head back and report. We can't stand here gawking at pretty colors all daz."

When they turned around to walk back to join the rest of the groups, they found the sight almost as captivating as the wall behind them. In addition to their lamps, they could follow back in the distance; they could also see the additional teams' lamps stretching off in various directions. Some were bright points of lights, while others were small and star-like. It was as if they were standing in space looking out across a sparsely populated starfield.

One other thing the explorers noticed while standing there — the string of lights went up, which confirmed even though they could not see it as they had progressed, they most certainly were heading lower into the planet.

"Damn, now we have to walk uphill, and hitchhiking is out of the question."

The Forge
Nully 27

It's not much; however, todaz marked the beginning of our next industrial age with the firing of our new metals forge. It did not take much work to get it going again since it had recently shut down about three cycles ago. Gases powered the factory in the past, but the engineers updated it for the Zolatron Generators. We are using about twenty percent of its capacity now; nevertheless, as construction progresses in the caves, we will eventually need the full one hundred percent. For our new community to succeed, we need to build tools to build buildings to build bigger factories to build larger equipment, and so on and so forth. I always wanted to use that old expression.

How many cycles long was the first industrial age? I do not remember from my history lessons, just the same, due to a lack of resources and a workforce, our industrial rise will be slow. We have the knowledge in books and on the main-cybez, but the workstations will not last forever, and it will be many decades before we have the capabilities to re-create the cybezs we have come to rely on so much for our survival.

A Cold Daz in Doxx
Autnar 18

I have heard many tanmen say, 'It will be a cold daz in doxx before I ever get espoused.' I have never been reluctant to get espoused, but yesterday on Autnar 17, Thereza and I got espoused, on a cloudy daz with temperatures only in the low 40's.

We were both anointed Athix, so we asked a tanmen in our towz who had been a Deaxon, to do the honors. Dr. Moxron walked Thereza into the main dining room of the Kiz Camo, which our friends had cleared and decorated for the occasion.

We had a small and short celebration afterward, a nice change from the usual activities. Thereza's friends all made unique dishes for our first meal together shared with all our friends. We have little to no, alcohol around here, yet someone did supply two bottles of wizen to share.

My friends held a bachelor party of sorts the nitz before, and as Arten had promised, it was old-fashioned. For drinks, we had bottles of locally produced, four-cycle-old ruxxbert, and the entertainment was an old contial film from over fifty cycles ago, shown on a screen made of a sheet, using an old projector. Where he got it from is still a mystery.

After the film, he brought out an old bottle of tezqula, with just enough for all of us to have a shot in my honor. With life still one big crapshoot, it is nice to know I have many friends.

Love, Contial and Work
Zelmar 13

It's been almost a mooncazt since my last entry. My espoused life has been keeping me even busier than before. I have been working with the underground mapping teams recently to cybeztize all the maps. We will use the maps to first layout ventilation holes and then plan the small beginnings of our underground towz.

We have been using some of our new tools to help excavate the caves to enlarge passageways and carve out our new towz. It is lengthy, hard work; regardless, we must start somewhere. We will be living a tight dorm-like existence below ground when twilight comes, just like we do now; all the same, it will be better than trying to live above ground.

Thereza and I have been settling into our new life together. What we have is not a camo; however, our double-size room is still a great place to have some quiet time together. Our friends are asking when we will have our first liltanz. I know we need to grow our community, but we have much to do before I can contemplate bringing a new life into this planet.

With certain supplies dwindling, we may not even have much choice in the matter. Currently, there is a voluntary moratorium on having liltanz. Thankfully there is no such rule against contial.

Reaching Out

Zelmar 24

Our communications specialists continue to monitor every daz for any radio or video signals as they have since our first mooncazts here in this region. It is often quiet and connecting to what little remains of the satellite network is hit and miss, mostly miss.

They have heard pleas for help along with some official-sounding announcements about remaining calm, most of which are probably recordings. I have been working in the communications center when some messages were received, and it leaves you feeling sad and ready to sit down and cry. Thankfully we have each other, our friends, and our community to keep us strong. The more we do here to rebuild some manner of civilization, the more we may help others who manage to survive in the future.

Espoused Life

Nemvaz 10

It's almost two cycles since Zeptulgar hit Tanacun. We have come far, but still, we have a long way to go if we are to survive. It's, in many ways, a daily struggle, even though most of us would probably say we are happy to be alive and glad to have each other.

The Council has planned a remembrance ceremony for the anniversary. So many individuals perished that daz and many have died since; we must not ever forget. The numbers, if anyone ever stopped to figure it out, would be staggering. If we survive, it will take decdecazs to rebuild all we had, and our total population may never recover.

On a happier note, for my partner and me anyway, we have been given a two-room accommodation in Kiz Camo. Being espoused to one of the big shot's assistants has its privileges. Dr. Moxron would also say it doesn't hurt; I am closer to the cybez center to make repairs at any time of the daz or nitz.

"Well, hello, stranger!"

Thereza greeted Johlnz as he returned to bed after spending a few late-nitz zakas in the cybez center. He spent a lot of time trying to make new systems out of old spare parts.

"I do not get to see you much at all as it is, and then they take you away from me."

"I think you should complain to the management. I understand you have a connection, which is how we managed to get these accommodations to live. If I have to be gone occasionally in exchange for being able to be with you, talk to you, and most of all, contial with you without our neighbors hearing, then it is worth it to me."

"Shut up and kiss me, Johlnz! Was it genuinely something they could not wait until tomorrow for you to fix?"

"Yes, this time, a server malfunctioned, and it would not let them access the few remaining satellites. After I fixed the problem, they tried to contact the orbital stations again, with still no response."

"Can they still be alive, Johlnz? I never paid much attention to the space program or what was happening with the stations and the expedition to Uberant."

"The stations had supplies, which should last about five cycles if there were no other problems. They could be gone, or it could be a communication systems issue. They both have multiple shuttles they could use if able, which would allow them to land back on Tanacun, but for now, they may be better off up in orbit."

"Enough talk, babe, kiss me!"

They spent the next half zaka in slow contial and cuddling together while they could, without distractions or interruptions. After a while, Thereza asked a question that surprised Johlnz.

"Johlnz, when do you think we will be able to have a liltanz?"

After a moment's pause, Johlnz responded.

"No one is preventing us or anyone else from having a liltanz; it is just not recommended until we get more stabilized. I would think probably after the first twilight, the Council will give their blessing. Not that they can or would do anything to stop someone from getting or being pregnant."

Johlnz paused a moment as his eyes widened in a look of realization.

"Are you trying to tell me something, my love?"

"No, I am merely wondering about it and about how you feel about the idea."

Johlnz answered without having even to think.

"I would love to have a liltanz, or two, or three with you; however, I feel we should wait at least until after the first twilight. I love the idea of having liltanz; nevertheless, I want to be able to bring our liltanz into an existence where they will not have to struggle for survival and have some real hope for a future."

He paused again, this time with a look of sorrow on his face as his eyes became moist.

"When I hear some of the messages, we have intercepted from individuals begging for help, not for them, but their liltanz—it brings tears to my eyes, and then I feel so angry, we can do nothing for them."

Thereza gently caressed Johlnz's face and kissed him as she saw a tear fall from his eye and realized his compassion for others was one of the many things, she loved about him.

Nemvaz 19

0002 AC

It's now been two cycles since Zeptulgar struck Tanacun, changing our lives forever.

The Council decided during last nitz's meeting; we would maintain two calendars in the future. One will be the traditional calendar marking the old mooncazts dazs, and holidays, and one will be a new calendar.

In our new calendar, yesterday was the last daz of our cycle 0001. Todaz is the start of cycle 0002. Nemvaz 19 is now considered our New Cycle Daz.

Since the planet continues to go around the sun in 310 dazs, we will keep the old mooncazts and dazs, but we will track the cycles of Tana and the cycles after the comet (AC) together. The warming season will no longer always begin in Eral in the north, and the cooling season will no longer start at the beginning of Zelmar. Someday we will probably drop the old dazs and mooncazts and replace them with a new system; all the same, it is too soon for such a change.

The town held the ceremony of remembrance yesterday, before the Council meeting, in the first large section of the caves, which will be part of the common area when the twilight time comes. Workers brightly lit the chamber with candles and colored floratine bulbs found in an abandoned warehouse a few zilos east of our towz.

The Council thought it would be an excellent place to have the ceremony so everyone could see the beginning of what will be our future camo. It was also the only place large enough for everyone to gather at one time.

Our population is now over 600, as every couple of dazs, a few more survivors arrive looking for help. We have little room to spare, but we can't say go away. Where could they go?

Hzalo-Multum - Gratuzes Auraltec
Nemvaz 25

We celebrated our second daz of gratmul todaz and began a new custom of using a local name for a similar tradition of giving gratmul for as the locals say, 'The blessing bestowed upon us by the Muzie.'

As part of the celebration, we officially welcomed seventeen new residents to our community. They made their way to us about a weez ago from Matabas after a long and terrifying journey, which saw ten fellow travelers die along the way. They were a group of missionaries from Guaz, a country in Iurox, bringing the Athix religion to a recently discovered tribe of Matabas Indugens.

When the comet arrived, they had managed to get most of the tribe to go with them to the top of a local mountain, which saved them from the initial tidal waves caused by the impact. Still, when the darkness came and debris began to fall from the sky, the natives saw it as a sign their Onemaz was angry. While the missionaries slept in the middle of the nitz, the tribe all jumped off the mountain in ritual suicide.

The missionaries waited on the top of the mountain until the waters receded and then started the long journey north. When one of our scouting parties found them, they were half-starved and a few close to death—now everyone is recovering and doing well.

The Fero-stoneworks
Tralmard 12

It's been a hectic weez in our community with new arrivals and the opening of the old fero-stoneworks.

As the planet continues slowly to heal, we also continue to spin in two directions at once, and as individuals have begun to realize this, they have started to travel as we did to the equator. It is a difficult journey for those without the proper provisions and armaments, but some do make it and find our byways, which leads them to our towz. The new arrivals, a few from the Provinces and Tezaci, have raised our population above 625.

We have teams working on ways to the north and south and clearing some already existing, which survivors are using to speed the end of their journey. Even though they are primitive in some places and barely passable in others, they help us with scavenging materials needed to build.

The rising population of our towz and the approaching twilight means we need more new shelters and homes above and below ground, and to build them strong and secure, we must construct them with fero-stone.

We have access to old stone scavenged from ruins, and we now will have fero-stone of our design. The new factory started production todaz. The output will be slow for now, and workers will use most to build a larger factory to prefabricate other materials and structures needed to erect our towz.

Special Council Meeting - Progress Report
Tralmard 20

I have just returned from a special Council meeting in which all the group leaders were to provide updates on where they are with preparing for the coming twilight.

I am one of the group leaders, and my responsibility is to move and protect the cybez systems and related equipment such as dishes and antennas, as well as being the citizen representative.

The meeting was long and full of important information I feel should be recorded somewhere, so I will add it to my journal as best I can.

Professor Kizermel approached the podium to start the meeting as everyone took their seats and prepared for their reports. After everyone sat, and the room quieted, he welcomed the group and started the meeting.

"In less than eight mooncazts our towz will be at twilight and will start the slow move back to a normal, but unfortunately temporary, light and weather condition. Getting through this period will not ensure our survival, be that as it may, getting beyond this first twilight will raise the chances our community, our towz of Nel Experza, will survive for many new generations.

"Our time to prepare is running out. The planet's tilt is now at over 67 degrees; our full dazlight zakas are becoming short, and our temperatures are plummeting.

"Even though twilight will be in the middle of Nemvaz, almost precisely three cycles after the comet struck, we must be ready to move into the caves no later than the beginning of Autnar, and we must prepare to stay until at least the beginning of Banlar. We do not know what will remain of the towz we have built so far when we emerge, but we know we will have much work to accomplish.

"Doctor Moxron, do you have any news in regards to the conditions above us and the efforts to contact the Orbital Stations?"

The Doctor stood at his seat rather than go up to the front since he had little to report.

"As you know, the skies are beginning to clear, and we now have more ability to see what is going on above the planet. We have not detected any large pieces of debris that look likely to cause us any direct problems, all the same, indirect complications of tidal waves and darkened skies are still a possibility.

"In regards to communications with others, we have nothing new to report. The messages we were getting from individuals looking for help have slowed considerably, and we have picked up no other video or radio messages."

He paused and was about to sit down when he recalled one more piece of news.

"We have been able to detect one of the Orbital Stations still in its normal orbit above us; nevertheless, we do not know which one and have not been able to make contact.

"Johlnz Zavix will give the update on moving our equipment down into the caves."

As Dr. Moxron sat back in his chair, Johlnz nervously walked up to the podium to give his report. He felt nervous, as he never liked speaking in front of individuals, and his education and experience were no match for most of those in attendance.

"We have begun the construction of a new central communication, systems, and cybez area in the main section of the Alpon cave, as we have started to call it for clarification, as we eventually move deeper into the cave system. The room will be climate-controlled as best we can, and we will drill shafts through the rock to run all the wiring and optical cable lines necessary for the dishes and antennas. We do have extra of what we need, so we will not have to cut communications while setting up the new cybez center.

"Work has begun on drilling the access holes necessary, and we expect to complete them in two mooncazts. The wiring and cables should only take an additional two weezs, and we should be up and running at least a mooncazt before we expect to move into the caves.

"Questions?"

He now felt much better and found speaking in front of a group of individuals was not as hard as he had feared until someone had a question. Jox Bartle, the tanmen in charge of some other construction projects, raised his hand and stood when acknowledged.

"Johlnz, what are you going to do to ensure the antennas and dishes survive the snowy conditions and high winds?"

"I am afraid there is not much we can do. Some natural protection surrounds the area, but the instruments do need a clear line of sight to function properly. We will put as many support cables on them as possible; however, we can't predict how they will stand up to heavy storms."

"So, what happens if we lose an antenna or dish?"

Johlnz hesitated for a few seconds before answering.

"If we lose communications, we can do little unless we can get out and up to the top of the hill to replace the equipment, which I do not believe will be possible. I wonder, though, whom will we need to talk to? Maybe this is a good time for a report on the expected weather conditions."

Johlnz realized he had accidentally taken control of the meeting away from Professor Kizermel, and he immediately apologized.

"It's is okay, Johlnz. I agree with your suggestion. Dr. Zarnikiyan, are you ready to report?"

"Yes, I am."

The Dr. approached the podium and took some time to organize his notes and clear his throat before starting.

"This planet has never seen anything like what is going to happen. There will be extreme temperature differences between what were the northern and southern hemispheres. Based on those extremes and the fact we will be directly between them, my team fears we will see many powerful storms, which will probably have winds as strong as the strongest storms of the past. We will likely see many pads of snowfall as temperature drops below what some here ever experienced in the past.

"In regards to Jox's earlier question, if we lose the antennas or dishes, which is very likely, I doubt anyone will be able to go and fix them. I know it sounds bad, but as Johlnz asked, who exactly are we expecting to contact?"

The question hung in the air, with no one willing to provide an answer as they realized how alone they probably were or would soon be on a planet once populated by a considerable number of individuals.

After a brief uncomfortable pause, Salerand Loxon stood up and said he would go next, and he went up to the podium to speak.

"Before giving my report, I would like to acknowledge all the help and expertise Johlnz has been providing on the construction side of the work going on in the caves. His knowledge of mechanical engineering has been beneficial.

"Work is proceeding on leveling out with crushed rock and dirt, the floor of the Alpha cave where we will be setting up the main dormitory spaces. We expect to be able to pour cemastic, of which we have a minimal supply, beginning in one weez, and then we will start to construct walls. We will erect most of the walls from fibrastic board, which means you will have physical privacy, but not vocal privacy. It will indeed be less private than dormitory living.

"There will be no ceilings in most areas, just the same; we will have a small space where we have ceilings to allow individuals to sleep who have to work during what we will establish as the nitz zakas. We will distinguish daz from nitz by using the lights to create an even cycle.

"In regards to protecting us from the weather, we will soon start construction of two doors which we will flank using fero-stone to make them strong. We will also have a stone-lined passageway connected to what we are calling the outpost. We will construct the outpost with reinforced fero-stone, with a double-sheeted metal and fibrastic board roof, which we hope will stand up to the worst conditions.

"The outpost has two functions, one of which is to offer help to those inside if weather conditions should cut us off, and to allow us to monitor conditions at times when the doors will need to stay closed.

"I am happy to report one thing, which is complete — the ventilation systems. They will allow us to vent out bad air and cooking exhaust as well as controlling the amount of fresh air coming into the caves.

"We are also creating some areas specifically for recreation. We could be in the caves for up to four mooncazts, and we need something to do, other than working on more permanent structures for the second twilight. We found another cave off to the side, earlier hidden, until we widened the passageway. It will be called the Ceton cave, and it leads to a large underground lake, which we can use for swimming if the water stays warm enough. For now, we are doing nothing with the lower-level Beton cave or the enormous Delton cave. They are reserved for large-scale permanent expansion in the future.

"That is all I have for todaz. I appreciate your attention, and I believe Loyst would like to go next."

"Hello, for those who do not know me, my name is Loyst Narstox. I had been a Geology student about to graduate when the comet struck. I know many individuals have concerns about the safety of the caves, so I have been checking out the integrity of the cave system as best I can.

"The first thing I wanted to check was the stability of the area above the cave entrance to look for signs of weakness. It appears to me that the area had been well overgrown with vegetation and is extremely stable. Even with a lot of the vegetation dead, I believe the site will still be secure, but I cannot give a guarantee. I have no way of knowing what the extreme cold we may see will do to the rocks. This area has never seen freezing temperatures in the past.

"I have also done some additional exploring of the cave system, and have seen no indication of any recent cave-ins or shifting of the cave structure. Again, I must stress, although they will be protected from the cold, these caves have never seen the extremes we may be facing.

"One more thing I would like to let you know is though I have tried, I have not found any additional entrances to the cave system. It doesn't mean they do not exist, only that I can find none now. It may be possible in the future to create entrances, and is certainly something to consider."

The meeting continued with a few other reports about food preparation and mezcaf hall areas to put together and a report on food supplies to get us through. Vegcamo structures with sunlamps are being built inside the caves to continue food growth while inside and be prepared to replant when the extreme cold weather has subsided.

There will also be an area for livestock, which we will maintain in the Ceton cave. The cave is off to the side of Alpon cave and may not be far enough away to keep the smell out of Alpon cave or the noise, be that as it may, we will have to learn to deal with it this time unless they decide to move them down to Beton.

Professor Kiz thanked everyone and briefly talked about the long-range plans for the caves and the intention to use the Delton, also known as the star cave, to camo the first permanent structures of our eventual new cizay. Delton is the enormous cave I helped to explore and light. The team gave it this name because of the shining rocks in the ceiling, which reflect our lights like little stars.

After the meeting, I caught up with Security Chief Marzco, and we talked a bit about our prospects for survival.

Hi Johlnz, I have not seen you for a while. Congratulations! I was disappointed not to be here for the celebration, but duty called. Personally, I think you arranged it just to get me out of the way so she would not change her mind. I am, after all, tall, extremely dark, and handsome, as well as a wonderful catch, or at least I would be if I could ever be here long enough to even talk to someone."

"Well, we know she doesn't go for your type, or I would not be espoused."

They laughed, which felt terrific to Johlnz after sitting through the long meeting detailing one problem after another.

"So, Marzco, what do you think of our chances?"

"I think we have a lot to be concerned about; this area has not been through these kinds of temperature changes, so we do not know what to expect. One reason why the building outside the cave is so important is the possibility of being trapped in the caves. Maybe there exists another reliable way out, maybe not, but it is something we must make sure we have for the second twilight.

"On a lighter note, Johlnz, I feel if we can get past this first twilight, we will be able to survive long term and build a proper society for the future. By the time the next twilight comes, I expect we will be a hundred percent more prepared."

"I agree, Marzco; if we make it through this one, I believe we are good, as long as the universe doesn't throw anything more our way.

"Well, I need to get back to the beautiful partner of mine before she does get tired of waiting for me and runs off with some other eligible bachelor.

The Spark Obelisque

Tralmard 22

The traditional Spark of Light Celebration Daz is approaching, and this cycle, we will celebrate. We have an Obelisque set up in the middle of towz, and we have even hung Lights Sparks and decorations made by some of our liltanz.

The Council felt it important to celebrate this cycle, and go into the caves, with a renewed hope for the future, from the merriment of renewal to be upon us soon. Even though we will not go into the caves for a few more mooncazts, the symbolism is important.

Unlike cycles past, this celebration will not be about gluttony or gifts. The gifts this cycle will be the gift of life and inner spirit, as was the original intention of the celebration.

The Spark of Light
Tralmard 24

If life had continued uninterrupted by the gift from the eternal darkness, todaz would have been The Spark of Light. Thereza and I returned from the lighting ceremony, and I wanted to update this journal before joining my partner for a much-needed sleep.

As I mentioned in my previous entry, the Council planned a small celebration, marked by a prayer meeting and a moment of silence, before the official lighting of the Obelisque. It was moving and beautiful when the Obelisque ignited. Most of the original residents of this region are Athix, as are some of us new residents. Still, the Council decided to keep the ceremony more straightforward and open to all.

"With the lighting of this Obelisque of Light, I hereby declare the beginning of the Celebration of The Spark of Light. May the light of the gift above, fill your body and soul, with joy and enlightenment, to be shared by all."

Council Chairtan, Professor Kizermel, flipped the switch to light the Obelisque and then proceeded to light the moat of fire that would surround it for the evening. The Council members passed candles to those gathered. After lighting their candles from the Obelisque moat, they proceeded to illuminate the walkways of enlightenment leading away from the Obelisque in three directions, as was the ancient custom amongst the Athix and a few other religions.

Johlnz gave Thereza the customary kiss of sharing, took her hand in his, and they proceeded to walk along the pathways now lit by miniature Light Sparks as snow began to fall from the sky.

"It's like a gift from above to bless us as we begin our celebration."

"Thereza, my love, it is your wonderful sense of optimism and hope, which makes me love you more each daz. It is beautiful, I agree, and it is far better than the other gift the eternal darkness sent.

"This snow reminds me of my dazs as a liltanz growing up in Rilodfia. We often had snow for the celebration . . . and I . . ."

"Come on now, Johlnz, hold it together. I need you to be strong for me; I can't hold myself together without your love and strength."

"I am sorry. You would think by now I would be past the sorrow, for there certainly is no time for it. Anyway, this is not the kind of talk to have on this nitz.

"The Light Sparks are so beautiful; the liltanz did a great job creating them out of the multicolored broken glass collected from the nearby ruins. I remember making some myself when I was a liltanz. I know you did not have snow for the celebration out in Arzonda, but did you make any Sparks when you were a liltanz?"

"Yes, Johlnz, I did, with my sibsom and my Muzie."

"We have been espoused for three mooncazts, and you have never mentioned your sibsom before. You never talk about your family, and I am always reluctant to start that conversation."

"It's okay, Johlnz; I think I need to talk about it, especially tonitz. On this nitz, it is good to remember those who have come before us in life.

"My Pypzie died when I was only five, even so, my Muzie and older sibsom always made sure to make the celebration special for me as I grew up, at least until they both died in a crash when I was twelve."

"I am so sorry."

Johlnz stopped and held her close while she steadied herself to continue. He could tell by her voice; the memories were painful.

"I was all alone on the planet; no other family."

"Except for your Onczle?"

Johlnz immediately recognized his mistake as he recalled the truth Thereza had told him what seemed like forever ago. Thereza gave him an odd look but did not say anything, other than to give him this time, the full story.

"Onczle Robarz had been my neighbor. He and his partner had no liltanz of their own, and they were like a real Aunz and Onczle before I lost my family."

Thereza walked a few steps farther along the pathway, stopped to look up, and let the snowflakes fall and melt on her face.

"Onczle Robarz petitioned the authorities to allow them to adopt me, and that is how I came to live with them. Aunt Luza died a few cycles later, and then Onczle Robarz and I moved east to Ohito, and I attended school at the Ohito Advanced Studies in Zeland.

"I do not know why I did not tell you all this before, but I am glad I now have. I feel so much better, and I know tonitz they are all sending their blessings to both of us."

"The snow is getting heavier; do you want to go back to our place?"

"No, Johlnz, I want to walk the paths again. The snow is laying around the Light Sparks and capturing even more of their beauty."

Johlnz grabbed her hand, and they walked along the paths for another zaka, enjoying the snow, and the light shining over the fresh powder. As bad as things were and could still be, Thereza thought this was the best Spark of Light she had experienced in many cycles.

Renewal's Eve

Tralmard 30

Todaz is—was, Renewal's Eve. Tomorrow would have started the cycle 3991. This will be the last time our towz celebrates the old Renewal's Daz. This cycle could be the final cycle of our lives, or it could be the beginning of the rebirth of our planet. Let me rephrase my last statement, for the planet will go on, no matter what happens to us. This could be the final cycle of our lives, or it could be the beginning of the rebirth of our civilization.

Thereza and I have been invited to a small gathering here in Kiz Camo, and I am waiting for her to be ready as I write this update. Hopefully, this time next cycle, I will be alive to write something a bit more optimistic and looking to our future even if we no longer celebrate the old tradition.

New Arrival

Banlar 03

Todaz, we held our Council meeting, filled with mostly updates on progress toward moving the population of our towz into the caves for twilight.

Council Chairtan Kizermel had just about finished his comments before radio tech Zuciano came into the room with his usual nervous energy. He was in his mid-twenties, tall, skinny, and always apprehensive around the leaders of the towz.

He waited for the Professor to acknowledge his presence and then approached with a piece of paper in his outstretched hand. They exchanged words, and Zayden, as I always call him, handed the Professor the piece of paper with extraordinary news.

Chairtan Kizermel stepped back to the podium with a small grin on his face.

"Radio tech Zuciano informed me, we have received a message from the Mazter of the U.P. SeaForce Super Cruiser, UPJS Zeltren."

Immediately the room erupted with questions being thrown out to the Professor. He raised his hands, asking for quiet so he could continue.

"All I know at this time is the Mazter has contacted us, and he will radio back in one zaka to speak to the person in charge, which would be myself. I do not know how long we will be in contact; however, I propose we adjourn for now and resume the meeting in two zakas. I expect to have many answers for you then. I know nothing of this ship as I never much followed the exploits of our Authority or the SeaForce, other than when we were conducting joint research projects."

When Chairtan Kizermel had finished, councilman Jox Bartle stood up and asked to have the floor.

"I do know of the Zeltren, and I am not surprised they have survived. The Super Cruiser class of ships, were the newest, most advanced, and most powerful SeaForce ships ever developed by any country. There were three under construction when the comet was first detected, but I believe the Zeltren to be the first and only one to be launched."

Jox paused for a moment to catch his breath and search his memory, as he was visibly excited about being contacted by the newest, strongest ship of the United Provinces fleet.

"They use the newest versions of the Zolatron generation systems, and they can go without refueling of any kind for up to twenty cycles. They are partially submersible and carry a small crew of sixty to seventy. I believe they also carry five vertical thrust, fighter jets, and a few helotransports, some large enough to move heavy freight."

"Equipped well enough to come here and basically take over, if they wanted," interrupted Councilman Predsen.

"Come on, Malcolz, do not go jumping to conclusions," the Chairtan responded.

"I am not Mr. Chairtan; I only think we need to be careful. I suggest you not give away our location, and propose a meeting somewhere away from our towz."

"You are probably correct, and I will be cautious. We will meet back here in two zakas."

(((*)))

Two and a half zakas later, Chairtan Kizermel finally came back into the room and was immediately hit with questions of concern.

"Everyone, please sit down and be quiet, I have much information to pass on to you, and we have much to discuss.

"The first matter of business. I have made contact with Mazter Calliaz Rourze of the Zeltren. He passed on considerable information about the condition of what's left of our planet.

"Most major Authorities have failed, and most of the bunkers the Mazter had contact with early after the impact, have now gone quiet, including the United Provinces. The ship has not been able to contact any planet Authority, SeaForce vessel, air system, or individuals for over nine mooncazts. The exception is, of course, our group, and I am pleased to say, the Orbital Station I."

The room immediately grew loud with questions, and again, the Chairtan had to ask for everyone to be silent.

"I will answer questions as best I can after I finish. Before detailing the rest of my conversation with Mazter Rourze, I first would like to give an update on the Orbital Stations.

"After my conversation with Mazter Rourze, I immediately contacted the Commander of Station I using the communication information provided. The Commander's name is Cazryn Forzzell, and she has confirmed the information given to me by Mazter Rourze. She informed me Orbital Station II had suffered severe damage and has since crashed back onto the planet. They were able to rescue only twenty-seven survivors from OS-II, even though over one hundred crewmembers lived on the station before the comet.

"OS-I is now the camo to one hundred and thirteen crew. The station can support them for about another five cycles. They do have orbital ships they can use to access and maybe repair some of the remaining satellites in orbit. The task is something they have not started since they had no reason. Now they know we are here, so they will try to repair some satellites so we can have better communication between us as well as access to weather situations, which will be critical as twilight approaches.

"They have enough landers to evacuate everyone on the station, but the problem is they've had nowhere to land that looked long-term survivable. After twilight, we will start working on a plan to bring them to our towz.

"Okay, now back to Mazter Rourze. They are five dazs away from the nearest port to us, which would be the old harbor towz of Bilwi, on the eastern coast of Donhurex. As we already know, there are a series of byways, which connect Bilwi to us, and the satellite views of the towz confirm the old stone docks remain. They are too large themselves to dock; nevertheless, they will be able to use their transports to ferry to the docks.

"We are under fifty zilos from the port, and we know from our reconnaissance teams the byways are passable for only twenty zilos from here. The Zeltren has equipment they can use to clear the byways, though it will take time. They will use one of their helotransports to scout the byways first and then will decide on a time to meet."

The Chairtan finished imparting all the information he had to give, and he prepared himself for the onslaught of questions he knew were about to be thrown at him.

"Any questions?"

To his surprise, they did not all shout at him at one time, and he was relieved to see Council Vice-Chairtan Johlant get up to ask a question.

"Mazjuen, how many crew members are on the ship, do they plan on staying on the ship or coming here, is the ship in good condition?"

"The Mazter did not give a number, but he did say they have rescued some individuals, and some families are also aboard the ship. I am not sure what his long-range plans are for the ship; still, he did say it remained in excellent condition even though it is presently overcrowded."

Malcolz was the next to stand, and Mazjuen knew where this was heading.

"How do we know we can trust them? How do we even know if the Mazter is whom he says? I urge you not to let them come here without meeting somewhere else first. We do not want them knowing where we are, not until we know more about them and their intentions."

"Malcolz, you have been instrumental in getting us here safely, and your caution has saved us many times, but this time, you need to relax. As far as where we are, they already know. Mazter Cazryn gave them our location when he contacted her about receiving our message. She vouched for him and mentioned she knew the Mazter before the comet. Could they be working together to take us over and take control? Yes, they could, though I find
it to be extremely unlikely. Why would they desire to take control of us?"

His answers appeared to make calm the security chief for now, and it seemed there were surprisingly no more questions, so he adjourned the meeting.

The flyover
Banlar 09

Tomorrow is the daz the representatives from the Zeltren will arrive in towz to meet with the Council. They anchored off the coast of Bilwi two dazs ago, inspecting the port and preparing to disembark. Chairtan Kizermel had a towz meeting yesterday, where he updated everyone. Most individuals already knew of the contact with the ship and orbital station; even so, I think they were still expecting a formal confirmation from the Chairtan of the Council.

Todaz one of the helotransports flew high over towz after completing its inspection of the byway, dipping its nose in a sign of friendship and respect before heading back to the ship.

As if today was not exciting enough, Tolz stopped by Kiz Camo to tell Thereza and me; he has asked Olania to be his partner. I am extremely happy for my friend—but maybe sad for Olania. Hopefully, Tolz never reads this journal.

The Meeting
Banlar 10

Todaz was the big daz, and not to be ignored, the weather had to cause some problems. We awoke this premid to several inches of slow-to-melt snow. It was not a problem for our bulk-transports, but it did make for some messy conditions around towz.

The inspection found the byways out of Bilwi to be in bad shape, so the representatives of the Zeltren had to take a helotransport fifteen zilos inland where a convoy of our best, most comfortable transports meet them. Since we came here mostly in army and freight bulk-transports, the nicest thing we have is a twelve-cycle-old limavan.

Commander Predsen and Dr. Johlant were sent with a security detail to meet the Mazter and others and escort them to towz. Malcolz had confided with me; he was going on the trip no matter what, so he inwardly rejoiced when Professor Kizermel told him to lead the group.

Many residents of towz came out to see the crewmembers. They greeted the crew with applause as we escorted them into the Council meeting room for a private discussion among the delegation and the Towz Council. Although I am not a member of the Council, I was in attendance since I am the Community Representative.

I am listing here the delegation members, since I do not think anyone else has yet thought of keeping formal records of our Council proceedings. The journal may be the only record to exist of how we survived Zeptulgar, assuming we do survive.

> Mazter Calliaz Rourze
>
> Second In-Command Frunx Neltia (First Scip)
>
> Doctor Rehum Zoensen
>
> Pypzie Malacha Yanez

The meeting began with Chairtan Kizermel presenting the Council, followed by Mazter Rourze, introducing his group.

"I would like to introduce my second-In Command, Frunx Neltia, who has served with me on my past commissions, Doctor Rehum Zoensen, our chief medical officer, and Pypzie Malacha Yanez, who joined us about a cycle ago. We rescued Pypzie, his staff, and fourteen liltanz when we sent a scouting party to check out what remained of Hondroxo Island. Pypzie ran an orphanage in the mountains; those who were at the orphanage were the only survivors. Pypzie is here to represent the twenty-one civilians onboard the ship whom we hope will be able to settle here in your towz.

"I am an Authority tanmen from an old Authority family, so I know how individuals think, and I want to assure you, we have no intention of trying to take over in any way. We are hoping for friendship, and if possible, a place to call camo when we are not on the Zeltren.

"We believe the Federated Authority of the United Provinces of Jantnel, no longer exists. We have tried to contact the Authority and Authority bunkers; however, the last contact was over nine mooncazts ago. They had extremely limited supplies remaining. We know the air support service planned to move individuals out of the Federated Command Bunker to somewhere south, but we never received confirmation. We still consider ourselves part of the U.P. fleet, even though the U.P. may no longer exist.

"When the comet struck, we had been in a sheltered area along the North, and our location, as well as the unique abilities of our ship, allowed us to survive the tidal waves the comet caused. Most of the planet's fleets and most of our own were not so lucky.

"We have met up with some other ships, both Authority, and civilian, and we have helped where we could; nevertheless, more recently, we have been greeted chiefly with hostilities. We have also made some landfall excursions for survivors, but we can only hold so many individuals on the ship. We have been looking for somewhere to create a settlement of our own; hopefully, it will not be necessary now.

"We know taking on additional survivors here may tax your supplies, especially with the coming of the dark time, but we have many capabilities which will help you all to survive in the caves you are working to make habitable.

"I know your Council Chairtan has gotten you up to speed on the status of the orbital stations. One of our priorities is to find somewhere they can land their emergency ships in the future. They can only survive on the station for another five or maybe six cycles.

"I have no further information to pass along at the moment; in any event, I would like to thank you for inviting us, and I hope we can work together to ensure the survival of the Tana race.

"Any questions for me?"

There were, as expected, a few questions, but not as many as I would have thought, based on the earlier reactions. The

Council members already approved the idea of allowing the civilians and sixty-three crewmembers of the ship to become part of the towz. They realized it was the right thing to do, plus the Zeltren and crew had much to offer.

Mazter Rourze requested to remain independent of the Council for the time being. He pledged to work with the Council to develop missions to be beneficial to the community. The Mazter also took the opportunity to remind everyone, should the ship encounter any official remnants of the U.P. Authority, they had sworn allegiance to them and would have to put their needs first. The Council understood any help we might get from the Zeltren could be temporary.

After lunch, the group decided the ship would stay off the coast and help with the towz's needs until the towz's individuals moved into the caves. The Zeltren would then head south to the warmer weather for about four mooncazts before returning.

My hands are fatigued and achy from all this writing, and I need to stop and join my partner in bed.

Changing of Priorities
Marwe 01

The Zeltren has now been here for almost three weezs. The civilians have been assigned quarters and jobs in towz, while the crew helps with construction; speeding the development of structures above and below ground. With the arrival of the Zeltren, the towz can focus on new priorities and opportunities. One of the opportunities is the ability to repair, and modernize some equipment, and utilize the expertise the crew offers.

They have two large tri-dimensional printers on the Zeltren, and a recycling system developed by the U.P. Authority. The system will recycle scrap materials into the material needed for the printers. All equipment no longer required on the ship will be moved into towz, and they are now re-stocked with fresh food and water for the crew remaining on board.

Traveling back and forth to Bilwi has been excruciatingly slow and difficult. One of our major new priorities is to concentrate on the clearing and rebuilding of the byways between towz and the coast before we move into the caves. We are also working on a clearing for the Helotransports to land near towz, which will greatly benefit moving equipment and handling emergencies.

Constructed close to the coast will be a new radio tower, so we can communicate with what someday will be our new harbor at Bilwi. The tower will also give us better communications with the Zeltren, but it will be difficult work that cannot start until after twilight when the weather warms. For the interim, communications between the ship and towz are going through OS-I, when the station's orbit places it in the proper position.

These new priorities will prevent us from starting some of the after twilight, planned factories, and slow expansion of the underground facilities. Be that as it may, the use of the tri-dimensional printers should more than compensate for the delays. Many are sure the open connection to the coast will be worth moving back other priorities since this will lead to the ability to have a fishing fleet and increase our fresh food supply in the future.

On another good note, Nuzen's team has discovered a huge new cavern below, with additional fresh water. The cave to be called Ezalon will allow for more significant expansion of our underground cizay when we have the resources to increase construction.

A Talk of the One
Marwe 16

I hate that I have not been able to write in this journal for over two weezs, but my life keeps me busy, while this journal helps keep me sane. I enjoy it when I have time to read back to the beginning and realize how far we have come; I also worry about how much farther we have to go to ensure our survival.

We all have been trying to keep up with the repair work above ground and the building below. The frequent storms are not helping as they are slowing down all progress on every front.

My workload may soon get a little lighter as one of the civilians rescued by the Zeltren is a cybez engineer, and another is a mechanical engineer. There are also a few engineers on the Zeltren, though they will remain the ship's crew for now.

I ran into Pypzie Yanez in the mezcaf tent, and we started a conversation while in line, which continued into lunch as we sat together. After a brief prayer of gratmul, something I had not done in a long while, we continued our conversation.

"Just look at the weather outside, Pypzie! It's as if the One is toying with us to make our lives miserable as best Itz can. Has not Itz done enough to us already? I understand the One challenges us to be worthy of the light of Itz grace, but enough already."

"I understand Johlnz how you feel and why you feel this way. It does appear Itz isn't looking out for us or helping in any way, just the same, I must ask you, should Itz? What do you believe—the One controls every little thing in life and bestows good things on individuals, or do you believe Itz created all and lets Itz plan run its course?"

"My Athix instructors told me, if I ask and pray, I would get an answer. I understand it may not always be yes; even so, I believe the One listens. I pray every nitz we will survive, and I will someday have liltanz who can be happy on a planet not out to kill them every daz of their lives."

"Everyone dies one daz, Johlnz."

"You know what I mean, Pypzie; I want to be able to have an actual life, not a life where I do not know what's going to happen."

Pypzie Yanez took another sip of his beverage while he waited for Johlnz to comprehend what he said.

"There are no guarantees in life, Johlnz; maybe we needed to be reminded. I do not personally believe the One gets involved with our everyday lives, even though it is what I am to believe and teach. I believe Itz created all; I believe when we do good, a part of the One's light and grace enters our soul, and I believe in the end, if we live a good life, we will become part of the universal light.

"What do you believe happened to those who died, Johlnz?"

"I believe some are in the light with the One, and some are in the eternal darkness."

"Then, in that case, Itz will has been done as planned."

Johlnz was about to answer when he heard a voice behind him, and his heart skipped a beat with joy. He turned around and stood up to greet Thereza with a hug and kiss.

"I wondered what happened to you. The meeting of the Grand Plan Envisionment Committee starts in fifteen minzakas."

"I know, I lost track of time having a discussion with Pypzie Yanez. Have you two met?"

"No, Johlnz, I do not believe I have had the pleasure."

"Pypzie Yanez, this is my partner, Thereza."

"It is a pleasure to meet you, Thereza. How long have you been espoused, if you do not mind me asking?"

"Not at all, Pypzie. We will have been together for five mooncazts tomorrow."

"So, you espoused after the comet. Did you know each other previously, or did you meet here?"

"Well, Pypzie," said Johlnz, "it is a bit of a long story. To make it brief, we met before coming here, though we did not start dating; I guess the term still applies, until after being here a few mooncazts. We were the first to be espoused here, but a few more couples have followed since."

"Great news, I would say. It means all hope is not lost here, and hope is one of the strongest emotions to help us survive."

"Pypzie, I have not discussed this with Johlnz yet, though I am sure he would agree; it would be an honor if you could bless our union. Deaxon Zerque espoused us, but I—"

"We," Johlnz interrupted, "would like to make it official in the eyes of the One"

Johlnz took Thereza hands in his and kissed her.

"I am sure the One can see the same great love between you, I see, and sure he doesn't need me to grant his blessings. All the same, I would be honored to bless you in his name. I ask simply one thing."

With some concern in her voice, Thereza asked what that one thing would be.

"I would ask we wait until we are living in the caves. I believe it will be great for the community to have something beautiful to witness during our time living there. I would like to open it up to all couples who would want to have their union blessed or renew their commitments."

"I think it is a wonderful idea, Pypzie. Is the idea okay with you, Thereza?"

"Yes, I guess so."

"You seem reluctant, or maybe just a little let down," Pypzie replied. "If you like, I can still do a private blessing for you at any time, but as I said, I feel the two of you have already received Itz's light, and nothing I can say in Itz's name will change your great love."

Thereza smiled at the compliment and turned a slight shade vermier in embarrassment as they bid their farewells and headed off to the meeting.

Council Meeting
Eral 01

I feel like I am always beginning my journal entries in the same way for the last few mooncazts. I am busy as usual, and it has been another two weezs since my previous entry. Work continues at a feverish pace to get everything ready for our move into the shelter of the caves. The weather is numbingly cold on most dazs, and we have had over a foot of snow the last weez, making progress impossible on some projects.

Todaz was our regular Council meeting, which began in the usual way until Professor Kizermel surprised me by making an announcement I was not expecting.

"Good pastmid, everyone, it is a pleasure to see so many new faces here in attendance. After a few announcements, we will go through the progress reports from each group leader.

"First, I would like to welcome Mazter Rourze and First Scip Neltia to the meeting. Mazter Rourze will be serving an advisory role on the Council, and Mr. Neltia will represent for the Zeltren crew.

"I would also like to welcome Pypzie Yanez, as the new Council Community Representative, and I would at this time like to announce Pypzie will be starting weekly Solndar services next weez in the mezcaf tent. He will also be overseeing the project to create a space for a worship center in the Beta cave. The project will create the first long-term permanent structure in Beta cave.

"As many of you know, Johlnz Zavix held the position of Council Community Representative. Since he will now need something to do, we have decided to keep him busy by putting him in charge of the cybez and communication center. Johlnz responsibilities are to include the design and permanent cybez installation in the Alpon cave and the design of the future cybez center and network facility to one-daz be an expanded permanent part of Beton cave.

"Thank you, Johlnz, for all your hard work."

The Chairtan led a round of applause while he winked at Johlnz, indicating his joke was all in fun, as Johlnz already knew. The Professor had gone out of his way many times to thank Johlnz for all his hard work.

"Thank you, Chairtan, and the rest of the Council as well for showing such great confidence in my ability. I will not let you down."

"You are welcome!"

After the second round of applause died down, the Professor began his update.

"Down to business. The planet's tilt on the axis is now at almost 80 degrees; our true dazlight zakas are becoming scarce, and our high temperatures are most often below freezing.

"Johlnz, please go first with your update."

"The arrival of the Zeltren has been beneficial to this project. I am pleased to report all the equipment, including new consoles from the Zeltren, have been moved into our temporary cybez and communication center. The center will only be for this first twilight period. It is our intention, and now my task to have a permanent center set up before the second twilight period is upon the towz.

"Again, thanks to the Zeltren, and their laser drills, we not only have the needed connections to the surface; we also have additional redundant connections in case of an emergency. The ship's crew has provided us with additional support structures for all the topside equipment, which will better ensure they continue to operate for the duration."

There were no questions, so as Johlnz sat down, the Professor asked Dr. Moxron to go next.

"Thanks to our communications with the Orbital Station, we can now confirm, no large pieces of debris are still encircling the planet. Although many smaller pieces, large enough to cause significant damage if they hit the towz, do remain in orbit, I believe, as does Commander Forzzell, we are safe from a significant tidal wave, which is good news for the Zeltren. The skies are becoming clearer, and we expect to have mostly flawless debris-free sunshine waiting for us when twilight is over.

"We are continuing to monitor communications bands, looking for other signs of life, but I have nothing new to report. If there are no questions, I believe Dr. Zarnikiyan is next."

"Thank you, Dr. Moxron."

"As predicted, temperatures have dropped to levels not seen in this area for tens of thousands of cycles, and it is killing off almost all native vegetation. The winds have also picked up, and we can expect storms twice as strong as the one that came through last weez. I requested the use of some space in the communications center to install radar and other equipment to monitor the weather conditions directly, in case we lose communications with the Orbital Station.

"I have nothing more for this report."

The Doctor quickly sat down without asking for questions. He hated speaking in front of individuals. It was the main reason he pursued being a behind-the-scenes scientist instead of an on-air personality.

"Salerand, you are next."

"Yes, thank you."

"Work has come to a halt in the Beton cave as we divert our attentions to the above-ground projects we hope to complete before we enter the caves. The snowstorms have hindered progress, though we have managed to clear seventy-five percent of the byway from here to Port Bilwi. The rest of the byway is mostly passable; however, we would like to accomplish much more to make it safer to travel for larger bulk-transports. I think it will have to wait till after twilight.

"I do have better news to report on our landing area for the Helotransports. We have completed clearing one ahead of schedule, and clearing two should be done before moving into the caves.

"The work in Alpon cave is also moving along well. The mezcaf will move next weez, and now it is my turn to thank the Zeltren for the use of their laser drills. We have cleared extra exhaust holes and installed a backup exhaust system. The system will guarantee we have clean, fresh air coming into the caves when needed.

"We are using the tri-dimensional printer installed in the caves to build a smaller laser drill to have in case we need to drill additional holes. It will also come in handy in the event of a collapse.

"The living quarters are almost complete, including the extra areas under construction to accommodate the new residents joining us who the Zeltren rescued. Work on the entranceway, including the doors and passageway to the outpost, will soon be completed. All in all, I am pleased with our progress.

"Thank you for your attention, and I believe Loyst would like to go next."

"This is starting to sound like a broken music disk, but I also would like to thank the Zeltren crew. They provided the ability to strengthen the cave openings and make the land above the entrance stable and less vulnerable to collapse.

"As I have mentioned before, I am constantly checking out the overall stability of the cave systems. Again, with the help of radsonar equipment from the Zeltren, I have verified the entire cave system explored to date is stable.

"We still have found no secondary entrances to the cave system. With the use of the drills, we will create additional entrances to the caves after twilight passes to better prepare for future construction.

"Are there any questions?"

No one had a question, and the reports continued with updates concerning moving the livestock, now to the Beton cave, and an update on the expanded vegcamoz already planted and growing.

When those reports were complete, the Professor acknowledged Mazter Rourze.

"Thank you, Professor; I am honored to be able to join this Council in an advisory position and look forward to being able to contribute to the growth and prosperity of this towz.

"Speaking for my crew, I want to thank everyone in Nel Experza, for welcoming us and making us feel like this has always been our camo. We have been in many ways alone out there for so long, we were beginning to give up hope, but now we know we have even more to live for and more to protect.

"Moving on to some business. As you know, the Zeltren will be leaving after everyone has moved into the cave system; nevertheless, we are a little short on crew. We lost nine crew members since the impact daz, and five will be staying behind in towz for medical reasons. Three other crew members will be staying behind to help out in case of an emergency, two of which are the pilot and co-pilot of the Helotransports remaining in towz. First Scip Neltia and I would like to leave port with a compliment of sixty-two, which leaves us short by seven crew members.

"We are hoping to fill our crew with volunteers from the towz. We will post a list of positions available and the qualifications needed. These are not high-tech or specialty positions, so we hope to have no problem filling out our crew.

"Thank you, and may the One's light fill you."

"Thank you, Mazter. I think it is we who owe you the most thanks. The support you provided may make the difference between success and failure.

"Last but certainly not least, Pypzie Yanez has a few announcements he would like to share. Pypzie, you have the floor."

"Thank you. I also would like to express my gratitude to the individuals of this towz for welcoming me and the other refugees rescued by the Zeltren. We will be forever in your debt.

"I want to make sure it is known; I am available to counsel anyone in this community. You do not have to be Jozna Athix, to come and bend my ear on any topic. I plan to keep our services as non-denominational as possible, so all will feel welcome.

"I do have an announcement, which I think will help with the wellbeing of our community while spending our first twilight in the caves. I will be conducting an espousal renewal ceremony for anyone who would like to renew their partner commitments to each other and the One. I have not determined a date, though I am thinking maybe between move-in daz and the Spark of Light Celebration. I will announce the details soon.

"If I may, I would like to end with a prayer."

There were no objections; Pypzie continued by raising his hands out above those gathered, a look of solemn reverence on his face.

"Giver of all life and light, protect us and guide us through the challenges we are to face. May you give us the strength we need to be helpful, respectful, and humble to those who are now our neighbors. May the One bless us all. Amen!"

Progress

Lant 05

With all the craziness and my time stretched to the breaking point, I have decided only to give brief once a mooncazt status updates for the next couple of mooncazts. As rudimentary as these updates are, I am beginning to feel they are a simple way to preserve and record at least some of the events transpiring. My hope is someday; a renewed civilization will look back and read these words and remember us all.

Progress continues on all fronts. The byway to the port is almost one hundred percent clear. It would not be a smooth ride for a basic personal transport, but it is good enough for bulk-transports and lisks.

All construction on the entranceway is complete, and we can close the doors at any time. All food service is now in the caves, and the open dormitories are ready for anyone who wants to move in early. The more private living areas are not prepared though they should be in another couple of weezs. Nuzen promised me, Thereza and I would have a place to live together when we move below.

The communications and cybez center is complete, and we installed several redundant systems to allow contact with the Orbital Station and handle internal communications. The Zeltren provided one hundred handheld communicators for use by the towz; the devices will be a great tool in the event of an emergency.

I had more updates I wanted to record while they were fresh in my mind; however, my communication device is going off. It appears my services are needed again—goodnitz planet.

Tropical Snow Storms
Nully 07

Snow, snow, and more snow. If that isn't bad enough, the winds have at times reached tropical storm strength. We had snow three dazs in a row, but it thankfully did not amount to more than a pad deep.

All essential equipment and supplies are now in the caves. I think the Council is delaying the inevitable because once the doors close, they do not plan on opening them again until it is time to leave.

There are still some dazs, which are not too cold and windy. We are close to twilight, and the skies are beautiful to admire, especially with someone special close to you to keep warm. Thereza and I spend as much time up by the now frozen waterfalls as we can manage. Pypzie has not announced the date for the renewal ceremony; still, Thereza and I are looking forward to the daz. Our only regret is the service will be below instead of next to the amazing frozen falls above.

We had a bit of a fireflames show a few nitz ago, as a group of debris pieces fell harmlessly into the western ocean. They were not large enough to cause any damage; however, it was a beautiful yet sobering reminder the sword of Danaga still hangs over our heads.

The Zeltren received an overwhelming response to the request for additional crew for the ship. The new crew members have been selected and will serve for two cycles. They are all currently living aboard the ship and undergoing education. Malcolz has also joined the crew for this trip as a senior security advisor. I wished them a safe journey and reminded Malcolz I expected him to use his hands if necessary to free us in case the worst happens and we are trapped below. He laughed and called me a flarzenren. I looked the word up when I got back to my cybez. I can't repeat here what it means.

Move-in Daz
Autnar 14

Move-in daz would not technically be the correct term for this daz in our history. Most of us moved in over the last two weezs, and all work above ground has stopped. What marked todaz, was the closing of the doors and the beginning of our life below ground. They held no official ceremony, yet everyone knew the time of closing. A few individuals did come to watch along with their liltanz as the doors were closed and secured.

The buildings above are secured, including the fero-stoneworks and the few other factories we had re-opened. Work will continue in the caves while we live here, which will keep us occupied. They are completing permanent walls to help hide the fact we are living in caves as our ancestors did millennia ago. Our caves are much more comfortable, but when you look up and see rock above your head, it is a stark reminder of all which has transpired over the last three cycles.

The Zeltren leaves
Zelmar 10

The Zeltren left port todaz, heading to the sunnier, warmer hemisphere of the planet. I am not sure hemisphere is the proper word to use now. North, south, east, or west does not have the same meaning even though the poles remain as they have been for countless millennia. The continually moving axis of Tanacun has not changed that aspect of our planet. The scientists worried at first, we would see polarity shifts or movement of the magnetic fields. I am relieved to say, it has not happened, and they are confident it won't change in the future.

Life in the caves has been uneventful so far, which is a good thing. I continue to have plenty of work to do with standard systems maintenance, working on plans for our movement into Beta cave, as well as my work on the GPEC.

I have more time to spend with my partner, which is wonderful. I also expect to have more time to update this journal, but will I have anything really to write? I am torn between keeping my journal a record of events or allowing it to be a diary of my life. Reading back, it appears to be both.

Lunch with Tolz
Zelmar 22

I did not intend to write in the journal tonitz; however, Thereza had to attend a meeting with Dr. Moxron, and I have nothing better to do at the moment.

Surprisingly, I do have something to write about anyway. I ran into Tolz this premid while we were both running to different meetings, and we quickly planned to meet for lunch. I expected one of us would have a change of plans and not make it; nevertheless, our schedules did work out this time. We both thought it enjoyable to have some small bit of downtime to genuinely talk.

"Hey, Big Verm, get your ass over here!"

Johlnz had arrived early and sat down at a table away from the crowd. When Tolz realized where Johlnz was sitting, he replied with two fingers; one to say I'll be there in a minzaka, and one to say screw you. He grabbed a sandwich and drink, but before sitting down, he stopped for a short conversation and then sat across from Johlnz without saying hello.

"You know Johlnz; I think I liked you better when you were quiet and shy. What happened to that guy?

"Well, let's see. He survived being hit in the head and tied to a bed. Rhyme not intentional, by the way. He then had to learn to shoot a machine gun and go on patrol. He was involved in and survived a few gunfights, was captured, and . . ."

Johlnz voice trailed off as he paused for a couple of seconds, and Tolz noticed his friend had a distant look on his face.

"Wow, I did not realize how much the incident still bothered me, Tolz, until I started thinking about it again. I am usually too busy to think about the past, especially the bad things."

"I am sorry, I did not mean to bring up old memories."

"Not your fault. I am the one trying to be a smart ass, explaining what happened to the quiet and shy guy, and unfortunately, the memories are not old enough.

"Anyway, on to better things. How is Olania? Is she still suffering from insanity? I do not understand what she sees in you."

"This would not be the proper place to show you, Johlnz."

That was not an answer he expected, and Johlnz almost choked on his lunch; as he laughed so hard and loud, the sound reverberated off the rocks above. He was so loud, a group of individuals he knew from the GPEC, were looking over and laughing at him as well with Tolz.

"You know you deserved that, and Olania sends her regards."

"I think it is time to change the subject. Have you seen Arten? I have not seen or heard from him since we entered the caves."

Johlnz took another bite of his sandwich, sure this time he would not almost choke. While he waited for Tolz to finish his mouthful and respond, Johlnz began to realize how much he missed his time with his friends.

"He is good. He is acting head of security, while Malcolz is on the Zeltren and has been busy with helping to explore the deeper caves as well as running the intensive physical training classes. I am going to join one of his classes tomorrow. I'll let him know you were asking about him. I am sure he will ask why you did not come to the class."

"And you can tell the knucklehead because I am not a security guard anymore and I get enough exercise just running back and forth between this problem and that, plus I also do some exploring of the caves from time to time. It's good; Arten is keeping busy with offering classes. Not much to do for security while we are in here waiting. What's keeping you so busy lately?"

"I have been working in the outpost and helping with exploring the caves. We are also considered the code in these parts since there is no one else to keep you all in line," Tolz finished with a huge grin on his face.

"Seriously, though, Johlnz, we have had a couple of security issues since we have been down here. Not everyone is adjusting well, and I have broken up some minor fights, nothing serious; at any rate, watching for those situations is now part of my job."

After another sip of his drink, Tolz continued with a more serious tone.

"As you already know, Arten has had a couple of meetings with the Council, and they decided security will now also act as an unofficial code enforcement department as the need arises. We do not do any specific patrolling, but we are to keep our eyes open for trouble."

"And what do you do, Tolz, if there is a real problem? We do not have any place to lock up anyone or a court system in place. I was not involved with those meetings, which is why I am asking."

"If someone needs more than a push along, we do have a temporary room where we can put them to cool off. Anything beyond is thankfully also beyond my pay grade."

"Mine too, so I completely understand. My small involvement with the Council has been enough to give me headaches, not to mention causing me to worry. Sometimes it is better not to know everything."

Tolz raised his glass as if for a toast. "Amen to that!"

"So has Olania picked a date for the espousal?"

"We," he stressed as he answered, "had thought about asking to have it as part of the renewal ceremony but thought it might be too public and too rushed. We are thinking sometime next cycle. I like the date Eral 4, if possible, so soon. It's when my parents were espoused."

"You've never talked about your parents before. Did they —"

"No," Tolz interrupted. "They had both died a few cycles before. I would never have thought I would be glad they died when they did.

"So, are not you and Thereza participating in the ceremony?"

"Participating? It was practically and unwittingly our idea. We asked Pypzie Yanez to bless our espousal, and it spiraled from there."

They both laughed; Tolz quickly finished his drink and stood up while stretching.

"I have to get back to work. Great to talk with you, Johlnz; we need to have a double date with the dins, maybe a little hike through some of the more interesting caves. The dins would find it romantic; I am sure."

They laughed again as they went their separate ways.

Ceremony of Renewal

Nemvaz 4

Thereza and I returned from the Ceremony of Renewal held earlier this evening, and I figured I should write this entry of events while fresh in my memory. I am also in a hurry to join with my partner to renew the contial of our espousal. I know, too much information.

The ceremony was beautiful, and it went beyond just the renewal of espousal commitments. Pypzie Yanez went out of his way to stress how much this was a renewal of life in general.

The Delton cave, nicknamed the chamber of stars, due to the crystals, which reflected every little bit of light, had been lit with a few tall candelabras. Seven candelabras with verm candles lined each side of the chamber entrance. An additional six held sanco candles stretched across the area where the chamber extended far above and off to the sides. Single starsow candles lined the edges of the rows of chairs set up for the ceremony.

The entrance area, well over fifty pads wide, and a small section to the left of the entrance, had been designated as a place to relax while looking up at the ceiling. The sounds of a small waterfall enhanced the atmosphere as it flowed down the cave side and into the adjoining chamber to join the waters of the underground lake. It was the perfect place for a ceremony of renewal.

A podium adorned for the occasion stood at the front of the chamber, decorated with flowers grown in the underground Vegcamoz. The multicolored flowers encircled Pypzie Yanez as he completed welcoming everyone to the ceremony.

"I have a few words before we begin the renewal.

"It has been an exceptionally trying time for us and all the other survivors out there on our planet. We have all lost loved ones, friends, and everyday acquaintances we knew only to say hello to as we passed on our way.

"Our planet has suffered tremendous loss, and we will never know why. We will never understand why the universe sent this catastrophe upon us, nor will we ever know why, as some would say, the One allowed this to happen. Be that as it may, I can tell you, the One, the bringer of life and light to the universe, has a plan that is not for us to know, and we cannot dwell on the past.

"We are survivors, and the future belongs not exclusively to us but also to our descendants. This ceremony is not merely a renewal of the commitments of espousal and the obligation they represent. This ceremony is a renewal of our determination to survive against all odds. It is a pledge to the determination to bring our planet back to life. I believe many decdecazs from now, the population of this planet will look back on us and praise us for our determination and will to survive.

"As you entered this evening, many asked the meaning of the different colors of our candles, bringing the One's light into the chamber. The verm candles, of course, represent the love you bring and share. The sanco represents the purity of espousal, and the starsow our One's true light. He who is the bringer of the spark that lights our lives and nourishes our souls."

Pypzie Yanez paused for a moment before raising his hands high over his head.

"Bringer of light to the darkness, you have made the bond of espousal a holy symbol of your light of life. Hear our prayers for all those gathered here before you to renew their commitment to their partner. With faith in you and each other, they again pledge their love.

"To those here renewing their commitment, please stand, face your partner, and join hands. I believe you all know where to insert your names."

Johlnz stood and offered his hand to Thereza as she stood before him. They joined hands, and he began his vowels as Thereza started to have tears form in her eyes.

"I Johlnz accept you, Thereza, to be my partner. I promise to be true to you in good times and in bad, in sickness and in health. I will love you and honor you all the dazs of my life, with the light of the One, forever."

"I Thereza accept you, Johlnz, to be my partner. I promise to be true to you in good times and in bad, in sickness and in health. I will love you and honor you all the dazs of my life, with the light of the One, forever."

To his surprise, tears began to form in Johlnz eyes as he kissed Thereza.

Twilight

Nemvaz 16

The position of our planet as it orbits our star and the tilt of our axis has now put us into our first full twilight. On the surface above us, it is not entirely dark or light, and the sun is a small spec along the horizon. We can't see the sun ourselves, though we have cameras mounted above, and satellite images sent down from the station orbiting in space.

What would have been our south pole is now pointing directly at our sun and will remain that way for many mooncazts. The combination of our planet's spinning on its axis and movement around the sun has made or will soon make surviving on this planet impossible. The exception is around the planet's equator.

The universe has a strange sense of humor, to have our first twilight occur almost precisely to the daz of the third anniversary of the coming of Zeptulgar.

Nothing much has happened in our lives since the Ceremony of Renewal. Life goes on as we adjust to living underground, which considering how infrequently we had seen the sun, isn't much of a change. Some have had adjustment issues, but most, including myself, are now fully acclimated to life under a stone sky.

Nemvaz 18, 0003 AC

It has now been three cycles since the comet struck Tanacun and changed the planet forever.

At lunchtime, the towz Council conducted a ceremony of remembrance in the chamber of stars, and it was, to my surprise, lightly attended. I think maybe individuals want to look forward and not look back, except in a way private and special to them. Even though I am espoused and madly in love with Thereza, I still miss Monharat.

During its next meeting, the Council will discuss the placement of a permanent memorial in the caves. Its construction will most likely not be a priority, though we should never forget our past, and we must remember all those lost.

Hzalo-Multum
Nemvaz 25

We celebrated our third Gratuzes Auraltec todaz—the first with our newest citizens who arrived on the Zeltren, both crew and civilians. The Zeltren crew was pleased to learn the custom of Hzalo-Multum they celebrated back in the

Provinces, would be carried on and enhanced to include all survivors.

All were invited to a feast similar to those the former citizens of the Provinces experienced in the past since the Zeltren supplied many of the traditional foods. The combination of the customary foods and new foodstuffs previously introduced made for the most spectacular feast this planet has probably seen since the comet.

A Conversation with Dr. Moxron
Tralmard 12

I have been busy dealing with one issue after another or helping out with little projects where I can, nevertheless so far, things are going well. We do, however, have occasional setbacks and worries.

Dr. Moxron requested I meet him in his office before returning to my quarters after my shift. I thought I needed to fix his cybez; actually, he wanted to talk and fill me in on recent developments.

"Hello Johlnz, come in. It's good to see you for more than just a quick minzaka in passing. We are always both so busy we never get to have an actual conversation."

"It's good to see you as well, Robarz. Are you having a problem with your system?"

"No, no, no. I just wanted to have some time to talk and wanted to personally give you some bad news before you heard it from the gravavine. We are trying to keep this to a need-to-know basis since we do not want too much upsetting news to travel around. At least the Council doesn't, all the same; I am afraid I have to disagree with their decision."

Johlnz pulled out the chair facing Robarz's desk and sat down, starting to feel a bit anxious about what the Doc wanted to discuss.

"You have me worried; what happened?"

"I am sorry to have to tell you; there was an incident in one of the newly discovered chambers in one of the deeper sections. Ruzicka Plaxco died when the floor collapsed below him, and he fell into a deep hole. I know you worked with him for a while when you were helping with the exploration."

"Yes, I did. How far did he fall? Was he recovered?"

"The hole was deeper than the others could see, and even when they sent down a drone probe, it started to get out of signal reach before they could see the bottom. I am sorry."

"Thank you. I did not get to know Ruzicka well. Does he have any family or a partner here?

"He was very close to a tanmen named Lyndian Szor; they were to share quarters. Lyndian is currently serving on the Zeltren as an advisor, and we did notify him of the incident. The Council, as I said, wants to keep this as quiet as possible, so our citizens do not start thinking the caves are unsafe."

"I understand, Robarz; nevertheless, I think it is a mistake. If individuals find out the Council is withholding information, it could lead to a greater panic. They need to trust the Council."

"Exactly what I told them, but I have been over-ruled. They are concerned because we have seen some minor incidences of individuals not adjusting well to living under the ground.

Dr. Moxron paused for a moment as he got up and started playing with the globe he had sitting on the table by the wall.

"Johlnz, I am worried, and I do not want to be too harsh a critic of the Council, and I do not want to tell Thereza, which is another reason why I asked you here. Even I need someone to talk to, so I can vent my frustrations and fears. I may be only a worrying old tanmen; still, I hope we can get out of here earlier than planned, but the snow keeps piling up outside, and I am now rambling on."

"It's okay, Robarz; we all need someone with whom to talk and confide. I am not ashamed to admit I talk to my cybezs when I am alone."

They both laughed as Robarz sat back down at his desk.

"Aside from talking to your cybezs, how are you handling everything, Johlnz?"

He sat there for a moment, thinking about what to say. Johlnz found it a difficult question for him to answer as it brought up again, memories he wished he could expel forever. His heart beat a bit faster, and he was feeling a little warm when he answered.

"Truthfully, I am happy to be alive. After what happened to me on our journey to this towz, even if we were all to die in here, which I have started to find extremely unlikely, I would be happy to have had the time with Thereza."

Johlnz quickly continued before Robarz could respond.

"I believe we will get through this first twilight, and by the time the second twilight comes in about seven and a half cycles, this will be more like a camo and less like a refuge. That is what my job is; to help make these caves a camo, and someday, a cizay."

We talked about meaningless odds and ends from there, like two individuals talking about the weather. I think we got precisely what we both needed from the conversation, and I did not even realize how much I did need it, until now.
Life goes on.

To that point, I am pleased to say our livestock has been moved away to the Helton chamber for the duration. A breath of fresh air, where there is little.

Spark of Light
Tralmard 24

We have been in the caves for almost ten weezs, and many were looking forward to this cycle's Spark of Light celebration. The Spark Obelisque is floating in the middle of the lake in chamber Ceton. The walkways of enlightenment are accessed by three different floating bridges lined by individual lanterns of multicolored Sparklights.

After Pypzie Yanez lit the Obelisque, the lanterns came to life electronically, and an oil line carried the flame from the Obelisque along the three walkways to the ends onshore. Those in attendance lit their candles from the oil, which they used to light small floating candles, individuals pushed into the lake.

The observance was a wonderful variation of the traditional ceremony and a great way to bring emotional light into the darkness of our lives. I must admit I stole the line from Pypzie Yanez's speech.

"Welcome all, may the spark of light be yours, and may the light of the One shine upon you.

"A little more than four cycles ago, this celebration would have unfortunately been all about gifts, gluttony, and drinking of spirits. Now, I have been known to drink my share of spirits, but not as a replacement for what is important in life.

"At the beginning of all, the One gave us the light of the universe, which led to our existence and many untold decdecazs ago, the One renewed his love for us by showing us the three lights in the darkness above that shone for our ancestors, sending us the eternal light. The special gift, the eternal light, filled the darkness above the planet for ten dazs, during which our existence was never dark.

"Todaz, we find ourselves surrounded by darkness; the darkness of spirit and absence of the light the One has given us. It is during this time of darkness we must embrace the light. This celebration is to be a way to bring emotional light into the darkness of our lives.

"We must remember the true meaning of this celebration. The light we celebrate awaits us all in this life and the next ones beyond. Our journey here is only the beginning and first of many."

Pypzie Yanez pushed the decorated button next to him, and the Obelisque came to life.

"With the lighting of this Obelisque of Light, I hereby declare the beginning of the Celebration of The Spark of Light. May the light of the gift above fill your body and soul, with joy and enlightenment, to be shared by all."

Life Goes On
Banlar 16

It has been tranquil the last few weezs with nothing much to write. Life continues, and I spend my time fixing the cybezs and servers as well as working on the GPEC.

The other engineers and I have also been working on expanding the system infrastructure of the cybez server area.

The work will allow for the needed future expansion into the chambers we will be living in the next time we need to move into the cave system.

I joined an expedition to help map out one of the newer chambers. An advance survey team checked out first to verify the cave was safe before the entire mapping team was allowed to proceed. The Council has been successful so far in keeping the death of Ruzicka quiet for now. I know it will eventually come out, but we will hopefully be out of the caves by then.

If we manage to acquire enough resources for food and medicine, the Council may start encouraging couples to have liltanz to begin rebuilding our population. Although the Council does not and could not even if they wanted to, force couples not to have liltanz, it has been discouraged.

Thereza and I have discussed liltanz, and we both are exceedingly eager to start a family, though also cautious. We wonder if it is fair to bring another life into a planet, which may not be survivable long term. The scientists say the worst will be over after we get past this first twilight, but it is more theory than fact like most of science.

Messages from the Zeltren relayed through the Orbital Station have confirmed there remains little left of the lands to the south. The crew has not been able to explore far inland; however, what they can see is now a barren wasteland. Some land has been overtaken by new plant life, with little to no animal life to be seen.

They have salvaged some useable material found lying in ruins and have even come upon a seaworthy fishing boat found floating abandoned in the ocean. They plan to bring the vessel back with them if possible.

An Espousal at Sea

Banlar 21

It has been a long daz, and I want to join my partner in bed, but first, one bit of important news. We received word todaz Malcolz and Ligaya Methuin, a tanwoz he met a few mooncazts ago, are now Tr. and Tiz. Predsen. Since both are stationed on the ship, they thought it appropriate to be espoused by Mazter Rourze.

Tolz, on the other hand, is still stringing along poor Olania, and they have yet to set a date for their ceremony. He will never see this journal, so it is safe for me to say, if she is smart, she will run while she can.

My comment is all in good fun; I wish them the best. Goodnitz!

Snowed In

Banlar 29

It's official, we have been snowed into the caves until the weather improves and the temperatures climb again. Satellite images and measurements have confirmed we have received over ten pads of snow. Another pad or two, and we will lose all communication with the Orbital Station.

An eight-pad by thirty-pad covering constructed over the access door leading from the outpost building has done little. The snow continues to blow under the covering and against the main entrance to the caves. Teams move out every twelve zakas to clear the snow from under the outpost covering, but they are running out of space, and it is becoming dangerous. A substantial drift fall made its way under the covering and buried two of the teams. One of the workers almost suffocated to death before being rescued. They are all doing well now, even though they have some minor frostbite on their hands and face.

Life goes on; while many are starting to worry, we will be in the caves longer than planned. Most are adjusting well, but when I spoke to Pypzie Yanez the other daz, he confided in me many more individuals have come to see him for counseling, and he fears trouble is coming.

Breaking Point
Marwe 14

The trouble Pypzie Yanez and Dr. Moxron feared has come to pass.

I was not present at or near the incident, however fortunately or unfortunately, Tolz responded to the threat, and I have tried to remember everything he conveyed to me. He remained distraught when I met with him, as anyone would be in the same situation.

"What is your name, somz?"

"I am not your somz. I have not been anyone's somz since that damn thing destroyed our lives. My parents, my sibsom and my friends are all gone. I am here alone, stuck in these muzie-fuez caves, which are going to come crashing down on our heads at any time. I know it. I feel it. I do not want to die in here; I want fresh air. I want to see the sun again."

"You are not alone; we are all here for you."

The tanmen in front of Tolz, looked almost still a tanwez, with verm hair and freckles. Tolz felt as if he looked at himself as he appeared over ten cycles ago. He put the thought out of his mind before continuing.

"My name is Tolz Bezler, and—"

"I do not give a damn about your name; I only want to get out of here. All those mooncazts on the ship mostly under the water, not able to see the sun, not able ever to know what happened to my family—how much they suffered."

The individual Tolz confronted, brandishing a knife, and holding an object he said was a bomb, began to cry like a lost liltanz. Tolz tried to get closer to him, but the tanmen noticed and immediately held out the knife and unidentified object.

"Do not come any closer, or I'll end it right now. One way or another, I am getting out of here."

"So, you served on the Zeltren, is that correct?"

"Yes."

Good, he is starting to have a conversation with me. The one thing I do remember from my negotiation training; get them to converse.

"How old are you? What's your name?" Tolz asked again.

After a brief pause, "I am twenty-two, a good age to die."

"And your name?"

"Andel, Andel Mel'Aknen."

"So, Andel, you must have joined the service right out of upper school."

"I did. I could not wait to join as a way to honor my Pypzie. He died in service when I was seven. Being in the service gave me a sense of accomplishment and honor; I loved it . . ." More crying, "Until . . . until it came and destroyed everything and everyone, I knew."

The tanmen pulled himself together again, briefly looking down at the object in his hand. The look on his face became a mixture of fear and confusion, followed by determination.

I need to bond with him; tell him of my service.

"I went to supreme school for two cycles, and found it was not for me, so I joined the service and never regretted my decision. My Pypzie told me it made him proud his somz served the Provinces. I was still in the service when . . . the planet changed. I lost many individuals I loved, but todaz . . . I go on. I go on in their memory to rebuild our civilization."

Hold it together, Tolz. It won't help the situation to let the memories and pain get to you; plenty of time for your grief later.

"You can do that too, Andel. You can honor the memory of everyone you lost. All you have to do is put down the knife and bomb and let me take you to get some help. Please!"

Tolz's heart beat fast and furious in his chest as if all his training had disappeared. This situation needed to end well, and he could think of only one scenario where this did not end badly. He needed Andel to put down the knife and possible bomb and go to the hospital.

Andel looked directly at Tolz with a new expression on his face, like a switch had been pressed, and Tolz knew he had lost him.

"It is time," was all Andel said before he turned to place the object against the first set of doors.

"Andel, listen to me. You do not want to do this. Stop, please—I can not let you do this! You need to put the knife down and step aside."

Tolz raised the rifle he had previously kept facing the floor, aiming it now at the back of Andel's head.

Dear One of light, please do not make me do this; please make him stop. He is just a kid, a scared kid.

Tolz was sweating as he stood in position—he felt his arms start to shake. He knew a crowd formed behind him, watching. He hoped there were also more security individuals behind him, someone else to do what might be required.

"Andel, this is your last warning; stop now!"

"No, time to go."

Those were his last words as Tolz did something he had never done before. He closed his eyes as he fired one shot, killing young Andel Mel'Aknen.

As the sound recoiled throughout the cave chambers, Tolz dropped the gun and fell to his knees in misery.

My good friend Tolz has spent the last two evenings sitting in the worship center praying. As I sat with him, trying to bring some comfort, he recounted the events of the daz. The last thing he told me before I left him with Pypzie Yanez was the bomb had been merely an old toy sphere with a symbol of Andel's family's crest.

Sharing A Bottle
Marwe 28

Two weezs have passed since the incident with Andel Mel'Aknen, and thankfully it did not have any lasting repercussions—except with Tolz. Last evening, we attended a small ceremony of remembrance for Andel. We all understand he suffered from mental problems due to all that had happened to him over the last few cycles. I am still amazed and thankful more individuals have not suffered mental breakdowns due to our situation.

Tolz is doing better. Arten, Tolz, and I spent a few zakas together last nitz after the ceremony, talking over a bottle of vintage Scurzt, Robarz gave me. He suggested we get together to help Tolz heal; it was, as usual, a good suggestion.

We talked for a few zakas about our friendship and adventures since we came to know each other. In another time and place, you might say we talked about the old times; however, the old times are gone forever—they were gone before we became friends.

Tolz and Olania have decided to put off their espousal till later, or maybe the next cycle. I know he loves her, but he is in no mental state to get espoused.

Snow Removal
Eral 12

It is the second weez of Eral, and still, no date has been established for when we will leave the caves. There have not been any snowfalls lately, and the sun is moving higher above the horizon as we leave twilight. Teams have begun clearing snow from under the outpost's covering. They expect to move most of the snow away from the main cave doors soon if we have no additional snow accumulation.

Hidden Truth
Eral 20

The Council called an unscheduled, general meeting to update the citizens on the progress outside. Many have become restless since we were to be out of the caves by now in the original schedule. Council Chairtan, Professor Kizermel was the first to speak.

"First off, I want to thank you all for your patience during this first time of twilight. I know we had anticipated moving out of the caves by now, but we did get a lot more snow than expected. For now, the snow stopped falling, and there is a warm breeze, which occasionally blows from the sun side of the planet. The sun, when visible, is starting to melt the snow; however, it will be a slow process.

"We have been in contact with OS-I, and they have relayed messages of encouragement from the crew of the Zeltren. Hopefully, by next weez, we will be able to open the cave's doors and experience some limited sunshine and playtime in the snow.

"I am pleased to announce; we will have elections to the Council, two weezs from todaz. The election is for all Council members as well as all representatives. All members are running for re-election, I have not given them any choice in the matter."

The Chairtan waited as the room filled with laughter followed by applause.

"Thank you, thank you all!

"If you wish to run for a Council member position, or a representative, please come by my office tomorrow and let my new assistant, Lezen, know your intentions. She will add your name to the ballot, which we will post in the main mezcaf hall."

Professor Kizermel paused as he collected his thoughts. To anyone who knew him well, it appeared apparent he felt nervous as he readjusted his papers for the third time before continuing.

"Before we conclude the meeting, we do have a sad announcement from Nuzen Hultztrand."

"Thank you, Chairtan."

"I regret to inform the community; we have lost one of our cave explorers and also a personal friend. Ruzicka Plaxco perished when the floor gave way below him while exploring one of the deepest caves we have found to date. Ruzicka, a native of Bousiana Province, worked as a Geologist for the Energy Ministry. He was twenty-seven cycles old, and he is greatly missed by many. We will hold a memorial service for him tomorrow evening in the worship center."

Nuzen moved away from the microphone, and the Professor had a few words.

"I did not know Ruzicka; nevertheless, I knew of his work. We have come far in our quest for survival, and I know Ruzicka is not the first member of our team we have lost and will sadly not be the last, but we must carry on. We will carry on!"

I noticed they made no mention of when Ruzicka died, be that as it may, at least they did acknowledge his death. I believe it is safe to write here since no one will be reading this anytime soon, if ever; the Council did not disclose the truth about conditions at the time. I met Tolz a few minzakas after the meeting, and he gave me the full story.

"It snowed again last nitz, Johlnz. Another two pads have fallen, and the winds are at tropical strength. The communications dish remains covered with snow, which means there has been no communication with the Orbital Station or the Zeltren."

"But the Professor just said—"

"I know what he said, and I hope it doesn't come back to haunt him or us."

Good News

Lant 3

It's been two weezs since the general Council meeting, and finally, some good news. It's nice to have good news to receive and write every so often.

My source, which I won't identify except to say he has verm hair, has told me the thaw is on. We have had no snow or even rain since the two pads, which fell a little over two weezs ago. The area around the outpost canopy is clear of all snow, and as of tomorrow, we should be able to open the main cave doors. Everyone is looking forward to experiencing some fresh air and maybe even a few zakas of sunshine.

Our towz's completed the election two dazs ago, and they posted the results this premid. As expected, everyone was re-elected to all positions. I almost hoped to lose since it would make my life easier; however, like all others, I ran unopposed. Daytime temperatures have been hovering near or above freezing; even so, the wind blowing in has brought occasional warmth a few degrees above freezing. Not that I do not trust my source, but I wanted to confirm myself, so I went to Robarz office under the pretense of visiting my partner.

Johlnz walked in and surprised Thereza while she was filing some papers, and he almost caused her to drop and scatter the stack of documents across the floor. Thereza, being used to bumbling visitors in the office, managed to grab them just in time.

"Hello, honey," she said, the frustration evident in her voice. To what do I owe the almost catastrophic surprise?"

"Oh, do not exaggerate so much. I merely thought I would drop in to say hello, as I passed by. Any new developments you can share?"

"This sounds more like a fishing expedition and not a casual drop-in to give the partner a kiss; she still has not received."

"Oops! When you almost dropped the papers, I became distracted."

Johlnz hugged his partner and gave her a huge kiss just as Robarz came out of his office. They ignored the Doc deliberately, hoping to get a rise from him.

"Hey, this is a workplace. Kiss on your own time."

"Sorry, Robarz, you keep her so busy —"

"Oh, Johlnz, it is you. I thought you were the other guy who is always coming around, giving out kisses."

Thereza punched Robarz hard in the arm and gave him a look of ice.

"Very funny, Robarz. So, what's new? Any more updates from the Zeltren?"

"Do not act so coy, Johlnz, you know damn well we stretched the truth at the meeting, but I am happy to say, as of a zaka ago, we have made contact again with the Orbital Station, and they relayed a message the ship expects to be in port less than six weezs from todaz."

"Wonderful news, good to share. You can only stretch the truth, as you say, for so long before individuals catch on. So, when do we get out of here?"

"As I am sure you already know, we plan to open the doors tomorrow, and as soon as we confirm it looks safe, we will let anyone who desires so to go out and play in the snow. I think it will be a few more weezs yet before we can live and work outside again. Hopefully, the damage was not too severe."

"Well, I, for one, will be expecting my partner and me to have some time off to play in the snow."

"I think I can arrange that for you, my dear Thereza."

PART 4 – Emergence

Sanco Wonderland
Lant 4

As promised by Robarz, the main doors to the caves opened today for the first time in almost twenty-five weeks. We were not allowed to venture outside yet except for the advanced teams. They were sent out with additional equipment to clear away more of the snow from the essential areas of the towz and inspect the buildings. Not many trees are still living, and the dead ones have never endured the weight of snow before, so the Council wanted to make sure the area was as safe as possible from falling limbs and branches. I can't wait until tomorrow. Thereza and I have our cold gear all ready to go.

Johlnz took Thereza's hand in his as they walked outside for the first time in many mooncazts. The sight greeting them looked spectacular. The daz started mostly cloudy with a light breeze causing little snowflakes to blow off the tree branches and fall to the ground.

Even though it hadn't snowed for over two weezs, a lot of snow clung to the trees, and Johlnz could now understand why the Council worried.

"Let us take a walk over to Kiz Camo, Thereza, and see if you still have an office to go to when the snow is gone."

"I hope so, honey; it is such a beautiful camo it would be a shame if it is damaged."

The work crews had cleared a path in the direction of the camo, and as they followed the cleared path, they could see some damage to other areas of the towz. A large tree had fallen on one of the buildings serving as a dormitory for the security forces and single tanmen. The tree caused damage to the roof and one of the walls, but it looked repairable.

A few yarzs farther on, the pair came around a large snowbank beautifully sculpted by the wind and saw a wonderful yet odd sight. Kiz Camo was standing and looked like it had suffered no noticeable damage from the front side; however, many pads of snow covered the roof and all the eves and porches. If not for the style of the camo, you would think you were looking at a mountain resort lodge in the Olpa Mountains.

As they stood admiring the view, the sun briefly came out from behind the clouds and illuminated Kiz Camo. The sun glistened off the snow causing little prisms of color to shine in various places. The scene became so bright they could barely look at the camo, and they both had to put on their eye protection. They looked around, amazed at the sunlight glistening off the snow in the trees and the distant mountains.

"I had forgotten how beautiful the sun and snow could be together, Johlnz. The land was mostly flat where I lived, so we only had large smooth fields of snow with only a few sizable trees around, but this reminds me of the one time I did get to go the Luraky Mountains with my Onczle."

"My camo in Rilodfia was only two zakas from the Zocanol Mountains, so I visited every couple of cycles. The mountains are not as spectacular as the Luraky Mountains, yet they were still always beautiful to see when covered in snow."

Suddenly from behind them, they heard the sound of something breaking and turned to see a large dead tree falling in the forest, which caused a cascade effect as three, other trees crashed to the ground damaging another dormitory building.

"Thereza, my love, this is beautiful, but I think it would be safer, for now, to go back to the caves."

"Do we have to Johlnz? I have not made snow knarels and zalenges since my tanzhood. Come on, let's lay down in the snow and have some fun."

Johlnz was about to relent when another tree crashed to the snow covered ground.

Damage Mounting
Lant 11

It's been a weez since Thereza and I had our outing in the snow. A few more trees and a large number of branches continued to fall over the next couple of dazs until the sun and warm temperatures had melted the heavy snow off the dead trees.

There is still considerable snow around, and it is too wet to start rebuilding what was damaged. Preliminary inspections of Kiz Camo show just a small amount of water damage. The electrical individuals plan to turn full power back on in Kiz Camo tomorrow, so we will soon start moving equipment.

The caves have experienced some minor water issues, as well. A few of the smaller caves we explored have started to have water intrusion. None of the caves are presently in use, but this could be a massive problem in the future.

Bad News
Lant 19

The deluge has begun. The water I mentioned in my last entry a weez ago has now become a full-blown flood. The caves are overflowing with water from the melting of the enormous amount of snow above. Thankfully, most of the living quarters and, more importantly, the cybez server areas were spared; however, some offices have not been so lucky.

The water is coming in through previously unseen or new cracks and flowing quickly down to the lowest level caves. The Ceton cave is entirely underwater and inaccessible at this time; fortunately, we had plenty of time to evacuate the livestock and those who were down below working before the water rose too far. Unfortunately, we have todaz lost one of our citizens to the flood.

Boz Floxian had been an electrician helping run the wiring to the lower caves before the deluge began. He was originally from the Provinces; however, he moved his family down to Guazemax, when his company offered him a high-level position as a supervisor in the new manufacturing plant.

His camo sat near the coast, so he decided it would be safer to bring his family to stay at the factory than to go back camo before the comet struck. Afterward, when society fell apart, the few workers remaining in the plant dormitories left to be with their families, while Boz and his family were left alone to survive.

Plenty of food remained in the commissary, much of it non-perishable. Two mooncazts after the comet struck, all power in the area had ceased, but he felt relieved they at least still had food and a comfortable place to live.

It was a mooncazt later when trouble arrived. A gang of tanmen from Tezaci had come to scavenge as much of the plant as possible. When they realized the plant had food, water, and shelter, they decided to stay and forced Boz and his family to be their servants. They did not mistreat his family, and he thanked the One the tanmen never abused them in any way; still, Boz wanted out.

A couple of mooncazts later, when the convoy arrived with Professor Kizermel, he knew their chance had come. He managed to slip a message to one of the convoy's deftanmenz, who immediately reported their situation to the Professor.

When Boz informed their captures he and his family were leaving, a heated argument started and ended later with gunfire. Boz and his family were caught in the crossfire; a projectile wounded his somz, and his partner broke her arm when she fell trying to grab their damza.

In the end, all the captures were dead, and the Professor's medical team cleaned and dressed his somz's flesh wound and set his partner's arm. Boz and his family knew they owed their lives to the members of the convoy.

Over the ensuing cycles, Boz became one of the group's most trusted electricians. He worked many zakas running primary cable wire down to the lower levels of the cave system to allow construction and further exploration.

When the meltwater started flowing into the caves, the workers were safe where they had been working. The cave in which Boz connected cable lines contained a channel that allowed water to flow into a deeper water storage cave. He and his two assistants had finished running guide wires across the water when they heard a scream from farther up the cave. They turned and saw what looked like a liltanz struggling while being swept along with the rushing water. Thankfully the liltanz had managed to grab hold of the still sagging guidewire.

Without any hesitation, Boz jumped into the water and followed the guidewire, moving hand over hand until he reached the liltanz. It was a young din, and he told her to put her arms around his neck. She remained frightened, but thankfully, after almost slipping away himself, Boz was able to grab her and guide the liltanz's arms around his neck. He slowly went back towards where his tanmen were waiting, almost losing his hold a couple of times. Finally, Boz managed to get her to safety as the tanmen grabbed and pulled her out of the water.

Boz started climbing out of the torrent when a piece of debris in the floodwaters struck him and caused him to lose his grip. The water carried the hero away as his team could do nothing but watch in horror.

Memorial Service
Lant 30

Two weezs have passed since we lost Boz Floxian. The Council held a memorial service outside under the stars since laying on the ground watching the sky had been one of his favorite past times when the stars were still clearly visible. The sky did cooperate for the service as the clouds parted to reveal one of the clearest nitztime skies I have seen in a long time. Since then, the water has slowed, and we have cleaned up most of the damage. The water is still higher than before in some lower caves, but the appropriate teams will address those issues over the next few mooncazts. Many video shots were taken, showing exactly where the water was coming in and to where it flowed. The next time we must go to the caves, we will be well prepared, and the snowmelt should not cause any issues.

Zeltren Returns
Nully 12

It has been a hectic few weezs. All the repairs from the flood and snow damage are complete, and the water level in the caves has returned to normal.

Everyone except security has moved back into their old quarters. The security teams will still bunk in the cave dormitories, and a new training and practice area is under construction adjacent to the dormitory area. Families of those on security have moved back to their old above-ground quarters. When not on duty, the security tanmen will be able to spend time with their families.

I understand what the Council is doing, and I know this is the best way for the teams to stay sharp and ready to go; all the same, it feels too much like the Authority. I understand we may, unfortunately, need an Authority structure for defense, but it was a part of the old Tanacun and Provinces I hoped we could let disappear forever. I remember the phrase, the more things change, the more they remain the same. I hope we prove it wrong.

We received word yesterday the Zeltren arrived back in port the daz before, and it was not smooth sailing. We were experiencing the most significant storm since leaving the caves. The heavy rain and high winds meant the ship had to anchor far off the coast, and they had to wait a daz before putting their transport in the water to come ashore. Even then, they almost ran aground out of control from the strong winds.

Mazter Rourze met with the towz Council immediately, and they are holding a community meeting in the premid to update the towz.

Council Update
Nully 13

The meeting this premid had a large attendance. Hopefully, I did not miss any important details.

The Council sat across a makeshift stage, and Chairtan Kizermel stood in front of the podium as he called the meeting to order.

"Good premid, everyone, and welcome to the first public Council meeting since the end of our residence in the caves. We have much information to share, and to start, I would like to recognize our newest residents, who are all standing behind you on the right."

I, the Council, and the entire towz welcome you."

Mazter Rourze will discuss the details of their rescue later. I have many updates and announcements — the first concerns the weather."

As you have noticed, it is becoming warmer, and I do not think we need to worry about any more snowfalls in this area. We will be heading into a period of warmth and heat. We do not expect the temperature to be as intense as it has been here in the past. Let me take a moment to explain."

Previously, our main concern was twilight; when would it come and how long would it last. While we were in the caves, the scientist up in OS-I predetermined the most likely future of this planet's dual rotation. Due to the combination of our position around the sun, the normal rotation, and axis rotation, if the planet continues as it has since impact, we can look forward to a prolonged time of temperatures, which will allow us to stay mostly on the surface."

A tremendous amount of applause and gasps erupted from the audience as the Professor's words set in. He gave them the first excellent news since the end of the floods.

"By the time we must move back into the caves, it will be a very different experience. More details will follow over the mooncazts to come; in any event, the next time we enter the caves, it will be to establish it as our main living and recreation area permanently."

A bit of grumbling arose from the crowd as one tanmen stood and began to speak.

"Professor, we do not want to live in caves for the rest of our lives. Why can't we build strong and permanent buildings out here?"

"I understand your concern; however, this long stretch of comfortable weather will not last forever. We will eventually experience a stretch of extreme cold weather lasting longer than the one we endured. Our long-term future is a cizay in the caves. As I said, much more information is to follow in later mooncazts, but I promise you all, you will not realize your camo is underground.

"I would now like to turn the podium over to Mazter Rourze."

The Mazter was surprised to receive a standing ovation when he stepped in front of the podium.

"Thank you all. I am not sure I deserve such a welcome camo; nevertheless, my crew does, and I can tell you for them, we are glad to be back.

"One of the objectives of our mission was to check out the Matabas Canal to see how much damage it has sustained. As expected, the canal is not passable. We made it as far as the first lock, which is close to the ocean. There is, of course, no power to the canal, the gates looked extremely damaged, and the lock itself contained much debris.

"Someday, with enough individuals and some heavy equipment, it may be possible to reopen the canal. Having easy access to the Narral Ocean will, I am sure, be worth the time and energy.

"We were able to salvage various oils and fuels found in fortified buildings and underground storage tanks. We also recovered many types of metals we can use for construction.

"The Canal towz and port of Cozon were heavily damaged, but the byways were surprisingly passable. We found no one living there as expected. Anyone still in the towz when Zeptulgar hit would have been swept away by the tidal waves.

"Now on to the good news.

"As the Chairtan has mentioned, we have brought back new residents for the community. The tanmen and families, all from the Provinces, had taken refuge in the mountains when the waves struck. They originally had enough supplies for a few cycles from a nearby factory; still, when we found them, they were barely surviving. Thirty-five individuals in all, and I can tell you from my time with them aboard the Zeltren; they will be assets to the community.

"I am also pleased to announce the towz now has a fleet. We towed back a barge we found floating in the ocean, and we used it to bring back the materials I mentioned earlier. The barge will remain in Bilwi and eventually be part of the rebuilt harbor. In addition, we also recovered and restored during our time away, a small skip and a fishing boat. They will both stay docked at Bilwi, and if we have no more large debris falls, the towz will have easy access to fresh oceanfood."

The last announcement from the Mazter got the individuals in attendance cheering again. Fresh oceanfood will be an extremely welcomed addition to the limited selection of food now available. I, for one, always loved oceanfood, and I am looking forward to having some again. It will be a mooncazt, or so I am sure, before the first catch. A crew needs to be assembled and trained on how to operate the equipment. I know from many stories before, the lives of fishertan are not easy, but then again, are any of our lives easy now?

I cannot explain why, but I have a new sense of hope for our future. I expect many challenges, but after all, that is life.

Quiet and Warmth
Autnar 29

I am afraid I am becoming lazy. I kept putting off writing in this journal because I was tired and had better things to be doing before going to sleep at nitz, especially now living back in Kiz Camo, where we have some additional privacy. Then when I wanted to write, I could not find the journal. I would not want to be pointing fingers, just the same; I think my partner may have hidden it from me because she likes when I am not writing in my journal in bed at nitz.

So anyway, because of the above, it has been six weezs since my last entry. I remain swamped with work as we all are, trying to rebuild a society and planning an underground cizay individuals will want to live in even when it is not necessary for survival. It is a prolonged process, but thankfully, the Zeltren crew has been more than helpful, with materials and expertise, yet we still need much. As crude as they are, our factories continue to grow gradually; regardless, we only have so many individuals to perform the work required. Everyone has multiple jobs and has had many kinds of training.

Our population is both a blessing and, at the same time, a curse. We have been out of twilight a few mooncazts, and the weather is warming, so our farmland is spreading. We can only feed and camo so many, but we need more individuals to build and create what we require to survive. Our livestock farms are also growing, and while most can survive the cold when it comes again, some will need unique barns heated to endure the cold period. We can't move them into the cizay next time.

Speaking of temperatures, it has been in the mid-fifties this last weez. It is nice to have warmer temperatures and more sunshine to fill our dazs. It has thankfully been tranquil the last few mooncazts, a welcome change. There have not been any noticeable tanaquakes or tremors in the area and no major storms.

The skies have been clearer than in the past, though still not normal, and as predicted, we have not experienced any major debris falls. However, we have had some excellent fireflames to look at in the evenings—a very romantic sight. My partner and I were able to have time together last nitz, lying on the rocks by the waterfall, watching the show in the sky.

"Look, there goes another one. The fireflames are so beautiful until you remember why they are so plentiful."

"We can do nothing about the past, Thereza, so we might as well enjoy them for what they are."

"When did you become such a philosopher?"

"I am just trying to learn to cope with things the way they are while hoping for what I want in the future."

"And what do you want in the future? Oh, I know; you want to contial with your partner while fireflames fill the sky above."

"Not that the thought isn't turning me on, but you know, security patrols are out there. Have you become an exhibitionist?"

They both laughed and kissed while Thereza was teasing him with her hand.

"Feels good, even so, if you do not stop, I may not care who is watching."

Again, they both laughed before the conversation became more serious.

"Thereza, what do you think about the idea of having a liltanz?"

"Whoa, what happened to worrying about security?"

"Not here and now, silly. Anyway, how long should we wait? I have been willing to wait, as the Council would prefer, at the same time I am getting impatient. Things are getting better, and we do need to increase our population for our race to survive. Yes, I know there are probably other communities of survivors around the planet, but I want ours to prosper. Our farms are growing, our livestock is growing, and we even have fresh oceanfood now and—"

"Okay, honey, slow down and take a breath. Are you trying to convince yourself or me?"

"Both."

"I would love to start a family, as well. Maybe I can drop a few hints to my Onczle to see if the Council has thought about lifting the voluntary ban on having liltanz."

"Like he won't suspect why you are asking."

"I am sure he will, Johlnz, that is why I want to ask. Now let's get out of here and go practice."

Warm and Rainy

Zelmar 10

Zelmar has brought warmer temperatures as we experience more sunlight each daz. Along with the warmth has been much rain, which has begun to cause problems.

The heavy rain caused many mudslides in the area, all of which have been far enough away not to cause any problems in the towz. The deep freeze and following snowmelt probably weakened the underlying rock, plus a lot of vegetation died, which once held the ground together.

Work teams have replanted many areas closer to towz to alleviate the problems, though it takes time for the vegetation to root. We can only replant so much, and the areas around towz and above the caves are the most important.

The heavy rain is helping to fill the new reservoir we built for irrigation, and extra water flows to additional basins in the caves, but sometimes it can be too much of a good thing. Rainwater started flowing into the caves from a rockslide, which opened a new channel into the underground system, very close to where they have been building future living quarters. Luckily, they were able to redirect the water flow before any significant damage.

A Short Trip South
Zelmar 23

The Zeltren left port on a short trip about seventy zilos south to the port towz of ZaCeixa last weez. They did not make it to the port on the previous mission because of severe storms at the time, and they were due back in towz. The ship returned yesterday with some additional supplies, and I had lunch with Arten todaz, and he filled me in on the trip.

Arten sat at a table already when Johlnz came in, and he grabbed a fresh fishcake sandwich and a drink before sitting with his friend. Lunch todaz would be his first time having any oceanfood since he first arrived at Reswoll Camo, and that was frozen. He hadn't had fresh fish from the ocean since before he left his camo in Nel Jerzana. The crap they had from the rivers on the way to the towz, did not satisfy his taste buds. It felt like a very long time ago and a different life.

"Yo, Johlnz, over here!"

"You did not have to yell; I did see you. How could I miss a large monster like you?"

Johlnz sat down as they both laughed.

"It's great to see you again, Johlnz, even if you are an insulting bastard. How is Big Verm? I have not had a chance to talk to him in mooncazts. When I am here, he is always gone or busy."

"And he is gone again. They sent a scouting team out west to see if any factory buildings remain standing that we could utilize. They are also looking for any additional survivors. It's not likely; however, this is the first chance to scout out the area."

"Enough about Verm; how was the trip down to ZaCeixa?"

"Uneventful but worthwhile. The port is on the inner bayside of a large peninsula, which partially protected it from the waves. Still, most of the harbor buildings were gone; nevertheless, we were able to dock the ship and explore the area."

"Sorry to interrupt—have you tried this fishcake sandwich? I had forgotten how good fresh oceanfood could taste."

"I just completed two tours on a ship in the ocean. I have had more than enough fresh oceanfood to last a lifetime. It's why I opted for the porlz. Freshly slaughtered game meat is what I have missed the most. Now, may I continue?

Johlnz remained too busy chewing to respond except with a nod of his head, so Arten continued.

"We found some construction equipment not too far beyond repair, as well as some protected liquid fuel storage tanks and two functioning zolatron generators.

The Mazter decided to leave behind a volunteer repair and security crew to try and get some of the equipment repaired.

"The Mazter is hoping the Council will approve sending additional repair and security teams to help; however, they will have to use a Helo because the one byway between towz and the port is completely blocked. Once repaired, we can probably use them to open the byway and then drive the equipment back to towz."

Arten paused to savor a bite of his porlz sandwich and take a drink. All this talking was making his mouth dry.

"Along the way, we also found some more repairable boats and left them docked so the crew we left behind could use them for shelter. Eventually, they will be fully repaired and moved to Port Hope."

"They prefer to call it Port Bilwi, Arten, as a nod to the local residents."

"Well, I prefer the Provincial name."

Arten paused a moment with a serious look on his face and leaned closer to Johlnz before continuing in a lower tone.

"The rest of what I am telling you is not for public consumption. Mazter Rourze and the Council do not want to cause any worry amongst the towz.

"We went north to see how things looked after the freeze and to try again to contact any survivors from the Provinces Authority. They did not pick up any signals from the Provinces; however, they picked up a disturbing signal from Guazemax. We picked up a radio conversation between two groups talking about attacking a towz and taking over."

"How did they survive the dark time? Do you think they were in an Authority bunker?"

Mazter Rourze thinks so; he will suggest to the Council we take the ship back north along with another Helo to do some investigating. He is also suggesting they send security teams up north to watch the area more closely. He feels we need to be prepared to fight off any militaristic groups from Guazemax, Donhurex, or any other place looking to cause trouble."

"Damn, I was hoping to have left all that behind. No offense—I am not too fond of the idea of the towz having any type of Authority. Be that as it may, I do understand the need.

"How about the Orbital Station Arten? Have they seen anything in the area, any sign of life?"

"They are looking but have seen nothing yet."

We had spent the rest of the time talking about our futures. Arten wants his next mission to be his last for a while. He wants to settle down in the towz, maybe find a partner, and have a family when the time is right.

I told him great minds think alike. His response, "Thanks, who is the other great mind?"

Four Cycles
Nemvaz 18, 004 AC

Tomorrow begins the fifth cycle since Tanacun changed forever, and in many ways, nothing has changed. The Chairtan held a special Council meeting this evening in which one person unimaginably suggested we attack another group of survivors. I am still shocked such ignorance has survived our planet's near destruction.

The towz held the Ceremony of Remembrance at lunchtime in the front common area of the caves where the permanent memorial is under construction. The ceremony planners decorated the space with candles, which have become a standard part of our remembrance. Pypzie Yanez said a few words of comfort, which they followed with a performance of the newly formed choral group.

They held the special Council meeting I mentioned, primarily to discuss the formation of what can only be called an army. Yes, the stated purpose is for our defense, yet I fear it will last forever, and our descendants might again fight wars over land and resources.

Mazter Rourze gave his full report to the Council to get the meeting started. The leaders already knew most of the details; the account was more for the benefit of those in attendance who were unaware of the intercepted communication.

Security chief Malcolz spoke next.

"If the Council approves, I will lead the reconnaissance team from the Zeltren. It is my recommendation we plan to leave next weez for a two-weez mission. The crew and security team will, unfortunately, miss the celebration of Hzalo-Multum. I know we promised the crew to be camo during the holiday, but I think we can't afford to wait. We are ill-prepared for hostile activity, and it will take time to create a defense force.

"Thank you for letting me speak to the Council."

Professor Kiz asked for comments from those in attendance, and there were a few. The first came from one of the original scientists who joined the team back in the Provinces before the comet impacted the planet.

"I thought our priority remained to build our towz so we can survive long into the future. I am thirty-three cycles old and recently espoused. I understand the need for defense, yet maybe we need to go on the offense instead. I feel it would be best if you used the weapons on the Zeltren so the rest of us can be building our future and not wasting time on patrols and looking over our shoulders. Thank You."

When he finished, an older tanwoz who had been a resident of the area before Zeptulgar struck and is now a citizen advisor raised her hand to speak.

"Yes, Mrs. Relaza, you have the floor."

"Thank You. Before the comet came, this area was always at war with someone, and when not, the local Authority remained strict and abusive. I have enjoyed the new freedom you brought here, and the idea of going to war with someone and having an army scares me. That is all I have to say. Thank you."

Quiet filled the room when she finished. When no one else asked to speak, Johlnz raised his hand to address the Council.

"I understand and support the need to be secure and to have the ability to defend ourselves. I could never, however, support the idea of using any version of the Authority to launch an attack against someone who is, in reality, unknown to us. No matter what may be happening up north, I am sure some innocent individuals would be unintended casualties if we launched an attack. Thank You."

There were no additional comments, and the meeting adjourned.

I just looked at the clock, and I see it is ten seconds to midnitz. 5, 4, 3, 2, 1, Happy Renewal! Goodnitz.

A Compromise

Nemvaz 6

I had a quick conversation with Thereza's Onczle when I met her at his office for lunch, and he filled me in on the decisions reached this premid by the Council.

They decided we would start training a more significant security force, which he said no one wanted to call an army or Authority. It will be comprised of both tanmen and tanwoz and will be called Alpha Force.

They also decided an additional twenty individuals would be sent down to ZaCeixa to bolster the security forces already in place. Half of the group will also help open the byway as much as possible to get the heavy equipment back to towz quickly.

After the Hzalo-Multum celebration, the Zeltren will be sent down to ZaCeixa to drop off the additional support and supplies. We are in constant contact with the teams already in place, and we have no immediate concerns. The ship will return to towz for the Spark of Light celebration, and afterward, be sent north to scout out the area with a Helo and listen for more radio messages. Other ports exist up north that the Council thought should be checked as well for any possible resources.

The Season of Light

Tralmard 35

The season of light, as some still call it, has come and gone. As you can gather by how long ago I last made an entry into this journal, I am, as usual, swamped with work. I have been spending much time moving equipment back and forth between Kiz Camo and the servers in the caves.

We also experienced problems with our communication equipment, which caused us to temporarily lose all contact with the orbital station and the Zeltren, docked at Bilwi. Thankfully, I identified a server protocol issue causing the problem, and after many zakas, I fixed it in time for Hzalo-Multum.

Between Hzalo-Multum and the beginning of the Spark of Light celebrations, preparations began for running server connections into the Delton cave. Delton someday will be our main living, working, and yes, at some point, shopping area. If all goes as planned, we will terrace the Delton cave with waterfalls running down the middle of the common areas. Some on the GPEC think we can complete this space before the next twilight time. I believe the schedule is much too optimistic; only time will tell.

As promised, the Zeltren returned a weez before The Spark of Light celebration. They had extra time first to make a short trip south and brought back more needed supplies in addition to supplies not required but appreciated. The patrols stumbled upon a half-destroyed factory, which made MusiPods and a large assortment of musidisks. Yours truly is tasked with downloading the music into our system to then distribute the MPs to those who want one. I guess we can consider it a Spark of Light gift to the community.

Malcolz assembled a new exploratory and security patrol team, and Tolz will be the group's mission commander. He had hoped to have more time in towz before being sent on another mission, but at least he remained for the Spark of Light.

He stopped by the server room in the caves yesterday to let me know, and we had a few minzakas to talk.

"Well, at least you were here for the Spark of Light, Tolz. I am sure Olania would not have been happy if you missed the celebration."

"True, especially since this one was extra special."

"You did not?"

"I did, again," Tolz responded with a huge grin on his face, which quickly faded.

"I am still sometimes haunted by his face in my dreams, and I fear they may never end. The memory has stopped me from enjoying what little of life I can."

There was a quiet pause, as Johlnz did not know what to say to help his friend.

"My guilt ends now; it has to."

Tolz continued as if the last minzaka hadn't happened.

"So anyway," he continued, his smile returning. "I got down on one knee and asked Olania again to be my espoused. She, of course, agreed and then smacked me for waiting so long to be ready. She is a very patient tanwoz, and fully understands I needed time after the incident with Andel."

Johlnz reached out his hand, then decided not to worry about what anyone would say, and instead of a handshake, he gave his friend a long hug and pat on the back.

"Do I see a tear in your eye, Johlnz?"

"Go to doxx. I am happy for you, not so much for Olania. After all this time, she must know what she is getting herself into."

"Very funny. We can't all be as perfect a match as you and Thereza."

"And do not I know it."

There became a bit of uncomfortable silence in the room except for the hum of the servers. Johlnz cleared his throat and spoke.

"Seriously, Tolz, you be careful and hurry back."

"We shouldn't be more than two mooncazts. We are taking one of the super transports as far west as we can along the old byway, which eventually leads to the coast. It's mostly a reconnaissance mission. After all the debris falls out that way, I do not expect to find much."

"Well, as I said, be careful. And by the way, I like the new look. What does Olania think about you losing the beard?"

"I did not ask, and besides, it is only temporary; I have two mooncazts to grow it back."

As I watched Tolz leave the server room, I had to smile. Big Verm getting espoused finally, proof no matter what, life can return to normal.

His news had been exactly what I needed right now. Tonitz, as I write this entry, it is fifteen minzakas before what used to be the start of the new cycle. Even with the happy news, I still am sad. Again, this nitz reminds me of all we have lost, more so than the Spark of Light celebration. I always was the odd one. Some things never change.

Reaching Out
Banlar 15

Our technicians have been monitoring for any radio or televid signals since our first mooncazts here in this region. At first, some broadcasts continued, mostly from personal radio operations, however, most times now, it is quiet. Connecting to what little remains of the satellite network
is very much hit and miss, mostly miss, even with the
OS-I in orbit.

The Council has decided to begin broadcasting a message via satellite connection and old-style radio when possible. The large radio tower in towz, along with the relay station in the mountains, and the one in Bilwi, do not reach very far; all the same, it is something. To improve the radio signal, we will build two more relay towers to the northwest along the byway used to arrive here, when further cleaned and rebuilt. We may construct one toward the south, but we will not likely receive any signal from that direction.

The new towers will be constructed about fifty zilos apart and located at higher elevation levels to get the strongest signal. Solar panels will power them, so they will not need much attention once operational. The work is expected to be done in a few mooncazts, weather permitting.

The towers will also be helpful with conversations between our various exploration and construction teams. OS-I is not always in the right location to assist in communications with the various groups in the field.

The message we will send is merely a call to contact. We will not give our position or give too much detail since we still need to be careful about attracting unwanted attention.

The Announcement
Banlar 29

When I came camo to our residence this evening, Thereza waited for me with a glass of wizen in her hand, and—well, let's not get into what she was wearing, or not. How she managed to get such a rare item as a bottle of wizen, I do not know; connections maybe?

The Council had a special closed-door meeting earlier in the pastmid and decided they would lift the voluntary ban on having liltanz, and encourage couples to start having families. She evidently heard, and we wasted no time getting started.

"So, do you think we will be lucky enough to have been successful right away?"

"I hope not, because then you will have to keep coming camo early so we can work on getting it just right," she laughed and gave him another kiss. "Seriously though, the preventor will take a few dazs to wear off."

"Perfect, I think I will need to leave the server room early every nitz."

After another few minzakas of cuddling, Johlnz asked for details.

"I knew they were thinking about it, but I did not want to say anything to you until it became a certainty. Professor Kiz called a meeting, and as my Onczle was leaving his office, he gave me a wink, so I knew; this was it, one way or another. Onczle filled me in on the decision when he came back, and I could hardly hold my excitement."

Thereza reached for the wizen bottle, filled both glasses, and sat on the edge of the bed before putting her glass on the table and re-joining Johlnz.

"I guess this will be the last wizen I have for a while."

"Well, it is kind of scarce right now anyway. Where did you get this wonderful bottle?

"Being the boss's relation has its privileges."

"Well, thank you. I have not had wizen since . . . never mind, not a good memory. Did your Onczle say what prompted the decision?"

"Yes, they decided since supplies are improving and the point of all we do is to have a future civilization, we would stop preventing liltanz and let nature take its course."

"Got to love nature," Johlnz said as he reached under the covers.

"Again? Really, Johlnz?"

"Got to keep practicing!"

Good to Be Back
Marwe 17

The daz started with a bang. As I headed to the cave server room to fix the latest issue with our primary system, a fireball streaked across the sky, heading northwest.

I later found out from Thereza, the space station confirmed the piece hit the western coastland of what were the provinces. They estimated it to be about 125 pads in diameter. Not huge though large enough, had it hit us, the towz and all the residents would be gone.

There was probably no one alive in the region to see it coming—nothing remaining beyond abandoned skyscrapers mostly destroyed now by the impact. The buildings, which hadn't already fallen, likely collapsed when the impact caused the fault lines in the area to shift.

On a brighter note, Tolz and the rest of the team arrived back early todaz. He sported an overgrown beard reminding us all why he is called Big Verm.

I ran into him while heading to have lunch with Thereza, and we had a few minzakas to talk.

"Well, look what the western winds have blown back to towz, the big tanmen sporting his new verm beard."

"Happy to see you as well, though not as happy as I will be to see Olania. She is busy with class, and I can't interrupt."

"Oh, come on, Tolz, you know I am much better looking."

"And you Johlnz have been working in the caves far too long. How is your, much, much better half?"

The two tanmen shook hands, and then Johlnz reached out and gave Tolz a big hug.

"She is doing fine; I am heading to meet her for lunch in her office. They have lifted the ban on having liltanz, so we have been busy—practicing. I can't believe I just said that. She would kill me. Anyway, how did everything go with the mission, any good news?"

"Some; the byway is mostly clear except for three cycles of overgrowth, all the way through the mountains. When we hit about twenty-five zilos from the coast, travel got tougher. Fifteen zilos out, there was no byway, no buildings, no sign of life, and only a small amount of vegetation re-growth."

"Did you make it to the port?"

"We did eventually. The tanaquakes and waves flattened almost everything in the port, other than the placreate docks, which are mostly intact and probably useable. I am sure the byway could be easily repaired for bulk-transports and lisks, but for what reason?" The eastern ports at Bilwi and ZaCeixa are much closer."

Big Verm waved at a passerby and scratched his bushy beard before continuing.

"We did pass many still-standing factories and found a lot of material we can bring back to help with the building, and here is the best part. The placreate factory was in perfect condition with a huge amount of old placreate substrate stored there, as well as the hydrospray equipment needed to use it."

"And how exactly are we going to get it back here in large enough quantity. I understand the stuff is heavy and needs specialty transport."

"You know an abandoned rail depot remains, ten zilos south of here."

"You have got to be kidding me?"

"Why, all we have to do is run a new rail line from the depot up to towz. All the needed supplies are available about thirty-five zilos west of here. The rail line follows the byway most of the way and leads into the factory."

"Oh tan, we can build a railway to the coast and go there for our holidays!"

Tolz laughed as he recognized the line from an old work of fiction.

"The railway did go to the coast; even so, most of it is long gone. I know it sounds like a lot of work; it will be worth it all the same. Stozzem thought it to be a great idea. He kept going on and on about beautiful sprayed archways in the caves and how wonderful and strong arches—"

"Yes, I know all about arches Tolz, even cybez engineers have to take basic engineering principles. I did not realize Stozzem went with you. He is a bit odd."

"I think all you engineering types are odd, but that is just me."

"Thanks! Anyway, as much as it is a beautiful daz for standing here talking with you, I have a lunch date, and you have almost made me late."

They parted, and as Johlnz proceeded toward Kiz Camo, he yelled back at Tolz, "Nothing can stop tanmen like us."

"Enough of the ancient fiction one-liners, Johlnz. Kiss your partner for me."

I am sure many of our fellow citizens who saw us yelling across the clearing would have thought we were an odd pair, and they might not be wrong. He was right; the placreate will be a tremendous help with construction in and out of the caves. I am sure the news will also change our direction at the GPEC meeting next weez.

Thereza was glad to hear Tolz and his companions had returned and scolded me for not asking him about the espousal date. I had to remind her he just got back and has not had much opportunity to talk to Olania.

This and That
Marwe 19

Two dazs have passed since my impromptu meeting with Tolz, and I am happy to announce Tolz and Olania wasted no time in setting a date for their espousal. They will join together as one on Tralmard twenty-two, above ground by the Spark of Light Obelisque.

I am surprised they are waiting so long to make it official, but I know they both love the Spark of Light celebration time of the cycle. Tolz told me rushing it for his parent's anniversary this cycle would be too hectic, and Olania absolutely did not want to wait till the following cycle.

Yours truly, and Arten, will share the best tanmen responsibilities. I, of course, teased Tolz about not being able to ever come to any quick decisions; however, I know it would have been a hard choice for him to pick one of us.

We had a short meeting of the GPEC todaz, where Stozzem laid out his ideas for using the placreate to build our new permanent homes in the caves.

"I propose we use placreate first to finish and make inviting the main entrance and all facilities in the Alpha cave. If we want individuals to live there all the time, it needs to be inviting."

Then we use it to enact our grand plan for the Delton cave. Imagine tall arches and arched bridges, allowing passage from one side of the complex to the other, all smoothly coated with different color hues of placreate. Its uses are endless and combined with the fero-stone and modular components; we will create a beautiful cizay, built to last many, many cycles into the future."

"Well, Stozzem, you certainly are enthusiastic, but I see a few issues with your plan. First of all, we need underlying structures of—"

"Excuse me, Salerand," Stozzem interrupted. "I know a lot about this material. The support structure needed is minimal; this stuff is stronger than most metals and can support a great amount of weight and stress."

"Yes, Johlnz, I see you are eager to add your opinion. Maybe he won't interrupt you!"

"Thank you, Salerand."

"Stozzem, I understand you propose to ship the materials here by rail from a factory thirty-five zilos away, and the closest the rail currently comes is ten zilos from towz. Is that correct?"

"Yes, it is Johlnz. Most of the rail line is in good shape, and I estimate we can build the extension into towz within two mooncazts of getting the old mainline up and running to the old depot."

"And how do we get the placreate into the caves and all the way down to Delton?"

Stozzem now appeared a bit nervous and started running his hands through his hair.

"Do you have an answer?"

"I admit, Johlnz, I did not see any pump towers or pump bulk-transports at the factory, but we did not explore the entire area. The facility has three buildings. If we do not find pumps, I am sure we can make them."

"More work," Salerand replied as he stood to address the entire group.

"This sounds like a lot of work, and it certainly is not a decision we get to make ourselves."

He paused a moment as he appeared lost in thought.

"I say it does not hurt to try, and at the very least, we should propose the idea of the rail line to the Council in the general meeting next weez. Let us also develop some firm plans of how we would use the placreate before the next Council GPEC update meeting. I believe the timeline gives us just about three mooncazts to prepare."

I think those in attendance were surprised after all Salerand's comments; he still agreed to go forward. Those who know him well understand he has always been the one to look at all sides of an issue. After his approval, everyone in the meeting agreed, so now I have more work on my plate. I will admit the vision he paints is worth the effort; now, we must get the Council to agree.

The Council Meeting
Eral 1

Todaz, I attended the Council meeting for the mooncazt of Eral. The meeting agenda mainly contained items about the everyday challenges and tasks needing the most immediate attention. The second part of the meeting they devoted to Stozzem, making his preliminary pitch to the Council. They liked the idea of using the placreate; however, the Council remains deterred by the upfront work needed on the infrastructure. Extending the rail line near enough to towz in addition to repairing all the other areas will be a daunting task; nevertheless, in the end, they approved the GPEC putting together a formal plan for the full update meeting in Nully.

Sad Daz
Eral 10

It's been over a weez since my last entry, and as I write this, I am fighting moments of despair. Many things have changed for us since the comet, but many bad things continue to remain.

In every society, a time comes when the pressure becomes overbearing for individuals, a time when hostility, bigotry, and or greed arrive. In this case, I believe it was just a combination of stress with maybe a touch of envy and prejudice. No matter the cause, todaz, we had our first taking of a life in Nuevo Esperanza.

I was leaving a quick meeting with Professor Kizermel about new server requirements when Security Chief Predsen entered the office and filled me in while he had to wait for the Professor to be available.

"Hi Malcolz, I have not seen you in a while. How have you been?"

"Hey Johlnz, good to see you. I imagine you have not yet heard what happened this premid."

"I have been busy, so no."

"Two workers on one of the byway crews got into a shoving and shouting match, and it quickly turned violent. When the fight ended, one tanmen, Parnec Morza, was dead, and Tizmon Ebertzel ended up in the medical ward in a coma."

"I hate to say it, Malcolz, but I am surprised it took this long to happen. We are all under a lot of stress. Does medical think Tizmon will recover?"

"Yes, he should; however, it will take weezs if not longer. I understand your surprise; all the same, we have had a few minor fights in the past. Supervisors, security, or other residents broke them up. The incidents get reported, and those involved we restricted to quarters for a daz or two. The system—my system has worked well till todaz."

"Your system works well. Do not blame yourself, Malcolz, for the problems caused by others."

"I know we need everyone working and helping in some way, so we never restrict anyone for long. We also do have a holding area, not secure like a confine, but guarded. We have only used it twice, and both times were because the person was drunk and did cause some damage."

"Maybe you know better Malcolz, regardless, to my knowledge, we have never had any theft or more serious crimes. We thankfully have not even had any complaints of contually related harassment, and you know what a problem that had been in the past."

"The question I think the Council needs to answer, Johlnz, is what do we do now? What do we do with Tizmon when he recovers?"

"Do we need a confine, a court system or codetanz, Malcolz? The answer to all these questions is, of course, yes, but I think we were all hoping it to be a task we could push off till later when we are not so busy trying to survive. At least, I had hoped.

"Do not take this the wrong way, Malcolz; however, I do not like the idea of the security forces acting as Authority within the towz. The Council needs to come up with a justness system. I would like to see us start a part-time Authority force and criminal penalty system, be that as it may, we cannot afford to have this be anyone's full-time responsibility. There is just too much work to be done, too much to do. We still, above most everything else, need to survive."

Malcolz told me he would include my suggestions with his own when he met with the Professor, and I will bring up our ideas at our next Council meeting if no one else does first. At the very least, we need to have a systemized set of codes that go beyond the basics every society knows to be wrong, like life taking, assault, and theft.

Corrective System
Eral 16

I despise the term, corrective system. It sounds like we have many hardened criminals to deal with, but aside from the incident last weez, it is usually peaceful.

The Council called an emergency meeting two dazs after the incident, and they decided we did need to establish a set of codes before we had other significant issues. By the end of the weez, they made a good beginning.

The towz will have a Sharoz's office above ground next to the building we currently use for our Council meetings. It had at one time been the camo servant's quarters, which only had junk storage items inside.

Our new Sharoz is Calliaz A Artsen. He worked as a member of his local Authority department before the comet, in his hometown in the Provinces. He was also one of the security guards at Reswoll. His Duzen will be Johlnzatu Yaxdan. He served as a PMO in the services before he resigned his commission about a cycle before the discovery of the comet. He had settled in Zexan Province and joined us on the way to Morcey-Sanchez. A third position will be created and filled in a few weezs.

None of the positions are full-time since the need is not there and will hopefully not be there for a while. All three tanmen have additional duties and responsibilities to keep them busy.

A small holding area is under construction in the Sharoz Building. The place is for simple disturbing of the peace situations, and we will build a more permanent confine facility below ground for anyone awaiting trial.

The Council members will for now serve as the Juaze and jurtany. They will work with Sharoz Artsen to formally codify codes and punishment guidelines.

Expecting
Eral 24

After the bad news two weezs ago, I am pleased to have some fantastic news.

I came camo this evening to find my partner waiting for me with two glasses of what I thought was wizen. I should have known better since wizen is still hard to find and a luxury. We have velpzs growing in the area, but cultivating them to make wizen, when we need them for food is a waste of a valuable resource, according to the Council.

Anyway, back to the more important news.

"Hello babe, it is about time you made it camo. I have been waiting for you for many zakas. Problems with the servers again?"

Johlnz sat next to his partner, gently putting his arm around her while giving her a kiss. He sat back and made the sound of someone who has had enough for one daz.

"We had an impromptu meeting to discuss the service for the underground—by the way, I have heard the Council wants to give it a name other than the caves or underground. I think it is a good idea, though I have no idea what name we could use."

Johlnz picked up one of the two glasses he saw sitting in front of them and was about to take a sip. Thereza gently put her hand on his and asked him to wait.

"I expect this is velpz juice and not wizen. When we can make wizen again, the accomplishment will surely be a sign of our success."

An expression of surprise and dismay appeared on his face when Thereza asked him to please shut up.

"It's hard to get a word in edge-wise with you on some dazs. You know I do not sit here waiting for you with drinks ready to go on just any old nitz; I have news."

Johlnz heart started beating a bit faster, and his hands twitched as he thought about what the news could be.

"Well, do not keep me waiting."

"Are you going to be this impatient with your first liltanz?"

As the words sunk in, an expression of pure joy appeared on Johlnz face, and the velpz juice he held spilled across the table when he haphazardly put the glass down. He stood up to grab a towel and then decided instead to lift his partner off the sofa and hug her tighter than he held her in a very long time. His eyes became wet as a few tears rolled down his cheek.

"I take it you are excited. I think you should sit down while I grab a towel. I do not need you to wreck the place."

Thereza walked away while continuing to talk, "So are you speechless? Do I need to get with liltanz every time I need you to quiet down and listen?"

"I love you, and I am so excited I do not know what to do. I want to run out and tell everybody. I—we have waited so long. When is the little one due? When did you find out, how far along are you?"

"I think I liked it better when you were in shock and quiet. I found out for certain todaz, and I am due in late Zelmar or early Nemvaz."

"I wish, babe; we had somewhere to celebrate properly."

"We do, Johlnz," she said as she removed her shirt. "The bed is a wonderful place to celebrate while we still can."

The Premid After

Eral 25

I awoke early this premid, even though I remained tired from last nitz's celebrations. I was almost as excited to tell Big Verm my news as I experienced hearing the news. With all that has happened over the last few cycles, it is great to have close friends again to share life's exciting moments.

We both had a full daz of meetings and tasks to complete, but I managed to catch up with him outside Kiz Camo. He was leaving as I was entering, as usual.

"Yo, Big Verm, I have been looking for you all daz. I have news, and if I do not get to tell you soon, I think I will burst and die on the spot."

"So dramatic! You high on something, Johlnz? You look much too happy for this time of the daz. I know I have—"

"Will you shut the doxx up so I can talk, Tolz?"

"Okay, okay, do not be so serious. It's not like—oh, oh, you are, you clar!"

"Do not you dare steal my thunder, Tolz!"

Johlnz quickly spit out his news before Tolz could say another word.

"Thereza told me last nitz; we will soon have an addition to the family."

Tolz raised his fist in the air and shouted, startling one of his fellow security guards and causing stares from others nearby. Without saying another word, he grabbed Johlnz and gave him the longest, hardest hug Johlnz believed he ever had before. When Tolz finally let go and stepped back, he had tears in his eyes.

"Really, Tolz, I did not even cry last nitz, sort of. I am sure this time next cycle, it will be you and Olania with good news. After all, my liltanz will need someone to play with other than Onczle Tolz. Tanz are going to love pulling on that beard, by the way."

They both laughed, and Tolz gave another shout of joy.

I am still sore from the hug Tolz gave me. I hope Arten doesn't do the same thing to me when he returns with the Zeltren next weez.

The Zeltren Returns

Lant 2

Before I continue, I must apologize. I wrote previously about the Zeltren arriving in port soon, and todaz as I sat to give an update, I realized I never mentioned the Zeltren left port. Good thing no one pays me to do this. Why I do this, I am still not sure; therapy, I guess. Anyway, here is the update.

The Zeltren arrived back in port Bilwi yesterday premid. Mazter Rourze addressed the Council at the standard meeting, which the Council opened for all to attend. The room was so packed; many individuals stood outside, frustrated they could not sit to listen. It reminds me to make sure our plans for the underground cizay include large meeting areas. I am sure the Mazter gave them an overview already to make sure nothing in his report would cause alarm.

Mazter Rourze stood on the small stage in the front of the room, flanked by his First Scip and Arten Luzas, to address the overflowing room. No matter what, Tanans are always curious and wanting information. It is what drove the planet's advances in the past.

"Thank you, Council Chairtan Kizermel, for the opportunity to speak to the Council and my fellow citizens.

"After stopping at ZaCeixa to check on construction progress and their supply levels, we traveled as far north as Canzun while listening for more radio signals, and as expected, the cizay was nothing beyond ruins. The wreckage of some of the taller hotels remains to mark the location, now nothing but a terrible ghostly sight. We did, however, manage to salvage some metals and other building materials from among the ruins.

"After Canzun, we started our trip south and sent an exploratory team into the mountains of Guazemax above Guaz Cizay. The cizay, along the coast at the base of the mountain range, was also gone—washed away. Some byways were clear enough for travel to get into the mountains, where we found no signs of life. While in the mountains, we stocked up on water, fruits, and a few game animals—some of which we brought back alive to add to our livestock.

"Farther south, we picked up another radio transmission from the area of Donhurex. The message was asking for help from anyone who could hear. We are not sure if they were survivors of an attack or attackers looking to their comrades for help. They did not provide a location, but we did send the halo in over thirty zilos yet could see no sign of life. While in flight, the Helo also picked up a weak S.O.S signal coming from the same area; however, again, they found no sign of life.

"While off the coast of Donhurex, we spotted a small ship on radar. It is doubtful they could detect the Zeltren; nevertheless, I did decide to back away before anyone could visually see us, just in case the ship had weapons. We detected no radio transmissions coming from the ship; however, we can confirm they were not adrift.

"I have only one more item to report. We found a barge floating off the coast and brought it back to port Bilwi. The crews in the port are doing some minor repair work. If sent on another salvage mission, we will tow the barge along.

"Thank you for your time and attention."

The Council has asked the Zeltren to stay in port for a few weezs so the crew can rest and offer assistance in clearing more byways and repairing more fishing boats, recently found washed ashore south of the port. The leadership will decide later what mission the ship should embark on next.

The only other major agenda item remained the rail line. The Council voted and authorized exploratory work to reopen the mainline without discussing the possible extension into towz.

I did manage to speak to Arten after the meeting. His reaction was not as loud as Verm's, but he also hugged me and kissed Thereza, who joined me at the meeting.

Pypzie Yanez was nearby as well, and when he overheard the news, he gave us a special blessing.

Tizmon Escaped
Lant 13

Tizmon Ebertzel escaped todaz from the medical facility. The Doctor and nurse both thought him too weak to do much more than stand next to his bed. He had been complaining about severe pain in his legs and vertigo when he stood.

The Doctor concedes Tizmon, likely faked the severity of his injuries planning to escape. Tizmon told Pypzie Yanez, he had started the fight; he was sorry and understood the need for some form of punishment.

I doubt there existed truth in any of what he said, other than having started the fight. We are better off without him, yet I wonder where he will go. Hopefully, he doesn't come back to haunt us, as my JarPypzie used to say.

An Anniversary
Lant 26

I am dead tired, but I feel I need to commemorate this milestone. Ten cycles ago todaz, OS-I became officially complete and operational. The station's crew had a small celebration, which they broadcast in the mezcaf for all who wanted to watch.

The crew is doing well, and supply levels are better than predicted. A plan to bring them back to Tanacun before their supplies run out is in the works. Our community has benefited greatly from the help above, and they have earned time to rest back on the planet of their joining.

Council Meeting
Nully 1

I am overloaded with work as usual, and even though I last posted a weez ago, I feel it is essential to record the Council meetings. I believe I am still the one single person keeping any log of events. It is something I think I need to address with the Council. We should have a recording secretary to take the minzakas of all meetings. I am working only from scribbles and memory, not efficient.

"Good pastmid everyone, it is a pleasure to welcome you to the Nully Council meeting and full department status update. After a few announcements, we will go through the progress reports from each group leader."

"I would like to start the meeting with the status reports and Pypzie Yanez. Could you go first, please?"

Pypzie Yanez approached the small stage and stood behind the podium with a huge smile on his face.

"I would like to start with a prayer.

"Giver of all life and light, protect us and strengthen us in our resolve to rebuild our society in the name of goodness, light, and truth. Bless us all. Amen!

"Thank you, Chairtan, I am honored to be the first to speak, for I do have good news to share. In the last three weezs, nine couples asking for my blessing and the blessing of their liltanz yet to join us have approached me. Doctor Johlant may have even more news to share on that front, as he is, in most cases, the first to know. Oh, excuse me for my mistake. He would be the second to know since the One is always the first."

There was some laughter and light applause from those in attendance before Pypzie continued.

"It is encouraging to see so many from our small community working to grow our civilization and show such firm resolve and hope for the future. I also would like to mention, my calendar for espousals is filling up fast. It's another good sign of our success in building an everyday life in the midst of what some may call chaos.

"I am also pleased to announce, the worship center is now fully finished and open to anyone for prayer, meditation, or even purely to relax and enjoy the quiet while it lasts. I say that because I also would like to announce the formation of a choir to sing at our ceremonies. If you are interested, please let me know. Thank You."

"Johlnz, you may go next."

"Thank you, Professor.

"Construction of the permanent server and cybez lab is well underway, and we have started working on space for future expansion of the facility. We continue to work on permanent underground connections to all the aboveground, permanent, and semi-permanent buildings. This project will ensure we do not have to reestablish the lines after each freeze period.

"I am also happy to announce our intention of providing the entirety of our future underground cizay with full connections by both hardwired and wireless airflex systems supplied by the Zeltren. The ship will be using its Tri-Dimensional printers to build all the necessary components. The task will take many cycles but will be worth the effort.

"Are there any questions?"

They had no questions, so as Johlnz sat down, the Chairtan asked Dr. Zarnikiyan to go next. He wasted no time getting started.

"The worst is over for now, and our climate should continue to improve. Eventually, we will see heat in this area that would have at one time seemed typical. Many of you will be wishing for those cold temperatures to return. Thankfully we will have the refreshing cool caves for the worst of the hot dazs. After the extreme heat, due to the combination of our position around the sun and continuing movement on our axis, temperatures will cool for many mooncazts before warming. Eventually, we will have a period of extreme heat followed by a gradual decline into the freezing temperatures and darkness of our community's second twilight.

"I have nothing further to report at this time."

The Doctor sat, glad to finish. He was getting more used to speaking in public, though he would never be completely comfortable.

"Thank you, Dr. Zarnikiyan. Dr. Moxron, you are up."

"Thank You, Kiz, ah Chairtan Kizermel.

"I am sure everyone has noticed how clear the skies have become since twilight ended. Commander Forzzell has detected a few remaining larger pieces of debris missed previously; however, after much studying and calculations of their orbit, we do not expect they will cause harm in the near future."

"Thank you, Dr. Moxron.

"Salerand, you are next up."

"Yes, thank you.

With both Helo-landing areas once again debris-free, we have turned our attention to two main projects.

"The first is building a landing strip for the lifeboats from OS-I to be able to land and bring everyone to safety. We have found an area large enough, and we will soon begin clearing the remaining trees and other debris. We have recovered two graders, which will help tremendously with both of our main projects.

"The second priority project, if fully approved, will be the reconstruction of the rail line and feasibility study of extending the rail line into the towz. The project would allow us to ship in placreate for use in the caves and the narrow landing strip.

"Work continues expanding the access in and out of towz and to the port at ZaCeixa. We have a tremendous amount of work ahead but feel we will meet all of our established timelines.

"I believe Loyst would like to go next."

"Thank you, Salerand.

"I am pleased to report; we have finished drilling all the necessary water drainage runs to alleviate the flooding we experienced after twilight. To further alleviate any problems, we have identified all past leakage areas, and they will be covered with the placreate if and when available. I can assure you the next major snowmelt will bring some grand waterfalls to our underground cizay. I think you all will be pleased."

"Thank you all for your reports. If there are no questions, I will give the floor to the GPEC, to give their full proposal on the reconstruction and extension of the rail line and plans for the placreate."

Everyone was eager to hear our report, so no one had any questions. The presentation lasted for almost a half-zaka before the regular meeting continued with the updates concerning food and water, at which time I fell asleep. I have been working late zakas, and the droning on of report after report became too much.

Finally, at the end of the meeting, the Council took a public vote, and the implementation of Stozzem's vision gained approval with merely one dissenting vote.

As I have written before, we need to have someone dedicated to being a recording secretary. My journal can only record so much, especially when I am tired.

Premid Sickness
Nully 18

I awoke to a round of cursing this premid from my partner as she was getting sick again in our bathroom. Eventually, she came out and directed the cursing towards my tanhood and me. According to Thereza, I am never to use it again. She has been dealing with the premid sickness for well over a mooncazt; however, this premid had been the worse so far.

Is all this cursing, trouble, and threat to my tanhood worth it? I can't say for sure right now, but I believe so, especially since I am not the one dealing with any pain. I love my partner, and I know she loves me too, yet I do not expect to hear her tell me for a little while longer. Goodnitz!

Trouble
Autnar 7

It did not take long for Tizmon to cause the towz trouble. Based on recent events, it looks like he may have found the group whose transmissions we picked up a few mooncazts ago. We can't be sure, they might have forced him, but he likely led them back to the towz. Luckily, they never made it beyond our perimeter defense teams. He will never be a problem again, even though some of his comrades did manage to escape back into hiding.

Johlnz walked past the medical building on the surface, on his way to Kiz Camo, when he saw Tolz coming out with a bandage on his head and a sling around his shoulder.

"What the doxx happened to you?"

"Oh, hi, Johlnz, it is not as bad as it looks."

"How does the other guy look?"

"He's dead, or at least a few of them are."

Johlnz's expression turned serious as he realized the injuries were probably from an encounter with hostiles. He motioned Tolz to sit on the bench next to the side of the medical facility.

"I did not realize this was something serious. We have not had any trouble, so I assumed an accident caused your injuries. What the doxx is going on, or can't you say?"

"We do want to keep it limited since the Council doesn't want to alarm anyone. We dealt with the problem, and unless there is a larger group lurking around, they shouldn't be a problem. The Helos will be doing routine patrols over the area. After twilight, not much tree foliage remains for anyone to hide below."

Johlnz shifted uncomfortably in his seat and rubbed his hands through his hair.

"The little one is due in a couple of mooncazts. This news worries me, and I am sure Thereza knows about it, and she will worry."

"Assure her, I do not think you have anything to worry about, they won't catch us unawares again, and that bastard is dead."

"Whom are you talking about?"

"Tizmon. He led them to us and helped them ambush the team. Cezeran is in serious condition, and other than me, everyone else got back without harm. We were patrolling ten zilos up the creek when Tizmon approached. He indicated he wanted to return and face his punishment; a few seconds later, all doxx broke loose.

I think there were more than a dozen fighters. They were, thankfully, not well-armed. Cezeran was the first individual shot, and I received a close call across the head, and the shoulder is from a large tree branch, which fell on me when they shot it down."

"They were no match for our weapons and training. I took out Tizmon and three others before dragging Cezeran out of harm's way. We called the Helo for backup, and they chased the remaining fighters up north until they lost them when they scattered. The Helo did some further reconnaissance but could not locate any camp."

"As I said, now that we know they are around, I do not think they will try anything again. The group, whoever they are, lost the element of surprise. We checked the

dead and found no identification or communications equipment. The guns were crap; even so, we took them anyway as well as knives and the food they were carrying. We dumped the bodies into a nearby ravine; something for the animals to eat."

Tolz finished and realized how angry the encounter made him, and he wanted to go right back out and chase down the survivors; nevertheless, he knew it would be a stupid thing to do.

"Hey, Tolz, wake up. What were you thinking about?"

"Revenge!"

"However, not todaz. The Doc said I would need the brace for a weez or two, and then I will be back out on patrol hoping to find a trace of them to follow."

I did not tell Tolz, but I was a little worried about his attitude. I understand his anger; be that as it may, we can't go out chasing a possible enemy for revenge. Hopefully, Cezeran will get well; if not, I am afraid of what Tolz will do.

On a happier note, Thereza is feeling much better after a few mooncazts of severe premid sickness. Now it is just the size she is complaining and cursing about to everyone. She only has a couple more mooncazts to go, and then the fun starts for real.

A Short Mission
Zelmar 5

The Zeltren departed todaz, heading north to the Gulf of Tezaci. They do not have any mission other than looking for survivors and listening for more radio signals out of Guazemax. I know many of us hope for the impossible—more survivors.

The land area around the gulf is extremely flat, so the waves went very far inland, wiping away most signs of civilization. No one thinks it is likely to find much valuable equipment, but we can always use more scrap metal and wire. The Orbital Station did detect a couple of what looked like boats floating around in the waters. They may be salvageable.

Tolz is back out on patrol, and all has been peaceful. He is not happy; he wanted to find the group Tizmon led to us and make them pay. Cezeran is out of danger; however, he will have many mooncazts of rehabilitation and will probably not ever serve on the security forces again.

Work continues on a variety of projects. The ways between towz and the ports are completely clear of debris. Some of the byways are constructed of only crushed rock and dirt; however, most of it is paved and easy to travel.

Any Daz Now
Zelmar 33

The Doctor restricted Thereza to bed rest for the remainder of the term; however, he thinks she will be early. She is not due until the middle of Nemvaz, which is still three weezs away. I am not sure I can survive; maybe I should volunteer to go on patrol with Tolz.

My Somz
Nemvaz 4

At the very beginning of this journal, when I introduced myself, I mentioned my JarPypzie Jacol. What I did not write at the time since it was not significant is the fact he joined this planet on Nemvaz 4; the cycle no longer matters.

Back before the comet, the United Providences celebrated Nemvaz 4 as the daz of the country's founding when our ForePypzie's declared independence from Guuz Iurox. My family used to have abundance feasts in the backyard and celebrate my JarPypzie's joindaz. Now I have a new joindaz to celebrate

My somz, Jacol Jantnel Zavix, joined us this premid. 7 lpz. 8 ozt. of blonden-haired and purplan-eyed new life for our community. Hopefully, he will live to have liltanz of his own on a planet renewed from catastrophe.

At one time, not too long ago, I would have never considered bringing another life into this planet, but now, we are making progress and feel there will be prolonged existence on this planet for future Tanans.

Light-Pypzie Tolz beamed with pride as if he were the Pypzie when he visited with his espoused. Olania can hardly wait to have a liltanz, and she even indicated if she were not

Athix, she would be practicing now. Tolz face was almost as verm as his beard.

Arten is encouraging Thereza and Olania to get moving and see who gets with liltanz first so he can be the next Light Pypzie. I informed him politely, of course, I would be the next Light-Pypzie, and I forced Tolz to confirm. I am sure he had his fingers crossed behind his back.

I expected I would have much to write when this happened, much to pass along, yet now… I am without words. You would think after four and a half cycles of keeping this journal, I would know what words of wisdom to pass on to my somz; all the same, I have nothing.

Excuse the small water stain.

What does it matter anyway? He will probably not care, not ever read it, and will probably forget it ever existed. Maybe a Jarsomz or Jardamza will care someday. I am sure no one else will. We will all eventually fade into history, forgotten. As long as we have a future history, nothing else matters.

Five Cycles
Nemvaz 18

I returned from the ceremony to remember all who died five cycles ago todaz and all those who have perished since, feeling a sense of great loss. I am not sure why the ceremony affected me so much this cycle. Various members of our community stood to speak of loved ones lost. I did not. I have told few individuals about my fiancée or her suicide.

It was a somber experience, and I am even now feeling a mixture of emotions. So much and so many were lost. Our civilization endures and continues to grow, but many still have a touch of survivors' guilt. Some feel it is a matter of time before a large piece of debris falls too close to us and wipes us out, even though the scientists say the danger has passed.

The scientists have reiterated; they are sure there are no longer any large pieces of debris circling Tanacun. However, an occasional fire-flame show of small debris falling back to the planet is a constant reminder of what could have been the end.

The Council took this opportunity to finalize creating two updated and simple memorials dedicated to all those who have died. One will be a memorial to commemorate all who lost their lives that daz five cycles ago.

We will build the memorial in a park area created in the aboveground section of our towz. The yet to be re-designed structure will include a plaque showing a map of the planet the way it existed before. The memorial will be covered by a specially built roof, which will allow it to survive through the brutal periods of twilight.

The second memorial of which I mentioned before in this journal, will be to remember all who have died since; the many who drowned from the waves dazs later, and the many who perished during the twilight to follow, a few cycles after. The plan is to construct the memorial below ground in a central courtyard planned for Ceton cave, near the reservoir lake. The spot will have natural light filtered down from the surface by a series of tunnels and mirrors. The memorial will include the names of all our friends, family, and associates who died on the journey here or have lost their lives while rebuilding our civilization.

The first planned memorial below ground, had been delayed. I hope this plan comes to be. Some of my fellow citizens think it a waste of resources, but most, myself

included, support the idea. Those who died should never
be forgotten!

I am excited and looking forward to Hzalo-Multum next
weez. With the arrival of my somz, I have renewed confidence
in our ability to rebuild. I am profoundly grateful to be alive with
a family, which I never thought would exist at one point.

Spark of Light
Tralmard 24

The daz after tomorrow is the espousal of Tolz and Olania,
which Tolz can never let me forget. Todaz, however, we took
Jacol to see his first lighting of the Spark of Light, Obelisque.

The Obelisque is set up in the same spot it had been for
this towz's first celebration. The liltanz again made beautiful
decorative lanterns, which lined the walkways of
enlightenment—a beautiful sight as always. Jacol gave
Thereza her first kiss of sharing, and he let out a little sound of
what I say was laughter as I gave Thereza my kiss.

Following our walk of enlightenment, we took Jacol to a
dark clearing to see his first stars shining on this special nitz.
He will remember nothing of this evening, but we will, and we
will treasure those moments for many celebrations to follow.

The Espousal
Tralmard 26

The daz had finally come. The only dazs more special to
me than this were my espousal and the joindaz of Jacol. It is a
great honor to be the best tanmen, even if I do have to share
the honor with Arten. Luckily the Zeltren arrived back in time,
so Malcolz and his partner could attend.

Having the espousal during the Celebration of Light was an excellent idea, lending a little bit more beauty and reverence to the celebration. The ceremony took place in front of the Spark Obelisque, minzakas after the sunset, providing a shimmering light to the festival.

Pypzie Yanez began with a prayer, welcomed all in attendance, and then began the ceremony.

Pypzie Yanez paused for a moment after his greeting, then raised his hands high over his head.

"Bringer of light to the universe, you have made the bond of espousal a holy symbol of your light of life. Hear the prayers from all those gathered before you to witness the joining of Tolz Bezler and Olania Aizal, as they start their new life together in your name."

Tolz offered his hand to Olania as she stood before him; she then offered her other. With hands joined, Tolz began his vowels as Olania started to cry tears of joy.

"I Tolz desire you, Olania, to be my partner forever in the light of the One. I promise to be true to you in good times and in bad, in sickness and in health. I will love you and honor you all the dazs of my life, with the light of the One, forever."

Olania followed with her vowels as Tolz began to show tears in his eyes.

Pypzie Yanez took the rings from Johlnz, blessed them, and briefly passed them through the fire lit behind them directly from the Obelisque. When the ring ceremony was complete, Johlnz and Arten's pledged their guidance.

"I Arten, I Johlnz, pledge to guide and assist you in your new life together, to be your protectors against the darkness."

Pypzie Yanez finished the prayers and declared them partners in the light.

Arten and I lit torches from the Obelisque and led the newly espoused couple and all in attendance to the caves where they held the reception in the cave of stars.

Shortly after we arrived in the cave came time for the part I dreaded.

"Fellow Tanans, it is my honor and privilege to introduce to you Tr. and Tiz. Tolz Bezler."

After the applause died down and everyone sat, Johlnz stood behind the couple, raised the small glass of wizen all had been served, and delivered his speech. The speech he had been dreading for many mooncazts. He was never comfortable speaking in public, but this felt worse because it needed to be heartfelt, and he needed to hold it together.

He rubbed his left hand against his pants, raised his right hand, almost spilling the wizen from his shaking.

"Tolz and Olania, we have been through much together, and recently your love has been a bright spot for all who know you. I . . . consider myself blessed to call you both friend and I—"

He had to pause to get control and wipe a tear from his eye.

"I wish for you all the happiness to be found on this planet and know Thereza, Arten, and myself, as well as all in attendance, will always be there for you. I—we love you both. Cheers!"

Tolz immediately stood up and gave Johlnz a long hard hug, and wiped his own tears from his eyes before sitting down and kissing his new partner as the glasses were ringing around them.

In the old dazs, before Zeptulgar, I probably would have made a drunken fool of myself, but with alcoholic drinks not being in much supply now, I just made a fool of myself dancing with my partner.

Life Goes On
Banlar 7

It has been a weez since the beginning of the old cycle. It would be the cycle 3995 on the old calendar. I do not even know why I mentioned the old cycle. I am sure it will soon be forgotten, just like all of us, trying to rebuild a Tanan civilization.

The Zeltren left on a mission to look again for the group from Guazemax. They will be listening for any communications and using a Helo to search for any signs of an encampment. The second part of their mission will be to explore Port Huozlan up in Zexan Province. Authority and civilian facilities existed throughout the region, and possibly some valuable equipment may remain in the Authority compounds. The area was well fortified and designed to withstand some amount of flooding.

The newly partnered are doing well. We hardly see them anymore, between workloads and them practicing to have their own bundle of joy. I may ask Tolz to take care of Jacol one nitz. He might change his mind.

I am just kidding, Jacol, if you ever read this journal. Muzie and Pypzie love you even though we never get to sleep much anymore.

We Are Not Alone

Marwe 3

The Zeltren returned a few dazs ago, and the Council encouraged all to attend the regular Council meeting for an update.

I was present in the office when Mazter Rourze made his initial report to Professor Kizermel and Dr. Moxron. We already know about the organized group in Guazemax; however, the Zeltren heard no further radio transmissions, and the Helo saw no sign of life. Whoever is up in the area they are staying low.

The communication they did intercept was unexpected. A group who may be the last remaining part of the Authority of the United Provinces contacted the ship on its way back to port.

"Thank you, everyone, for your updates. The last update will be from Mazter Rourze."

"Thank you, Council Chairtan Kizermel."

"Last weez while on the way back to port Bilwi, we intercepted a communication explicitly directed at the ship, from a person identifying himself as a Josuex Nauzton, a representative of the United Provinces of Jantnel. I acknowledged the call without giving my name and spoke to the person at length.

"Josuex claims to be a Jantnen and the head of a small joint research team with members from the former country of Tezaci and the Provinces. They are located in a settlement in southeastern Tezaci, which they identified as a research station.

"I know of no research facility of that name. I checked the ship's records and found no mention of a facility in Tezaci, and I found no records of any joint ventures;

nevertheless, they did provide valid security codes. Josuex told me they had plenty of food, water, and equipment in the station, and we were welcome to join them. He indicated most of the facility is built underground, which was how they could survive the waves and what he called the dark time.

"I did confirm our identity as a Province ship since he already knew, though I am not sure how he knew our true identity. He instructed, since we were a Jantnen Authority ship, we had a duty to report to the station. They asked us to dock north of Xuncan at a port, still good enough to accommodate a small ship. He said they would send transport for us and escort the team to the station, located two zakas away from the coast.

"I strongly suspect that they have overheard our communications, which is how they knew of our existence. In the future, I suggest we send all communications through the Orbital Station.

"I confirmed we would bring the ship as ordered and cut off communications. I doubt they have any ships since they are so far from the coast, but thought lying would give us more time to head away from the area just in case."

"No additional contact was heard or made during the trip. We searched for additional signals along the full communication spectrum, including citizen band, regular radio, and video. The search teams were able to recover a good amount of scrap and also another salvageable small boat to add to our fishing fleet and more zolatron generators."

"Thank you for your time."

There were many questions, most unanswerable, and nothing of note.

First Scip, Neltia, gave a more detailed report on what they found in Zexan. The search teams recovered a good amount of scrap from the area, including large amounts of electrical and optical cable.

After many dazs of trying to break in, they did obtain access to the Authority facility. They recovered multiple types of munitions, cybez equipment, compact, portable power sources, and other equipment vital to the ship's operation.

A Great Honor
Eral 12

Todaz we dedicated the first of the two monuments to those who have died over the last five and a half cycles. The ceremony was well attended and held at the above-ground memorial, which includes a park filled with evergreen trees, which hopefully can live through the extreme temperature shifts.

Todaz became special for another reason. After the ceremony, Dr. Moxron and a couple of other Council members approached, and they invited me to join the towz Council as a full member.

They feel my work in planning the below-ground facilities, my time as a citizen representative, and my experiences over the last few cycles make me an excellent choice to join the expanded Council.

There will be a simple yes, no vote put to the citizens of our towz to approve the expansion and the new members invited. If approved, the Council will now have fifteen full members who represent various backgrounds of experience and expertise.

I, of course, said, "Yes."

Voting

Lant 1

We voted today, and all nominated were elected; however, a small handful of citizens voted against the expanded Council. Some did not think we needed a larger controlling body, and others had personal grudges against some nominees. Professor Kizermel and Doctor Johlant will continue in their positions, pending a Council vote in Tralmard.

I have mentioned before other citizens elected to the Council, including Pypzie Yanez, Mazter Rourze, Nuzen Hulztrand, Salerand Loxon, Loyst Narstox, and Doctor Zarnikiyan.

The selection of new leaders for the Council will occur during the first meeting of the post comet, new cycle, in Tralmard. Only Council members will vote. At some point in the future, we will need to establish a standard form of Authority, but I feel the process needs to wait for a few more cycles.

Before the vote, the existing Council decided we would make no further response to whoever contacted the Zeltren, claiming to represent what remains of the Province's Authority.

It's Official

Lant 10

Todaz was the swearing-in ceremony, which made me an official Council member. I have decided with my new duties and access; it is essential for me to update this journal at least once a mooncazt.

Although we do now have a recording secretary, his job is to document the meetings only. We have no official record keeper or records of any kind. If we are to build a true civilization, it will be important to keep track of births, deaths, espousals, and everyday events. I feel we owe it to those who will hopefully follow to leave as much information as possible.

One new thing I learned todaz was the extent of our security forces. The Zeltren has a fast response security team of thirty, and our land-based force is growing faster than I realized. The surprise attack a few mooncazts ago caused many tanmen and tanwoz to volunteer to be trained and serve part-time. We now have over one hundred tanmen and tanwoz dedicated and trained to protect us from any possible trouble from external forces or even ourselves.

We have heard nothing more out of Guazemax, and hopefully, whatever happened up there will not work its way south again to attack our security forces. One of the Helos makes daily patrols of the area north and south of our community.

A New Mission
Nully 12

The Zeltren was sent out on its latest mission last weez. The Council—my first time voting on a motion—has asked them to head up north along the former United Provinces coast on a scavenger hunt. We do not expect them to find any survivors left in the Provinces, and anyone who did survive would not be near the coast.

The secondary part of their mission is to look for surviving vegetation. Now that we are in the warmer time again, we hope the teams will find young seedlings of tree species not existing in this area. Hopefully, we can transplant some species and start new forests of different varieties down here to help our community. They will also be looking for fruit trees and other food type plants, which may have survived the most recent cold spell. I personally do not expect much success.

It is expected to be a short trip. Up and back in three weezs. They will continue to monitor communications from Guazemax and now Tezaci and any possible signals from the Provinces. All communications between the ship and the towz will be through the Orbital Station since we know at least one group is listening.

The Zeltren is Home
Autnar 2

The Zeltren returned a couple of dazs ago, and I a moment ago came back from the Council meeting where Mazter Rourze gave his report. They were late returning due to a massive storm of almost tempest strength. The storm forced the ship to lay low close to land, anchored in a sheltered bay to wait out the weather.

The trip was a successful scavenger hunt. They brought back a significant amount of usable wood and a large variety of metal for construction, including large spools of wire and many different types of industrial and commercial batteries. Not everything can run with zolatron and portable fuse generators.

Most important, some would say, are the trees and food plants they were able to find. The crew brought back almost fifty very young trees consisting of six varieties, which should be able to flourish in the area with care. Everyone was amazed they survived the twilight and started growing.

In addition, they found cosson, poyams, larrotts, casbean plants, and a couple of fruit trees we can try to grow in the underground area with sun lamps and natural filtered sun when available. The additional plants will help to diversify our gardens so we do not lose significant amounts of food to blight or other diseases.

The Mazter also reported they picked up no signals from anyone. Both the compound in Tezaci and the group in Guazemax have been quiet.

On a personal note, my somz has been crawling for a weez and sleeping a bit better. My partner is fully recovered and talking about a second liltanz already.

Tezaci - No Longer Silent
Autnar 19

Being on the Council now gives me access to information I would not typically have. One such piece of information is, the Tezaci compound, or station as they call it, has been broadcasting a message for the last couple of dazs.

"I called this special meeting to disclose a situation, which has developed we must address. I understand that not everyone could be here at this time. One of the reasons we nominated so many new individuals to the Council was to allow for such situations."

"Now, to get to the point. Two dazs ago, we started receiving the following message from a person identifying himself as Josuex Nauzton. The message repeats every zaka on the zaka."

"This is Josuex Nauzton, former Chief Executive of the research arm of the United Provinces of Jantnel, Supreme Intelligence Agency. Our group is, we believe, the last official survivors of the U.P. Authority. We are at the former joint research facility in southern Tezaci, eighty zilos southwest of Xuncan. Our facility is called Caztona Station. We are offering

refuge to any survivors who hear this message. Our facility is underground, protected from the elements and any possible additional tidal waves. If you hear this message, please contact us at frequency 100.10."

"For us to hear the message, they have to be using a very powerful and tall transmitter, or they may have a relay station or satellite in orbit. We believe they intercepted our communications with the Zeltren in the past. We are convinced this message is directed at us, even though no mention is made of the Zeltren or the towz."

"We have not divulged this information to anyone outside the Council and have asked our radio technicians to keep it quiet. We will have a special meeting tonitz to decide how to proceed."

"I ask you to please hold all questions and comments till this evening."

After two zakas of heated debate at the evening meeting—I am beginning to not like politics—we decided to contact the Tezaci facility with some ground rules.

Commander Malcolz voiced his concerns first, as was usual for him.

"We should not give our location until we know more about those individuals. Merely the mention of the SIA disturbs many individuals on this Council for good reasons. We should not divulge our belowground settlement, and we should not divulge our entire population. Until we fully understand the situation, we must be extremely selective in what information we impart."

From those in attendance were heard murmurs of agreement as Pypzie Yanez stood to speak without being recognized. You could tell watching the expression on his face—a mixture of contempt and confusion; he disagreed.

"I like you, Malcolz, but you Authority types have always angered me; why be so mistrusting? They are offering help to those who need it and—"

"And they are lying by omission. The station knows we are here, and they are trying to lure us out. It's been over five cycles; why wait so long to offer help?"

Malcolz's face turned verm, his anger becoming apparent, while Pypzie Yanez continued in his usual calm manner.

"Malcolz, everyone, the only way to build trust is with trust. Not many of us are remaining on this planet; we must be as one, or we shall surely perish in groups."

Johlnz requested permission to speak and stood to address Pypzie Yanez.

"Pypzie, I understand what you are saying, but individuals must also earn the trust; we lose nothing by being cautious. I believe, for now, we say we are a small group surviving well with the resources at our disposal, living in caves when necessary."

Chairtan Kizermel banged his gavel and suggested they move on and let Mazter Rourze speak next.

"Thank you."

"I am in the middle. I do not see any problem with divulging a bit more information. Certainly, we should not mention the Zeltren, even though they might already know who we are, and maybe, where we live. If they do mention their communication with the ship, we can say the Zeltren did contact us a few mooncazts ago and said only; they would check on us the next time they were back in the area."

Jox Bartle motioned to follow Mazter Rourze's lead, and Johlnz second the motion. The meeting continued until all in attendance approved the plan.

We agreed to contact the station in the premid, and every member of the Council was invited to the communications center. I am not afraid to admit the contact makes me nervous. It is great others are alive; however, I have a terrible feeling spinning in my gut.

The Storm and Conversation
Autnar 30

We had our first conversation with Tezaci, Caztona Station, last weez, but I am not writing about it till now because of everything else, which has happened since.

As we were finishing our meeting with the station, an officer from the Zeltren came in to inform us their radar picked up a massive and violent storm heading our way. Mazter Rourze immediately confirmed the information and asked for permission to take the ship out to sea toward the south to get away from the impending storm.

We had an emergency Council meeting and gave the Mazter permission to go, with instructions to check out the coastland along the remnants of Veneztuz, to look for more usable salvage materials.

It's a good thing we have the Zeltren here with working radar. Without their warning, we may have lost lives and had more damage. We moved everyone except essential patrols down below and prepared everything above as much as possible.

The unprecedented way our planet now moves causes storms to appear and grow at a tremendous rate. The OS-I was not in a proper position to see the storm, and with a limited number of functioning satellites, they had no warning. On a side note, they have managed to repair two of the damaged satellites still in a functional orbit. They hope to be able to fix at least three more before returning to the surface.

Having lived through some tempests in the past, I would say it was precisely what we experienced to some degree. When the storm ended, three dazs ago, we began the cleanup. We have significant damage to the Vegcamoz and barn areas and some minor damage to additional structures. Fallen trees in some spots are again blocking the byways, which were never considered good, to start.

Thankfully, we lost no lives, and no one was hurt. We can only hope these storms are not an ongoing occurrence. Yes, someday we will have a wholly contained cizay below, but we need farms and grazing areas for the livestock. They cannot remain down in the caves for long periods without problems. Twilight was about as long as they could go before developing medical issues, and many are concerned about the length of the next twilight period.

I just had to feed my crying somz, so my partner could get some needed sleep. With the task complete, I can document the conversation with Caztona Station held back on Autnar 20.

Josuex responded to our call about five minzakas after we started broadcasting and sounded excited to be hearing from other survivors. Many on the Council began to distrust him immediately since they believed Josuex already knew we were here.

"This is the Council Chairtan, Professor Mazjuen Kizermel, of Nel Experza settlement, trying to contact Josuex Nauzton, of the research facility Caztona Station. We intercepted your transmission; please respond."

He repeated the message a few times and then waited. Five minzakas later, as they were about to repeat the message, Josuex responded.

"Hello, it is great to hear a new voice. This is Josuex Nauzton, of the research facility Caztona Station. We have been trying to contact other survivors for many mooncazts, most of the time, without any success. How many survivors are in your settlement?"

"Hello Josuex, it is a pleasure to speak to you. There are over two hundred survivors here at the settlement."

Malcolz stood off to the side, nodding his head in agreement that the Professor hadn't given their real population. He picked up a notepad and quickly jotted down some additional notes for the Professor.

"More than half of our population is from the Provinces and Tezaci. We are primarily former research scientists who were following the condition of the planet after Zeptulgar. We knew we had to head south for any chance of survival."

"I am also from the Provinces, Chairtan Kizermel, and I was an SIA regional director in the southeastern region before Zeptulgar hit. Our team realized things would worsen when the Authority slowly went silent about eight mooncazts after the comet. My team and others from that facility were aware of this station, and I suspected it to be where an old friend of mine served.

"I gathered together the tanmen and tanwoz still trying to restore order in the area and convinced them to come. We did not have much food remaining, and if we did not move on, we would have been fighting each other for survival. We heard reports of gangs a few zilos away from our position, and we had very limited armaments to defend ourselves.

"We were able to get a few Authority bulk-transports, and started heading down toward the station. After a few minor fights and the loss of three of my friends, we made it to the station about two mooncazts later.

"I was correct; my friend did work here and was the head of the station. We were amazed to learn the station to be self-sufficient, and we began helping those already here to find more survivors. My friend died from a major infection about two cycles later. I was soon after elected to the position of Chief Director, which I consider to be more of a Malodal position."

As Josuex continued, non-stop, many in attendance whispered they agreed he sounded like a Malod, always talking, never believable. There were groups of three to four individuals, quietly discussing how much of the story they should believe.

He continued, talking about the facility and what resources they had available. He did not mention boats; however, he later referenced docking facilities, which confirmed he either knew the connection to the Zeltren or was fishing for confirmation.

When Josuex finished talking, the Professor gave some more information about the towz. He did not mention the underground facilities, the actual size of the community, or the Zeltren.

Josuex suggested they should try to meet either at the station or in the towz.

"If you do not have the means to travel, we could come to you. We have Authority bulk-transports, and my advisors say the trip to you would be possible. We are near the ocean, so if you prefer, and you have access to a seaworthy boat, we are about two zakas from a dock where we could pick you up and transport you to our facility."

Professor Kizermel advised Josuex he would discuss it among the residents of the towz and would be in touch. After some other pleasantries, the communication ended.

The Chairtan stood, trying to think for a moment, but to no avail, as the room erupted with questions and arguments.

"How do we know he is telling the truth?"

"What if they want to steal our resources?"

"What if they come here and kill us all?"

The sound was deafening until Popsie Yanez yelled, "What if they want to help?"

The room quieted a moment, and the Chairtan used the opportunity to ask for motions of how to proceed. Before they could begin, a crewman from the Zeltren interrupted with information concerning a massive storm heading for the area.

No decision has been made yet as to what answer to give or how to proceed. Our first priority is to repair the damage from the storm. The Zeltren will be back in port in two dazs, and we will have a full Council meeting the daz after.

The Professor had the radio tech send a message to Josuex to let him know we had to postpone our decisions due to a severe storm.

Plan of Action

Zelmar 2

After many dazs of discussion—should have known one meeting would not be enough—they decided todaz we would send a delegation to Caztona. We still need to determine who and how many will go; however, we did finalize all other details of the trip.

Taking bulk-transports overland would take too long and be too dangerous. We have no idea what additional gangs or marauders may survive between here and Tezaci, so instead, we will take the larger fishing boat. The trip is slightly over four hundred zilos, but the vessel will not go alone. The Zeltren will tow the boat up to about one hundred zilos from the Caztona dock area, saving on fuel and making the trip safer.

At that point, the fishing boat will proceed on its own with the Zeltren following along fifty or so zilos out to sea, within radio range, just in case the boat gets into trouble.

We will tell Josuex we are more than five hundred zilos away, so they will not have any idea of our towz's true location. We also will say we are leaving earlier than we plan. The deception will cover the fact of how quickly we will get there with the ship towing the fishing bout most of the trip.

If we were taking the fishing boat, the trip would take around twenty zakas of nonstop traveling. In reality, we will be able to make the trip in about twelve zakas.

Delegation
Zelmar 8

It has only been a weez since my last entry; however, the Council has finalized the plan for the visit to Caztona, and I may not have an entry for some time.

We contacted Caztona and told them we would be coming by a fishing boat we had recovered and restored. We told them we would be leaving in two dazs on Zelmar 10 with a group of seven individuals, five from the Council, and two or security.

They provided the coordinates of their docking facility and gave us a radio channel to contact them when we were about three zakas away.

As discussed by the Council, we told them our location was about five hundred zilos away and expected the trip to take twenty to twenty-five zakas. We advised them to expect the delegation on the premid of Zelmar 11.

So, who is going on this trip? To my surprise, Professor Kizermel and a couple of other senior members of the Council nominated me to go. I think I am happy to be going yet also a little nervous, as those feelings in my stomach I mentioned earlier have not subsided. I am not a politician or a diplomat; nonetheless, times they are a-changing, for sure. They want me to go to observe and report back on Caztona's level of technology from an engineer's perspective.

In addition to myself, the group includes three security guards, one, my friend Tolz Bezler. He will act as our resource manager. Also included, senior Council member Jox Bartle, one of our radio technicians, Branin Zomplant, and the Zeltren's second in command, Frunx Neltia, who we will say is another senior Council member who had boating experience. Since they may know his name, we decided he would be Rozer Johlant on this trip.

Although I will not take this journal with me, I will keep notes on my trip and add them when I hopefully return. I hate having to leave my partner and my somz. He is getting so big and starting to walk on his own. I miss them both already.

PART 5 – Caztona and Beyond

Transcribed Zelmar 13

Zelmar 10

We gathered our group together at 3:00 in the pastmid and started our travels to Bilwi, where the small shuttle boat waited to take us to the Zeltren. The trip was uneventful, slow, and bumpy, thanks to the recent storm. Our little convoy consisted of three transports in all, with Tolz and I together in the middle.

"Nervous Johlnz?" Tolz asked his fidgeting friend.

"Should I be? After everything I have been through these last five cycles, this should be a cakewalk, Tolz."

"Says the tanmen sitting here tapping his foot and playing with his hands. I have known you long enough to see your nervous hand movement many times."

"Okay, I admit, I am nervous—and worried. What if something happens and we do not make it back? I have a kid and a partner now."

"And Olania is—"

"Yes, and you have a partner. We both have a lot to lose now. All the same, I do have to admit I find this exciting. Engineering a cybez network and doing repairs can get a bit boring."

"I can always recommend you go back on the security team if you are thinking occasionally getting shot at might prove more exciting."

Johlnz said nothing but gave his friend the look of death as they both laughed to relieve the tension.

We arrived in Bilwi three zakas later to see our fishing boat set behind the Zeltren and ready to go. I had never seen the

Zeltren before, and until this daz had never been on an Authority Sea Vessel. The ship sat tall in the water—an impressive sight. I was happy to see they still proudly flew the stripes and crossbow but had it set at half-mast to commemorate the loss of so many.

We planned to depart around 7:00, so I had time to settle into my quarters before going to the conference room for a briefing scheduled for after we were underway.

They assigned me a compartment reserved for guests; however, the room was smaller than my original quarters back in towz before I espoused. The room had two beds, and I would be sharing with Jox for the nitz.

Jox came in, dropped off his bag, and we went up to walk around the deck before the meeting. He admitted he also felt a bit nervous; even so, he had a feeling this contact would be beneficial. He confided the towz needed some crucial supplies and hoped Josuex, whoever he was, could help.

We stayed on deck while the ship pulled away from the coast and went below for the meeting as the still low on the horizon sun set behind the clouds.

"Welcome, everyone. I hope you like my ship.

"Muster time tomorrow premid will be at 6:00 for your breakfast. At 8:00, we will place you on the fishing boat, at which time the Zeltren will head about fifty zilos out to sea ahead of you in case you need assistance. We will also deploy Helo One to ensure no surprises are waiting ahead of you and scout the port before anyone should be on-site. Branin, you are to contact Caztona as soon as we pull away and let them know you expect to arrive within three zakas.

"There will be no radio contact between any of us except for an emergency. You will ping us three zakas after you leave Caztona dock for the trip back to our port.

I know I am leaving you in competent hands with Frunx. No offense to our security team. Enough talk, time for dinner."

"Mazter Rourze are—"

"Johlnz, thank you for the respect, but you are guests on my ship and friends. Please call me Calliaz."

"Okay, Calliaz, are you sure they can't detect the Helo?"

"Absolutely . . . not. I suspect they can see this ship and probably the Helo. I believe Josuex is playing coy to feel us out. They may be as nervous about meeting us as you are about them."

"See Johlnz, everyone knows about your nervous hands."

"Shut up, Tolz."

"This is not something a Mazter should admit; even so, I am nervous as well. It is a different planet; what is left of it anyway. We could be heading into a trap. I doubt it, but as an Authority tanmen, I am always cautious. Let us continue the discussion while we eat; you would not want to be around me when I am hungry."

The galley prepared a meal consisting of a selection of various plates of oceanfood; still, I could not help wondering if it would be my last meal. We had great conversations at which time I got to know more about Calliaz and Frunx, as they both insisted we call them. Each tanmen had lost family while out to sea when Zeptulgar struck. Both had families living in Ronfolx, and most likely lost them to the waves or the extreme cold. Neither knew what really happened after impact.

We ended dinner by 10:00, and we went immediately to our quarters to sleep.

Zelmar 11

We were awakened at 6:00 in the premid as promised, and I still felt tired. I did not sleep well, worrying about so many things.

Jox and I went to the mezcaf for cazzaa, where everyone else already had their second or third cup; I always was the slow person in our family. We had some conversation to pass the time until one of the crew came to tell Mazter Rourze, they were ready for the transfer.

The young crewmember I never met before led us up to the main deck, where our fishing boat waited alongside the ship, ready for us to board. Two crewmembers lowered our group, one by one, down to the boat's deck via a bozon chair —quite an experience I am not looking forward to repeating for the trip home.

Frunx piloted the boat away from the Zeltren five minzakas later, and Branin promptly sent a message to Caztona, letting them know we were about three zakas out from the dock. Josuex quickly answered the message personally, and he assured us he would be waiting at the pier.

We had decided to have our full breakfast on the boat since we had nothing else to do, plus we had to make it look like we were here the entire trip in case they came aboard for some reason.

During breakfast, we decided our vessel needed a proper name; as Frank had mentioned, it could bring bad luck to be at sea on a boat with no name. The fishing boat had a name at one time; however, time and weather damage had wiped the label away. The only writing still visible was the script E. After some thought, we decided to name the boat Holxanlaz. It's a mouthful to say, but appropriate, we hope. The name is an old lurox name meaning, 'the bringer of good fortune.'

We arrived at the dock a bit after 11:00 in the premid. No other boats were in view; though, it quickly became apparent this dock had been fixed up and could accommodate about four vessels of our size. Josuex, and two additional tanmen, one with a machine gun, were waiting at the end of the dock to greet us. After the third tanmen assisted with tying up our boat, we disembarked to find a broad smile and outstretched hand.

"Good premid, and welcome to Caztona Station, or at least our dock anyway. I am Josuex Nauzton, and it is a pleasure to meet you."

Josuex did not introduce the tanmen standing to the side, holding the gun—obviously former Authority. Josuex, however, looked to the group from the towz, like a person you would find working in an office pushing papers. He was tall and skinny, with short-cropped blonden hair and a barely visible mustache.

Jox and Johlnz stepped forward ahead of the rest of the group and took turns shaking hands. Johlnz noticed a small tremor in Josuex hands; he made a mental note to discuss with the group later.

"Hello, Josuex; I am Jox Bartle. I, along with Johlnz, are representatives of our Council. I would like to introduce Rozer Johlant, our boat Mazter, manager of our dock, and also a Council member."

Josuex reached out and shook Frunx's hand with an odd expression on his face.

"You guided everyone here safely, so you would appear to be excellent at your job."

Jox continued with the introductions.

"This large tanmen here, whom we like to call Big Verm, is Tolz Bezler. He is one of our resource managers. And this is Branin Zomplant, our radio technician."

Like Josuex, Jox did not introduce the other two members of the group. They both carried pistols at their side but were far less imposing than the tanmen with Josuex, holding an Authority-style machine gun.

Josuex reached out to shake their hands without further comment and led the group to the waiting vehicles. They were old-style mini-lisks, which could accommodate eight individuals each, and thankfully the air-conditioning still worked.

At the transports, another individual waited. Josuex introduced him as his right-hand tanmen, Marzco Bisbee. Marzco had a much darker complexion and probably had been raised in the southern regions. He was shorter than Josuex and of larger build—likely former Authority. Waiting with Marzco were two more guards with holstered sidearms.

All the guards, including those from Nel Experza, went in one transport, and the rest of the group went in the other. Josuex did make sure everyone was okay with the arrangement, to which Jox did nervously agree.

The trip to Caztona Station took almost two zakas on byways well maintained, which led Frunx to believe they made the trip often. Josuex spent most of the time talking about the events leading to his arrival at the station, including conversations about conditions at Caztona and questions concerning conditions at our towz.

"We have a large group of refugees here which is straining our resources, or more accurately, the ability of the station to support so many. We have an abundance of medicines and medical supplies, though food can be an issue, even though we have a large amount of farmland.

The problem with the farms is the weather and lack of irrigation. I am hoping maybe you can help us with food, and we could offer medical supplies."

Jox thought carefully before responding.

"We are certainly low on medical supplies, however with twilight behind us, we have been able to establish some farms, and we have livestock. We do not at this time have an overabundance; even so, I am sure we could work out some mutually beneficial arrangement."

As they neared the station, they saw a large area of farmland, though some of it looked dried out and sickly. Josuex was eager, however, to point out the hezzle, porlz, and zraap the group could see in various holding pens.

"We have caves in the mountains you can see in the distance, where we heard the livestock during the hottest and coldest mooncazts."

Caztona station or towz, as Josuex did say a few times, consisted mostly of a bunch of makeshift buildings, he explained, they used for storage of transports, fuels, and heavy equipment. No fence or visible security surrounded the immediate area.

At the center, bounded by a high, heavyweight fence with a gate patrolled by security, was a heavily fortified, sizable main building, which Josuex explained was the aboveground portion of the facility. He further clarified the structure to be more of a warehouse than anything else, with some offices, meeting rooms, utility, and communication rooms.

The small convoy entered the structure, and after parking the vehicles, Josuex guided the group to another secured door leading to the elevators. His guards headed off in another direction and into one of the offices. In front of them were two elevators, both with the doors open and large enough to accommodate the entire remaining group together in one.

"Ten levels, make up this facility, three of which we converted into makeshift housing for the survivors. They used to be part of the research labs, no longer required."

"What kind of research did the scientists conduct here?"

"This facility, Rozer, acted as an Authority station, being jointly managed by the Tezaci and Provence's Authorities. I would hate to speculate, and my friend never did confide in me. He did, nonetheless, assure me the facility was safe."

"Two levels devoted to utilities, one exclusively for supplies and the rest are an assortment of labs, workspaces, communications, and offices. At this time, most of the labs and offices are unused."

"With labs now being used as dormitories, they can't be too comfortable. I remember when I slept on hard floors with no bedding. I certainly can relate to how the refugees must be feeling."

"Yes, Johlnz, it has been a struggle, but things are not too bad. The facility did store a large number of cots and bedding. I am not sure why. It's another thing my friend did not explain before his passing."

After descending, according to Josuex, four hundred pads, they emerged into a large corridor that looked much like an office lobby. He explained the area was the location of all the command offices, as well as the large meeting rooms.

Josuex directed the group to one of the meeting rooms, which had a guard at the door, and he instructed everyone to have a seat and relax. Josuex left to arrange some refreshments, and the group made small talk with Marzco while they waited. A few minzakas later, Josuex came back, followed by others bringing in some water, cazzaa, and tea, as well as sandwiches.

Josuex sat at the head of the table and gave them more information about the station's history.

"This station primarily focused on research but also served as a listening post directed at the southern instability regions. Morzan, my friend, never would elaborate on the exact research they conducted; at any rate, he did say he was glad it would never be used."

"If he confirmed it to be safe for refugees it could not have been too bad."

"Tolz, I believe."

"Yes."

"Tolz, he did confide in me they disposed of everything potentially harmful before I arrived. There are huge furnaces below he used to destroy all dangerous substances and chemicals."

Josuex paused a moment, then asked the group's security guards, who had been standing, to relax and take a seat. They were reluctant until Jox instructed them to sit. Josuex stood, and Marzco stood by his side. Josuex appeared a bit nervous as he clasped his hands in front of himself.

"I must first apologize for a bit of subterfuge on our part, but I assure you there is nothing to fear from us. What everyone here wants is to work together to forge a partnership to help us all to survive. So, to that goal, I believe it is time for full disclosure and honesty from all of us at this table."

Josuex looked over at Frunx and said, "Welcome First Scip, Frunx Neltia to Caztona Station."

Josuex picked up his water glass with his slightly shaking hand and took a long drink of water. His guests remained silent while his disclosure sank into the group, and before Frunx could respond, Josuex continued.

"We have been able to intercept all your messages, which are how we knew about you and the towz. As I said, this facility partially served as a listening post, and some support structure remains. We also have records of all the ships and crew under the Provincial Sea Authority command structure and the other branches of the service. Mostly all useless now — almost."

Josuex continued to appear nervous, moving his weight from one foot to another as he stood before the group, not making eye contact for more than a second or two.

"I assure you, I have no delusions of grandeur, and I do not consider myself as any representative of what remains of the United Provinces. My order was a ploy to try and get you to come here so we could meet. I figured Mazter Rourze would be more likely to come if he thought my request to be an order. In reality, the Mazter would have rank over everyone at this station, including myself. The Authority services always outranked the intelligence agencies of the Authority.

"Tolz, I hope they did give you some background of what resources your towz has available. I am sure your actual part in this mission is to be an additional security person. You do not spend as many cycles with the SIA as I have and not recognize trained security.

"I am sure you now realize we do know the Zeltren escorted you here and is waiting out at sea for you. We can contact them later to let them know everything is okay, and there is no longer any need for any deceptions. One of the things we have here that still works is access to one of the remaining SIA spy satellites.

"I assure you, gentleman, all we are looking for is a chance to work together. We have much to offer and hope you can help us.

"I will sit and shut up now, for I truly am interested in your towz and how you managed to survive the cold period."

Jox, as the senior official of the delegation, spoke up first.

"Thank you, Josuex, for your honesty. I, for one, am somewhat surprised and also hopeful all you say is true. We did have suspicions you knew more about us than we would have liked, and it made a few of us here and on the rest of the Council nervous."

"I understand their concern. We do not have much of an Authority structure here, but my advisors were reluctant to make any contact. With just the firepower and personnel on your ship, you could easily take control of this station by force."

"It is a shame with the planet and Tanakind facing extinction; we still can't let go of our fears."

Jox let his statement sink into all before he proceeded. He then gave more information about Nel Experza but did not provide complete details about everything. They spent the next half zaka discussing various specifics about the towz, the station, and surrounding areas. Josuex was impressed and delighted because, as he indicated earlier, he needed help from the towz.

"We do not have a lot of firepower at our disposal, and after some trouble early on, we still worry about security for the aboveground facilities. No one could get into the station, be that as it may, for the station to survive with the number of individuals here, we need the surface facilities."

Frunx acknowledged the Zeltren did have weapons and munitions they could share and should be able to help out if the Council agreed. He also pledged to offer additional security training and personnel if they could be spared and approved by the towz Council.

One of the many things Caztona had to offer were medicines and access to a complete medical facility. They had a few doctors at the station as well, and one had volunteered to return with the delegation to help at Nel Experza if needed.

Josuex continued and explained the facility had an extensive supercomputer system with a vast database of scientific and other knowledge, much of which would be needed to build a new civilization. He went on to say what they needed most was fewer residents. They were able to welcome anyone they found wandering around; however, the facility was not meant to hold so many individuals, and it strained the systems and resources. Josuex hoped at least some of the families at Caztona could be relocated to Nel Experza to live.

"I will have to get approval, but I believe we can take some individuals back with us and possibly many more in the future. The caves we lived in are extensive, and we are working on building a full infrastructure in them to survive future twilights."

"Thank you, Franz; any help you can give will be much appreciated."

Josuex was excited to learn of the work below ground and wanted to know everything we were willing to disclose. A zaka later, after a lot of logistics discussions, Josuex suggested they go on a tour to see the rest of the facility, and then he would give them time alone to talk. The facility looked impressive, and the group's excitement rose to see much that would help build larger settlements at an accelerated pace.

The towz representatives unanimously decided to trust Josuex since they discovered no apparent reason not to, and invite as many as they could handle to move to the towz. They became so caught up in everything they had forgotten Josuex's offer for them to contact the ship. The Mazter was surprised to receive the transmission yet delighted to hear of the developments.

"We will be spending the nitz here as originally planned, Mazter."

"I will contact the Council, provide them with a report, and ask for permission to bring some of the refugees back with us to towz. I will also ask them, Franz, to give you full ability and discretion to negotiate and disclose whatever you believe is appropriate."

"Thank you, Mazter, for your trust and confidence."

"Have a good evening, Franz. Zeltren out."

In the evening, they had a relaxing dinner where they met more of Josuex's staff, and they spent some time discussing the events of the last few cycles. Another benefit Josuex could provide was a variety of alcohol, of which they had a bit too much of that evening.

Zelmar 12

We met with Josuex and Marzco the following day to work out details over breakfast.

Our sleeping accommodations the nitz before were only slightly better than our ship, however after drinking, it did not take long to fall asleep, so we all appeared well-rested.

During breakfast, we discussed many things. Josuex expressed his pleasure to learn of the survival of OS-I. They only had access to one satellite, and they could not reach either station with the frequencies they knew to try. He offered to give control of their satellite to OS-I so the station could add it to their existing network.

We then discussed Guazemax specifically and security generally. Caztona Station knew of the trouble in Guazemax, yet was not in a position to provide help. Josuex confirmed, whatever events were transpiring, the area had quieted down, and their satellite did not see any current activity or clear indications of life.

"Some of the refugees here came from down south, many from Guazemax, and they told us many horrific stories of theft, rape, and slavery; such a waste. Not many of us remain to rebuild, and such behavior makes our tasks so much more difficult. One of the last groups told us most individuals were dead and lying in the streets. The fighting between the two main factions had left no one much able to survive. Security locally has not been a problem; just the same, we are always on guard to be safe. With one twilight behind us--I like your term, by the way, Johlnz—it is not likely anyone else will be coming for good or bad."

Johlnz responded. "I read many stories when I was younger about the end of the planet, surviving plagues, zoms, and alien invasions. The reality seems so much worse than the speculation in the stories of what life would be like."

Tolz put down his drink and wiped his mouth before responding to Josuex and Johlnz.

"The two of you are depressing me. Sure, many bad things have happened to the planet, and we all have probably seen many things we would like to forget. Now, it is time to put the past behind, remember it, so we do not repeat the same mistakes, and rebuild from the ashes."

"Gee Tolz, when did you become so passionate and wise? Must be that partner of yours."

"Espoused life agrees with me. Who knew! I am surprised, Johlnz; you do not have a quote from one of your old storybooks to share."

"You asked for it."

'It was the beginning of the rout of civilization, of the massacre of Tanakind.'

"I hate you, Johlnz."

"I know!"

Josuex stood with a smile on his face.

"Let us pray to the One, that Tanakind survives this particular massacre. I want to thank you all for raising my spirits with your joking and close friendship. I hope we can all be close friends in the future, and I look forward to meeting all your friends and family in Nel Experza.

"I need to go make arrangements for medical supplies for you to take and discuss who will be joining you for the ride to their new camo. Please enjoy the rest of your breakfast."

The Council leadership unanimously agreed to give Jox complete discretion to negotiate and begin bringing some survivors back to towz. We spent the rest of the premid working out the details.

Over four hundred refugees were living at the station, including over fifty liltanz, some alone, they wanted to relocate. In exchange, Josuex suggested some individuals from our towz could come up here to use the research facilities and database. We could not take everyone to Nel Experza at one time since we did not have enough room on the ship or even yet in towz. We would take a few families back with us; then, in a few weezs, we would take some more individuals starting with families and orphaned liltanz, followed by those with building or other needed skills.

Branin suggested the station could become a training area and education center for advanced studies needed to help us grow in the future. The database would be a great resource, and we discussed the possibility of a satellite link between the two settlements.

Considering the incident with Tizmon, Jox also suggested the existing facilities at Caztona could confine anyone needing to be held for trial or sentenced to confinement for a long duration. I surely hope it will be a long time before any such facility is necessary.

If we are to have a confinement, we need to have a complete court system. We will have a Juaze, since Dranzlin X Bartzan, a former Juaze, was one of those coming back with us from Caztona. We do not yet have codetanz, and I am not even sure we need them. The only code, for now, will be the code of the Council for many cycles to come. When the need arises, we will have to decide how to proceed.

If approved, the Zeltren would be used to transport materials and individuals back and forth until better options became available. Caztona did have, as we expected, a couple of large fishing boats, which could also serve as transport if needed.

We contacted the ship and arranged a return time frame, and included instructions to prepare space for a few extra passengers. In addition to twenty-seven new citizens, we will bring back medicines, food supplements, and additional cybez equipment.

Later, five lisks and two bulk-transports made their way back to the docks. It took a couple of zakas to ferry the individuals and supplies out to the waiting Zeltren. The crew again positioned our fishing boat for towing, and we were on our way camo.

It's been a long daz, and I look forward to getting camo and seeing my family.

Good to be Home

Zelmar 14

I woke up a moment ago from an excellent sleep. As rustic as our camo may be, it is still camo, even though it had only been three nitz; being away from my partner and somz left me feeling alone and uncomfortable.

The trip back was uneventful. We contacted the Council again to give them a heads up, and they decided to have a meeting to provide a full report at 10:00 this premid. I copied all my notes over to this journal late last evening, and now it is time for breakfast, then off to the Council.

Council Meeting

Even though the Council's decision to give Jox full ability had at the time been unanimous, we knew there would be some on the Council who would not be happy about the complete disclosures made at Caztona Station. We also expected others would not be happy about the additional individuals coming to our community, but mostly our report was well received.

Some members feared the first group was sent to spy on us, cause trouble, or sabotage us from within our community. They were vocal about their displeasure and even called for the removal of Jox and me from the Council.

After a long, heated discussion, Council Chairtan, Kizermel spoke about the need for calm discussion and thought. He admitted he had concerns; nevertheless, he trusted our decisions and told those who wanted us removed not to rush to judgment.

I stood and asked to address the Council, which again caused some to exclaim they heard enough from us already;

even so, the Chairtan instructed them to be silent and granted my request.

"I understand your concern; I felt the same way at first before we met with Josuex. However, we feel they are truthful, and they do want to have an open exchange of ideas, resources, and assistance. It is a new planet, much smaller in a way, much larger and foreboding in another.

"We cannot grow our civilization with nothing beyond fear and mistrust, not if we are to prosper and build a better civilization from the ashes of the past. We are most certainly not the exclusive survivors of the comet tragedy, and this will probably not be our first contact with others. It may take cycles or decades before we contact those in other parts of the planet, and we cannot do it in fear and mistrust. We must be vigilant, but we must also be welcoming. We must rebuild and grow together, or we all will probably die as a civilization."

It became quiet in the room after Johlnz's speech, and the first person to stand and speak next was one of the members who asked for his removal.

"I must first say I am sorry for allowing my emotions to get the better of me. I apologize for asking you to be removed and truly commend you for being willing to go and meet with those at Caztona Station without knowing what to expect. I think I have allowed my fears to take control of me. I am an old tanmen, maybe still living in the past. I vote to move forward with our hopefully new friends at the station."

After the member spoke, the Chairtan led us in a much better debate of the situation. The almost unanimous decision to proceed with bringing the Caztona Station refugees into our towz passed soon after, and we began the process to establish a formal relationship with the station.

We contacted Josuex to let him know all the plans we discussed were confirmed. We scheduled another meeting for two dazs later to work out how to bring the individuals into the towz without overwhelming our resources.

Quick Update
Zelmar 28

Work demands much of my time; nevertheless, I have a few minzakas for a quick update. In addition to the new individuals added to our community, Caztona has also sent additional much-needed medical supplies and supplementary communications equipment.

Josuex had expressed a desire to come to towz to see what we have built. We decided to have him and some other higher-level representatives from Caztona come right before the anniversary, so they may participate in our remembrance service. The Zeltren will bring their delegation and some more new citizens on that trip.

My Somz's First Joindaz
Nemvaz 4th

Todaz is my somz Jacol's first joindaz. We will celebrate tonitz with a small cake, some new blankets interwoven by a group in our community, and a little wooden toy made by one of our new citizens from Caztona.

The 'woveners,' as they call themselves, provide a blanket to each liltanz on the daz they join the planet and on their first joindaz. The blankets are a welcome new custom, which helps us to feel even more like a community, progressing through life instead of holding on for dear existence.

Okay, I exaggerate, life is not that perilous, but after what happened, we can take nothing for granted. I think back on the early dazs after the arrival of Zeptulgar, and I cannot believe I did not lie down and give up.

Anyway, toys for the liltanz are hard to come by, although we have scavenged some over the cycles, and we now have the woodworker I mentioned who makes toys out of wood we recovered. All liltanz need to play and need toys to help them develop.

I look at my somz, and I am excited about his future. However, at times, reality sets in, and I ask myself, what have I done? How could I have brought a liltanz into this precarious existence; pride, selfishness, a need to leave something behind? I do not know. I think about what Pypzie Yanez would say, and then I come upon the answer, love. Love can never be wrong, and the existence of a liltanz from love is a blessing no matter the state of the planet. If Tanakind is to survive, we need to be brave, and we need to have faith.

On to other news, after I dry my journal.

A convoy of heavy equipment from the west arrived about a weez ago. I do not know much about the machinery, but I do know the six new pieces of equipment will be a significant help with our construction projects, especially the railroad expansion and rebuilding.

The byway to Port Bilwi is completely clear again and widened, so traveling to the port will be much faster. The Zeltren will bring more equipment and supplies from Caztona, which we will now be able to move more swiftly to towz.

Nemvaz 18th, 0006 AC

I finally managed to get Jacol to sleep. It has been a busy daz for all. Todaz was the sixth anniversary of the comet, and the towz commemorated the event with a short prayer service and candle procession to remember all who perished.

The procession started at the entrance to the underground cizay and proceeded to the monument at the surface park. The routway chosen symbolized we will never forget, even when we move on with life in our new cizay. Chairtan Kizermel spoke a few words, including recognition of our guest from Caztona, followed by Pypzie Yanez, who spoke a few words of comfort followed by a prayer.

I suspect this may be our last official cycle commemoration of the event, and we will only have a special service every five to ten cycles. At some point, we need to be thinking more about the future and less about the past. Even this cycle, our community leaders emphasized our upcoming celebration of Hzalo-Multum, to remind us of all the good things happening, the future we are all starting to see, experience, and feel.

Josuex and his group arrived two dazs ago. They are amazed at all we have built here in so little time. I watched him, and he appeared genuinely moved by the ceremony. He later told me they had nothing at Caztona, no memorial and no services, and now felt it to be offensively wrong.

After the remembrance ceremonies, we had a joint Council meeting with the representatives from Caztona. We discussed our collective future and developed plans on how to grow our civilization together.

"Thank you, Chairtan Kizermel, and thank you all for allowing us to join you on this daz of remembrance.

Those we have lost; we should never forget. I am ashamed I needed this great community to remind me of something so important."

Josuex paused a moment. He did not want to be emotional in front of those in attendance; all the same, the ceremony had a tremendous emotional impact on him. His shame and guilt of not ever before remembering or thinking about all the friends and family he lost affected him more than he was willing to admit, even to his close friend, Marzco.

When composed, he continued.

"As I walked around the last two dazs, I have been amazed at all you have accomplished. You should be proud of the community you have built, and I know our friends and family who are no longer with us would be equally impressed.

"It is my hope and humble request, at some point in the future, our two communities will exist as one entity, one country, working together to rebuild from the ashes. I envision a robust and vibrant future for us if the universe will leave us alone and not throw any more catastrophes our way.

"The community at Caztona stands ready to offer all assistance and equipment you need to help build and grow your wonderful community into the future cizay you have envisioned."

He immediately received a standing ovation from the Council, and some who initially fought against the mission to Caztona, walked up to shake Josuex's hand.

I did not speak at the meeting; however, I am uneasy about the idea of a country. Tanans fought many wars in the old dazs over silly things as nationalities and borders. I do not know how many other settlements and refugees remain; come what may, I believe we should go forward as one planet united together.

After the meeting, which I attended with Thereza, Josuex came over to meet my partner. He told us he had decided to stay for the celebration of Hzalo-Multum. He was, as he put it, overjoyed to hear of our continuance of the tradition and looked forward to next cycle, introducing the custom back to Caztona.

Hzalo-Multum
Nemvaz 25

I had too much wizen at dinner this evening—now that it is readily available from Caztona—and I want to get to bed. What I am trying to say is this will be short.

We celebrated Hzalo-Multum at Kiz Camo, with the Professor and Thereza's Onczle, Doctor Moxron. Josuex and Marzco were also in attendance, and it was Josuex who had supplied the Wizen, as I think I already stated.

Professor Kizermel and Josuex spoke a few words of gratmul before we enjoyed a dinner, which included some traditional favorites from Caztona station.

Happy Hzalo-Multum, and good nitz.

A New Council
Tralmard 1

Todaz, during our regular Council meeting, we elected a new Chairtan and Vice-Chairtan to the Council. For this two-cycle term, the Chairtan will be Dr. Andrez Johlant, and Vice-Chairtan will be Doctor Robarz Moxron. Professor Kizermel will still be a part of the Council but declined to be among the foremost leadership. He is tired and is looking forward to a small amount of rest.

At my urging, Vice-Chairtan Moxron put forth a proposal to create an official recording secretary position to record all regular and special Council meetings in the future. The proposal was second by Popsie Yanez and unanimously passed. After being nominated by Popsie Yanez, the Council voted and elevated Haszex Hoanzt, one of the citizen Council members, to the now-permanent position.

They will officially start in Banlar, so I have till then to set them up with a portable system to automatically archive to a general repository, with multiple backups. On a personal note, this will free me up from my self-imposed job of trying to record every important aspect of the Council meetings in my journal.

The new Chairtan's first official act was to dedicate the second memorial now completed in the underground. We dedicated the monument to those who have perished on the way to making this a viable community. Part of the ceremony this evening was to add names of those who were part of our community back in the individual camoz, who perished during the journey here or lost their lives trying to rebuild our civilization. The Caztona delegation attended, as well. They will be returning to the station tomorrow aboard the Zeltren.

Josuex learned of the crew's plight on board the remaining Orbital Station while here, and after confirming with Caztona Station, he brought fantastic news. A few zilos north of the station is an extended landing strip designed to allow the landing of large Authority aircraft. The station verified it is in a good state and can be brought to a safe condition in half the time it would take us to finish the landing strip we were trying to build.

Spark of Light

Tralmard 24

The Spark of Light celebration grows every cycle to be a bigger and livelier part of our lives. We had some decoration contests, including some more old-style Sparklights, found in a warehouse fifty zilos to the south.

The celebration is an excellent time to pause and remember; we can still have joy on this planet. Even with the old Renewal celebration a thing of the past, this still has meaning for me, as I am unwilling emotionally to give up part of my former life.

All overflow residents from Caztona have moved into the towz. We are still struggling with housing; however, the last group was made up entirely of singles, so they will be housed in a barracks above ground. Some of the scientists in towz have moved up to Caztona Station, where they will have access to better equipment and more advanced cybez systems.

Caztona has helped us improve our new belowground medical facility, but the main medical facility will be at the station. Anyone needing specialized testing or non-emergency advanced services will go to Caztona for treatment. We are working on several things to improve the trip.

The station also supplied us with additional cybezs to be used exclusively to access the vast network of information stored at the station. They also provided a significant number of personal cybezs, which I need to update and integrate with our systems. I have a great idea of how we can best utilize them—more to follow.

I am now off to the beginning of the festivities with my partner and somz. Tonitz, we will attend the Spark of Light celebration. My somz Jacol, the pride of my existence, loves the Sparklights, and all we will hear all nitz long is, "Oh, Pypzie, the lights!"

The Zavix family finished walking along the walkways of enlightenment, and Jacol loved all the additional lanterns and Sparklights strung around the towz. Johlnz was not happy about celebrating the holiday with such warm temperatures as he missed the customary snow. He made the mistake of commenting to Thereza.

"Would you prefer we all be freezing to death in many pads of snow? You should be happy, Johlnz; we are all alive and doing surprisingly well."

"I am happier than I could ever be in this new life of ours, but I miss my snow. I am sure you will remind me of my statement when twilight returns, and I am complaining about being cold."

They both laughed as they sat on the little bench, enjoying the customary holiday sweets made by one tanwoz who recently moved to towz from Caztona. Jacol enjoyed it as well, and it kept him from repeatedly talking about the Sparklights. They were about to head camo from the evening when Tolz and Olania came strolling up, followed close behind by Arten and a tanwoz Johlnz did not recognize.

"Hello, Zavix family, Cheery Spark of Light to you all!"

"The same to the Bezler family, and hello Arten, I thought you disappeared; I have not seen you in so long."

The group exchanged hugs and some customary kisses as Arten explained he had been working way too much coordinating security with Caztona.

"Yes, I hear congratulations are in order, Security Chief Luzas. How is Malcolz enjoying his new position on the Zeltren?"

"Why do not you ask him yourself, Johlnz?"

Malcolz and his partner, Ligaya approached the group walking hand in hand. Another round of hugs and kisses followed before Malcolz answered Johlnz question.

"I am enjoying my new position as Team Leader, even though it keeps me extremely busy. I am training and coordinating security and strike teams on the ship and at Caztona, along with Arten."

"I, on the other hand," Ligaya said, "am not enjoying it so much. Between his schedule and mine, we do not even see much of each other while in port; however, change is on the way in a few mooncazts."

"Do you have something to tell us?" Thereza asked while a huge smile appeared on her face.

"Yes, since you inquired. I am resigning from the Zeltren and will be living in the small community at Bilwi. A ship is no place to have and raise a liltanz."

Ligaya waited as what she said sunk into everyone, and shortly thereafter, they all stood to give the happy couple kisses and handshakes of congratulations, adding more joy to the nitz.

"Anything you want to tell us, Tolz?"

"Not yet, Thereza, not yet."

"Arten, are you going to stop eating the sweets long enough to introduce your friend?"

"Sorry, everyone, I do love these things and really missed them."

"Obviously!"

Arten gave Tolz the look of death.

"Everyone, this is Chaizen. She recently moved here from Caztona."

Johlnz gave Chaizen a hug. "I am sure I speak for everyone when I say welcome to the towz. Did Arten ever tell you about the time he hit me on the head and tied me to a bed?"

Yes, the rhyming was unnecessary, but Chaizen enjoyed my story, and after some more conversation, we headed camo to anticipate Light Daz premid. Tolz and Olania invited Arten and Chaizen to spend Light Daz with them and join them for the feast. I am sure they will have a good time.

I am glad Arten has found someone special, and I hope they end up becoming something more permanent.

Upside-Down
Banlar 2

No major update tonitz; I have been too busy.

Only routine status updates at the standard Council meeting this premid. Yes, old habits die hard. Recording Secretary Hoanzt officially started his position todaz, so why should I even mention the Council meeting.

I realize I am mainly writing nonsense, proof I am tired.

One thing of interest, not mentioned at the Council meeting, as of todaz, our planet is officially upside-down, compared to what was at one time normal. I never knew much about the stars, so I did not notice the difference other than the sun moving west to east instead of east to west.

Temperatures are what I would consider hot, though the area's original residents say it is cooler than normal. Thankfully I can take refuge in the refreshing cool air below.

Cave In

Banlar 24

We have been through so much, but at times we still get complacent.

Things have been going well, considering what life has become. We started the process to assimilate the new citizens from Caztona. We also brought down some of their livestock and developed revised plans to make our byways and port better, considering they will get more usage.

Unfortunately, todaz we have had an accident in the part of our towz under construction in the caves. I was down below when it happened, discussing the new expansion area with Salerand and Nuzen while showing them the changes we had made in the Council, when all doxx broke loose.

"I think Salerand; this will be a great place to build a cybez facility for all the cit—"

The discussion was interrupted by an immense sound of rocks falling, along with screams coming from deeper in the cave system. Johlnz ran behind Salerand as Nuzen went to alert others and get help.

"Nuzen, grab some respirator masks if you can. I am sure there will be a lot of dust. And bring some lights as well," Salerand yelled back.

When they arrived near the scene, a wall of dust confronted them. Johlnz pulled a cloth from his pocket as he started coughing; however, it was too late. He had to move back out of the cloud while tears were falling from his eyes, and he fell to his knees, gasping for a clean breath, unable to breathe properly.

Johlnz felt arms around his body as Salerand helped him up, and they moved back away from the dust to wait for lights and respirators. A few seconds later, Nuzen arrived with the respirators and head lanterns, plus, thankfully, additional workers.

Johlnz rushed into the dust, now starting to settle, to find a large pile of rocks had fallen between Helon and Iroz caves. A bloody hand extended out from the pile, and he knew they would find more than just one body below the rubble. Everyone started carefully moving rocks while more debris continued its occasional fall from above.

"Johlnz, move back; it is not safe!"

Salerand, there could be workers still alive in the rubble!"

"I know, Johlnz, just the same; if we get buried under additional rock falls, it will make the rescue team's job even harder. We need to move back."

Johlnz reluctantly backed away and was almost hit with further rocks crashing from the ceiling while they waited for additional help. The ceiling clearly remained unstable, and Johlnz felt now, no one could be alive beneath the rocks. The realization upset him, and he started to feel sick as he again began to uncontrollably cough. Nuzen knew Johlnz needed fresh air, so he pulled him away as the sound of additional rocks crashing to the floor reverberated behind, and they both stumbled as Nuzen almost fell flat on his face.

Cave In

Banlar 25

Salerand informed me this premid, seven workers in all were inside when the collapse happened. Three were far enough into cave Iroz to escape without major injury and were simply temporarily trapped.

It took eight zakas of careful digging to get the entrance opened and temporarily braced. The rescue team pulled three bodies from beneath the rocks, and thankfully the fourth only sustained a broken leg.

Before returning to my residence to clean up and rest, I almost passed out from all the dust I inhaled. Nuzen suggested I go to the medical building, but I decided I wanted to be camo when I felt better. I desperately wanted to see Thereza and Jacol.

Two of the tanmen who died were from Caztona, and both had young liltanz. The third, a tanwoz who lived in this area before Zeptulgar. She was not even twenty-three cycles old and in preparation to be espoused.

After all, I have been through; I would almost expect to be immune to tragedy and sorrow; even so, this has me quite upset.

I think it is time to hug my partner and somz again.

Burial

Banlar 31

Todaz, we buried and held a remembrance service for the three victims killed in the cave-in last weez. Their names have already been added to the memorial recently dedicated in the Ceton cave. They will not be forgotten.

Using materials supplied from Caztona, we have been able to properly brace and support the area where the cave-in took place, and work has begun again. Thanks to the special bracing, we now have a stronger, more secure entrance, which will one daz have a plaque in remembrance of the three who died.

We cannot keep using the Zeltren to run up and down the coast for material transport. Luckily, we have some experienced boat builders in our towz who, using the resources of Caztona, are building new boats specially designed for heavy material transport between the two communities.

To ensure better communications, we are going to build another radio tower. This one will be between our towz and Caztona. We will locate the tower in the ruins of a coastal mountain towz in Guazemax, called Hicaque. The towz is on the other side of the mountains and over one hundred zilos away from where we had detected radio signals in the past.

Getting Crowded Around Here
Eral 1

It has been over four weezs since I wrote in this journal—stop reading if you heard this before. Just kidding, if you stuck with me this far, I am sure you want to know the rest of my life story. Do not you love my optimism that anyone in the future would actually care about anything I write?

Anyway, life, my work, and my family keep me exhausted. I see this journal sitting on my desk, but the brain is not willing to make the hand move to write. This evening is different since I want to record my recollection of todaz' events.

It is starting to get a little crowded around here, as todaz we received a radio message from a person claiming to be a representative of the Nizarax Authority.

They contacted us directly by name, which makes sense considering how far our signal goes with the tower we put up farther south of towz. We constructed the tower to facilitate better communications with our southern resource and security teams when the satellites were not in range.

Their towz is located in the mountains fifty zilos below Port Bilwi, only a couple of zilos from the Matabas border. They probably picked up our communications recently and were as surprised to hear us as we were to hear from them.

We were in our Council meeting when a radio technician came in to tell us about the message. He did not answer because he did not know what to say. We told him not to acknowledge the message until we decided what to do.
If the person were from the Authority of Nizarax, it could have been a problem since our towz is in what was part of the pre-comet country.

We quickly decided we could not ignore the message since our continued survival could depend on the actual situation down south.

Before the Chairtan and a few other senior-level members went to the radio room, we voted to authorize an expansion of our security force in case we needed them to defend our southern border, whatever or wherever that may be.
We would reconvene two zakas later to get updated on the conversation.

Chairtan Johlant came in the door and stood on the podium to address the Council.

"Everyone, please take a seat, and I can review with you the conversation I recently completed with Mazia Luiza Morcex."

The Chairtan grabbed a glass of water as he waited for everyone to take a seat.

"Thank You.

"Maria claims to be the senior representative of the Nizarax Authority. She acknowledges the title means little but thought it necessary since she believes she is the last remaining member of the Nizarax Authority. She is, however, now head of the Council of the towz she called

Nel Juizes, a small vilogge according to our maps, west of Lake Rivaz, about twenty zilos from the Battal Ocean.

"She was excited but cautious when she first heard our communications and had been listening for about two mooncazts before deciding to make contact. She wanted to be as sure as possible we were not a threat to her community, as I am sure all here can understand."

"How far away are they Andrez, can we send a Helo to check them out?"

"I think Calliaz; the approach would be a bit rash and not a good first impression for us to make toward someone who could be a vital friend.

"To answer your first question, the towz is about one hundred zilos from here, about fifty zilos south of Bilwi. They are in the mountains overlooking the lake, which is how the towz managed to survive the waves, which destroyed Manazua and many of the other coastal cizaes and towzs."

"Are they asking for any assistance from us? We are already stretched thin with all the new individuals from Caztona."

"No, Zelena, they have not asked for any specific help. They have electricity, water, and ample food supply. They have slightly less than eight hundred individuals currently living in and around the towz. The pre comet population in the area was only six hundred, so their biggest problem appears to be shelter. More survivors were living lower in the valley by the lake; however, one of the early tanaquakes caused a landslide, which killed most.

"She wants to keep an open dialog to which I agreed. There is never any harm in having open communication. She did mention trying to meet, and I agreed it would be a good idea; however, she indicated the main byway between the towz and Bilwi is completely blocked, and the main byway north, which passes a few zilos west of us, is open for only five zilos beyond their community. We have cleared about ten zilos south along the same byway and had no immediate plans of going further. I did not mention our capabilities, but if we decide to make full contact, we can use a Helo to send a delegation to the towz.

The Council debated for a zaka and finally decided in principle to, at some point in the future, let her know we could fly down to the towz for a meeting. It is not, though, a priority.

Airport Needed
Nully 14

Over the last two mooncazts, we have exchanged much information with our neighbor to the south. It turns out they have a small undamaged airport and three small planes at their disposal. They have not used them in the past since they had nowhere to go and did not want to waste fuel.

We have nowhere to land a plane yet since we halted work on our landing strip when we found out the crew of OS-I would be able to land at Caztona after repairs are complete. Work will be restarted on our landing strip to make an area to land their airplanes. They are small planes and can land on a rough field, so we only have to make it level and clear any debris or overgrowth. Josuex informed us Caztona also has a small landing strip north of the station, and he knows there is much fuel of the type the planes could use, still stored at the facility.

After much discussion, everyone agreed there existed no immediate need for us to meet since we have excellent radio communications. Maria told us the planes would be available if needed, and we disclosed our access to the Helos.

The Council expressed our understanding of shelter being a concern. We offered the possibility of residents moving up to our towz in the future when we are farther along with the underground construction. I believe many will take advantage of the offer before the next twilight.

All of this is detailed in Haszex's reports, yet I was surprisingly bored and felt like doing some updates. Jacol is growing and sleeping through the nitz except for an occasional bad dream or something. He wakes up crying but doesn't talk enough yet to tell us what is wrong. My partner has not been feeling well. I think she works too much with taking care of Jacol and me, plus still working for her Onczle.

I do also have what I consider a sensational development. Yes, I may be exaggerating, but after two cycles of construction, todaz, we finally began to receive placreate shipments via the recently completed rail extension into towz. We will start to hydrospray the placreate into our already constructed framework tomorrow.

A Sickness, A Sight, and A Baby
Autnar 23

I have been busy again lately, pulled in multiple directions. GPEC meets every two weezs now to review all construction progress, and I occasionally inspect the hydrospray work and make sure all system connectivity continues to function properly. The workers do sometimes make mistakes and cut the lines or damage the receptors. Of course, they also still come to me for other engineering help and overall system repairs to keep me on my toes.

I initiated a new procedure where all GPEC meetings will be documented in the system and have set aside construction archives for all plans and documentation for future reference. We were, at times flying by the seat of our pants, which is not good on a major construction project.

I am starting to feel a bit stressed and under the weather. My partner keeps telling me to get checked out and start delegating my responsibilities; nevertheless, do I listen? Does any tanmen listen to the wisdom of their partner?

Feeling under the weather is better than the epidemic they were having down in Nueva Juizes, a couple of weezs ago. They were struck with a respiration type of sickness, and it hit fast and hard. It is similar to Moniasar Disease, but thankfully not showing any signs of being connected to the Monuasatan Plague that struck our planet about fifty cycles ago.

The medicines they had were not working, and they asked for help. We do not have anything much or special here, though Caztona station has a good supply of different and stronger medicines we thought might be more effective.

Since the only way to quickly get the medicines was to fly, Maria decided to send a team to Caztona. Josuex and Marie coordinated the flight, and after a frightening trip through a storm, the pilot and co-pilot were able to bring back the medicine. On the way back, the pilot flew over our towz and tipped his wing.

I have not seen anything in the sky other than a Helo for a long time. The sight gave me a good feeling of hope for the future.

Luckily the new medicine worked, though not before two individuals died.

Speaking of hope for the future and on another exciting note, I found out todaz, my partner, and I are expecting our second liltanz. Our new addition is due at the end of Marwe.

Jacol is only a little over one and a half cycles old; it should be fun.

Enormous Storm
Zelmar 24

I spent the daz helping to inspect the aboveground areas of our towz after another huge major storm. The storm brought near tempest-force winds and a tremendous amount of rain. So much rain fell, we were afraid the dam would breach, and we would lose our aboveground water supply, which we will need for our crops and livestock. After inspection, it was deemed safe; however, they did release an extra amount of water to alleviate some stress.

Commander Forzzell from OS-I notified us of the storm three dazs in advance, so we had time to prepare. They might have missed the storm if not for the fact the remaining spy satellite Caztona controlled had been added to the network. Gaps in radar and communication remain, but they are now less frequent. It will be many cycles before we or anyone else on this planet can launch new satellites.

Thankfully the early warning gave time for us to get everyone and everything we could, secured or moved below. The storm looked to be huge but centered about fifty zilos northeast of us. Its track was also beneficial to the residents of Nel Juizes since it moved far enough away, they could shelter in place. The individuals of the towz, built their camoz many cycles ago to handle major storms, and they had enough room in the nearby caves to hold their livestock.

Nel Experza did not have any significant damage from the storm. We performed some minor repairs on a few of our structures in towz, and we will need to clean up along the byways leading to the ports and radio towers, nothing new. Work crews are in the process of cutting down dead or dying trees near the byways, so storms do not put as much debris in our way.

I have been feeling exceedingly tired lately. I do not know if it is the long zakas or just overall stress. Thankfully Thereza has not had any premid sickness yet, and she is feeling better than me right now.

I need to take some time to get to the infirmary for a checkup soon. I am hoping it is not a flare-up of my Moniasar Disease. I have not had any eruptions in over ten cycles; however, it has been known to lie dormant and come back later in life.

Another Anniversary
Nemvaz 19 – 0007 AC

Good news. I have only personal updates to record. Life is ordinary.

We celebrated Jacol's second joindaz a couple of weezs ago. He is getting so big and never shuts his mouth. Pypzie, what is that, what is this, on and on? I hope he keeps his inquisitive nature as he grows.

The Zeltren brought back over fifty personal systems from Caztona to distribute first to the Council and then to all supervisors and foretanz.

All will now be required to use them every daz or at least every few days, depending on their role in our community, to record all daz-to-daz and significant events. It is also encouraged that everyone maintains a journal of their life for future generations to know what we have done.

I wonder where that idea originated?

I had wanted to do this with the shipment we received last cycle, but there were not enough systems, and we needed them mostly for research and education.

Continuing with the extraordinary, ordinary, it is another anniversary.

It has been seven cycles since the daz the planet changed, and glad to say this daz is slowly being forgotten and replaced by the celebration of our unofficial New Cycle.

The Council has started officially discussing changing the calendar, a conversation I started, to make Nemvaz 19, the first daz of our cycle.

More Stress and Dreams
Banlar 13

The celebration time has come and gone, and it is a little better every cycle. The Sparklights are more numerous, and individuals are generally more upbeat about life and the future than they have been for many cycles. My family, as well as my friends, had a great time together in celebration.

Just the same, not all is good, at least not for me. I used to dream a lot back before my life changed so drastically. Most of the time, my dreams were fun, interesting, and made little sense; even so, I enjoyed them, and at times, looked forward to going to bed for the opportunity to dream and escape the reality of life.

After Zeptulgar, my sleep became restless, and what little dreaming I had was more like nitzmares. I would dream my espoused was falling off a cliff while the comet came directly toward me, and I stood frozen with fear.

Over the last couple of cycles, my life has become more, for lack of a better word, routine, and my dreams have gotten better. No more nitzmares; only dreams about the towz, my work, and my new family.

My dreams changed a few nitzs ago. I dreamt I walked in our towz, but the towz was empty, and I stood alone. I could see, yet the sky was dark, and the stars moved like the planet spun quickly out of control. Then I saw one star moving swiftly toward me, growing larger and larger.

I awoke with a scream so loud it woke Thereza and Jacol. After the shivering stopped, I spent the rest of the nitz snuggled close to my partner while I hugged her tightly.

I had another bad dream last nitz. This time I saw my former espoused as she looked before I buried her, wearing the dress I bought for her last joindaz. She stood in front of me with one arm outstretched, pointing at me. Her lips were moving; however, I could not understand what she tried to say. I looked up at the sky and could see the comet fall off in the distance, hit, and send walls of flame heading toward me.

Having these dreams reminds me of my Muzie. She used to have vibrant dreams, and many times they would come true in the future. Good things, though, not like the nitzmares I am having. I can only hope the cause is stress, and they are not some advanced warnings like what my Muzie experienced.

None of my dreams have involved Jacol, but the other daz he was hurt playing right in front of me as I watched. He tripped over a rock and almost broke his nose. I cried for nearly as long as he did. I wonder if maybe my dreams are about our second liltanz to join us soon? I wonder if I am afraid I can't give myself to three individuals as much as I have given to two.

I do have some good news to add to this otherwise depressing update. Tolz and Olania are expecting a liltanz in

Zelmar. Tolz confided he is hoping for a din. I admitted it would be nice to have a din as well. Time will tell.

Emotional support
Banlar 28

The nitzmares have continued. Sometimes Thereza is part of the dream, and at other times it is my former espoused. They never include Jacol, which I do not understand, but I am grateful. Last nitz I dreamt my partner was in labor, and as the liltanz joined the planet, a comet crashed over the horizon, and a wall of fire approached as I awoke covered in sweat.

Thereza has suggested I talk to someone. I do not want to go to our one and only therapist, so I did decide to speak to Pypzie Yanez todaz.

"Hello Pypzie Yanez, are you busy?"

"Never for you, Johlnz. How are Thereza and Jacol?"

"They are both fine, and Thereza says to say hello. She has not had any premid sickness this time and believes it is due to your blessing."

"I am simply the instrument; all good fortune comes from Itz."

"How are you, Johlnz? You look a bit tired?"

"Yes, Pypzie, that is why I am here. I have been having trouble sleeping. Over the last few weezs, my sleep has been disturbed with what I can only describe as nitzmares. It may be medical, all the same—I feel I would prefer guidance from you before seeking medical or mental help from anyone else."

"I am grateful, Johlnz, you hold me in such high regard since I know you are not a strict religious individual. Tell me of your dreams, and maybe I can help ease your mind."

Johlnz sat across from Pypzie Yanez's desk and told him of all his dreams. The entire time he spoke, Johlnz played with his hands and repeatedly ran his hands through his hair. His old signs of insecurity had returned.

When Johlnz finished, Pypzie reached across his desk and asked for Johlnz hands.

"These hands, your strength, and your mind have helped tremendously to build this community. Maybe you need a little rest. You cannot do it all on your own, and no one is expecting you to.

"Do you feel depressed, Johlnz?"

"No, I do not believe so, just exhausted . . . and maybe anxious. I feel like trouble is coming. I feel like things are too good, which is odd considering our life."

"Is it Johlnz? Yes, we have work to accomplish, but we have survived. We have survived what I believe is the worst. No one knows the future beyond Itz, and even in the past, good and bad things happened; that is the way of life."

Pypzie Yanez sat back in his chair and gave time for Johlnz to think about what he told him, and then he continued.

"It is okay, Johlnz, to be happy. You have earned the right to be happy; you have much to be happy about, even a new liltanz on the way. You are not guilty because you survived. You are not betraying those we lost because you are happy. You have a life given to you from the light above. Relish that life, enjoy what you have and be happy without guilt."

Pypzie's words brought tears to my eyes. I dried my tears, and we talked a little longer. When I left his office, I felt better. He might have hit the nail right on the head. Yes, after some thought, I believe he is correct. I do feel guilty when I am happy. I have much to be happy for and about, including my new liltanz soon to join us on this planet.

Music and Memories
Marwe 3

My conversation with Pypzie Yanez last weez appears to have been beneficial. I have not had nitzmares since, only the common dreams about my family and an occasional dream about my work and responsibilities.

As I walked down to the server room from todaz' Council meeting, I heard something I had not heard in a long while, a song from my dazs in supreme school.

Of course, we have music, live music, and music on the players some had brought with them. I have also been in my limited spare time building a database of musical selections.

I spent a few moments standing alone listening, recalling better dazs, and I started to cry. Now, as I write these words, I realize how important it is to save some of the culture from our past. I intend to ask the Council to start a program of preservation; collecting any recoded material we have or find and making digital copies for our future. I know Caztona already has some music, videos, and books, saved on their servers, so the selections there will be my starting point.

I envision a depository of music, videos, and a library of physical and electronic books for our future generations to enjoy. I do not know how I will fit this into my over-packed schedule, but maybe my staff will volunteer to help.

And now, for something you will truly like, some personal observations from the Council meeting.

Work crews have made steady progress in cleaning up the byway between our towz and Nel Juizes. Along the way, the teams have recovered and repaired a few mini-transports, two bulk-transports, and an old backhoe loader. They even found a medalance that ran off the byway, probably during one of the tanaquakes. Inside the vehicle, they found many medical supplies, undamaged and usable.

I stopped by the building where they were fixing the transports and found myself amazed. One of them was from model cycle 3971. It had been the model of mini-transport my Pypzie used to drive for his sales job before he started his own company. I know you think I cried again, but I did not. This time I smiled and laughed to myself as I recalled the happy memories of my life as a small liltanz.

Enough for todaz; Thereza just put Jacol to bed for the nitz, so we have time together. Goodnitz!

Say Goodbye to Marwe
Eral 1

Marwe came, and Marwe went, with no liltanz in sight. Thereza is feeling good even though she feels like a jorzen. She has gained over thirty pounzs this time, and she is way beyond ready.

If you want to know about this evening's Council meeting, look it up in the archives. Haszex is doing a great job; a little dry, though. He only gives details and facts, no commentary.

One thing I do want to mention; the results of the election yesterday are in, and everyone was re-elected to the Council.

Two Somz are Better than One
Eral 6

Todaz is a wonderful daz. Our second liltanz, another somz to carry on the family name, joined us at 2:24 this premid. His name is Johlnz Moxron, and both liltanz and Muzie are doing well.

He is the third liltanz to join us in our towz this cycle, and there are ten other tanwoz with pr-liltanz who will be giving new life over the next four mooncazts. It is still a delicate balance; at any rate, if our civilization is to survive, we must grow our population.

Speaking of growing the population, maybe it is time for a damza? I think I'll wait a while before bringing up the idea. I know my partner was secretly hoping for a damza this time, so she might not be opposed to the idea—in a couple of cycles.

Normal Life and Death
Nully 10

How does one describe normalcy—living, eating, life, death, as dazs go by one after another with nothing unusual or out of your control? It's this normalcy we strive for in rebuilding our civilization, and part of normalcy is death.

We had what I believe to be our first natural death todaz. His name, Rafael Berndez, age seventy-seven. He died in his sleep last nitz. He was a native resident, already seventy when we first came here to build our towz. He had been a teacher in a past profession, and he continued as a teacher working in our school. It is sad, and we all will miss him, but it is also a sign of success; he could die of old age instead of freezing or starving to death.

Finally, with both liltanz asleep, my partner and I had time to spend together with a glass of wine. Considering they were a research station, Caztona certainly had an abundant supply of wizen, and other forms of alcohol.

"I love them to death, Johlnz; however, it is nice when they are asleep."

Johlnz nodded as he sipped the wine Theresa poured from the bottle Josuex gave them during the celebrations. Thereza sat behind him and gave him a big kiss.

"Did you hear the news todaz?"

"I heard lots of news todaz, some good and some bad. You know I am a member of the Council and the GPEC, so there is always news."

"If you did not have a glass of wizen in your hand, Johlnz, I would smack you upside your head.

"Well, I had lunch with Olania, and she informed me of our towz's first set of twins who joined us yesterdaz. The proud parents met in towz. The Muzie was a citizen of the provinces, and the Pypzie joined the planet in the Provinces, then moved to Tezaci, as a youngtanz."

Johlnz sighed, but not from exasperation or weariness. His was a sigh of contentment, and Thereza knew him long enough to recognize the difference.

"We have come so far, Thereza, to be able to sit here and enjoy a relaxing glass of wizen together and not have to worry about freezing or frying to death or if a rock is going to fall on our heads."

"And no more bad dreams, no feelings of guilt?"

"No—I still occasionally feel sadness, but the thoughts and feelings are quickly pushed away by our times together."

I did have a dream last nitz; I would not call a nitzmare, yet it left me anxious. It was not about the comet or the end of the planet; as I told Thereza, those have not returned; this was about war or some secret Authority mission.

I enlisted applications for some new specialty service, and of all the individuals, my commander chooses me to lead the team. In the dream, it felt like I was solely responsible for the mission and the lives of those who would be joining.

When I looked around at those I would lead, the clothes and uniforms were something I had never seen before. They reminded me of something I had seen in a future dramy about outer space—even the weapons looked futuristic.

I remember looking up in the sky, which looked nothing like the sky we see, and thinking—they are coming. That is when I woke up in a cold sweat.

Thereza did not wake up, and I do not believe there is any reason to tell her or Pypzie Yanez. I am sure he would say it is more survivor's guilt; however, I feel it is familiar but out of reach.

This and That
Zelmar 1

I have no major news to write about this evening. I only have a bunch of boring updates. How wonderful it is; I feel these updates are tiresome. I believe it to be a sign of a growing safe society, daz-to-daz life being boring?

Well, it really has not been tiresome or non-exciting to me; nevertheless, I am sure whoever reads this journal in the future might use it to help get some sleep. At times this reads like a bad sci-fi novel trying to be something worth reading. It makes me wonder who will ever read this outside the family?

These thoughts remind me to bring up to the Council the need to have a database to record the tedious things of building our new society. In addition to the minzakas of our Council meetings, we need to document rules—I hate to say we now have codes—joining's, deaths, and everyday life. It could be valuable in the future. The individual logs the Council members are now asked to keep on the personal devices I gave them, and the notes of team leaders need to be categorized and assembled into a permanent database.

Are you asleep yet, whoever might be reading my ramblings? If not, I have more.

I had more strange dreams in the last few weezs, nothing terrible, just weird, and a little fun. I dreamt we had a train I was riding to Caztona. The dreams had made me think about looking over satellite images Caztona might have on file to see what rail lines, if any, exist in the area. Maybe we can clean them up and have a rail line between us in the future.

Speaking of rail lines, the second engine is now in service on our placreate line. I always loved trains as a liltanz, so I sometimes watch as the carries arrive in towz.

Little Johlnz is already sleeping through the nitz. I wonder if it is time to mention the idea of trying to have a damza? Well, that is it for now. Hopefully, I have not bored you too much.

A Future Damza-by-code
Zelmar 22

Tolz and Olania welcomed a damza onto the planet todaz. They have not picked a name yet since they both want to honor their respective Muzie's.

She is beautiful, and I am already playing matchmaker. She would make a perfect partner for Jacol someday; however, Tolz is unsure of the family. Something about the Pypzie being a little off.

Reflections on Life

Nemvaz 18 – 0008 AC

Eight cycles, and thankfully, life goes on. We attended a short, lightly attended prayer service in the worship center this evening. We held no large-scale remembrance ceremonies at the two monuments; however, individuals did leave flowers and notes around the structures. We can never forget, but we must move on and not ever feel guilty about our survival.

Thereza and I spent our lunch up by the waterfall talking about and remembering those who were close to us and no longer a part of our lives. New plants grow along and around the stream, and many should survive the coming twilights and heat. It is beautiful and a reminder; life can find a way, especially with help.

The Council has not entirely bought into the idea of changing the calendar. Hang around for the tenth anniversary is what I am unofficially told. Like I have somewhere else to go! A trip around the planet is not a possibility.

We celebrated Jacol's third joindaz back on the fourth, with ice cream and cake. Yes, you read that correctly. One of the new workers in the mezcaf, who came from Caztona, was an accomplished baker before the coming of Zeptulgar. She made us a small cake and a pint of ice cream. She hopes to be able to offer both to everyone for special occasions.

Light Celebrations

Tralmard 7

I have been lax with my journal, mostly because I am busy keeping up with the official record I am required to keep. Whose idea had this been anyway? My colleagues never let me forget the idea was mine, requiring everyone to record all key events.

The celebration of Hzalo-Multum continues to grow, and I am looking forward to the Spark of Light holiday.

I won't bore you with details since, thankfully, boring you is everyone's job now, including me, but things are going well. You can read the details in my official towz log I mentioned above.

I am feeling better than I had earlier in the cycle. Little Johlnz is crawling, and I spend some of my free time chasing around Jacol, which helps renew me as much as the activity wears me out.

I do not have nitzmares anymore or the odd dream about me leading an Authority mission. I did, however, the other nitz dream about my old liltanzhood neighborhood decorated for the Spark of Light celebrations. The dream was a pleasant, yet also sad memory, of what used to be.

The Spark of Light celebration is expected to be bigger, livelier, and brighter than last cycle. Pypzie Yanez has already been reminding us of the true meaning of the event.

I know you can read this in the official Council meeting minzakas; all the same, I wanted to add my thoughts. The Zeltren will begin a series of more extended missions to look for additional settlements now that we have different vessels for basic tasks back and forth to Caztona.

The first such mission, which will start next mooncazt after the celebrations, will be to head east to see if anything remains along the Orisa coast. The assignment could be dangerous since Orisa had not been one of the safest places to be even before the comet. I know I will worry about my friends, including Tolz, onboard the Zeltren for the trip, but at least we will all be able first to spend the celebration time together.

Devastated Mezosso
Eral 10

My two liltanz may be making my hair fall out. Well, that is whom I am blaming anyway because I can't blame Thereza. The idea of a third liltanz is losing its luster as the two I have, are wearing us both out.

We celebrated Johlnz Moxron's joindaz with the usual gifts from the woveners and our local toymaker. We had to dry his tears and explain to Jacol why he was not getting a toy. Oh, the joys of being a parent.

Officially, the Zeltren made it to Mezosso, Orisa, and found nothing except severe damage. There are no individuals around; however, they found ojize trees growing and are going to bring back some ojizes and maybe a tree or two. I look forward to something new and familiar to eat from my old life.

Unofficially, Olania told us Tolz misses his family as well as ours. He told her he even misses Arten. Olania was thrilled to inform him Arten and Chaizen are espoused as of a few daz ago. Hopefully, the ship will be back in time for the ceremony. The couple has not picked a date yet; however, they want it to be soon. Neither one wants a long espousement.

I had the dream again last nitz about being in charge of an Authority mission, but this time I had to rescue Tolz. I wish I knew what it means, assuming it means anything at all. Thankfully on most nitz, I dream about everydaz things like living underground, and for some reason building a snowman while the snow falls in the Star cave. I guess the heat is getting to me.

Survivors

Nully 5

Before you say it, I will, even though I will never hear you for obvious reasons. Yes, all this is in the official record; all the same, this I feel is important enough to be repeated in my journal.

We heard from the Zeltren todaz, and I think we all let out a sigh of relief. I know I, for one, worried about Tolz and Marzco. They were silent for almost two weezs due to radio and storm issues. They had to go down low in the water, which is why the station could not locate the ship.

All is well with ship and crew, and they expect to head back next mooncazt. Recovery teams found more survivors in an old Iurox Authority underground facility in the Olda Mountains. They secretly built the facility to ride out any Authority or financial turmoil.

It turns out the facility did not stay a secret. When the comet came, a group of survivalists overran the place; however, they brought much-needed equipment, food, and knowledge with them. The experience, more than anything else, helped them all to survive.

The survivors have limited resources but are trying to expand. The Zeltren gave them food and medical supplies to help. They do not have access to satellites or long-range communications, so we will not have any way to communicate. They do have short wave radio able to reach far down into the Orisa continent; even so, they have not heard anything for over three cycles.

The Zeltren salvaged a lot of old equipment and resources from former U.P. Authority bases in the area. They found evidence some individuals did survive at the facilities for a while but did not last long. The crew buried any remains they could find and had a remembrance ceremony.

I am happy to hear of other survivors, and hopefully, in the future, we can communicate. I am disheartened, though, to find out Authority bases we thought would have survivors were empty and lifeless.

Another Espousal
Autnar 14

Todaz we celebrated the espousal ceremony of Arten and Chaizen. They arranged a small ceremony performed by Chairtan Johlant since neither of them is Athix. Pypzie Yanez did, however, offer his blessing to the couple and blessed the meal.

The Zeltren is in port, so Tolz was present for his duties. He would have been devastated if he could not share in his friend's special daz. All is well, and I hope it stays that way.

Four Cycles Old
Nemvaz 4

We celebrated Jacol's fourth joindaz todaz. Torliaz, our resident baker, has recently been supplying cakes for all celebrations in towz. Her work is excellent, and it is a reminder life goes on.

Jacol is getting so big; I think he may be taller than me someday. He has started taking much more interest in the welfare of his sibsom. He is also great at taking little Johlnz out to play. He is a great big sibsom.

Muzie and I are doing well. I am as crazed as always, as you can read about in my official log if you need something to help you sleep.

The Friendly Skies

Nemvaz 16

Our landing strip is complete, and todaz we welcomed the first flight from Nel Juices. Malod Mazia Luiza Morcex and two other Council members arrived from Nel Juices to meet our Council and tour the towz.

We included the visitors in our usual scheduled meeting, and they, like those from Caztona, became amazed at all we had accomplished. We promised them to accept one hundred new citizens from their towz during the next cycle, if any wanted to come.

The visitors will be staying for a small remembrance ceremony in two dazs to remember all who died nine cycles ago. Mazia told me they have a small worship center in her towz dedicated to those who died; however, she also is more interested in looking to the future.

The Zeltren will be taking a short trip to Caztona to bring back equipment the smaller boats cannot transport. I will be going with them to install some special software I wrote which will enable our two systems to communicate efficiently with shortened lag times. I am looking forward to the little vacation.

The liltanz

Eral 6

As you can see, I have been lax with my journal entries. My old journal, which you are reading, has become more of my personal thoughts and less about life. If you are interested in our daily lives, you can check out the official diary of Councilman Zavix.

One detail I always like to write about is the liltanz, in both my handwritten journal and official record. Jacol continues to be a great help with his sibsom when he's not teasing him by taking his toys. He is now four and a half cycles old and growing like a weed. He looks like his JarPypzie and—okay enough for now. Some memories are still too painful.

Those of you paying attention surely realize todaz is Johlnz Moxron's second joindaz, and we celebrated in the usual way. The little milestone is the main reason I dug this journal out from all the official paperwork piled on top of it for many mooncazts.

Jacol had his first date with Elizamaze Bezler todaz. Yes, only a play date, but you never know what the future will bring. Her name is a combination of both Jar-Muzie's names.

Tolz, if you ever read this journal, I want you to know the name is precious, though you should have just given in to Olania.

A group of tanmen and tanwoz came to the last Council meeting to ask for permission and materials to build small bi-planes. Two from the group used to build and refurbish old bi-plains before the comet ended their hobby. They feel they could construct one a cycle we could use for emergency trips to Caztona or Nel Juizes to supplement the planes in existence. The planes Mazia has are old and will not last forever. We gave permission and complete support. I include it here because I plan to get involved. It sounds like fun.

They Are Home
Lant 17

Yes, you could read all about this in the formal record, but this moment touched me so much, I had to add it to my old journal. Besides, writing by hand is good for my motor skills.

All one hundred and thirteen crewmembers aboard the Orbital Station returned to the planet, landing at Caztona earlier todaz. The six emergency escape landers arrived at the Caztona airstrip starting early this premid. One ship landed every half zaka, and they broadcast it to anyone who wanted to watch and had access to a monitor.

Since probably no one will ever read this journal, I will admit I did cry when the first and the last landers made it safely to the ground. The first was the joy of knowing they were safe and the beauty of seeing the lander glide in, right on target.

The most emotional moment for me was when the final lander came to rest, and I realized this planet would not see such a sight again for a very long time. The best we can expect to see is an old prop plane now and again and of course our Helotransports.

Someday, long after I am gone, I have confidence we will again leave this planet and maybe even colonize Uberant or one of the other planets. I am sure the plans of all the spacecraft are stored somewhere in the Caztona archives.

Unfortunately, the ship and team sent to explore Uberant have never been heard from since days before Zeptulgar struck our planet. Maybe we have a colony on Uberant already if the ship ever made it there and landed.

I have faith in the individuals I will someday leave behind on this planet, and if the universe will leave us alone, we will one daz again reach up and say hello.

Ten Long and Brief Cycles
Nemvaz 18th, 0010 AC

It has been almost five mooncazts since I last updated this journal. It fell behind my desk, and I never had the time to care. All the details of my life, all my thoughts, and feelings, are now in the system record along with the official records of my work and responsibilities.

Thereza asked me tonitz why I am still wasting time handwriting in this falling apart journal. Yes, this entry is basically a duplicate of what I wrote earlier todaz in the system record; however, this is a special occasion, and I feel this journal could not be complete without this probably final entry.

Todaz we acknowledged a special daz of remembrance. It has been ten long cycles since Zeptulgar all but wiped out all Tanan life on the planet; nevertheless, we are a strong race, and you can't get rid of us easily.

It has, in a way, also been ten brief cycles. It sometimes feels like only a short time ago; I wandered alone across the provinces before I came upon a camo that, for some reason, looked odd and inviting to me. Little did I know my decision to investigate would be the beginning of my new life.

Tomorrow we start our second decaz. I could never have imagined all those cycles ago when I started this journal, I would be part of a brand-new civilization thriving and growing, yes slowly, but growing, in the country the planet knew as Nizarax. Most of its original citizens are now forgotten; however, we continue.

Although it has been over ten cycles, I feel like it was merely a few short cycles ago I lived in Nel Jerzana, preparing to get espoused. Occasionally I still dream of my prior espoused, standing beside me watching the sun come up over the ocean from one of the Nel Jerzana beaches.

I mentioned previously, many mooncazts ago, about a new calendar. The Council is still working on it, and I am head of the committee charged with making it happen; however, we did officially pass a resolution making tomorrow, Renewal's Daz. The one thing I know for certain is the first mooncazt of our new cycle, will be known as the mooncazt of Jantnelnu to recognize my former country. Acknowledging my old country is something I insisted upon as the head of the committee.

Another thing I think important to mention in this journal is our population. There are now almost fifteen hundred citizens in our combined communities, including Caztona and the ports. Another eight hundred live in Nel Juizes. More than enough to rebuild our civilization without any mutational issues, but we will need to keep detailed records of tanealogy.

One last development to write in this journal is another ray of hope. As we get ready for the next twilight, coming up in eighteen mooncazts, the scientists at Caztona have announced their latest findings. Their research suggests that some daz Tanacun will begin to slow down and maybe even stop spinning out of control. Too soon to tell for sure what the future holds. Stop back in a hundred or so cycles for an update.

So now I am at a loss for words. This journal started as a way to pass the time until what I thought would be my end; its time has come and gone. What to do with it? I could transcribe it to my cybez journal—probably the best thing to do when I have time.

An Espousal

Lantnu 22, 0024 AC

A couple of dazs ago, I found my old journal buried in a trunk of clothes, long since too small and forgotten. I had put it away after the tenth anniversary as Thereza thought it silly I kept handwriting in this old thing when the system was available.

I occasionally thought about the journal, wondering where it disappeared and lamenting never having transcribed it to the cybez records. A second chance, maybe?

It is fitting; I find it now since I have something to add just for nostalgia. After all, others and I will fully document these coming events in cybez records, personal and public.

Our oldest somz, Jacol Jantnel Zavix, is getting espoused tomorrow. His future partner is my best friend's damza, Elizamaze Bezler. If you read the earlier entries, you know I joked about this the daz she joined us on the planet.

What is the old expression; the truth is stranger than fiction? In this case, the truth is stranger, or shall I say better than prediction. Thereza and I are ecstatic, as are Tolz and Olania. All of us are doing well, by the way.

Our renewed civilization has grown over the cycles and is now almost twenty-five cycles old. I no longer serve on the Council, as the task falls to the younger to lead and guide. I am fifty-two cycles old, tired, but busy working below, designing the new cybez center. It will be three times as large as the one I designed when we first moved underground.

So, what do I do with this Journal? I started it to stay sane, never expecting anyone ever to read it or that it would go on for so many cycles. Will anyone ever read it? Who would want to? If I transcribe it into the cybez records, it may just become more files no one will ever need or want to read.

I may give it to Jacol for safekeeping. He heard me mention it a few cycles ago and found the concept fascinating—his word, not mine. He thought about starting his own journal, though it never happened as far as I know.

Yes, it is vital to have records of our towz, which we have now in abundance, but who will care about my words or thoughts? Who am I? Or should I say, who was I?

It is time for bed. Big daz tomorrow!

Personal Note from the Publisher

Johlnz Dezlond Zavix *II*

The entry from the daz before my JarPypzie's espousal was the last in my great-JarPypzie's hand-written journal. His thoughts and personal feelings continued for a few more cycles in the system record, but eventually, his personal recollections and musings ended there as well. He never transcribed the journal into his personal cybez record — thankfully, we have it now for all citizens.

I hope you appreciated reading his intimate account of the re-founding of our civilization. I know I enjoyed reading his words and putting this book together for future generations to enjoy.

I took the liberty of dividing his journal into parts to indicate, in a way, the path his life took after Zeptulgar. Also, on the next page, you will find a note from his partner, my great-JarMuzie, Thereza. I'm sure Johlnz never saw the note, as I believe to be her intent. She wrote her thoughts toward the back of the journal and glued the page onto the next. I only found it by accident.

In his last entry, he asked, 'Who am I, and who was I'?

He was no one special, and he, at the same time, existed as a unique individual. He lived as a tanmen of mental and moral strength, who helped us survive and flourish among many others. To Johlnz Dezlond Zavix *I*, and to all the others, I would like to say thank you!

My name is Thereza Zeleton Zavix. Johlnz Dezlond Zavix is my partner, my rock, and the love of my life. He is the Pypzie of my liltanz and, in many ways, my hero.

I have watched over the cycles as he struggled with his doubts while also spreading strength and encouragement to others. I did not know him until he stumbled upon our camo in Reswoll, but I knew then he was special.

He helped in many ways, even when it made him uncomfortable with who he became because he knew the most important thing was survival. Yet, when needed, he was there to lend a certain logic and morality to discussions and situations, which could have led us to become a different assemblage.

When you read this journal, you can feel his sense of loss, commitment, determination, and even guilt. His conversations with Pypzie Yanez, only a portion of which he documented, helped him resolve his feelings of guilt and strengthened his determination to do all he could to build a new and better planet.

When I watch him with our liltanz, my love grows even stronger, and it gives me strength. I never burdened Johlnz with my insecurities and fears; I did not have to. Holding his hand, feeling his touch, is all I ever needed to feel better and endure. The strength he gives me continues to this daz.

I watch him write in this journal, and I further admire his commitment to passing on our struggles to future generations, so no one ever forgets how close we came to extinction. His writings give a voice to many who history will forget.

Personal Journal of Calliaz B Solomant

Nel Lozdox, Uberant – Oventer1, 300 AC

Three Hundred Cycles After – Three Mooncazts Before

It's been a long time since I read the journal of Johlnz Dezlond Zavix I. The first time I read the journal was in school at the age of ten. The journal became required reading as he is one of our historical heroes from the time when this planet almost became extinct.

Was he a hero? He did help re-build, he did give us some of what we have todaz, still and all, he was also just an ordinary tanmen pushed headfirst into an unordinary life of survival. Many individuals at the time were doing great things to keep our species alive. He's only one of the many who brought us to where we are todaz.

What made him so special? He was the only individual to write down the events he witnessed and the one individual to give firsthand accounts of life after Zeptulgar. Yes, the second Council, to which he served, began to keep official records all at his urging: even so, only Johlnz D Zavix I, gave us insight to life three hundred cycles ago.

I'm re-reading the journal now because it seemed fitting to remember what happened before, just in case. Various publishing companies have reprinted the journal—yes, an antiquated word in todaz' digital holographic planet—many,

many times, over the cycles, all the same; I never bothered to care until now.

I'm also drawn to reading his journal because I recently discovered I'm a descendant of Johlnz's via his second somz, Johlnz Moxron Zavix. My Muzie, Jeanx Zavix was his many times Great-JarDamza.

I feel drawn to them and the individuals of the first community. For that reason, I have decided to start this journal of my own. I don't expect any great tragedy or triumph to line the holographic pages of this journal. Still, I feel it's important to continue the tradition, as I discovered many of Johlnz's descendants have done over the last three hundred cycles.

As we all know, Tanacun did eventually correct itself and end up with a stable axis. Almost two hundred cycles after Zeptulgar, the planet's spinning out of control, slowly stopped.

Fifty cycles later, the planet finally settled into its new tilt of 19.75 degrees. Even todaz, our scientists are trying to figure out if it is a huge coincidence to be so close to where it rested before; or if some force we have yet to discover is controlling the position.

Our dilemma at present is another comet coming out of the dark of space. Unlike before, this time, we had a two-cycle warning, and because we are a space-faring civilization, we were able to determine where it was heading early during its approach.

The universe must hate us because it's heading directly for Tanacun. The scientists have disclosed they believe this comet started its journey towards us at about the same time as Zeptulgar struck. A coincidence, some believe it isn't, as they think we were and are targeted.

It's funny in a way, how the universe works in cycles. In any event, this cycle, we are well prepared, and we have choices. We can destroy the invader, alter its path, or leave the planet and live on Uberant or one of the other colonies we are building. Wasting Tanacun would, of course, be silly, and destroying the comet could backfire, so those in charge devised a plan to change its trajectory.

The plan is working; a few more mooncazts of pushing and the comet will pass safely away and not be a problem again for well over three thousand cycles.

As for me, I decided a few mooncazts ago to move here to Uberant. Not because I feared for my life, although something could go wrong, but because I wanted to set a new course for my life. Our great civilization, built from those ashes three decdecazs ago, has choices, and I choose the spaceship Zeltren.

I doubt my journal will ever be important or read by anyone other than my family, if I ever have one, however, this is its beginnings and it will be available on the halo net for all to enjoy, or not.

To be continued…

About the Author

J J Eckhardt is a former direct mail marketer with a degree in art and advertising production. A fan of everything Sci-Fi, Fantasy, and Horror, he started writing almost twelve years ago. A strengths analysis suggested that writing could develop one of his skills, and a new writer was born.

He has completed four novels—of which this is the third to be published—and a grouping of short stories to be released in the future as a book of dreams.

Born and raised in Philadelphia, Pennsylvania, J J Eckhardt now lives in Burlington, New Jersey.

A Note from J J Eckhardt

As my bio says, I began writing over eleven years ago. The thought of someday publishing my work was the farthest thing from my mind. It wasn't until I had written a few short stories and finished my second full novel (the one you just read) that I even considered the idea of publishing.

If you would like to read about my personal journey to this time in my life, please check out my blog on my website.

J J Eckhardt

JJEckhardt.com

Other Novels by J J Eckhardt

Psychic Storm, The Overlord

A dark look at future humanity that has gained psychic powers. After a breakdown of society and many deaths, one individual arises from the ashes to take control of Philadelphia with an iron will; few can resist.

Jonathan Bartram and Stephen Estrada will be brought together through psychic abilities they never asked to receive.

Jonathan uses his new power to enslave survivors of the event and take control of Philadelphia. He becomes the Overlord of Bartram Fortress and reigns with cruelty never before seen in the city.

Stephen begins his journey into adulthood through a fallen world. He must accept the death of his family and wrestle with the choices he makes to survive.

Four years after the event, their paths cross as Stephen works with Sanctuary and an Abolitionists cult to destroy the Overlord.

Adult Content

Softcover available from Amazon and B&N
eBook available from Apple Books, B&N, Kobo and Amazon.

A Journey Toward Tomorrow – The Beginning

A Journey Toward Tomorrow – The Beginning, is a science fiction novel with a touch of romance that takes you on a journey as new life begins from the forgotten ashes of the old.

Unknown to Humanity, the Earth's sun would soon release a tremendous amount of formerly unknown radiation destined to destroy all life. The galactic community of space-faring species, of whom Humanity had no knowledge, discovered the impending doom, and developed a plan to rescue a portion of Humanity from extinction.

Those rescued would begin a new life on a world terraformed with Earth plants and animals to sustain human existence. The survivors had memories of Earth and their former lives erased to ease their transition.

One man's journey begins when he awakes in the middle of an unfamiliar landscape. When he finishes his adjustment, he meets aliens and other human survivors—but one feels familiar.

Warren Estridge meets Laura Blanched, seemingly by chance. Together, they must both endure the sometimes-painful re-occurrences of their old memories, learn how to come to terms with the truth emotionally, and adjust to a world they don't recognize before building a life on their new home.

Softcover available from Amazon & B&N
eBook available from Apple Books, B&N, Kobo and Amazon.

Novels Under Development
Psychic Storm II – Common Enemy
A Journey Toward Tomorrow II – Building and Discovery
A Journey Toward Tomorrow III – Mission Earth

www.ingramcontent.com/pod-product-compliance
Lightning Source LLC
Chambersburg PA
CBHW071225300726
48975CB00002B/304